Silent Violence

Dawn Marie lives and works in London.

D. M. Samson has had numerous articles published. He lives with his wife and two daughters in Germany.

Copyright © David M. Samson 2007

The right of David M. Samson to be identified as author of this work has been asserted in accordance with the Copyright, Designs and Patents Act 1988.

All rights reserved. No part of this work may be reproduced or stored in an information retrieval system (other than for purposes of review) without the express permission of the publisher in writing.

First published in 2007 by David M. Samson, 20 Arundel Road, Bath, Avon BA1 6EF.

Printed and bound by Lulu.com.
Lulu Enterprises Inc.
860 Aviation Parkway
Suite 300
Morrisville, NC 27560
United States of America

ISBN 978-0-9556796-0-5

British Library Cataloguing in Publication Data.
A catalogue record for this book is available from the British Library.

Cover design by David M. Samson.

Many thanks to Bernie and Mike Walsh.

For my family.

David M. Samson, October 2007

Contents

Dhahran, 1405	**10**
Sand Rose Farm	**43**
Colony	**129**
Anoud	**210**
Oil and Water	**274**

Follow the advice of any book on novel writing and you will be torturing yourself looking for that attention-grabbing opening sentence. Go for the jugular, they shout. Furthermore, you will be told to start your story at a turning point or a moment of conflict. Hurl a shower of question marks like hooks into the mind of the reader.

My initial reaction to this advice, when beginning my story some twenty odd years ago, was to shout back: this is my life not a novel. Since completing the first, second, fifth draft, and in so doing discovering the turning points and moments of conflict, I have been persuaded to reach a wider audience. However, rather than scouring my story for a suitable beginning I found I had too many. So I decided upon two: a turning point and a moment of conflict. The first turning point has to be my arrival in Saudi Arabia. The moment of conflict I have chosen is the immediate aftermath of the disaster. What about the elusive opening line? Here too I had the problem of too many candidates. So I will let you choose.

These opening sentences come from when I was re-reading the only English magazine in prison. The old Indian gave it to me. It was a women's magazine, a brittle five years old and still curling. There was a competition in it, with one of those why-I-chose-this-product-in-fifteen-words-or-less tiebreakers. At the time I made up my own competition.

Order the following sentences according to their appropriateness at describing my story. Good luck.

A. *Saudi Arabia destroyed my life.*
B. *The country killed my husband.*
C. *The greed of others stole his life.*

And when I think about it I could add the more nebulous:

D. *A clash of cultures caused his death.*

Of course you can't order the sentences. You haven't taken my journey. Anyway, all of these statements are true and the order is subjective and therefore irrelevant.

Still, the tone is set. And yet before the tragedy there was levity, perhaps gaiety. There was at least a semblance of normality, under the circumstances. There were no real warnings. Of course, with the benefit of hindsight I can see the clues. But at the time they were buried under one of the very things that helped us through daily life in Saudi. If it's not at the top of the list of qualities required by expats then it certainly occupies second or third place. I'm talking about humour. Humour was the habitual opium. In the face of adversity laughter was a balsam. A laugh a day keeps the blues at bay. This, taken with the tedium of the farm and the fact of my isolation, gave any clues the deep-six.

I can see I'm digressing.

I must start with my arrival: an arrival that on the face of it was quite mundane. And yet it was at once ordinary and extraordinary like only a birth can be.

Dhahran, 1405

Learning to breathe. That was how it felt at the door. My face was at an open oven and I was gagging in front my famous fig cake at gas Mark 5. I was so surprised I hesitated. The cabin-controlled air had lulled me. The airhostess with the wraparound teeth said "thank you for flying British Airways". All the hostesses could have exchanged the aisle for a catwalk. I wondered what presents and marriage proposals they had been offered. Was the route revered or reviled? I don't know. I smiled and stepped out into the heavy heat.

They never returned my journal but from a letter to my parents I see that it was 23°C. This was surprising because it was twenty to ten at night. I knew this meant serious heat, not the fun-loving Mediterranean sort. And I always thought it became rock-cracking cold at night.

An old diary notes that on this very day British Summertime ended. Here endless sunshine was forecast, but unfortunately not endless summertime.

The journey had taken its toll. My husband and I had been up at six for my parents to take us to Heathrow. Friends were there to see us off too. "Printing money in the sun," was what they said. Mike had given up telling them that it was hard work. Our weariness was shared. Being purged from the bright, cosy conviviality of banter and booze precipitated a silent vulnerability. An unspoken consensus was made and we quietly fell into line, wary and weary; raw recruits after a long haul, straggled into combat interval by the weight of hand luggage and eyelids.

As we walked across the tarmac towards the building stadium floodlights put our star-fished shadows on stilts. The quartz sparkled with the muted iridescence of lamplight upon snow at night. I remember thinking of asking Mike whether it was quartz I was seeing or diamonds.

A soldier with a machine gun slung over his shoulder indolently followed our progress.

When we got to baggage collection and I saw we were not going to get through customs within the hour my heart sank.

* * *

Unlike other airports where potluck or bad-luck depicted whether you were selected by the customs officers, here nothing was left to chance.

After retrieving our baggage and loading the trolley we joined the line of jaded travellers. Another plane must have arrived for there was already a long queue of Asians to our right.

Arab nationals were whisked through a third line.

In the queue well ahead of us was a drunkard. Drink had been flowing and free on the flight and many had drunk as if there was no tomorrow. He was not loud and reeling, but I could see that his disgruntled mutterings were affecting neighbouring people. Those in his vicinity wished for hats, high collars. They fussed with their bags, became absorbed by a wall or verged on slinking away. When his turn came and he heaved his cases upon the counter and opened them I expected a scene. I don't know whether respect or fear came into play, but like everyone else he knuckled down and was meek. Yet, his mutterings and overall dissatisfaction remained with me. They spoke of an antipathy that I would see again and again as an undertow of cynicism, an invisible force: the gravity of which required jet-propulsion humour to escape.

Then there was only a young man in front of us. He opened his case on the counter and turned it to the official. The official pulled out a white plastic bottle and stood it next to the case. "Contact lens fluid," he said brightly as the official unscrewed the top and sniffed. He put the bottle back on the counter in such a way that it was obvious it would not be packed. He went back to rummaging. The youth looked at us and I raised my eyebrows sympathetically.

Mike had told me not to bring any perfumes for they could contain alcohol. Medicine and make-up could be regarded as drugs. Videos would be confiscated for viewing. All *Marks and Spencers* labels had to be cut off and anything else pertaining to Jewish companies or Israel itself had to be erased or better still left behind. Pendants with crucifixes or any adornment that could be construed as an object of worship were not tolerated. For just as there are no natural rivers in Saudi Arabia so too there are no churches or places of devotion other than mosques. Yet, non-believers are not tolerated. "I'm sorry," the agency representative had said. "They won't accept your form. You've got to believe in God. Let's put Protestant, shall we?"

The official spoke loudly into the boy's last case. He turned it for the boy to close. The bottle of contact lens fluid was the only thing he had put aside. A guard or soldier the official had apparently summoned appeared and took the bottle. The youth was about to protest but shook his head instead.

When Mike and I reached the counter I was shocked to see the official standing on a carnage of printed material, all flesh and eyes. I realised that some of the eyes were not eyes but nipples. Booby Babs and sexy Sadi shone heroically through the trodden mosaic. All manner of offensive pictures had been ripped from magazines, newspapers and books. Revelations as mild as a soaring slip of leg or a plunging décolletage were considered improper. A girl in lingerie was scandalous and there were few contemporary magazines without one.

The official went through everything, right down to impassively rifling through my smalls. My supply of paperbacks was scrutinised - perhaps he expected to find an imbedded phial of sherry. When he came to the Koran I looked to him for some emotion, but it was not forthcoming. Finishing one case he slid it to one side and gestured us to open the next. To close the inspected one, we had to rearrange the contents. Nothing was said, but there was no surliness either. There was nothing. Only the cases existed. We were not present. We merely transported the cases. Even he did not exist. He was expressionless, dead-panning the monotonous stream for articles of abuse.

There was no narcotising supermarket music, but there should have been. It would have lifted the grim silence jarred by intermittent sounds of tearing paper.

There was a significant, if unsurprising, absence of women. In the Asian queue I counted five waifs with downcast eyes. Their timidity was such that had they been told that breathing was not permitted they would have turned blue and died on the spot. On our flight there had been only one other woman. She was also a westerner and had been noticeable in the waiting lounge at Heathrow because she was travelling alone. Yet, despite the presence of so many men she did not seem intimidated. I got my fair share of sideways glances, but she was constantly being devoured. Throughout the flight I did not see her. Then, just after the pilot announced that we were nearing Dhahran airport, she marched down the aisle. When she re-emerged from the toilets at the back of the plane I almost did not recognise her. Gone were her tight blue denims and colourful blouse. She was enveloped in a sheer black cloak, an *abaaya*. Her head was uncovered, but she had put her hair up - no doubt in anticipation of concealment. The woman in London with the air of independence had prepared herself for anonymity.

An hour and three quarters after touch-down we'd got our luggage chalk-marked by one official, had them verified by another at the exit, and were through to the other side to be confronted by a lively regatta of bold lettering on cards and boards and placards. Some were flagships sporting the company motif; others plain white modest yachts and still others on ribbed cardboard like junks. Amongst the disorientating mass Mike spotted our surname.

The man holding the card introduced himself as Pat. He was Irish.

"You're probably knackered," he said.

"We left Heathrow at noon," said Mike, "but to get there we were up at six."

"I'm sorry, but we have to see the chief rag-head first." That was the first time I heard an Arab referred to that way. At the time I found it offensive.

He led us down a corridor bustling with people despite the late hour. A devastated Indian dressed in white was pushing a trolley of bin-liners, buckets and cleaning implements. Every so often he would spot a speck of dirt or even as much as a cigarette stub and laboriously gather it up. The place looked spotless, but he could not be idle and was programmed to perpetually sweep and wipe.

Dhahran airport was the first building I saw in Saudi Arabia and was of the modern Arab architectural school. Without resorting to gaudy ceramics, horseshoe arches or onion domes, which could have been a mockery in such a contemporary structure, the architect had endeavoured to lend an Arabic flavour. Outside there was a liberal helping of pointed arches, but inside the ceiling resembled the groined vault that one sometimes finds in a castle or below a church. The building was low-level and like most buildings in the country, respecting the intense heat, the windows were absent, deep-set or sheltered.

* * *

Pat knocked upon a partially opened door, peered inside, gestured for us to wait and went in. A moment later he ushered us in, pointing to the orange plastic chairs that lined one wall. "Give me your passports," he said and handed them to the man behind the desk. Mike couldn't bring the trolley with our luggage in and parked it near the door. "Nobody'll take anything," Pat said quietly. "Crime is virtually non-existent here. But I've got to wait outside anyway."

There were two men in the room. One sat behind a large teak desk in a padded leather chair. Another sat in the corner on a chair like ours. He was tall and thin in a charcoal-grey uniform and carried a holstered pistol. I could not tell whether he was a police officer, ranking customs official or airport security man. By the way he was slouched in the chair I could tell he was not cultured. His eyes were coal but his thinness and grey suit reminded me of a pencil: hard and thin: H3. He was inspecting his nails, occasionally stealing smouldering glances in my direction. For fear of catching his eye I looked elsewhere. The man behind the desk was conversely stockier and dressed in Arab attire. Although dark, almost sinister, he was a more passionate man, cultured, incongruously soft, of eyeliner consistency: 4B. He was the first real Arab I had seen. On the plane most of the dark-skinned men had been in crisp business suits. Even then a European jacket spoilt 4B's Dickensian nightshirt known as a *thobe*. The contrasting outdoor heat and the aggressive refrigerator setting of the building's a/c made the jacket necessary. "It can't be healthy," I had remarked and Mike had said that I'd get used to it. The tails of the Arab's white headdress had been flipped on top of his head. His dead-eyed gaze could have knocked the pips off that of the best London commuter.

  4B's watch on a gold link bracelet was loose, more a bauble than a timepiece, and it tapped the desk as he examined our passports. He looked at the important pages, he looked at us, he looked at some papers and then he returned to the passports, turning every single page. It seemed that the only qualification for his job was a doctorate in meticulousness.

  The uniformed Arab mumbled something and the man at the desk let slip a half smile. I grew angry. He'd been scrutinising our passports for a full ten minutes, a long time when you're exhausted. And I didn't like the sideways looks H3 was giving me. I believed that H3 had made a snide remark. I looked to Mike and his expression said patience.

  I surveyed his spartan office. There was the obligatory picture of King Fahd, a map of Saudi, the Saudi flag and a calendar. Sunday 28th October 1984 was 4 Safar 1405. The Arab New Year was into its third month.

  I was tempted to reflect upon the state of Europe in 1405, the end of the middle Ages. We too lopped off hands for theft. We also branded and flogged and although we didn't behead we hung without the drop technique, effectively strangling the wretch. Naturally, such comparison was cheap. It was arrogant to believe that we'd risen above this level of barbarity. For one would have to dismiss that bastion of the Western World, USA, with its electric chairs, gas chambers and lethal injections. Many in the Arab world condemned Britain's long terms of imprisonment. They claimed confinement was unjust. Whilst one soul suffered, another thrived and even expanded upon his criminal knowledge and connections. Arab punishments doubtlessly embraced the deterrent factor more closely. Only those who had experienced prison could say what it was like, whereas the lasting effects of having your hand cut off were relatively easy to imagine. Unless you were victim of an unfortunate accident, you were also branded for life. I didn't know whether the Arab way was an effective deterrent, but I did believe that a high proportion of the British populace would welcome the return of capital punishment for a child murderer, for instance.

He closed our passports and placed them one on top of the other. Still he said nothing. Then he looked up and feigned surprise when he saw we were still there. Whereas H3 was shallow and could be physically cruel, 4B was deep and psychologically damaging. "You may go." And with a limp-wristed wave of the hand one might use to flick dust off one's shoulder, his gold bracelet rattling, he repeated: "Go."

I got up and being nearest to the end of the desk where our passports lay, I made to retrieve them. Casually he placed his hand on them and I paused, my hand in mid-air. He did not look up. Such was his confidence.

"He keeps them," said Pat from the door. "They'll get sent on to the company's Riyadh office."

There was something profoundly disconcerting about giving up my passport. For the majority of the time it sat in a bureau or locked drawer. When I had it in my possession I guarded it like an appendage.

Our belongings had been scrutinised, a part of our personalities laid bare and it seemed now our identities were being confiscated. We had queued and been processed. Had George Orwell ever visited this country? Ha, even public intimacy was banned. It was truly 1984.

Outside had turned surprisingly cold. Then again it was almost one o'clock. I was glad that I had not anticipated heat and kept the sweatshirt I had donned inside.

When we were out of earshot making our way to Pat's car I voiced my anger. "Things would have gone quicker if we'd slipped him a few riyals." I never got to speak about giving up our passports. A week or so later we would receive our *iqamas*: identity cards.

"I doubt it," returned Pat. "It's always like that. Things get done, but at their pace."

"*Inshallah*," added Mike.

"Exactly," smiled Pat. "You sound genned up."

"I worked out here a few years ago."

I knew Mike had been dying to announce it. He wanted to know what had changed. So for most of the journey I sat quietly in the back of the car. As far as I could gather from their banter, not much had changed. I was too weary to keep up and my naïvety at the time made me an outsider to their rapid conversation. To his credit Mike tried to involve me by occasionally explaining what they were referring to when they dropped euphemisms and abbreviations. I appreciated his effort and had I had the opportunity I would have told him not to bother. I was too tired to listen.

There was not much traffic and the roads looked pristine, bathed as they were in a lamplight that hazed the surroundings. The hush was conspicuous and isolated us in the vehicle. Although the motorways were modern - there appeared to be no roads only American-style freeways - they were bewildering in layout. Four, six, eight lanes it did not matter, a small track would join at ninety degrees. And then the motorways themselves would merge from the left or the right and sometimes both at the same time. We did not traverse a spaghetti junction, but we did a couple of suspicious turns. By the time we reached our destination I was utterly disorientated.

* * *

I throw the mesh door aside. It judders and the buzzard perched upon the roof of the opposite demountable looks over. The bird is so startled it just stares. Does it see the pieces of an ill-fitting puzzle that was once my face? It takes flight with slow confident flaps of its wings. But I do not see its majesty. My surroundings have been reduced to a backdrop of tissue-paper consistency. Such is the enormity of what has happened. And yet although I am numb and cannot focus I absorb everything. The farm is as still as if the lads are out working. The presence of the buzzard has banished all other birds.

I should run, but I just stand at the top of the wooden steps. They creak with my indecision.

There is a small pain, sharp like a hypodermic puncturing my heart. Thirst has egg-shelled my lips and I am about to lick them, when a noise on the threshold of my imagination pinches me for attention. I deny the sound and my attention is about to implode when I hear it again: a groan and then a rasp of sand. I focus on Abdul's cruiser standing in front of me before his demountable. There is no sound for a long time. But I'm focused on it, frozen by it, waiting for its confirmation. When the groan comes I know I have to act, but I'm petrified. Curiosity tussles with dread but eventually I move forward.

My approach is weird. I walk over to the cruiser, but I do not move purposefully. I feel the young sun perforating my skin with tiny scalding needles. A streak of cats has dabbed the sky in a stampede of off-white paw prints. I am strolling over, almost looking nonchalantly this way and that for distraction or observation; almost abstractedly kicking the dirt. Weird.

I move around to the right, the front of the vehicle, allowing myself ample distance.

At first I don't recognise the battered face in the shadow of the cruiser. Whoever it is presents no threat. I step closer but stop when eyes snap open and stare at me.

My heart aches with angina.

Exhausted though I am, my emotional time is not over. I am still going through a myriad of emotions at lightning speed. Occasionally, I can reach up into the gale and hold a thought before it is torn away. One such thought is clear like a splash of ice water in the face: I should kick him. Not for who he is, but what he represents.

His lips part and he speaks. Then I'm standing over him and the word he is repeating is water. His eyes plead with me. One side of his blood-red face is pebble-dashed with grit.

After a while I realise that he's fallen silent. Still he looks into my eyes. I give him nothing. I am not there. Caked lips mouth something, but I do not bend to listen. Has he resumed his litany? Is he gasping for water? Can't he see that he cannot get sense from me, let alone water? I do not bend to listen.

Some distant urgency is mounting. I don't know why at first. Then I hear them: the wailing of hysterical ghouls. And they are getting louder. Stillness carries sound.

No, he isn't asking for water. He is speaking English, using a word I recognise, but one to which I can attach no meaning. The wailing of the banshees is obvious, but I hesitate, as if the word is the most important thing in the world. This new word is not like his plea for water; this word is not for him, it is for me. When I flee I don't remember the word. Much later, under interrogation, when they are trying to establish my part in the killings, does the word come.

Now I run.

I see the multiple blitzes of distant vehicles trying to strobe the daylight. Banshees becoming sirens.

I run round the kitchen building and race across the courtyard into the old greenhouse. And I wait, hidden, cowering. Not thinking about Abdul's word. The word that was his attempt to reach me, his attempt to span the void between us. The word he knew I knew. The one he thought could explain the inexplicable.

* * *

Despite the late hour at which we had hit the sack, we were showered and dressed when Pat called for us at seven-thirty.

"It's my house-sit," he had explained as we neared the whitewashed house the previous night. Mike had been to the Aramco (Arabian American Company) camp before and had already explained the concept of housesits to me. When the occupants of one of the more luxurious houses left a pet to go on holiday, there were queues of volunteers ready to look-after the place.

Outside I could see the house more clearly. It was a concrete block, identical to the one next to it and the one next to that; a small community of about a dozen buildings surrounding a car park, not unlike a housing estate.

The furnishings within made up for the lack of architectural style: on-suite bathroom with massage shower, walk-in cupboards and a well-stocked refrigerator also walk-in size. Modern appliances were in abundance: ice maker, coffee and espresso machines, video machine, cinematic television, food processor. Everything one could want. The sense of home was apparent, yet I could not appreciate its warmth. There was a dislocation founded in the feeling that the building could not yield to the occupants' efforts. Like a film set or a show-house there was a stylised almost unlived-in aura. Individuality had merely been tacked upon the frosty walls. Remote-island rugs dappled the sea of nondescript carpeting. Solitary artefacts and ornaments from travels afar seemed displaced.

The deserted clean-swept roads enhanced the sterilised toy-town feel.

The stillness was conspicuous. "Does anyone live here?" I asked as we clambered into his car.

"Everyone's at work."

We were on the Aramco compound known as main-camp, Pat

informed us. The very reference to a camp added a temporal feel to the place as if civilisation was bivouacking on the harsh land. There were other camps, notably North camp, an ex-army array of demountables where the majority of the foreign male workforce was housed. This was where Pat lived.

"Women are not allowed there," he lamented.

"Too bad," I joked.

Mike gave me a scolding look and smiled.

The light from the new sun was zinc: a bluish-white metallic brilliance. The blinding exposure was not complemented by intense heat. The warmth was young and pleasant, late evening rather than early morning. But in still moments the threat of blast-furnace heat vaporised the pleasantness.

Nature's elemental heat and light cauterised the striving civilisation: paling colours and flattening shapes. Unquenchable strips of grass and hardy trees were already being sprinkled. Their colour was dust and parched green.

There was ample parking and we stopped outside the main refectory.

Inside the place was as unobtrusive and practical and as unimpressive as a burger-house. It was large and it too was deserted. The smell of ketchup and chewing gum adhered to the furnishings. I suspected the place was built in the sixties but modelled on the rock'n'roll fifties and revamped in the seventies. Efforts had been made to broadband the clientele, but eventually calibrated to attract the fifteen year olds. The paper place mats, a flowered border with the motif "Live one day at a time and make it a masterpiece" rejected jocular youth and sent the barometer up to the sixty-year olds.

Again, the cold was fierce, but the contrast was not as defined as yesterday evening and I was not chilled to the bone. Nonetheless I folded my arms against it.

The head of the company that employed Mike met us. Firm handshakes were made and then Pat bid us adieu. He hastily arranged a meeting with Mike for the transference of our luggage.

Smith was smartly dressed in a white shirt, sober tie and pressed trousers. He was not fat, but his reddish face was mildly bloated. He appeared to be a stereotypical businessman unsuited to the Middle East. He had a mildly worried face hinting at blood vessel bursting restraint: the perfect cardiac candidate. In an effort to appear casual his shirt was short-sleeved.

He led us to a table were a woman was drinking a cup of coffee.

"My wife June," Smith announced.

"Hallo," she greeted. We exchanged glances and I thought hers dismissive. "I need a kick-start in the morning," she said, referring to her coffee. Had I misread the contact?

We seated ourselves and a waiter brought us the large glossy menus. Mike and I ordered hearty breakfasts.

"I thought you two could go shopping," explained Smith.

So that was why this woman with the fragrant bouffant hairdo was here. I was not to see the hydroponics greenhouses with Mike. This was our reason for flying to Dhahran and not to Riyadh; a mere fifty kilometres drive from our farm.

June looked as if she was about to present a range of cosmetics rather embark on a shopping expedition. On camp one was relatively free to dress as one wished. Her attire was more suited to a ball or some other social event. Admittedly she was in a wine dress-suit rather than an evening dress, but she was undoubtedly a prestige shopper. She was no Christmas tree but her jewellery was out of sync with the mundanity of shopping. Gold was predominant, but matching her outfit were rubies.

Mike knew my disappointment, but I knew there was no protesting. One did not challenge the husband's boss on the first meeting.

I looked at June and forced a smile.

"The maid always forgets something," she said haughtily and I shrank from her.

Was I to be a mere helper? Drastic action was necessary to make or break the morning. "Sherpa Dawn at your service."

Mike chuckled, Smith gave a half-smile and June blanched. My enthusiasm was vulgar. The morning was ruined.

"I'd love to see what you can buy out here," I went on. "I'll probably be doing some cooking on the farm."

"There's not much else," June said with a vicious smile.

An earring flashed. I'd mistaken the stones for rubies. They weren't stones at all, but clots of enemy's blood, trophies among the charms.

"It's only for six months," I said, but her smile remained. As if she knew something that I didn't.

Mike registered the skirmish and galloped into no-man's land before we became fully entrenched. "Dawn's brought enough reading material to open a small library."

"Here there's a little more to do than on the farm," Smith confessed, unaware of the scuffle. "I thought you could set off late afternoon when it's cooler."

Mike nodded.

Small talk followed. It was so small that silence would have been less of an embarrassment had it not been our first meeting. We scoured the corners for something to magnify. Smith was socially inept and his wife was content to ignore us. Thankfully our breakfasts arrived and gave us reason for silence.

As we finished eating we foundered on more small talk before the cavalry in the guise of a third party arrived.

He was a tall thin man in a chequered shirt and slacks. An ill-matching tie betrayed him. Either he had no dress sense or his attire displayed admirable rebellion in the face of his superior. Whatever, because he did not fit in with these people I awarded him ten sympathy points.

Smith introduced him as Ted. He was the overseer of the hydroponics centre.

"Ted the head," Smith joked. He also shot up in my estimation. Evidently despite his dress sense Smith admired Ted. Ted was the man who brought results. And I could see him in overalls and wellies grubbing about in the soil.

The remark caused Ted to redden and his uneasiness won him further points.

"Coffee?" Smith offered.

"No thanks, I've, er, actually had breakfast."

"Don't be fooled by Ted's modesty, Mike. This man is a tower of knowledge. He could argue a case better than a lawyer. And he carries his books around in his head." Perhaps Smith had also been disconcerted by the small talk. Although I felt the comment was more for his wife's benefit, as if to say: "Excuse him, he's a genius in disguise."

Ted coughed and shuffled in his chair. He gave me an awkward smile.

I was giving away points like confetti when Smith announced that it was time to go. My thoughts scattered like threatened insects. Condemned to the best part of a day with June, subservience or a sham-fraternity seemed the only options open to me. She not only had better established fortifications she had the high ground too. I was completely disadvantaged. At the first opportunity I hastily whispered to Mike: "I don't know how I'm going to get through the day with her."

* * *

I'm in the old green house crouched behind the fan of Elizabeth I's collar. Distant reason tells me that a greenhouse is a glasshouse and although I am not throwing stones I am obvious.

They are at the door. Two, maybe three? They're speaking. Talking to me? I know they've seen me, but I cannot accept it and I tighten myself further. Trying to become smaller. I dare not look, but I know they're approaching. Two, maybe three. Have I closed my eyes against their presence? The sweat and shivering have given way to primal vulnerability. I still believe that if I don't move they won't see me. More words, closer. Their movement is cautious. They speak and I know they have separated and I know that the words are not for me. Have they noticed I have no use for words?

Movement, not verified by shadow but by changes in the light. I want the clumps of green in the rejecting sand to help me. But clinging to the sand is all the plants can do. They offer me nothing.

Trousered legs are before me. I look up: a frightened child. The face contorts and the expression is supposed to be benign. The uniformed man crouches and his hand reaches out: a sham offering to coax a wounded animal. The eyes look up and beyond me, and the face is a command that has dropped its benign expression. The eyes fix on me, and the smile returns, but I am wise to the deception.

I allow his clammy fingers to take my wrist. They are damp and reek of spices. I want to recoil, but I am cunning. I rise with him. Turn with him. His soft steamed fingers lead me to the door. Nobody speaks. One stands at the door. One walks behind us. I make no effort to resist.

The one at the door steps aside. He chooses to step aside and not outside. Only one can step through the entrance and I lead the way. They are all behind me. My moment has come. There are others by the farm vehicles to my left, but to my right is freedom. I rip my arm away and run. Orders are barked. Noise and commotion. The wind is in my heels and I soar. A smile captures my freedom, a smile that fades as I drop to running, a smile that falls to pain as I am reduced to jogging. But I remain free, moving between pivots of green. Could the huge tractor-like wheels of the pivots offer me shelter?

A motifed vehicle pulls out in front of me. I am as startled by its appearance as if by a rhinoceros. I change direction with a suddenness that causes me to fall. I'm up like a sprinter. Sallies at my heels. The beast roars towards me. Another cuts off my path and I stumble into the tall grass. Knees coming up as if wading through snow drifts. Hands flailing to maintain my balance at this speed. Cats' tongues rasping my shins. The vehicles disgorge gangly beasts, as gangly as me in the grass.

I drop to the ground and curl up. Fear is shutting down systems. The heart has burst and breathing is becoming negligible, sight is extinguished, hearing too. Taste has not been needed for some time and touch knows something that it is keeping to itself.

* * *

The refectory was not open and I sat outside on a bench in the shade reflecting the day with June, wondering how I was going to break the news to Mike. About me were unidentifiable plants and trees, but also Peepul trees, a hibiscus shrub and nearby the thick green and yellow flames of monstrous mother in laws tongues.

Shopping had not been what I had expected. We had driven - on camp women could drive - to the commissary where she spent almost an hour buying foodstuffs. One required a laminated Aramco I.D. card and thankfully her husband had obtained a temporary one for me. Otherwise I would have had to bide my time at the entrance or in the car, either of which would have turned out to be on a par with shopping with June. Casual meetings with other female shoppers punctuated the event. At the first encounter I was introduced and a few strained pleasantries were exchanged. But my small talk reservoir was exhausted. I was introduced again the next time, but all but ignored as they talked of mutual acquaintances, arranged a barbecue or a dinner and spoke of past events. Eventually I wandered off.

I browsed the magazines and newspapers, which for the most were not butchered, merely strategically filled-in with black marker-pen. This censorship was either finely done or as a frustrated scribble over the offending picture. I found yeast and sugar, non-alcoholic beer and red and white grape-juice in bottles with wired, porcelain tops and rubber seals. These resealable flip-top bottles gave the game away. All that was missing were the demijohns. (At one time local camp brews were openly tolerated. There was even a booklet "The Blue Flame" produced to stop people poisoning themselves. Outside pressure eventually banned moonshine and the booklet.) The commissary wasn't big enough to get lost in, and on the fifth or so meeting I chose to stand nearby and fume, smiling sickly when glanced upon by the stranger.

Then it was helping June load up her station wagon with the numerous packages and American-style handle-less brown-paper bags doubled up for strength. As we drove off I was livid. On the one side was the fact that she had agreed to share her morning with me. Also on that side was Mike's future - I didn't know how much influence she had but I felt that she was the dominant figure in the marriage. The other side was the beastly - a word out of her immediate vocabulary - way I was being treated. I was merely a lackey. I wasn't Sherpa Dawn. A Sherpa shared, was even respected, and was therefore a Himalayan step above my treatment. I was a lowly beast of burden: a yak. I sat in tight-lipped anger, opening my mouth to issue the occasional innocuous observation. "I didn't expect it to be so green. It's nice that they went for low-level housing. And you have theatre and film and a golf course."

After unpacking her goods we sat in the studied lounge and drank coffee. I was subdued by the prim silence of her porcelain. She saw no need for conversation and it wasn't until we'd finished drinking and we were in the kitchen that she spoke.

"I'll take you to the pool this afternoon. Have you anything to read?"

She could see I carried nothing. Subtlety was not her strong ground, but I had gone this far for the Oscar nomination in my role as wide-eyed naïveté - she would no doubt say bimbo - that I could not break character. "Not with me. Could borrow something of yours? Do you get the *Tatler* or *Country Life*?" I knew over-acting had blown the nomination, but what the heck, like Gregory Peck I would have given the bauble away.

Before she could answer the cat-flap clattered.

"Blossom," she exclaimed joyfully. "My darling." The animal ignored her and sauntered in. She scooped it up. "Isn't she adorable?"

Reconciliation was on order and although I didn't care for cats I mumbled a yes.

With Blossom still in her arms June opened a wall unit and fetched a tin of cat food. Blossom started meowing. One-handed she clipped the tin under the electric can-opener affixed to the wall. June and Blossom waited cheek to cheek for the tin to open. "Patience, patience, my darling," she said placing the cat on the floor and retrieving the tin. Probably because she was under the influence of overflowing adoration June volunteered a piece of information as she spooned the cat-food into a bowl.

"Can you believe some maniac is going around decapitating the camp pets?" I was shocked. A distant bat-squeak issued from a sudden crack in the perfect-town facade. "But nobody's going to get you, are they my darling? You're too clever." Then as an afterthought: "Of course it could be something put out by Rumour Control to keep pets indoors, but I don't think so."

"Rumour Control?"

Presumably because I had spoken and reaffirmed my presence, the tiresome green horn, June came out of her trance and after a moment of surprise her face clouded over.

"It's a department within Aramco that dispels and perpetrates rumours," she said, making no effort to hide her weariness. "I don't know whether they exist as a department, but they're mentioned officially in my husband's weekly Communication meetings."

I was about to suggest that somebody influential had read Orwell, but she spoke first. "I'm going to take a bath." Rather than glance at me she looked at Blossom before leaving the room.

From then on searching for conversation was like searching for oil. All we had were toothpicks with which to prod the desert for something to lubricate the friction between us. Such were the odds of striking lucky and hitting gushing conversation.

* * *

An insect as large as a sparrow flew into the bush before me and I left the shaded bench to take a closer look. Before I could find out whether it was a locust or a dragonfly a taxi pulled up and a familiar face that for a moment I could not put in context leaned out and waved me over. I had been told that we were being picked up, but I was surprised to see a taxi.

As I got in the back, to sit alongside Mike, the man in front next to the Arab driver turned around and introduced himself. He was handsome in an innocent way. Perhaps it was his large brown eyes or the fact that despite his dark complexion - he had blue-black hair - it appeared as if he did not have to shave. He was slight, a man with a boy's frame. He was a Filipino and like all the Filipinos on the farm he had a nickname.

"People call me Scab," he smiled. It was difficult to hear him for the windows were wound-up and the a/c was blasting away like the rush of an aeroplane's engines. Perhaps it was faulty. Conversation with him would be a constant battle with Vickers.

"Scab?" I repeated incredulously.

"Yes," Mike confirmed. Alone with Scab in the farm's kitchen I would attempt to explain that his wasn't a pleasant nickname. He argued that it meant healing, something good. To my: "Yes, but it's ugly." He answered: "Beneficial things are not always beautiful." Age was not in his eyes, but it had taken generations to get them that soulful.

"Are we going all the way by taxi?" I asked, maintaining my incredulous tone.

"Yep."

"I thought somebody was coming out to pick us up."

He gestured towards Scab.

"You know what I mean."

"Scab's come from the farm. He hasn't got a driving license." The poor man had travelled the best part of two hundred kilometres only to turn round and travel all the way back. His outward-bound journey would have been in the searing midday heat too. "Still, the company's paying, apparently."

I couldn't believe we were going to do the whole journey by taxi. The extravagance pushed at the boundaries of reason. Yet, looking about me I wondered whether extravagance was the right word. Mike followed my gaze and gave a resigned smile.

The seats were done in fleece; the ceiling was carpeted in a patterned fringed carpet, as was the dashboard. Trinkets, mainly Bedouin jewellery and some camel saddle adornments hung from various points, predominantly the rear-view mirror from where they jingled. Arab women's jewellery was meant to be heard as much as seen; protocol demanded that they announced their approach. Jewellery served another purpose. It was insurance in a time of war: when widowed they were not immediately destitute. The entire rig was exotically overdone and had I not been in Saudi I would have said that it was a mockery.

I detected no unpleasant smell. In fact I initially caught an inoffensive aroma. When we were underway I realised that the taxi driver was perfumed.

"It's like travelling inside an adorned sheep," I said quietly as we slowed to a mild chime to pass through the main gate of the camp.

Mike shushed me and then asked about my time with June.

"No, you first," I said. Despite having gone over my interpretation of events I still wasn't ready to tell him. "What did I miss?"

"That doesn't sound too good." He paused, possibly waiting for me to speak, but I waited him out.

He told me about the hydroponics centre where the plants were not grown in soil but in plastic tubes containing running water with dissolved nutrients. Cucumbers were harvested five weeks after planting, he enthused. A lot of his day had been in discussion. Mike was interested in the experimental side of agriculture. Food and water were at a premium in Saudi Arabia and for some time the government had been backing experiments in the cultivation of edible salt-water plants, for instance. The greening of Arabia was an important and long-term venture. Self-sufficiency underpinned this strategy.

Mike had worked on a Saudi farm before returning to Britain for further study. Armed with more qualifications he had hoped to join an experimental station. But a place had not been available. Then a sudden requirement for someone to manage a farm had come up. With the promise that the next opening at an experimental site would be his Mike agreed to take his place. As a form of compensation and good will we were flown to Dhahran to view the progress. I was glad that what he had seen had whetted his appetite rather than tortured him. Having studied returning to a farm was not a forward step.

The journey from Dhahran to our destination was inland in a southwesterly direction. Dhahran itself was situated practically on the coast of the Arabian Gulf, formerly the Persian Gulf but often renamed for geopolitical reasons.

Leaving the Aramco camp was like leaving a moon-base: a sophisticated bubble-land of cleanliness. I could see the landscape much better than on our arrival. Roads were stamped on the wilderness. An occasional high-wall barricaded a villa or whatever from the wasteland. A rusting hulk of a burnt-out car, shreds of tyre, cans, bric-a-brac, the blemish of so-called civilisation were strewn alongside the strip of road adding to the sense of waste. Bitty shantytowns clinging to an ancient well or oasis were a mess of old and new. A sparkling, tarmacked petrol station would be an incongruous addition to these one camel towns;

their incomplete and makeshift buildings clustered about the dome of a mosque. Nothing of the beautiful oriental architecture I had envisaged was in evidence. The random appearance and sense of isolation of these collections of soulless buildings was akin to those forsaken gas stations you see on American highways.

Even the sand was initially disappointing. There appeared to be little of the romantic rolling *Lawrence of Arabia* sand dunes. Here was just a defying expanse of compacted ground. I realised that you couldn't build roads on shifting sands. However, the deeper we went into the country the more the landscape became the Arabia I imagined. Voluptuous Henry Moore curves and graces.

Many of the dunes nearest the road were tar-topped in an effort to stop them rolling. I could not help feeling a twinge of sadness at the way the ugly black stuff capped the beauty of a dune. Unfortunately it was necessary. Not only were the dunes dangerous for road and rail, they threatened habitation, agricultural land and oases. Like most methods, this one was not totally successful. Other partially effective techniques were oiling, covering with stones, shells, broken glass, dry camel dung and fencing. The most effective method was to grip them with plants, but this was not always practical.

Mike concluded his monologue with the confirmation of the promise that we would be on the farm for no more than six months.

It was then my turn to talk. Many scenarios had passed through my head after June had dropped me off at the refectory. I had visualised her at dinner with Smith moaning about the terrible day. Or better still sipping sweet sherry with her contemporaries at some soirée talking of the dreadful woman her husband had dumped upon her. "So plain and common."

Euphemisms to minimise the adversity between us were tantamount to lying. Not saying anything was also out. Should anything get back to Mike I would have a tough time explaining myself. Honesty was the only policy.

* * *

They don't seem to know what to do with me. I'm sitting in the back of a car. A guard at my side. One stands nearby. A man in white slacks and shirt comes over. He's just carried Abdul on a stretcher into the ambulance. He opens the door and speaks but I don't understand. He smiles and nods and reaches for my breasts. I hold myself and perhaps scream. A well-dressed Arab hurries over and there is a rush of talk. This Arab speaks to me in my tongue but his gold tooth robs his words of meaning. The man in white approaches again and the guard pins back my arms as I try to protect myself. The tension in me evaporates and I'm limp as he unbuttons my blouse. His touch is tentative but during these moments I abandon my body. He redoes the buttons and is gone.

When I take possession of my body again the ambulance is gone. There are many uniforms that don't seem to know what to do. Suits walk in and out of the kitchen building. There is gesticulating and solemn talk too. A finger is pointed in my direction. They should put the a/c on in this car. And they should turn off the flashing lights on that one over there.

This is a scene I've witnessed in umpteen episodes of *Kojak*. Urgently parked cars, lights. What's missing is the taped-off crowd. I imagine what is happening in the kitchen. Is someone chalking a multi-limbed creature? Then I'm in a *Twilight Zone* episode. So familiar and unreal. Oh, let it end happily. Sweat beads my forehead. They should put the a/c on.

My insides jolt as the car door is opened. I glance up to see others climbing into other vehicles. Then we are moving in convoy. I hate the way the suspension makes me slide on the seat. Hate the smell the a/c puts in the air. Hate these silent men. Hate the brightness of the day. Hate the sand. Hate the clouds. Hate the world. Hate life.

***

"It goes unsaid that I would have preferred coming with you. That woman treated me like the maid." I explained the cold-shouldering when buying her groceries. "When we got back to her place she paid more attention to her cat." We spoke of the pet-killer and Rumour Control. "Then she said she simply had to take a bath and left me for an hour and a half. I heard her upstairs telephoning friends."

"It wouldn't surprise me if that was her routine."

"Maybe, but she was just dreadful." Something had rubbed off and I couldn't help using the adjective.

He nodded sympathetically.

"Before we went to the pool she offered me a pulp-fiction paperback. Can you recommend it? I asked. She replied that her husband's secretary had left it when they had a company do. I could keep it. I thanked her and then said that I had found something to read. Whilst she was soaking I'd checked out her books." The pristine condition of some of the magazines suggested they were for show. This fitted perfectly with the menthol cool room's attempt at warmth, for there was a pedantic neatness in any untidiness, as if the untidiness itself were deliberate. *Arab News, Aramco World, Arabian Sun, Saudi Gazette*: I glanced through them all. "I'd spotted a decent book on Arabia and asked whether I could take it to the pool. It was one of those glossy hard-backed coffee-table books." I glanced at Mike. "I know this is all petty but that's how it was the entire time: a constant flow of niggling remarks. Anyway, she reluctantly let me take it.

"At the pool we had lunch but I was treated in the customary way. She left me to talk to friends and acquaintances. I hired a bathing suit - apparently she didn't have one that would fit me - and did a lot of swimming."

"That must have been nice."

I mentioned that she didn't swim, but it seemed puerile to tell him that she had heavily doused herself in a perfume. Using it sparingly it could have been pleasant, but instead it was as pungent as fly killer.

"Yes. You get the picture. Our unspoken pact was to ignore one another. Anyway, it was on one of those rare occasions when we were together on our loungers..." I again saw the pool's palpitating web of light. The day had moved from zinc to molten copper and everything was sharpened and detailed with shadows reduced to eyeliner. The only children at the pool were a girl and boy, both seven or eight years old. They started water fighting and splashed the book that I'd left open on the table between us, our Berlin Wall. A woman from the far side shouted their names and hurried over. Between scolding them she apologised. Her apologies and smiling pleas met cold granite in June. In her search for forgiveness she explained that they were new arrivals with one week's grace to acclimatise, although her husband had already started work. This explained why the children were not at school. June said it was an expensive book and the woman offered to pay for it. Then I offered. But June didn't want money; she wanted guilt and suffering. Out of her sight I tried expressions of understanding, all the while using a towel to dab the buckling paper that had lost its sheen. Doubtless to rid herself of the tiresome woman a fissure that was supposed to resemble a smile broke on the plinth that was June's face. The woman gathered up her kids and fled. I hoped to catch her alone later, but the opportunity didn't arise and I never saw her again.

* * *

Once on the open road, a straight slightly undulating blacktop striking out ahead of us, the driver became kamikaze. Yet the more road he ate up the more appeared before us. This was the land of the automatic car.

For the majority of the time there was nothing on the matt road and it seemed as if it had been laid exclusively for us. Once, as we neared habitation Mike asked me whether I wanted to stop and rest. I was as fatigued as yesterday but like the fanatic at the wheel I just wanted to get there.

I regarded the clouds at the horizon. They were careless brushstrokes and yet they were with design, like an abstract Japanese picture. Of flames and dragons, chunky Siamese fighting fish and trailing Portuguese man-of-war. Never overhead: forever on the horizon.

We were making good time when the driver said something and pulled off the road. I gave Mike a questioning look and he shrugged. I assumed the man wanted to relieve himself and I looked away vainly searching the empty landscape for thought. The boot opened and he walked to a point beyond the front of the car where he unfurled a small carpet. Returning he again said something and sitting sideways, with his legs outside, he slipped off his sandals and used water from a large plastic jerrycan to wash his feet and hands and arms. He then glanced at a plastic ball compass stuck on the dashboard and then towards the lowering sun. He returned to the carpet.

We got out and Scab turned his head and spat.

Fascinated I watched our driver follow the timeless ritual. He stood, bowed and then began. He genuflected, prostrated himself twice, forehead to the ground and then sat for each unit of prayer, all the while silently reciting portions of the Koran. His open hands first covered his face to shut out evil, afterwards they were a plea or together as a pretend book.

It seemed discourteous to stare at his personal communion with God. Yet, he had chosen to undertake a private function in a public place - albeit not Piccadilly Circus - and we were forced into voyeurism. Seeing him unashamedly subjugate himself to his God I understood why his awesome devotion frightened me. Islam means to surrender and in the Koran it means to surrender to the will or law of God. I was a consumerist individual, westernised, selfish and unable to give myself up so utterly. I could only rationalise his adoration in terms of fanaticism.

Therein lay my fear. Popular images of en masse worship magnified my unease. There was an unsettling collectivism, not quite embracing the lynch-mob potential but leaning that way. Women ululating shivered me to the bone.

When he began rolling up his carpet I asked Mike if he would change places with me. A whiff of the Arab's perfume was okay, but the jet engine seemed to direct it at me and it had become nauseating. The carpet and jerrycan were returned to the boot and we resumed our white-knuckled race. To my dismay the perfume honed in on my nostrils like a heat-seeking missile.

We stopped a short time later to tank-up. Whereas some ten minutes earlier there had been evening light, the zinc and copper having alloyed in strata of bronze, almost at the flick of a switch it was now pitch dark. We all got out to stretch our legs, but none of us left the vicinity of the car. Down an opposite side street a woman was throwing a bucket of water on the walls of her house to douse the heat and settle the dust. At the time I was surprised. Either she was flouting some law or water was not such a luxury. Scab said something to the driver who went round and opened the boot for him. Scab spat and beckoned us to him with a gesture that was an inversion of our own: performed palms down as we might brush crumbs towards us. From a small cool box next to our luggage he offered us cans of lemonade. The name of the make caused me to roar with laughter. I pointed to the can and Mike could not help but smile. Scab looked hurt. The driver returned and scolded me as if to say guffawing was an impropriety. As likely as not it was, especially coming from a woman. As I entered the car I made a mental note to explain to Scab. He was hamstrung by his own self-consciousness. I was out of control as we drove off. Maybe I needed to release the tension spawned from my time with June.

"A can of Zit," I exclaimed, unable to suppress my mirth. "Given to us by Scab."

The word was of course an American one for spot or pimple, but ever since our arrival everything I had seen of western culture was American. So the thought came readily.

"I think we're on the outskirts of Riyadh," said Mike, some time later.

I too had noted the vestiges of the civilised world. Shreds of tyre had appeared first. Then a rusting ball of wire, like tumbleweed from a Wild-West set. A bush adorned with fluttering snared plastic bags. And then all manner of abandoned and dumped, decrepit and decaying bits and pieces.

I knew the capital to be about fifty kilometres north east of the farm and that we would probably only traverse the outskirts. Like much of what had so far transpired I was wrong.

* * *

I don't remember the drive from the farm to the police station. That's one of the memory blackouts. I've tried to piece it all together. Was it a police station? I don't know.

I've been put in a room with a guard who leans against the wall nearest the door. He doesn't look at me. The room is spartan: an interview or interrogation room. I'm sitting on one side of a simple desk: wooden top, wooden legs. My tears have dried and I want to ask for a glass of water but I have no voice.

The door opens and activity intrudes. The guard reacts as if a poker has a shoved up his bum and he strains with the tension it puts in his back. A man briskly enters. He barely notices the candlestick guard and is smiling at me. He probably introduces himself, but his aura and midnight eyebrows remind me of 4B. Two further guards follow him. The outside is shut out and I am alone with four men.

This 4B sits on the only other seat in the room on the other side of the desk. He doesn't carry a loose bracelet watch, but wears a fat gold ring with a turquoise stone. He leans forward, talking and smiling. What he's saying is nothing to smile about. My silence frustrates him. He leans back. He ponders. He leans forward and offers me a cigarette. He fingers the packet on the table. Smoke fills my nostrils and I'm in the kitchen again. My sore eyes burn and tears come to them. 4B speaks. He snatches the packet and puts a cigarette between his lips. My look stops him from lighting it. He speaks again. A guard leaves. We all wait.

The door opens and the guard reappears with a glass of water. It is placed before me. I look at it and my palms sweat. 4B is disgusted and mutters something before taking a sip from the cool glass and placing it again before me. His smile broadens encouragingly as I move a hand to take the glass. He urges me on with nods and soothing words.

I gulp the water greedily. Too greedily. I suppress a splutter. Rivulets form at the edges of my mouth and roll towards my neck. When I replace the glass I am groggy rather than refreshed and I begin to sway, my eyes getting heavy. I don't know what time it is, but I haven't slept for at least thirty hours. The door opens and I'm jarred into life. I pull myself up but continue to sway.

4B barks at the newcomer, a guard who promptly stands aside. A studious looking little man comes in. He carries a small leather bag and resembles a mole. 4B gestures in my direction and speaks to the mole. The mole sniffs and is disapproving. 4B is affronted and powerless. A white woman in nurse's attire enters. Her eyes, like her bearing, are subjugated. She looks at me but cannot communicate. I try a smile that I know is not a smile and I feel myself keeling over.

There are two shouts before all is blackness.

I'm being dragged upwards. The dulcet tones of English in an Irish accent are soothing like a stream over polished stepping-stones. I don't know what she is saying but the voice and the words are so comforting that I can't stand. My legs become liquid and heavy like molten toffee. I think I babble something. I'm being taken out of the room. Through another door. It's an adjoining room. Again a desk and chairs. The door is closed and I am alone with the nurse and the mole. I'm made to sit as he burrows blindly in his bag. The nurse strokes my hand and then takes my pulse at the wrist. I say something and see that she smiles. She speaks but the mole snaps her shut.

His stethoscope is as cold as his manner and I look to the nurse. My mind is suddenly clear, a flush of oxygen to the brain.

"Please," is all I can muster. Please what?

She speaks softly and pulls my sleeve. I give her my arm before my concentration wanes.

There is a burst of laughter from the other room. The mole is fussing in his bag again. He brings out a small-labelled bottle of clear liquid and a syringe. I stiffen and the nurse speaks again. She is pulling something over my head and for a moment I cannot see. Then my head is through the *abaaya* and the doctor is closing his bag. Have I been injected? I look at my forearm, but see my clothes crumpled on the table. The ochre stain on my blouse confuses me until I see scarlet on the cuff. There is another burst of laughter that is accentuated by the mole opening the door. It dies almost immediately. I'm brought to my feet and led into the room, which is now full of smoke. My eyes burn. I feel a sudden vulnerability: my clothing is barely adequate. I'm being led to the gynaecologist's operating table. My vision blurs. A face from the past, Khalid, smiles through brake lights and fumes and I struggle to leave the room. But I am weak and my efforts are no match for the nurse. The mole raises his voice. A guard grabs my arm. Spicy fingers.

Suddenly there is a lot of movement, the door to the corridor is opened, and the bustle outside pops our world. Guards are leaving. There is much talk and I am forced to sit. The nurse is trying her best to sound comforting, but she unnerves me, like a dying accident victim being reassured that "everything's going to be all right. Just keep still, don't look down, just look at me." My arm loses the arm wrestle and is pinned to the table. After a cold cotton wool dab, the needle slides in with clinical viciousness. I feel the alien substance enter my beleaguered system. I speak before slowly collapsing in on myself.

* * *

We had left the Aramco camp just after three thirty. Had we driven directly to the farm we could have arrived around six thirty. Instead we pulled off the macadam road a little before nine. I was as exhausted as the day before. The car veered off the road onto the wasteland at a point significant only in that other vehicles had left the road at this point. Later I would notice the faded sign and the cairn. Needless to say the manoeuvre caught me unawares and I can't remember whether Scab said anything or whether the driver remembered from the outward journey.

For most of the trip I felt as if we were in the middle of nowhere. Now that we had finally arrived I felt no different.

I didn't notice the buildings until we passed one to our left. The meagre light and their beige colour effectively camouflaged them. We stopped in front of a building that was parallel to the one we had passed. About thirty metres separated them. The first building was in darkness. The one before us offered dismal windows of light.

We got out and I suddenly felt drained.

Scab spat again. I was getting used to him doing it at every opportunity. All the Filipinos spat. Mike had visited Indonesia after his first Saudi stint and said that the locals did this too. He thought it was due to the dust.

They were not really buildings. They were prefabricated structures: demountables. Indeed, they were raised off the ground. Each one was the length of a long container, the sort transported by articulated lorries. There was no doubt in my mind that such a vehicle had dumped these wooden structures out here.

I felt numb. I did not want to meet people. It was as if entering the buildings would confirm their existence and somehow my acceptance of this abysmal situation. Earlier I had seen oases of civilisation, which despite their size seemed huddled together, shrinking from the implacable expanse of desert. By comparison this was a frontier outpost, literally beyond the edge of civilisation. Nothing more than a few temporary buildings stuck in the desert. I was reminded of the television series *The High Chaparral*, isolated in the harsh wilderness under the scorching Arizona sun surrounded by hostiles. Here, of course, there were no hostiles, or so I thought at the time.

We had travelled for the best part of five hours in a vehicle done-out like a sheep to arrive at this pitiful collection of buildings.

Numbness turned to dejection as I sluggishly helped retrieve our baggage from the boot. I could see June triumphantly smiling to herself. My time with her seemed like decades ago and definitely not part of the same day. Not only did she now belong to another time, she belonged to another world.

Mike had warned me that I'd have months of nothing in the middle of nothingness. I was not permitted to work. And I knew that he was watching me, looking for reaction. For the moment the dimness afforded me shelter.

I heard later that coloured light bulbs had been strung from demountable to demountable, but visiting trucks had so often brought them down that they'd been permanently removed. Had they been up my dejection would have been more profound. I would not have found them cheery. Truly, all that was missing was a banging shutter, as forlorn as the toll of a bell of a fog-bound vessel.

Scab was getting the driver to sign a piece of paper, when the door to the building swung open and a young westerner as thin as our Filipino companion stood illuminated in the entrance.

"Hi," he greeted us. "What happened Scab? Get lost?" Before waiting for an answer he was down the steps and introducing himself. "I'm Ian. Come on in. Leave your baggage there." I hesitated. "You can leave it there all night, nobody's going to steal it."

I braced myself for the onslaught of conversation as we clambered loudly up the wooden steps situated in the centre of the structure.

At the entrance a further face appeared. This time it was a Filipino. "That's Tass," said Ian. "Short for something. I can't remember what. This way."

We were in a corridor of sorts. The building was structured like the carriage of a train: the main entrance opening onto a short corridor offering numerous compartments. This was the communal building.

A cloying animal stench of fry-ups and sweat, urine and farts, contrasting the creeping sweet nausea of the taxi driver's scent, assailed my nostrils and besieged my thoughts. It was all I could do to stop myself careening against the walls.

Ian led us to the kitchen, right of centre. Despite its banality, flayed to greater heights by the strip light, it radiated warmth. The entire crew had congregated here, having awaited our arrival since dinner, I assumed.

Ian gave in to a new lead man.

"Well, it's the freshly deloused couple," exclaimed the stocky Englishman sitting at the Formica-topped dining table. "We were beginning to wonder whether you'd come to your senses and taken the next flight out."

The stark light and joviality was a slap in the face. I was unprepared and felt vulnerable. Moreso, because Mike could be appraising my demeanour and interpreting it as dejection.

My husband was not normally quick-witted, I was the one with the tongue, but he bravely rose to the challenge. This role-reversal would be the shape of the rest of the evening: he soared and I slumped. "No such luck, mate -" he never used the word mate in a friendly way, but he was not being aggressive "- we're here to help you out."

"Not me," he smiled. "In eight weeks I'm out of here. Just in time for Christmas," he gloated and then as if remembering his manners he got up. "Welcome to purgatory. My name's Bob." He had a comic-tragic face. Although he was not chubby, full cheeks made him appear cherub-like. His hair was in a perm that suggested dissatisfaction. As if he was not at ease with himself. He shook my hand and then Mike's. "That lump over there is Pav. He may look like the Philippines answer to the *Amazing Hulk* but he can seduce the flavour out of a pair of old shoes." Pav was the stocky, no-necked, muscle-bound type. His hairy arms were covered in tattoos that to me spoke of time at sea or in prison. His mouth was wide and his smile displayed a full set of healthy white teeth. In fact he could have had more than one set, because his mouth protruded slightly, as if stretched in its effort to contain the multitude of teeth. It made him look as if he were continually having amusing thoughts and contradicted his brutish physique. Overall he appeared more a benign frog than a grouchy toad. "You'll sample one of his legendary chicken curries. Anything to flavour our scrawny excuses for birds. Talking of scrawny excuses, you've met Scab, no?" The last word was added in mockery and caused some laughter and a smile from the victim. "Ian and Tass have already been introduced. That sulky fellow in the corner is Diek, although we call him Sparky. No prizes for guessing his job."

There was a large flip top bin, the plastic bin-liner oozing over the side like a vane of crumpled coal. Two flies patrolled the area. I recoiled. Of course, although I had no farming background, even I thought it ludicrous that a farmer's wife should be appalled by flies.

I was reeling from the severity of the situation and could find no solace in their joviality. Yet, I could not slink off to bed straight away. As I surreptitiously looked from face to face I became detached. So here we were with two Englishmen and four Filipinos in a flimsy building in the desert, with little or no communication with the outside world.

I was not quite the Gorgon in their midst. I gave no one a stony stare and they were not reduced to forming their impressions of me from the backs of teaspoons, the black window or any other reflective surface. Nonetheless I was not one of them.

Rather than shrink from the frugality of the kitchen I tried to see possibilities for improvement. Typically the lads had done nothing. My efforts were undermined by the nagging suspicion that I was trying to fend off defeat, as if I'd thrown in the towel before the fight had begun. And then, merely thinking that I was about to enter a contest, a contest with boredom, seemed the wrong approach.

I was determined to make a go of my time here. For what was at stake was more than giving in to boredom. Mike knew of my mother's ailment and its latency in me. But I had convinced him that I was a fighter. Seeing in the flesh what I was up against filled me with doubt, but I shrugged this off as fatigue.

From the entrance one could look out through the large window. Running the length of the right-hand wall was the kitchen itself: cooker, sink, workspace, standing unit and wall units. In front and a little to the left, dominating the floor space, were two Formica topped tables shoved together and surrounded by eight metal-legged chairs in chocolate-brown plastic. On the wall adjacent to the entrance hung a simple clock.

There were no adornments, no relief from the basic and functional. On the table were their cups of tea or coffee and a couple of empty tea plates. Standing alone was a Rubik's Cube. This solitary object spoke volumes. It spoke of time idled away.

I felt burdened. If the housing on the Aramco camp had appeared cut out of a film set, then these were the temporary quarters of the film crew. That is the film crew and definitely not the stars.

* * *

Bright oversized lozenges fly overhead. Their regularity takes me back to a late night car journey with my parents. Lights from the motorway came into view from under a flyover and my tiny mind thought they were magically appearing. Their appearance is silent and to the wonder of my parents I gave them noise. "Ping. Ping. Ping."

But I'm not in a car. I'm lying flat on my back. A nurse walks briskly at my side. It's the Irish nurse who'd accompanied the mole. She's having trouble with the orderly pulling the stretcher. I move to change position and realise I am tied down. I lift my head to see thick straps holding me in place. I let my head fall back.

I feel breath on my forehead and look up. An Arab orderly is wheeling this end of the trolley. But he is not just any Arab he is Khalid. He smiles and I panic. His expression changes. He is worried that I am going to give him away. I begin to struggle against the straps. His presence is a stranglehold and I can only hum urgently. My writhing becomes painful and the nurse's voice assumes the urgency I seek.

Then I am wheeled into a bright white and steel room. The orderly is gone and there's only the nurse and a doctor. Is it the mole? I can't remember. The nurse is talking all the time. Her fine skin is bereft of make-up and her pure complexion is lavender. She reminds me of Julie Andrews. "Just a spoon full of sugar helps the mescalin go down, the mescalin go down, the mescalin go down." The doctor is pulling on latex gloves. The nurse is undoing the straps in a most delightful way and my face is a plea. A blanket is removed and only a flimsy *abaaya* protects me. I try to speak, but my mouth moves like a fish out of water. "Your turn fish face." She's unstrapping my chest as I begin my fight. The strap remains and there are raised voices. The strap at my waist is redone and I clamp my legs together. They will not be pried open. A syringe appears and I die.

When my heart beats again I'm still in the stretcher. Now I'm outside in the glare of normality. With a clack of metal I'm in an ambulance. I close my eyes until we're underway. A red light on a machine nearby winks away the seconds. I try to synchronise it with the rocking of my head. I give up and I mouth a word in my head. Ping. Ping. Ping.

* * *

"We expected you for dinner," said Bob, when we were seated at the utilitarian table before chosen beverages.

"Our driver took us the scenic route," said Mike. "I didn't recognise where we ended up. Somewhere in the north-west part of Riyadh."

"You've been here before?" said Bob.

Mike nodded and Bob put on an expression of exaggerated incredulity. "A second tour of duty? I don't believe it." He looked to the others. "I thought the effects of the sun wore off when you escaped the Great Sandpit."

He made it sound as if we were entering a war-zone and I wondered whether he was going to offer us uppers and downers. He could only require downers. Bob was the kind of guy who didn't need pills to get high. He was always flying; the kind of one-man-show you either adored or loathed. The lads were avid fans.

Mike described how the driver took us across Riyadh. He toned down our disorientation and our attempts at asking whether this was a short cut. He made light of our anger when we stopped outside a high-walled villa in residential suburbia.

"How long?" Mike asked, as the driver climbed out of the car. "Scab, ask him what's happening. How long he's going to be." But I could see Scab was consumed by fear. His grasp of Arabic was weaker than Mike's.

The Arab muttered something.

"What did he say?" I asked.

"I think he said he wouldn't be long." I don't know whether Mike caught what he said.

I slumped back in the seat like a petulant child and Mike took my hand. "I'm sure he won't be long. He's left the keys." The a/c was low but on.

"We're totally at his mercy," I said.

The street was one high sandstone wall fronting another. Wooden, double-garage sized doors, with an inset door, permitted access. Housing was like the fortress of one Mafia clan butting that of another. The Arab had disappeared through just such an inset door and for a second I glimpsed a shaded courtyard of cool stone and magnificent foliage. The sound of running water reached my ears.

Mike suggested giving the man ten minutes. They came and went. After a quarter of an hour he told Scab to hoot the horn. Scab pretended not to hear him, but Mike persisted.

"I believe we should wait, Mike. No?" he said.

Scab was the archetypal Asian, unbearably polite and brimming with humility.

"No, Scab, no." But our companion did not budge and eventually Mike leaned forward and banged the horn three times. The sound jarred the air and my nerves.

"This is ridiculous," Mike exclaimed. "We should have arrived by now."

"Perhaps he's having his dinner," I suggested facetiously. "He's had a long day."

"So have we." Mike's anger was enough for both of us. He leaned forward and gave the horn five long blasts. The sound rankled me more than the waiting.

The driver appeared at the door with another Arab. Scab spoke without turning around. "I think my goose is cooked." He thought the Arab would blame him and I felt a twinge of sorrow for him when the driver turned to us. Whether he was cursing or moaning as he entered the car I'll never know. I must admit it was very effective at disarming us.

Even Mike was deflated. He tried to express his annoyance, but there was no real venom in his voice. His limited Arabic forced him into English and it was debatable whether the driver understood.

If one counts the man who checked our papers at the airport this was my second encounter with Arab mentality. Their pace of life was more casual than ours.

Bob told us of how he arrived at Riyadh airport with no one to meet him. He knew no Arabic and had no money. On top of all that he was drunk. Possibly he was not as blind, stinking drunk, as he would have us believe. "Pissed as a newt," was the phrase he used to describe his state of inebriation. Being alone was something I could not even contemplate. To cut a long story short he changed some money, language was not really a problem at the airport, and telephoned the only number he had. He detailed a bizarre conversation that had us chuckling. He eventually got in a taxi and plonked himself on some official's doorstep.

For all this easy conversation I couldn't help feeling that I'd missed a members' only plaque at the door. Was it in my sense of their unity? Our intrusion upon their established routine? The talk seemed colourful wallpaper that did not quite conceal the pits and cracks. Or was I being over-sensitive? Was I merely the first woman in a men's only club?

Ian wrenched me into conversation. "Did you bring any paperbacks?"

"What? Yes, sorry. I'm not all here –"

"None of us are," laughed Bob. "Or we wouldn't be here. If you get what I mean?"

"We're both very tired," Mike admitted.

"Of course you are. And we've got an early start tomorrow. Come to think of it we've got an early start every day. To the cells then!"

We packed up and Bob led Mike and myself out into the black night. Our ears were greeted by insects sand-papering the dry abrasive air. Two moths fluttered about the closing door, seriously unaware of our presence.

At the door I was struck by the multitude of stars. The sky was a magical fog of silver, a myriad of sparkling holes, pinpricks of daylight in a curtain of black satin. The night was terrifyingly vast. My eyes had not adjusted and it seemed exceptionally dark at ground level.

Through the fused light at the entrance I noticed small clumps sitting at the ends of the top step. I had not seen them earlier and for a moment I thought they were creatures: squatting monstrous sand crabs, if such things existed.

"What are those?"

Bob turned and followed my gaze.

"Sand roses."

Sand Rose Farm

The early morning was primordial with a low sun casting a gentle light and pleasant warmth. Clouds shrivelled into a far atoll charted on cerulean parchment. There was an unnatural stillness as if this was one of Earth's first days: the dawn of the *Homo sapiens*. Mild breezes fluffed up the meagre top sand, lifting and gathering it into tiny whirlwinds that swirled and gyrated between the buildings. These evolving djinn highlighted the barren landscape, contributing to its bleakness.

Two things irked me that first morning on the farm. The first was something I could do little about. The second was what I'd heard before dropping off to sleep.

"You were out like a light, but I heard somebody murmuring last night," I said to Mike as we dressed for breakfast.

"Who?"

"I don't know. But it was outside our door."

"What did they say?"

"I don't know," I admitted. The incident was so slight I was not sure I had not imagined it. Our a/c ran all night. We'd all retired at about the same time. The speakers had waited at least an hour after all was quiet.

My husband had no answer and shrugged. "Don't worry about it."

"I'm not," I retorted, offended. But I was bothered by it. What was so important that it couldn't be left till the morning?

Everyone was in the kitchen when we arrived. There were vestiges of the ill at ease I'd sensed the previous evening. It was as if they suddenly fell silent when we appeared. Like schoolboys caught smoking in the toilets there was a defiant guilt lingering in the air. Again I erroneously put these smothered dynamics down to the upset in their balance. Newcomers on board. Indeed woman on board. And they were shuffling to accommodate us. Yet, there was a tinge of wariness in their welcome. They'd not gone into a rugby scrum, but they'd certainly moved shoulder to shoulder. My desire to alleviate their caution was uncharacteristically forced.

Pav was at the stove, tending the spluttering fried eggs and crisped 'American-style' streaky-bacon. Everyone else was at the table that was laden with toast, jam, cheese and baked beans. Morning greetings were exchanged and Ian gave me a look of mild surprise.

"I wanted to be on Bob's tour," I said, to explain my presence at the ungodly hour of 5:30. I had forgone the Turkish bath the shower unit had become after Ian and my husband had used it and simply washed my face and added a dab of make-up. I was at breakfast not simply out of curiosity. After my lukewarm arrival yesterday evening I wanted to assert myself. I turned to Bob. "I know I'm not supposed to, but I was wondering whether I could do some work."

"If you do and the old Rag-head catches you, you'll be back in Blighty before you can say: '*Indak Kabreet*'".

"What's that mean?" I asked.

"Oh, it's just one of those useless Arabic phrases you pick up: Have you got a light please?"

"And you don't smoke."

"Right."

"Maybe I can do something when our Saudi overseer's not on the farm?"

"That's most of the time," Bob admitted. "But his minions appear from time to time."

Bob resumed setting the order of the day. He finished allocating duties with a statement to Ian: "I'll join you at number seventeen between seven and seven-thirty. Oh, get the cruiser out for me too."

I was seeing another side of Bob: the jester becoming foreman.

Sparky had a plate of orange segments before him. Beside the peel was a saucer into which he poured a liberal helping of salt. He began dunking the segments in the salt before popping them into his mouth.

"Coffee?" Ian offered, reaching for a black thermos flask.

"Please," I smiled. Mike nodded.

"It's normally self-service," said Ian. "But it's your first morning and I'll make an exception." He smiled.

"Very gracious," I said, dismissing further analysis.

"Where's the menu?" Mike asked.

"There's no need for one," answered Bob. "Right Pav?"

Pav grunted.

"It's always the same," said Ian.

Bob took over again. "Bacon, eggs and beans."

"No cereal?" I asked.

"You didn't think the word health preceded farm, did you?"

"If I'm to be under house-arrest -" I hadn't accepted that I couldn't work "- I'll have to watch what I eat. Otherwise this kitchen won't be big enough for me and the rest of you."

Smiles encouraged me.

"House-arrest is a little exaggerated," began Mike. "I'm sure as long as you keep a low profile there'll be things to do." The latter half of his statement was a question for Bob.

"Washing, ironing -"

"No, thanks," I protested.

"Fair enough."

"I'll do my husband's and maybe occasionally some extra. I'm not going to be your washer-woman." I looked to Mike for support. It was critical that there be no misunderstandings.

I sipped my coffee so that he only had my eyes.

"Like I said," smiled Bob, "fair enough. But even if you've burnt your bra, it's a man's world here. And I don't just mean on this farm." Then to Mike: "I hope you warned her."

"Don't worry, Dawn can look after herself."

I caught a smile in Ian's eyes. I didn't know him well enough but sensed an opening. His appearance was not unpleasant, but somehow weak. Taken individually his features were average; together they were thin and characterless. His smile accentuated this weakness. His lips never quite peaked at the ends and remained rounded, making his smile banana-like, beguiling him with both clown-sincerity and insecurity.

A plate of bacon and two eggs was placed before me.

"Scab does most of the laundry," Ian explained, finding self-effacement in banality. "Although we all do our own ironing."

"Or not," Bob corrected, pointing at small creases in his shirt.

I tucked into my breakfast. When Mike's plate arrived I took the opportunity to compliment Pav. It was weak congratulating a cook on the way he made bacon and eggs, yet I felt I ought to say something. The stocky Filipino nodded and returned to the stove.

"I thought maybe I could cook once in a while." Pav kept his back to us and made as if he had not heard me. My proposition clogged the air. Everyone was lost. Even Bob gagged. I stirred disorientating eddies into it all by verbally reaching for Pav, who clung to a pan in the kitchen sink. "It'd give Pav a day off."

Mike forged a path through my faux pas and the others followed him. "We'll have to see how it goes. There'll certainly be something in the greenhouses for you."

"We can never completely get rid of the pesky aphids," said Ian.

"The chickens too," suggested Scab.

"The aphids don't bother them, Scab," said Bob.

"Stone the crows, Bob," smiled Scab. "I know that."

Everyone chuckled. My chuckles were related less to the comment and more to Scab's archaic phrase. I later discovered that Bob had been feeding him pure bull.

"You could tend them when the old Rag-head's not about," Bob continued.

I smiled through my dejection.

Sparky was the first to rise and leave. Ian, Tass and Scab followed.

Bob noisily pushed his chair away from the table, grabbed a piece of buttered toast from his plate and slouched back awkwardly as if the moulded plastic chair was upholstered.

"Now for the real orientation. I'll start now if you don't mind listening over breakfast."

* * *

The blindfold is removed. I'm standing in a reception area like that in a police station. There's a uniform behind me at the entrance. There's one in front of me talking to the anonymous woman behind the screen. She wears an *abaaya* and veil.

A form has been signed, papers exchanged.

The one behind me removes my handcuffs.

An alarming buzz is broken by the opening of a door to the left of the room in which the anonymous woman sits. Two further pawns enter the area. They sandwich me, holding my forearms. And then I'm taken through the door.

I had spent two, or was it three, nights in the police station. Most of my time I was in a spartan cell. Otherwise I was in a room with 4B. He asked a lot of questions, but I didn't have any answers. I just looked at him. He lost his temper on at least two occasions.

So here I am, unbeknown to me, my home for the next eight months. I've been questioned and physically examined. Now I'm a rag doll, too exhausted for anything.

The further we go the gloomier and dirtier and louder it seems to gets. There are no windows, just heavy wooden doors with riveted metal frames and peephole slides. Then there is an open area to our left. As if one of the cells has been removed.

The appalling stench of sweat and urine cramps my stomach and I feel the warmth running down my leg.

My guards remove their *abaayas*. There's a woman like them also in a khaki uniform sitting at a desk. One of my guards converses with her.

The guard leads me away from the madness. She takes me further down the corridor. We stop at one of the wooden doors. She pulls back a bolt and coaxes me into the room. There is little in here: a brown blanket on a flimsy bed, like a camp bed, an ancient wooden desk with an empty enamel bowl on top. There is no chair, no sink or toilet. The walls are grey concrete. A barred window gives away the thickness of the wall.

I stand for a long time; long after the guard has gone; long enough for my leg to dry. Eventually I go to the bed and sit down, fearful that it might collapse. I sob.

Something wakes me.

I can see the moon through the barred window set too high in the wall. A solitary door opposite is the only other break in the walls. The moon is a pendulum at full tilt, frozen like my world. A block of ice sits in the pit of my stomach and my fists hug the blanket to my chin. I'm in an Edgar Allan nightmare. The single light bulb, itself in a cage, burns with a low hum.

It's late but there is talking and somewhere a baby cries. Occasionally there is the clang of metal, a door bangs or something is moved. And there are low rhythmic moans next door. Sex and madness. I want to die.

I doze. I'm too weary to think let alone worry. When I wake stars replace the moon. I doze off again and wake when the door is opened. It's lighter now. A woman comes in and speaks. I get up. I'm still in my *abaaya*. She takes me by the elbow, keys jingling in her other hand.

We move down the corridor, passed the open area beyond which is a courtyard. It's early morning. A few sorry souls shuffle about. I'm taken into the neighbouring room where a wooden chair set in the middle of the room is the only difference to my cell. The bedding is ruffled but the lovers are gone. The woman sits me in the chair and picks something off the bed. The buzz is a magnified light bulb. Then she is going over my head with a hard beehive, pushing my head this way and that as clouds float to the floor.

I'm returned to my cell. My head is cold, sensitive to every breeze, sensitive to motion.

Later, when the day is blazing at the window, the cell airless and hot, I am again taken. This time the guard appears in an *abaaya*. There are no words. I simply go with her. We enter a room like my cell. It too has a door with a bolt, although the door remains open. Inside there is a desk with two chairs. 4B sits on one and I am offered the other on the other side of the desk.

The questions start and I drift. I mumble, I nod, but I never really answer. And he goes through the routine we both know so well. He reasons, issues veiled threats, expresses disbelief, drops to anger, spits blatant threats, and descends into exasperation until finally I'm returned to my cell.

This happens a further two or three times over the next day or two. I thought he would have had enough at the police station. At one time a doctor examines me again.

These days are lost to me. I don't think I was eating. I recall a guard admonishing me. But I don't know whether it was for not eating or soiling myself. By the time I thought about knocking on the door to be taken to the toilet it was often too late. I clearly gave them headaches those first couple of days.

When the bolt to my cell door is pulled back I look up and know something is different. The guard is not wearing an *abaaya*.

This time we go to the open area, separated from the courtyard beyond by floor to ceiling bars. Although it is light the area is dim with the press of bodies at the bars. Some are my side of the bars. The ones behind the bars are in rags. They are forced back by the opening of the door, itself bars. The guard gestures me inside and I step towards the crowd. She nudges me further so that the door behind her can be closed. I stand where I am left, wasted. But the inmates jostle for a position at the bars and I am brusquely pushed away. Things are being exchanged. Packages are pushed through the bars into greedy hands.

Not all of the women are at the bars. Some are further back sitting or even lying upon the ground. For surprisingly the floor is sand. There are at least twenty bodies waiting here. The majority are Asians, but a few Arabs are also present. All are bald and clad in *abaayas* or blankets. It's cool.

The guard pulls me through the crowd. The room opens out

onto a courtyard aflutter with lines of washing. This is not a room, but a covered area, as if a ground floor room has been removed. She stops at a desk behind which sits yet another guard. They speak.

It must be late evening for it is not dark but not quite day.

I stand entranced and devastated, ready to collapse, ready to die. Wanting to die. Although I am on the edge of the courtyard the claustrophobic dimensions of the room give me no distance from the madding crowd. A withered Arab woman appears before me. Where did she come from? Her face is covered by a rural woman's *yashmak*: a piece of gossamer cloth hanging from a velvet band across her forehead. Two close-set rectangular windows expose her opaque eyes. A dark leathery hand comes up and two henna'd fingers, chain-smoker yellow, lift her veil. A sneer reveals gapped teeth. My focus drifts. The vast solitude in this place full of women consumes by the time she spits in my face. Warm saliva, cold froth, camel spit, a glass of chilled water.

* * *

"We work everyday," Bob began. "Although we try to take things a little easier at the Muslim weekend, Thursday and Friday. As the great Merv the Perv would say: 'Today's physical Tuesday, but logical Thursday.' He's a friend of mine, a programmer in Dhahran. Everyone gets a day off a week. We start at six and finish more or less at five. There's an hour for lunch, which we don't always take together. We have a rota for maintaining the generator and working in the greenhouses. The greenhouse is no breeze, but it's easier than outside. There are no hard and fast rules and sometimes one of us goes with Pav to help with the shopping or collect the post."

He noticed that we'd finished eating and took our plates to Pav.

He returned with a tea tin from one of the cupboards, which he upturned on the table. I winced at the clatter and then smiled through embarrassment. He began, separating the notes from the coins. "This is our dinner money box. Pav tells us when and how much he wants us to put in. I don't want to play tiddlywinks I want to give you a rough idea of the layout of the farm." Two coins, one above the other represented the kitchen and the old rag head's demountable and made the stem of a Y. The arms were made up of the Filipinos accommodation on the left and the westerners' accommodation on the right. Capping this Y and making something of a courtyard were the greenhouses. But the arms of the Y went beyond the greenhouses. To the left was the workshop and store and further up the sheds and petrol pump. Moving on from our accommodation on the right was the generator and farther still the silos. He took a few notes and laid out the road. "As you can see we're too close to the road."

"What do you mean?" I asked.

"Well-planned farms have central buildings." I felt foolish. "This one has grown away from the road and so we're lopsided."

He looked at the spread on the table. "We've a few kilometres of perimeter fence running north and south, otherwise we're wide open."

Bob packed up the coins and notes and suggested going to the lounge.

"What's this for?" Mike picked up the brass horn that sat upon the refrigerator. It was a single fluting loop of brass of the type you might find on an antique motor vehicle or as a prized student union possession.

"The next best thing to one of those ranch-house triangles." I made to squeeze the thick black rubber bell. "That's strictly forbidden. It's for outside use only. Give it a blast if you want. I doubt if anybody will come now." The temptation was too much and I took it to the front door. The first squeeze produced a sigh. A second sharp squeeze let rip a honk that would have sent me up the wall in the confines of the kitchen.

Mike and Bob were in the corridor behind me. I nodded agreement, my hair settling down again. "Strictly for outdoor use."

"It's a good call to dinner," he said as I returned it to its place. "Although we use it to call Scab some mornings. He oversleeps. He plugs his ears with cotton wool." He continued to talk as he flicked the light switch of the lounge. For a moment the overhead strip-light strobed the room. "They say on a quiet night you can hear Pav's snoring in Riyadh. Scab's got the bedroom next to him." Scab would say that his internal clock woke him on time, but he would doze off waiting for Pav to finish showering.

* * *

We seated ourselves in this neighbouring room. "We have a telephone," he waved to the wall nearest the door, "but it's only good for local calls. The nearest phone for international calls or anything beyond Riyadh is at the Masstock dairy, about twenty kilometres from here. They're also our nearest neighbours. You'll have to pay them.

You'll get to know the boys there. They use our grass - I mean the green stuff, for their cows. Occasionally we're invited over for the evening. Somebody has to stay here though. We draw lots." He glanced at me. "There're about forty-five guys there. Six Irish. The rest are Asians."

"Did Scab draw the short straw yesterday?" Mike asked.

"No, I sent him."

"But he seems the most vulnerable of you all," I pointed out.

"That's exactly why I sent him. I want to build up his confidence." He reflected. "Okay, that's not strictly true. He's probably the least experienced on the farm and therefore the most dispensable. He's also the only one without a driving license. We all drive on the farm, of course. Anyway, I couldn't spare a vehicle and I couldn't afford to lose a good man for more than a day."

"You didn't need to send him at all," said Mike.

"The old Rag-head wanted it."

"But we could have travelled to Riyadh - even by taxi - and met there."

"The old Rag-head wanted it."

"There was no reason for the taxi to travel all that way to pick us up."

"Do you want me to repeat myself a third time?" I knew Bob wasn't telling us the whole truth. "I should say something about the lads. If you go by the rule of thumb that you need one worker per 1,000 acres then you don't have to be Einstein to know that we're one man short. We did have a Filipino: Eddie -"

"At last a decent name," I exclaimed.

"He went home in July because his father's ill. Cancer, I think. Anyway it meant that we've been one short for a while. I don't think he's coming back. I can't say I'm too unhappy about it. I think it was him who made so many long distance calls that the company or Abdul decided to make the telephone good for local calls only." He paused. "Pav helps out. It's surprising how little he knows about farming. He's a whiz with our a/c units, though. Out of all the equipment on the farm I think they give us the most trouble." He smiled. "Mainly because of unqualified maintenance." He glanced in my direction. "So it sometimes gets a little sticky." He teased the dirt under his nails. "We've a Cummins generator that supplies the workshop and living quarters. It's checked every morning. Touch wood, it's given us no problems. Sparky is our official electrician - he hasn't a clue about a/c. He's not lazy, but damned slow. Bright doesn't precede his nickname. But he somehow muddles his way through. The last time he touched something and it worked first time we heard the beating of pigs' wings. Tass is our official mechanic. He's also our unofficial hairdresser." He looked at me pushing at his hair. "How do I look?" I gave him a pitiful look. "They're all machine operators. Ian shirks responsibility, but is otherwise a good worker. He's also a mechanic." The latter statement was an aside and I was right in thinking that his abilities were questionable. I had no illusions about this aspect of farming. An able farmer was also an able mechanic.

Then they spoke of the general workings of the farm and amazingly, I unconsciously absorbed a lot of what was said. I smiled at his talk of winter and summer seasons which could be distinguished by being hot and hotter.

This month had been busy with deliveries of seed and fertiliser and with land preparation. November would be taken up with the sowing of wheat, one of the two main crops of the farm.

Ultimately my mind wandered.

The lounge had drawn curtains at the windows. They were of a thick material in lacklustre brown. Their drabness blocked the early morning light and made the room dingy rather than subdued. A chink of the day glowed at a gap in a pair of them and I spied a slip of window. Someone evidently took the trouble to clean the large window of the kitchen for these ones were grimy. I later discovered that they were not proper glass but Perspex similar to that used in airliners. Sand had scoured them with tiny scratches. The blind eye of a large television set dominated one half of the room, with the settee and easy chairs arranged in positions of homage. The other half was taken up by a table and chairs a single aesthetic level above those of the kitchen. A stack of canned soft drinks on their cardboard palettes took up a corner.

* * *

As the lads clattered down the steps I took a moment to look more closely at the sand roses. One was a doorstop, holding back the outer mosquito-net door. The sand roses were indeed clumps of sand. Of course they looked nothing like roses, except for the fact that their jutting segments could be the tips of thick petals. For that was all there was to these enchanting formations: a jumbled knot of segments. But they were like crustaceans, their natural wonder bestowing them with beauty.

We made our way across the loose courtyard formed out of the three demountables and the greenhouses before us. The lads used the area to park the vehicles during lunch. Their proper housing, in the form of open-mouthed sheds that were also used for storage, existed beyond the greenhouses on part of a paved area. On the other side of this area, were the twin grain silos, each with a 20,000 tonne capacity.

"We produce about 28,000 tonnes per year," Bob explained, "but there're always delays in issuing delivery licenses. Last year's entire yield hasn't left. And we've begun harvesting."

In the cool of old greenhouse the madding cacophony of the chickens supported and muffled by the generator was barely noticeable. The distinguishing factor between the two parallel 100 by 25 metre greenhouses was that one used PVC and the other glass. The former had been built first and the Perspex had turned milky in places so it looked worn and was appropriately called the old greenhouse.

The green was a pleasure to the eye and the sound of water quenched some mental thirst. "It's another world in here," I said in a lull in Bob's monologue.

"Scurvy's not one of our problems." We walked beside the rows of tomatoes, lettuces, peppers and cucumbers that were planted in the ground and were in various stages of growth. My thoughts again wandered. To call the place lush would be an exaggeration. But for me this was what a garden truly meant: a place to relax. So whilst Bob explained the organisation of the plants I sought a place to set a chair.

A few days later I would be working in the greenhouse and not being sure of something went in search of advice. I thought I'd go to the kitchen, ask Pav and make myself a cup of coffee. On the way across the courtyard I notice somebody moving in the workshop. So I changed direction, thinking I could offer this person a cup of coffee as a reward. When I entered there was nobody to be seen. Were they bending down behind a bench working on something on the floor? "Hallo?" I called as I began to walk the length of the room. The only exit was the entrance. The lack of reply stopped me and the silence was a ratchet that cranked up my senses. I strained to hear pins dropping. Without moving I craned to look behind the benches, the lathe and other equipment. "Hallo?" I waited. The strain yearned for release and I shivered. Why hide? "I know somebody's in here." Was it one of the lads? I backed away. Something irrational crossed my mind, like the shadow that had crossed the workshop window. Had I imagined it? With the possibility of strangers on the farm the workshop was locked when not in use. There were expensive tools here. It didn't make sense. I left and hurried to the kitchen building. Once there, even Pav was not about. I filled the kettle and looked over at the workshop. Distance now made it difficult to be sure, but again I thought I saw movement. The kettle boiled but I did not take my eyes off the workshop. Pav entered the kitchen and I jumped. "I didn't hear you," I mustered and shakily spooned coffee granules into a mug. As I poured in the water I again looked over at the workshop. Sparky came out and went off in the direction of the petrol pump. Why would he hide from me? I was confused, so much so that I did not immediately tell Mike of the episode.

After the greenhouse Bob pointed out the chicken coop next to the generator.

The chickens were a scrawny crew of two dozen or so birds living in a makeshift structure in the shade and the unbearable roar of the generator. "The building's in two halves. One opened, one closed. We've got the UV-sensitive crop chemicals in the closed half. As you can see the generator occupies the open half. We won't go any closer. At 125 decibels it isn't far from a jet engine at take-off."

I'd heard this grey monster last night on the way to our demountable. In our room, however, it was thankfully obliterated by the ubiquitous a/c.

Mike and I had single beds; we were too tired to push them together. The room was not exactly a cell, but despite the desk and chair it was mono-functional. There was also a sink and mirror, but this was a bedroom. I had assumed that all the rooms were of similar size. This was not true. The structure was the same size as the communal demountable. Here, it was split into two pairs of rooms, each pair sandwiching a toilet/shower unit. So every room had two doors, one onto the corridor and another to the shared conveniences. The two adjacent middle rooms had centrally placed doors that opened onto a short corridor. Each end room cut off the corridor with their doors. Therefore, unlike the middle rooms, none of their area was taken up by corridor space.

"Honeymoon suite number two or three?" Bob asked. Naturally Bob and Ian had housed themselves in the larger end rooms: numbers one and four. "They're both the same." He stood in the corridor to the right of the entrance, effectively offering us the left of centre accommodation.

"Is this two or three?" I asked looking about the austere room.

"Yes," he answered facetiously.

Mike went in and opened the cupboard.

"That bulging door is the karzy. You'll be sharing with Ian." I understood the strategy of his position in the corridor. He had cut off the room that shared his amenities. "Shall I bring your stuff in?"

"I'd like to see the other room," I said, looking directly at him. A glint of eyes was the flash of sabres.

After satisfying myself that the other room was indeed a mirror image of this one and looking into both toilet/shower units I held my tongue, but not before hinting at its sharp-witted edge. "There is a difference," I said, straight-faced. A flicker of movement in his cheeks betrayed his teeth clamping against an assumed assault. "The stench in Ian's doesn't make my eyes water." As if he had misheard me he was stunned. Then he saw me for the first time that evening and he laughed loudly.

If I had not established myself in his eyes then I had at least shown him that I would not be type cast. I had also shown him that his colourful language was not going to bring on a fainting spell and that he did not have a monopoly on vulgarity.

Mike heard my remark too. And as if he were waiting to exhale all evening, his laugh was a welcome sigh. Then he said to Bob: "James, our baggage please."

* * *

Food is often a soup of fish and rice. One would think something so simple could not be inedible. Although the cook has been heavy handed with the salt it is not the taste that puts me off. It is the fact that the fish have been butchered. Awkward bones lurk in the whole, from needles and spines to full blown combs. The heads are easy to spot, but not the razor shell that covers the gills.

At first I ignored the soup. This was not to protest the slops or my treatment. I simply made no conscious effort to eat. I took it when it was given and held it. Eventually one of my fellow inmates would speak to me and, receiving no reply, relieve me of it. At the time I felt nothing. As if I could not be bothered to eat or partake in life's daily necessities. The only time I returned from my absence was when I went to the toilet and due to my lack of intake this became less frequent.

I'm no longer in solitary.

One day the small dark girl took the bowl from me and teased a spoonful of the fluid between my lips. She knew I had shut down all functions. These functions did return. The first to leave would be the first to reappear. Along came taste, followed by smell and hearing, then sight and finally speech. Physically I had forgotten how to eat. Shock has a limitless wardrobe.

My lips offered no resistance. But then my mouth was inoperable. The jaws didn't move and the soup dribbled. The girl tried to move them on the meagre substance. I might as well have been comatose. My senses had emigrated to Catatonia: an austere Salvadorian landscape sparsely filled with isolated Technicolor aberrations as forlorn as the mammoth sun-washed highway billboards in the middle of nowhere.

Just as I am a prisoner of my body, so my mind is a prisoner of what it can comprehend. Life for me is a galaxy within, plugged into the universe about me. My galaxy had been severely damaged by the death of another. And I had imploded. The space-time continuum had collapsed. History had been rendered obsolete. My mind was a singularity at the beginning of time. There was no explosion, no expansion. That would come much later, after many psychiatric sessions. I know I had visitors: 4B and then someone from the embassy. But they had not reached me. My mind was compacted into a black hole, neither shedding nor receiving light: a hard kernel of existence that didn't even harbour the instinct for survival. Oh, there was no drama here. No thrashing, no passionate fires, no walking through glass, tearing out hair, no emotional conflagration burning me down to charcoal and ashes. What happened was much more devastating.

The police, 4B, tried kindness and then threats. At that time the inadequacy of language effectively gagged me. How could I talk? I had been forced to swallow something horrendous and indigestible. It refused to stay down. I was continually on the brink of regurgitation. How could I explain it? Whenever I thought I could begin sharp splinters of memory filled my mouth with blood and caused me to choke and blubber. So they gave up and sent doctors and diplomats.

I was probably ready, maybe yearning, for the jolt of the familiar that turned a small cog in some obscure recess in the mystery of me.

Fully covered guards escort me through the visiting area. It's not visiting time. I'm taken down the corridor to one of the rooms. I am transfixed and stand limply in the cell into which I've been brought. There's a desk and two chairs on either side. I stand. The guard turns me to the door and the voices there. There is another *abaaya'd* guard in the cell, just inside the door. But in the doorway are familiar faces that cause an infinitesimally small movement. Pat and big Pat from Masstock are standing there. I think they're speaking. They look horrified. Is it my haircut? Although I have been staring at them for I don't know how long, it was minutes later that they had to leave. I don't know what they said to me. I think they left knowing they'd reached me. The tiny internal creak caused silent tears to run down my face. I think big Pat - bless him - began crying too.

I'm not sure whether this happened or whether I imagined it happening. But long after they'd gone, as if trying to put names to their faces, a voice echoed from afar that they were the cowpats and I began to laugh hysterically until the big inmate from the top bunk at the window slapped me.

* * *

I only spent a few moments in the workshop before fleeing. My husband popped his head out to check on me. "I'm okay. I just felt a little dizzy." Not only was it unbearably hot, there was also a sickening stench of waste oil and burning metal. Dark stains marked the hard floor. The room was chock a block with equipment: gas and electric welding gear, a lathe, air compressor, tyre repair equipment, hydraulic lift and scarred workbenches. Scab and Tass looked up from a brutal chunk of metal, apparently a pivot engine. "At ease men," said Bob. Then to us: "This is the hub of the farm. This is where it happens." I didn't wait to hear about what happened and stood outside in the shade of the concrete building waiting for them to emerge. Even outside the smell edged towards the intolerable. It didn't seem to bother the flesh-coloured gecko that was stuck high up on the wall. I watched him for some time marvelling at his stillness, willing him to move, and as in the children's game, I glanced away and then looked again, thinking he might move when unobserved, but he remained uncannily motionless. In one of the moments when looking away I was caught by markings next to those of our footprints. They resembled a fossilised sea anemone and I knew what had made them and frantically scrutinised the immediate area.

I was beginning to relax, returning to the gecko when the door opened and their talk burst my thoughts.

Mike gave me a smile that I answered with a nod of "everything's fine." Perhaps he suspected there was more behind my fleeing the room.

"What turned your stomach were the fumes of a can of gasket sealer," said Bob.

"Is that what I think it is?" I asked when he closed the door.

He looked at the markings in the sand. "A side-winder," he said a little too loudly. He went on, his voice taking on a casual relish that was boyish. "You don't see many of them. Sand vipers are more common. They're all poisonous, I'm afraid. They'll stay out of your way. But they don't like getting stepped on. Then, who does? And here's an anecdote for you. Last year some Arab hob-knob from the Grain Silos and Flour Mills Organisation, to give them their full title, came here in open-toed sandals and stepped on one. We rushed him to hospital." Pause. "Never saw him again." Another pause. "He survived."

Before we moved on I took a last look at the lizard. He was still a fixture.

"And you've no idea where the key is?" my husband asked, evidently picking up on some unfinished conversation.

"Nope," Bob replied. "It's always been locked." He was silent for a few paces. "As far as I know it's empty."

"Empty or not we could use the space."

There were two storerooms in the workshop. Unlike the workshop, which did not have a/c, these rooms were temperature controlled. Both were locked and the storekeeper and mechanic held the keys. "Otherwise some of the spare parts would get up and walk to the Philippines." But one of the doors had no key. I readily accepted the inaccessibility of this room. Part of this was because it was of no interest to me, but the main reason was that since my arrival I'd been bombarded with the new. There was an exciting and unsettling haphazardness to everything. Anything was possible. And I'd grown accustomed to accept and learn rather than question and appear green.

"Maybe Ian and Tass should have a good search for it," said Mike.

"Eddie's probably got it. I'm sure it's empty."

"What with the telephone, this Eddie's got a lot to answer for," I said.

A light went on behind Bob's eyes. "Anyway I've never had to go into the spare parts storeroom. The end of month stock-taking always adds up."

"Always?" questioned my husband. Bob's affirmation led to another question. "Who plays accountant?"

"Scab." Bob's smile was that of a snake-oil salesman. "And you can bet your bottom dollar he's conscientious."

He pointed to the no smoking sign and mentioned the capacity of the buried petrol tank. We passed the open storage sheds in granite-cold grey concrete with their stacked bags and sacks and he mentioned scorpions. "Black and white, both dangerous." Then he listed the farm equipment. "We've got a four-wheel drive centre-pivot service vehicle, three 450hp articulated tractors, three 12 metre seed drills, two 10 tonne fertiliser spreaders, one land ripper, two land planes, three 15 tonne grain trailers and one 30 ton grain truck."

"Right," he said finally, "let's go and see the farm."

* * *

My returning senses stress my appalling condition. I am dirty, my hair uncombed, teeth woolly and I have diarrhoea. But I'm not much worse than those about me. I share a room with eight other girls: one from Sri Lanka, one from Bangladesh and six Filipinos, one of whom has a child of two. Five bunk beds line the walls and leave enough standing space to allow you to reach out and touch all of the beds. There is nothing else in the room. A rickety a/c unit is attached to the ceiling above the door. It works, but sounds as if it's on its last legs. A small window high on the opposite wall ensures that the cell remains in semidarkness even in broad daylight. A 40W light bulb set in a cage in the ceiling does little to diminish the shadows. The bedding is a hotchpotch of the cheap and gaudy. The sheets patterned with faded flowers, and heavy dark blankets rough like mats. Personal effects are stashed in or under the bed. There is no privacy here.

Even the toilets offer no privacy. The doors there have no latches. But they are not places for lingering, let alone contemplation. The vile stench is an infinitely more potent version of the stink of the toilet in the communal building when I first arrived at the farm. And to think I chastised the boys for leaving to the toilet seat up. Anyway here I cannot squat for long before the smell makes me sick.

"Rita and I took care of you," says Pip.

Rita is a big Filipina, a challenge to the Sudanese, who rarely speaks. No one bothers her. She's top dog in our cell. Top dogs get the privileged bed. So the beds give away the pecking order in every cell. Top bunks are better. But the top bunk at the solitary window is the best place. The window is shuttered, but the air is good. And you can look at the stars. When Rita's not lying on her bunk she's at the door smoking infernal thin black cigarillos.

I can only assume that Rita bothered with me because Pip asked her. She's the one who slapped me out of hysteria. I'm not sure why she bothers with Pip. She doesn't seem the caring type. She's hard-boiled, undoubtedly suited to this place. Perhaps she has a soft spot for Pip's child.

Pip is a contrastingly petite Filipina with small lips and a button nose. She looks so young she could be her daughter's sister. We're sitting on my bed watching her daughter playing with small stones. Children up to the age of two and a half stay with their mother. Pip is filling in the cracks of my first days. "You were in shock and not eating or drinking."

"And now I'm eating I've got diarrhoea."

She nods. A scarf covers her close-cropped head. She told me that the prison population had their heads shaved only a few weeks ago after an outbreak of lice. I've seen my Death's head in a small make-up mirror. I can do nothing about my sunken eyes, but I too have taken to wearing a scarf. It keeps my head warm.

I have two other possessions. One is a prison issue toothbrush; a cheap plastic thing with bristles like steel, the kind of gift an airline might give to passengers for one-way use. The other is a half a cake of soap, whose rounded edges say that it's been used. I later notice that Rita has a full unused-looking block.

Since coming out of my delirium many prisoners have come to talk to me. I guess I'm something of a rarity here. But please not a celebrity. Some speak in broken English. And I wonder at the phenomena of how my English becomes pigeon to meet their level. They tell me of time in Britain or tenuous British connections, distant relatives or even a tourist in their country. It doesn't matter. They all want the same thing. They want to know if I can speak to my embassy about their plight, whether my embassy can contact their government, for instance. No, I'm no celebrity, but I'm suddenly very proud of my nationality.

All these women have the glaze of hopelessness in their eyes. Some newcomers still burn with desperation. But their eyes are glazing too. They're all fishermen's wives: condemned women, already widows, waiting on the wharf for ships that will never come in.

Pip and I are alone in the room. All the others are outside. The cells or houses open onto a courtyard; one end of which goes into a corridor of sorts, ending at the bars where visitors are met. Washing lines criss-cross the other end of the courtyard. She sees me gazing at the women playing volleyball over them.

"Don't ever try to stop them playing. Even if it is your washing. They'll gang up on you and if they don't get you straight away they'll get you in the toilets." Her face darkens as she continues. "Stay away from the Arabs. Don't bother anyone, but especially the Arabs." My look urges her to elaborate. "They stick together too. I don't know about you, but Asians are the lowest here. The guards and Arab prisoners are the top here. The guards use some of the Arabs to control us." Like asking the lions to look after the gazelles, I muse. "Don't mess with the Sudanese either. They are a crazy lot. Always fighting." I'd noticed the big shiny black women already. "If you can help it, don't go to the toilet after dark."

"I have to go all the time. Aren't the cells locked at night?"

"No. They're only closed. If you want to go out you can open it and signal to the guard at the end of the courtyard."

"Why shouldn't I go to the toilet at night? Surely if anything is going on, it's going on in the houses?"

"Mostly. Some of the guards are having affairs with the prisoners. They use the empty solitary cells, or go to the houses. But the toilets are meeting places and places where things are settled."

I mull over what she has told me in the silence.

"What do you do to pass the time?"

"You can work. A lot of them sew." I've seen them traipsing through a door in the far corner. A guard marks their numbers off. "They get ten riyals a month. Then they can buy things from the shop." I wait and she goes on. "I can't leave my child. The others help me out. And I don't need money." She's not the only one. The older women don't work. And I don't think any of the Arabs do.

"Okay. So what do *you* do to pass the time?"

"Keep my head down."

"There's a television somewhere. I've heard it."

"Yes, in that far building. But it's always set to the Arab channel."

"And you said stay away from the Arabs."

She smiles and nods. Her smile is sour. They've housed the wolves with the sheep.

I draw strength on the belief that I'll be out of here soon. I have enough worries without taking on her problems.

Now that I can communicate someone comes to see me every other day. It is either a law official or a doctor. The various doctors examine me physically, talking my pulse, blood pressure, checking my eyes, mouth and ears. I've given urine and blood a couple of times too. The law officials simply sit on the other side of a desk and ask me questions. The police want to hear my story. I've asked to see someone from the British embassy. All this time, easily two weeks now, I've only seen the police and doctors.

"Don't you go out?" It was not warm, but pleasant in a sweatshirt or blanket.

"A little."

"Shall we go out now?"

"Let's wait for Rita." I don't think I've ever seen her go out alone. I know she is afraid of something. Rita appears to protect her. She'll tell me when she's ready.

* * *

We traipsed back to the courtyard. I was again dazzled by the starbursts that jewelled parts of every reflective surface: the sun arc-welding pieces of itself to them with painful brilliance.

We headed for a Japanese four-wheel drive land cruiser. The vehicle was modern, expensive and oversized: you needed a stepladder to look under the bonnet. There were only two doors and naturally I went to the wrong side.

"I'm afraid you can't drive," said Bob.

"Oh," I exclaimed, noticing the left-hand drive. Even out here, in the middle of nowhere, I could not get behind the wheel of a vehicle. I moved round the front touching the body as I did.

"You won't be able to do that in a couple of hours," said Bob, reaching up to the door.

"What?"

"Touch the metal. By mid-morning it'll be hot enough to fry an egg on."

I was a little peeved at being treated like a child and forced myself to let it go.

I climbed in the back, approving of the furnishings. It was

decked out with all the mod cons: plush upholstery, stereo, beautifully comfortable seats. The air was musty. The warmth coaxing smell from the furnishings fooling one into thinking the vehicle was brand new.

Bob set the a/c to hurricane force. Then he unhooked a paper blind pulled across the front windscreen and eased it into a roll on the passenger side where Mike was seated.

"When I drive you need seat belts," he said. He was right. On the farm and on the open road everyone drove like maniacs. "It's my ambition to hit sixty before leaving the courtyard."

There was no road but vague tyre marks marked a route.

"You can go back to sleep, Dawn," he said. "We're going to be talking testicles - technicals, again."

"You're incorrigible."

I was impressed by the size of the farm. Mike had spoken of seven thousand acres, just under eleven square miles, but the scale of the operation was something I had not visualised. The farm fanned out in all directions from our cluster of buildings. Apart from the main road, which flattened one edge of the circle and some arbitrary fencing, there was no boundary and everything merely gave itself up to the desert. Again, there were no rolling dunes, merely shallow undulations or a layer of loose carmine coloured sand topping hard, compacted ground.

Bob turned down the fan. The interior was a lagoon of coolness.

"We grow a lot of grass for the Masstock Dairy. We've sown Rye with Rhodes so we can supply all year round." Mike explained to me later that Rye grew under thirty degrees Celsius and Rhodes above thirty. "We do the harvesting. Sometimes we deliver it too. Normally someone comes out for it."

"How many central-pivot systems are there?" I asked, before he really got going. I had been waiting to show some understanding.

I met his glance in the rear-view mirror. "Thirty-five," he answered, forsaking wit and so disclosing his surprise.

He recovered quickly. "Some of the older ones are hydraulic, but most are electric, with power supplied by skeeko, the Saudi Commercial Electric Company, S-C-E-C-O, skeeko. We sometimes have 'skeekos' on the farm. Do you know how the pivots work?"

A simple yes was out of the question and I gave him a textbook rendition. "They pump up the water from underground reservoirs" - which had been discovered when drilling for oil - "and feed it along slow-rotating arms which sprinkle the ground."

"Done your homework, then," he complimented. "Do you want the technicals?"

"Preferably those," I smiled wickedly.

Mike laughed, although I wasn't sure of his sincerity.

Textbook Bob's delivery was in monotone. "The pumps pull the fossilised water up from aquifers about three hundred feet below. The irrigation arms are 1,640 feet long or 500 metres and cover 200 acres each."

"What's the delivery rate?" Mike challenged, tongue-in-cheek. He knew it all.

I expected a "piss off" or some such sentiment, but Bob was silent for a moment. "Around fifteen hundred gallons a minute."

We all laughed.

The arms were linked stretches of piping supported by towers on chunky tractor-style wheels. From the piping hung an array of sprinklers of the type one sees in modern buildings. On a twenty-four hour rotating cycle their movement was negligible.

There were no crop sprayers. All herbicides, fungicides and insecticides, plus nitrogen fertiliser and micro-nutrients were injected through the irrigation system."

We met Ian at number seventeen which was marred by a pond-sized puddle. "You can see our problem," said Bob. "There must be a large stone or some obstruction under the surface. There's enough good area to warrant its continued use, we just need to watch the growth of the pool. If ever they decide to grow rice, we've got a paddy. I think Pav called it Saudi's answer to 'the stairways of the Gods'. Apparently that's the name of some rice terraces in the Philippines. A little bit of culture for you."

"Rice or not it's a great breeding ground for mosquitoes," said Mike, clambering out. "Still, if this is the only one then it's no real problem. We were plagued with flash floods coming down the *wadis* (gullies) on my last farm."

"We've *wadis* off to the west, but they give us little trouble."

We looked over the pivot and I touched the grass that was rough and surprisingly dry like a cat's tongue. The misting sprinklers suspended a piece of rainbow in the air. Rather than being enchanted I was repelled. The odour of sulphur reminded me of the second thing - the thing I could do nothing about - that had irked me that first morning. I'd only washed my face, but the hot water was also pumped up from underground and was untreated. Washing had not been pleasurable. When I showered, I would use more than double my normal dosage of shampoo to neutralise the dissolved solids. As I entered the kitchen that morning either the smell of sulphur or the memory of it lingered. Whichever, the farm was making its indelible, diabolical, mark on me.

Mike and Ian stayed at number seventeen and Bob returned me to the demountables.

On the way he remained convivial, but strangely serious, almost as if he had lost confidence. I was hurt. Was I still under assessment?

"As you can see there is more than enough for us to do. Being one man short doesn't help. Forget the sowing and reaping, there're a multitude of mechanical problems too."

"Mike's very able."

"Yeah, he seems to know where he's at."

Even here I couldn't help reading between the lines. And again I cautioned myself, dropping asking whether his observation was meant to highlight that I did not know where I was.

He stopped in front of our demountable and ejected me with a "have a nice day" that was flippant and at the same time sincerely meant, but didn't quite make either.

* * *

I spent the rest of the morning unpacking. All my belongings took on ration significance. Lightly taken choices now acquired the weight of circumstance. My books, especially my books, became cherished objects. They didn't take on Bible-like reverence. I would lend or even give them away. Rather they became treasured, affording a cord to a familiar world, linking me to reminders of another existence.

I began to confront the problem of filling the endless hours. I listed ways to melt in with the farm's daily routine and keep occupied.

Waiting in the wings was a more threatening enemy than boredom. My mother's depression was part of me. One of my earliest encounters with her illness was when I was a toddler. I remember being scolded by her, but I wasn't the one to dissolve into tears. Seeing her break down profoundly disturbed me. A pillar of adulthood I had unconsciously come to rely upon turned to mush. Her scolding me was not unjust, but the extent of it was out of proportion. The experience was dreadful and my minor misdemeanour filled my tiny mind with guilt for many years.

I was growing tired when I heard vehicles approaching. The boys were returning for lunch. Strange that I should refer to them as boys, I did not feel remotely motherly towards them, but part of me had apparently adopted them.

Only in the evening did they bother to wash and change. For now they just dusted themselves off outside and washed their hands. This was why the kitchen resembled a sand pit. The Brits wore their own clothes but for some reason the company supplied the Filipinos with overalls.

Until everyone was about to return to work, lunch passed without much note. Most of the time the talk was about the workings of the farm. I was pleased that Mike had been readily accepted into the fold and general bonhomie. This was not surprising. Not only did he have gender in his favour, he was also their future leader.

I was asked how I had spent the morning and then it was suggested that Pav take me shopping tomorrow. I jumped at the idea. Pav remained characteristically impassive, but he was not openly against the proposal. The journey would provide the opportunity of hacking through his stoic mantle. So far only Ian seemed to make any real effort at extending the hand of friendship. Yet, inexplicably I warmed to everyone but him.

"Do you think I could do a spot of sunbathing?" I asked, as their hour was almost up.

"I'd advise after three thirty," said Ian.

"Out of sight of the old rag-head," added Bob.

"You can't expect me to stay in all the time," I bristled.

"The Saudi isn't often here," said Mike.

"About once a week," said Ian. "It depends how busy we are."

"He comes just when we need him," added Bob, "sticking his oar in when we're up to our eyes in it. He's not the only one who comes. Apart from truck drivers we get other overseers. They send any old Tom, Dick and Hamed. Some don't know anything and just watch. That's fine. It's the ones who think they know that are dangerous. Abdul's like that. Sometimes you can persuade him, other times he's heard or read something and wants to sound knowledgeable. You have to be pretty diplomatic." Although Bob didn't say so, I knew that impatience quickly dried up his diplomacy. "He's like Tolstoy, coming to see the serfs."

"Tolstoy knuckled down and helped," Ian pointed out.

"We're spared that honour, luckily. Like most of them, he doesn't like getting his hands dirty. It'd be havoc if he got behind the wheel of a combine harvester." He brightened. "We're not like serfs either. We work ourselves till we're blue, so we're more like Smurfs."

"Am I'm expected to become a Muslim woman, then?"

"Almost," said Bob, a tinge of exasperation edging his voice.

"Nobody's stopping you sunbathing," said Mike, "but this is Saudi Arabia."

"Don't I know it."

A gaping silence opened up between the rest of them and me and nobody met my eyes.

More was behind my mood than this restriction. I had already asked Ian about the milkiness of the Perspex of our shower unit. Before he could answer Bob had contributed his two-penny worth. "Mine's the same. Sometimes when I'm under the shower and get the urge, I scratch at it with my thumbnail. Let's face it Dawn, what's the point of cleaning it? In a week or two it'd be back. And we've got enough to do." I would scrub our unit. I could live alongside their sties, but I could not live in one. But one of the main sources for my discomfort lay in the concoction of smells that came from the communal toilet at the end of the kitchen corridor. The cubicle housed a very civilised porcelain throne, exceptional for the prefabricated building. Fittingly a cheap black plastic seat and cover crowned it. These had been left up, to help circulate the stench and reveal the revolting yellow stains. Bachelor-hood at its best. The plastic bottle of disinfectant was a dud: not simply empty but dried out. At the moment I was frustrated into conforming. There were limits and a few days later I would suggest that the seat and cover remained down. Pav bought an air freshener and disinfectant. And I certified the building safe for naked flames.

"We'd better get back to the coalface," said Bob. For a moment nobody moved as if waiting for me to approve or for an echo to return out of the chasm.

Tass and Sparky got up together. Their movement gave the others an excuse to break out and I was left with Pav's back and a lonely afternoon for company.

In our room I was too angry to cry. Naturally, I was angry with myself. Lethargy took me and I fought through a few pages of a novel before falling asleep; solving the question of sunbathing for the time being.

* * *

I'm sitting outside our cell next to the old Indian who has been here since 1974: more than a decade. We're mindful of the general goings-on, especially the volleyball game over a line of washing. Like her I'm on my haunches huddled against the wall. Long silences punctuate over conversation. We have all day. She tells me that between the cells there is a hierarchy too. There are about a hundred women here and the stagnation has congealed them into gangs. Safety in numbers. Nationality plays an important part in the comradeship.

There is more than a fair share of idiots in here. A woman wanders passed us. She talks aloud to herself. I avoid her eyes for fear she might address me. Is she mad or just lonely? I don't want to know. I have more than enough problems of my own.

She notes my reaction. "Most of these women shouldn't be here. But there are murderesses." She doesn't hide the weariness in her voice. "Most of the Arabs are accused of murder or being found with drugs or alcohol." We watch a tall black woman slam the ball at her opponents. "She's in for pushing Qat." Without looking at me she anticipates my question. "A narcotic common in Yemen and countries of the Horn of Africa."

This prison was some kind of army barracks. It is fort-like in its structure.

"There is another group. A small group, but one of the most powerful. You should keep out of their way." I follow her gaze to the old woman who spat at me. Another three are also shrouded. Otherwise there are women hanging around them like bodyguards. They look upon the courtyard like personages above the horde. I don't understand why they choose to be veiled in the presence of women.

I allow the woman her silence. Eventually she continues. "They are the ultra-religious ones from Asir in the south or Burayda in the Najd Province. Their allegiance can't be bought through marriage or bribery. They say the country's rulers are corrupt. And accuse the al-Sauds of putting modernisation before Muslim values."

"What have they done?"

"I don't know. Perhaps nothing. But they are the mothers or sisters or wives of men who have issued a *fatwa* against the al-Sauds. Some may be related to the men who seized the Grand Mosque at Mecca in 1979."

"What happened?"

"They held it for three weeks. The Saudi army killed them or they were executed."

We watched the women. "They're not rich or well-connected. Otherwise they wouldn't be here. They'd have gone to al-Malaz, instead of here. I'm surprised you're here. This is where they - how do you say it? - lock the door and throw away the key."

The workers are returning from their shift. They struggle in from the door in the corner, passed the guard with the clipboard, moving along the walls of the enclosure. Beyond the door there is a hall of sewing machines. I believe there is a laundry with presses there too. There are two four-hour shifts a day: early morning and late afternoon. Every month they're paid ten riyals. A few of the women work in the kitchens and administer the food. The old, the children and as far as I can tell, the Arabs too do not work. How they earn I don't know. Of course money is not the only currency.

The marauding gang of Arabs are moving purposefully across the open space. They've singled someone out. The guard has seen them but concentrates on her clipboard. They're attacking a Filipina. If she'd had hair they'd no doubt have pulled it. Instead she is pulled by her rags. The Arabs are shouting; their victim is on the ground. For a moment I don't think it's going any further than this, but then the girl replies in some way. Perhaps she doesn't speak. Whatever, they begin kicking her. They're yelling and screaming so much I can't tell whether the girl is making a noise. I look to the old Indian. I know her answer. Eventually the Arabs are done. Mercifully the whole incident is over within seconds. But they are long seconds and the victim remains appallingly still: a clump of rags.

A guard has left her desk at the visiting area and clipboard is also moving to the clump of rags. The Arabs linger until the guards are almost upon them. Then they casually disperse. A guard crouches and lifts an edge of cloth. I'm sure she's talking but I can't hear her. The rags move and then the woman is helped to her feet. She's red in the face, but I can't see any blood. She limps along the wall. Another girl takes her from the guard. They disappear in a cell and with them the incident is forgotten. The volleyball resumes and the buzz of voices increase.

It's nearly visiting time and we watch the Arab group move towards the corridor bars. These kin of Saudi dissenters are the only group that are not allowed visitors. Yet, they remain powerful. Even the guards seem frightened of them. They go to the bars to see what comes through.

Visiting time is the highlight of the day, not simply because of the visitors but because of what they might bring. Most of what circulates enters this way. I suppose the guards take their cut or are bribed. They too deal in contraband. They sell things to the inmates for belongings or favours. At least one of the female guards is having an affair with an inmate. It's not all corrupt. One guard is good to Pip's daughter, regularly giving her sweets.

A low always follows visiting time. There's a lull in the courtyard. It's not a good time to walk. Nerves are frayed. A couple of hours' later things have risen to the pre-visiting-time level.

Essentially every day is the same. Squabbling is put on simmer at sunrise. There it remains bubbling just below the surface. Sometimes during the late morning or early afternoon it erupts in physical form.

There's a bored Arab at the opposite wall. She too is sitting with her knees at her cheeks. But she's playing with a mirror, reflecting the light of the sun on our wall. She's following imaginary lines; sometimes in a slow investigation, others in an erratic swiftness, dizzy like a fly. And the light flashes across our eyes. Then she torments, the light ever more frequently crossing our eyes. The Indian quietly tells me to ignore her. The mirror is a hypnotic strobe, slapping light in my face. Slap, slap, like the urgent blitz of a police car.

"Don't become bitter," says the old Indian. "Bitterness will eat you inside out."

I look at her in wonder. The Arab with the mirror becomes history. How can this woman sit there and tell me not to be bitter? She's been incarcerated here for more than a decade. I know her story. She was employed as a maid. One day she came upon a man stabbing the woman of the house in the kitchen. He turned on her and told her to mop up the blood. She was young and terrified and simply obeyed. The man left and the police arrived. Nobody believed her story. And that was that. Here she was. End of story. Her government was active, but were accomplishing little; procrastinating the inevitable.

* * *

"Filthy lucre," answered Bob. "What else?"

We were a group of four at the kitchen table, the Filipinos having retired to talk or gamble. Yesterday, they had remained in the kitchen to welcome us. Normally they left after dinner, Pav preferring to let the dishes soak overnight. Sometimes they went to the lounge, but mostly they went to their demountable. On the pretext of bringing a message from Mike I once went to their rooms. Bob had suggested they were bum-chums, but I did not believe him. He had left Saudi by this time and I wanted to prove to myself that he had been wrong.

I apprehensively entered their building. They were very noisy, possibly arguing, and did not hear me enter the main door. So I knocked loudly on the door behind which they were congregated. The silence was immediate and shocking and I was filled with misgivings.

Sparky opened the door and although I was not unwelcome I felt like an intruder.

There was a lived-in smell in the room: a mixture of body odour and pistachio nut induced farts. There was an additional sweet sickly smell I couldn't identify. I remained at the doorway. A table lamp weakly illuminated the den.

They were huddled before crumpled piles of toy money and jealously guarded mah-jong bricks. We had to fetch the money from them when we tired of Scrabble and wanted to resurrect the farm's tattered Monopoly set. I suspect the money represented the real thing.

Traces of fading animation were extinguished by my first words. "I thought there was a cockfight in here."

I don't think they gambled every night. They couldn't afford it. They wrote home, read, slept or took a collective trip into Riyadh. They never made such excursions alone, Pav's shopping being the exception. But tonight was Thursday evening, the Saturday night of the Muslim weekend and I think they ritually gambled on this night. I see now that these once-a-week late-night sessions took their toll, especially on Scab who didn't have the stamina of the others and periodically overslept.

So we Brits often found ourselves alone after dinner.

"I'm here to make as much as I can as quickly as possible," Bob continued. "But I'm not gambling with the Filipinos. Mark my word they'll fleece you. But if there's any way of bolstering my salary I'm there." I was not sure what he meant.

My husband had grasped his meaning. "On my last farm - it was further out than this one - there was some weed growing." He never did contact his old farm. All his colleagues had left. "One of the shower units was always out of order and these plants started growing in there. They flourished so much they grew out of the window. Some grew on the pivot perimeters. Just before flowering they were harvested and left to dry in the sun."

"Was it a business?" Bob's eyes sparkled at the possibilities.

"No way. Too dangerous. When I arrived I virtually put a stop to it. It didn't make me very popular, but the amount of damage to the farm equipment went down. I allowed them a little to keep them happy."

"And you?" I asked Ian. "Why did you come here?"

"The same. Lolly."

Bob and Ian exchanged looks.

"Ah, that's not totally true," Ian admitted. "My, er, fiancée left me." His afflicted eyes snared upon mine before scurrying off like frightened animals. "I needed to get away." He managed an embarrassed banana-smile.

Ian, at twenty-four, was the youngest at the table. The rest of us were in our late twenties.

"And this is certainly *away*," remarked Mike, denying moroseness a grip on the conversation.

Bob bulldozed his way through Ian's personal Armageddon with his acerbic wit. "Don't worry, there're no sharp instruments in his room and I've removed his shoelaces. I suppose you two came here to study the mating rituals of the camel in its natural habitat."

We smiled and I fought to keep from looking at Ian.

Mike spoke about experimental farming, but couldn't quite whip up interest in them.

"I'm surprised we haven't met the old Saudi," he eventually said.

Bob's answer was raised eyebrows as if to say: "Are you?"

I felt Bob was to blame for Ian's reluctant admission and current abstraction. "What happened between you and the rag-head?" Slandering someone I had yet to meet scotched my sensibilities and I regretted not saying: "old Saudi." Was he old? To tone down my bluntness I added: "I mean, it's no secret, is it? And it's the reason you're leaving."

Mike regarded me.

"No, it's no secret," said Bob, casting his eyes down to inspect his bitten fingernails. He looked up and his look was an accusation. "The guy's an idiot. He hasn't a clue about farming. He's just another of those entrepreneurs. Probably a prince to boot or at least related to the House of Saud. They all are."

His statement about our Saudi overseer's farming knowledge was not as disparaging as it sounded. The Saudis had embarked upon self-sufficiency after wielding the oil weapon against the West in a 1973 embargo and then realising that they could suffer an equally crippling grain embargo. The Ministry of Agriculture and Water was immediately consigned to achieve food security irrespective of cost. Free land was distributed and the government agreed to pay half the start-up cost for farming it, the other half being supplied by interest free loans by the Saudi Arabian Agriculture Bank. Influential businessmen and some of the five thousand or so princes saw the fast buck and jumped in. Agreements were made with various companies to secure farmers. Hence the liaison between Abdul and Smith. Many of these businessmen had less farming knowledge than me and this was my first farm.

"Turning the entire populace into one big happy family is one of the ways the monarchy maintains power," said Bob.

"Tribal culture," said Mike.

Bob looked at me. "When I first came out here I was full of respect like you. I complimented the old rag head -"

"Yeah, like calling him a great merchant," said Ian.

"It's not my fault if he doesn't understand cockney rhyming slang. Anyway he was pleased - proving my point." His smile of satisfaction faded into the silence. "I made a mistake. I lost my cool a while back. I told him that we were understaffed. Eddie had been gone a couple of months. To meet the schedules we were working longer hours and cutting into our days off. He disputed this and I lost my temper."

"Tell them what you said," said Ian, his hurt having receded.

"I told him I thought that his type had been abolished with slavery in 1962." He skewered us with a hard stare. "His English was good enough for him to get the gist of the insult. He went pale and walked off. Since then the atmosphere between us would blunt a chain-saw."

"And the rest," Ian coaxed.

"Yeah, I forgot to mention that some top brass type from the Ministry of Agriculture and Water was with him at the time."

"You were a bit tactless," I stated.

"I thought I could use the brass to jump-start some action."

"You were probably too harsh."

"I'm not the arse-licking type."

"Why didn't you apologise?" I persisted.

"I just gave you the answer." He smiled. "Hey, only a squeaky wheel gets oiled."

"Or replaced," Mike pointed out.

I later learned that Bob had used under-staffing as a reason not to lose a vehicle or a good man to pick us up. I can imagine Bob's obstreperous attitude exasperating the old Saudi to the point of reluctantly agreeing. "We didn't see eye to eye from the word go." He began picking at the dirt under his short fingernails. "I can't remember when it was. At the beginning of my time here. He said he'd meet me the following afternoon. And like a typical Arab he didn't turn up. I wouldn't have minded except for the fact that it was my day off. After that I did my own thing. There was no apology or anything. They're just not reliable."

He reflected. "Look, a year and a half out here is more than enough. I've made my million anyway." Did he earn more than my husband? I couldn't believe the company paid so highly. I decided he was talking figuratively. "It gets to you after a while. Maybe that's why I flipped out. Something inside old Bob was saying it's time to get out. It's very easy to stay here. The money's good and you're almost your own boss. You get lulled into a routine. And only sometimes do you see it's not a routine, but a rut." He had grown very solemn. "But don't let me put you off," he said caustically. Then his gaze at me softened. "It'll be harder for you."

I had apologised to everyone at dinner. And they said that they could find me work. I could help in the greenhouses. Tend the chickens, if I didn't mind going deaf. I could also take on some of the paperwork too. One of the lads might have to front for me when signing for deliveries. That was something I was going to have to live with.

"I was thinking this afternoon - and yes, I'll have a lot of time for that - I was thinking, I could take a taxi into the city."

Bob smiled and shook his head. Ian looked on pityingly.

Full of sympathy Mike turned to me. "It'd be too dangerous."

"Why?" I didn't have visions of becoming an intrepid Gertrude Bell, but I thought I might absorb some of the culture. By comparison today's dangers were far less than in her day.

What hadn't my husband told me?

"Many of the Arabs think western women are loose," said Bob.

"What?"

"This is a Muslim country," said Mike, as if that explained everything.

"As far as I've seen it's westernised."

"Oh, it is. All the twentieth century things are here. But it's their mentality. They have a different world picture. Particularly those not educated abroad."

"And let's face it, Dawn," said Bob, patronisingly, "a taxi driver is hardly going to have an Eton education."

Mike continued. "As far as they're concerned our society is promiscuous." He knew that I was annoyed. Such statements were not enough. "There's more to it than that. The general belief is that women, if left to their own devices, are sexually uncontrollable."

"You mean western women?" asked Ian.

"I mean all women." This was one of the things that had initially attracted me to Mike. He was modest, but knowledgeable. After his stint in Saudi he had taken a year to return to England. Doing an extended Asian tour. Indeed, he had spent a sizeable amount of what he had saved. "Women are like children, incapable of controlling their desires. They're not to be trusted. That's why they're kept behind the veil and closed doors."

"It'd be heaven on Earth if all women were nymphs," smiled Bob.

I wasn't ready for his levity. Of course I had been warned, but all my efforts at trying to make the best of a bad situation were being thwarted. Tired of playing the naïve one I lashed out. "So I'm expected to reduce myself to a silhouette too."

"That's the way it is," said Bob, resignedly. "You're in the land of the *sharia*. Islamic Law. There's a twisted logic that blames you if the taxi-driver has an accident. It goes that if you hadn't hired the taxi it wouldn't have been where it was and there wouldn't have been an accident. You hired it and so caused the accident."

I thought of the guilt I had felt when June's coffee-table book was splashed. The Saudi logic was then an extension of this sense of responsibility. The reasoning was not twisted just extreme.

"Anyone for a cuppa?" asked Ian.

"I don't want to stay up too late," said Bob, exchanging looks with Ian.

"I'll second that," Mike added, oblivious to the exchange.

"A night-cap then," said Ian.

After Ian filled the kettle Mike took up the thread.

"It's all to protect the honour of the family. But Dawn, most Muslim men treat their women well. She's for the man and for the family and nothing more. She has her place."

"I don't care what anyone says, about honour or whatever, there's no getting round the fact that women are second class citizens."

"Madam, you flatter yourself by forgetting the camel," said Bob.

Mike smiled reassuringly. "I don't think that's true today."

* * *

"Look, I can get you into a hospital. As a trauma patient. Depression, if you like -"

"Paranoia? Psychosis?"

"What?"

I smile.

Others have been to visit. Two men, I think. Sending a woman is an obvious ploy. They are to blame for my cynicism. They are too diplomatic. I'm surprised it took me so long to realise that they can talk a lot but say nothing. A direct question meets a "I'll try to find out" or a blank "I don't know". Then there is the buddy-buddy approach. They speak of their difficulties with the Saudi authorities. It's almost as if they want to belittle my problems. I'd respect them more it they'd give me a straight *Inshallah*. No, that's not true. Honesty would be refreshing, though.

"I'm trying to help. You'll have your own room," she continues. "You'd be out of here, at least."

I know this too is a form of interrogation. When she is reduced to being blatant she turns her back to me and looks out of the window. She can't face me and lie. There is the merest ripple in the back of her jacket, enough to betray her hard fin and expose her circling strategy. Sending a woman is a clever move. But like them all from the British Embassy she's a shark just the same, and she will get nothing from me. I am doing the taking.

I've been here for three weeks and I'm sick and tired of the waiting. Time and again I've fobbed off with "these things take time". I can smell the impotence of these diplomats. I can see it in the tired eyes and insecure smiles. I'm just another line in their weekly report, at most a topic of conversation over cocktails and cucumber sandwiches.

This place is dragging me down. I've tried to detach myself from life here, but as time passes I feel it draining me. In prison you're initially faced with two reactions: fight or flight. Fight quickly burns out. So you end up with flight all the same. And flight can only be mental, which means drawing inward. You deny the world about you and build a personal reality. Maintaining this inner sanctum also requires effort. You're continually reminded of where you are.

At the time I thought it couldn't get any worse. But it did get worse: much, much worse. With hindsight I can now add another sentence to my magazine competition: E. Saudi ground me down to my most primitive self. A savage capable of murder.

She's standing, pacing. I'm sitting, relaxed.

I have got nothing from the Arabs. But then I have not tried.

Of course they extracted everything from me. What happened? What part I had in the killing? And then strangely: what friends did Pav have off the farm?

So now this diplomat is having a go. She wants to know about Pav's off-farm friends. Of course her route is circuitous. She talks generally about shopping and then cooking, before moving on to shopping for food. It's all so obvious.

I draw out her discomfort, delighting in weirdness. She could easily spite me and I'd crumble, but then she'd be left with debris. She is trying to extract information from a child, a child delighted by the power and the knowledge that there is no information. Using her hunting powers to the full, her tiptoe approach nonetheless breaks eggshells.

* * *

I was lying in bed trying to escape the throb of my heart in the mattress when I heard them. Not them, but the creaking of the floor.

I'd slept during the afternoon of that first day so although it was night I was dozing more than sleeping. Also remnants of jet lag were upsetting my sleep.

Mike was long gone; distantly chopping logs in the land of Nod. That first day on the farm had knocked him out.

Was I worth less than a camel? Of course not. But behind every joke there was an element of truth. Out here I was not sure where I stood.

The sudden absence of creaking and a single crack on the wooden steps outside told me that they had left the demountable.

I waited before getting up and slipping on an XL T-shirt. I crept to our door and opened it quietly.

Like the kitchen demountable there were foggy windows either side of the central door. One of these windows was in front of our door. I glanced at Mike before stepping into the corridor.

I didn't go any further but remained transfixed at the window. To move could betray me. For now I was merely a shadow amongst shadows.

There was movement outside. Two or three figures. One was clearly Pav. They were pushing a cruiser. When they were practically out of sight, beyond the demountable I heard the engine start up. Somebody wearily returned, either Sparky or Tass. I watched him go into the Filipinos building. Then all was still.

Where were they going? It was the dead of night. Why the secrecy? They could have only pushed the cruiser so we wouldn't hear the motor.

Back in bed my mind began to spin out various scenarios.

* * *

Pav was a mountain, presenting me with a face so sheer I could find no handhold. I had realised this earlier, shortly after leaving the companionship of base-camp. My questions had received abrupt replies, one word answers, restricting the conversation to small talk.

"How long have you been here?"

"Three years."

"Do you like it?"

He shrugged and even this was an effort. For a moment I was at a loss as to how to tackle his unscalable demeanour.

I was irked that I was not going to Riyadh. I had spent time thinking of my choice of wardrobe: a long, formless summer dress, inoffensively plain: white, delicately spotted with pastel blue forget-me-nots, a loose jacket to cover my arms and a scarf ready to enwrap my head. But it wasn't my attire that was the stumbling block. I would need an *abaaya*. It was the fact that Pav and I weren't related coupled with the fact that I could present no form of identity. I didn't have an *iqama*. It was too risky. Mike initially thought I could get away with it, but the others persuaded him to err towards safety.

My consolation prize was a trip to the Masstock Dairy. Pav was going to drop me off on the way to the city, buy me an *abaaya* during his shopping, and pick me up later.

Later would I have the letter from the old Saudi, explaining my right to travel with someone other than my husband and giving a telephone number should things get complicated.

As soon as Pav took us off the farm I exerted myself in my effort to befriend him. We mounted the blacktop between the cairn of stones on one side and the solitary board bridging long stakes on the other. I'd missed these things when we arrived. The board was sun-bleached and the name of the farm was barely readable, the colours of the lettering and symbols had turned peculiar like a Calcutta film poster. Of course this was a symbolic entrance, as useful as a turnstile in the middle of a fenceless field, and because it was a sharper turn off the road it was more bypassed than driven through.

By asking more demanding questions I tried to coax longer answers out of him.

"Why did you come out here?"

"Money."

"Is that all?"

He nodded and I looked away. I was irritating him and his brusque attitude was scotching me. Waving a white flag of honesty was my next option.

"About me cooking, I'm sorry if I upset you. I thought I'd be a help."

He grunted.

"You can understand that I want to be useful, can't you?"

A nod. The road was straight and there was nothing upon it except us. Driving did not warrant the concentration he wished to present. The steering wheel looked puny in his meaty hands. And his poise betrayed the effortlessness with which he controlled the vehicle.

A puddle that we could never reach moved ahead of us. This was not water, but a reflection caused by hot air sitting below cold; a mirage, indeed as its etymology would have it "something to wonder at." Funny how heat mimics water. Funny too, how pertinent this puddle was to Pav's unreachable attitude.

I was able to prize out a few nuggets information. He was not married and had an uninteresting past. His mother and father were farmers and he had two brothers.

I decided that his impervious attitude could take the claws of the grapnel I had started to swing. I hurled it high, sending it crashing through all decorum.

"You don't like me, do you Pav?"

If I had known him better I could have been more certain of the broadening of his private smile. But he was impossible to read; his features were cast in the leathery-tan of an Eskimo.

"You talk too much."

This was a shower of razor-sharp shale meant to wipe away my finger probing and strike me down. I reacted fiercely. "I can handle it if you don't like me." My neck was afire. "I just like to know where I stand." Nonetheless I had been dashed on the rocks and thrown into the sea.

As if conceding something portentous he said: "Women are trouble."

I was cut and angry and in no mood for such claptrap. Now it was my turn to be aloof. I huffed and let the strained silence echo the closing of doors and turning of keys.

The heat in my neck had risen to my face. During the lull it passed through red and into white. I wanted to pound him. Contrary to securing victory with his landslide, I flourished in the silence and I grew and rose above him. I rose up like Poseidon, not to save the Argo in the film *Jason and the Argonauts*, but here to crush the mountain under the heal of my hand like a nub of dry bread. Supreme indifference was achieved when I pulled out a paperback from my bag.

He dropped me off at the Masstock dairy a short time later.

The lads here made time for me. Their welcome betrayed the tedium. The dairy was a big operation. There were over fifty workers with six Irish expats. Three of whom were called Pat. Leading to the names Pat, big Pat and small Pat. "The first person we met at Dhahran airport was called Pat," I remarked in our kitchen, complaining that should I meet any more I'd have difficulty separating them. "Lump them together," suggested Bob. "You can call all the dairy Pats the cow pats."

We had tea and a tour. There were 5,000 milking cows and 5,000 replacement stock: saleable female stock and beef stock. Altogether 10,000 livestock units, as they referred to them. There were four milking units, a milk processing plant, maternity unit, clinic and cooled housing.

The merciless Arabian sun confined the poor animals to a life indoors. Yet, the lads assured me that they were well looked after. Indeed, happy. "Diet and temperature are all that matter," said big Pat. "Four to twenty five degrees C. Below or above that they get stressed and production suffers." The milking sheds were damp with misting fans that maintained this temperature even during the fifty-degree summers. For all that I couldn't help feeling sorry for the dumb beasts. Their taut hide of monochromatic sky said they should be drifting over pastures. Instead they were interned behind steel cages. I despaired of their stupid nonchalance and something within me wanted to scream at them.

When Pav picked me up late that morning he had softened. He asked me about my time on the dairy. I was friendly and thankful when he told me he had procured an *abaaya*. His softening could not compare with the hospitality I had just received. I denied him any truce. It wasn't that I was not ready to forgive him, more that I could not be bothered with him.

* * *

At dinner the novelty of our presence had worn off and we broke up early. I had spoken of the lads about the dairy and how I had spent the rest of the afternoon writing letters. Apparently this activity twanged guilt-nerves and Bob and Ian retired to write.

"The day after tomorrow we'll go to Riyadh," promised Mike when we were back in our room. The likelihood of being stopped was slim. The worst that could happen would be spending some time in custody. We were married. Mike was at the desk, having also been bitten by the letter-writing bug. "I'll take the morning off." I can count the times he had a full day off on one hand.

"That's great." I was sprawled upon the bed skimming over a "What to see in Riyadh" magazine Bob had lent me. Riyadh meant the 'Gardens' in Arabic. "Perhaps we can buy a wicker chair for the old greenhouse. It'd be a great place for me to read." I flicked through a couple of pages of advertisements. "Don't you think it strange the old Saudi hasn't come to see us?"

There were a variety of markets to be visited. I was dying to see the Gold *souq* and the Bedouin *souq*. The Women's market also enticed.

"He could be away on business," Mike eventually said.

The Museum of Archaeology and Ethnography promised a few full days of occupation. Pav could drop me off and pick me up after shopping.

"What do you make of Pav?" I asked.

"He can cook."

"That's not what I mean."

"He's okay. Distant, maybe."

When I didn't answer he turned to me, sucking the end of the pen.

"There's something dark about him - and I don't mean the

colour of his skin," I smiled.

"You mean sinister?"

"If you like."

He dismissed this with a huff. "He's just private. Like the rest of them. Just because he's built more solidly doesn't make him a gangster."

"So you think so too? He's got that shady mobster dignity."

"What? No. At most he's a bit of a rogue."

"But what if he is a criminal? What better place to lie low?"

"As a cook?"

"He's no cordon bleu chef. And he's hardly likely to advertise the fact that he's a bank robber or hit-man."

Mike shook his head. "If he's either of those I can't see how he got out here."

"Maybe somebody pulled some strings?"

His laugh was akin to throwing his hands in the air. Then a moment later he said: "Goldfinger?"

I laughed. But yes, squeeze him into a bursting suit and top him with a bowler and he'd be Odd-Job. He even went about like a child playing aeroplanes, his delta-winged arms never hung vertically.

"Do you really think they go to the red light district?" This was our conclusion to the crew's nocturnal activity. I was still intrigued. How did they come to find out about it? That such a place existed surprised me. As always Mike had his priorities.

"I don't really care, as long as it doesn't effect their work."

* * *

"He raped me," says Pip quietly. We sup more of the thin soup. The food is as uninspired as the days. An endless cycle of fish soup, chicken, rice, and salad. We're sitting on the edge of my bed. Her daughter is behind me and I'm afraid she might spill her soup on my mattress. She hasn't heard her mother. Nobody in the room can hear us. Our heads are together. "Then I became pregnant." I don't ask how often she was raped. "In some ways I am lucky."

I can't conceal my astonishment.

"If I had given birth to a boy they would have taken him from me." She speaks impassively. Being here has eroded her hate. Funny how some become resigned and others fight on. In which category do I fall? I'd plumb for resigned. But deep down I know I am procrastinating. The bitterness and call to fight are swelling with each passing day.

Eighty percent of the girls are here for getting pregnant, being with a male that was not a husband or relative, or because they lodged a complaint against their employer with the police. The girls in my cell tell variations of the same theme: stories of intimidation and abuse. They are often alone in a Saudi house. Like all the females in an extended family they're open to the will of the menfolk. And the womenfolk don't exactly welcome them with open arms, especially if they're pretty. These girls have to obey them too. There're rapes and abortions. I can't believe it happens in every household. Otherwise India and the Philippines would dissuade their people from coming. Perhaps they do.

A clatter causes us to jump. Rita has thrown her spoon and empty plate on the floor. Nobody protests. She doesn't wait for reaction turns on her bunk, presenting us with her back. I meet indifference in the others. Pip smiles weakly. I watch Rita reach through the bars of the window to the shutters. Her hand brings in a sliver of metal. I shift to see what it is. She lies on her back and looks at it before using it to idly pick the dirt from under her nails. I see that she is holding a spoon the wrong way round. The handle has been sharpened to a point and from the way it glints I suspect the edges are also keen. I am shocked that she toys with the weapon openly. A guard could pass by. If she's not suicidal then she's burnt out. She is always unpredictable. Nobody knows what goes on in her head. Any attractiveness in her face is held in check by her stony expression.

I have seen one of the Arabs with a spoon bent into a knuckle-duster; others have honed an edge of their make-up mirrors. The loose slats of the shutters double as wooden knives and I've seen a woman hit another with a sock full of stones.

"Rita is good to me," Pip says suddenly.

"Who's she protecting you from?"

"The Arabs."

The Arabs are second only to the guards in the pecking order of the prison.

"Why?"

She looks at me for a long time. "The man who raped me is dead. His wife killed him." There's no trace of gratification in her face. "She is here."

The consequences of this dumbfound me. This Arab woman blames Pip for her misfortune. Her husband is of course the true culprit. Pip is the true victim. This woman would see it as Pip's fault. Again there was that twisted Arab logic along the lines of: if Pip hadn't arrived her husband would not have been led astray. It's maddening.

I have not missed that she said Arabs. Many are out to get her. It seems there are always the types that look for trouble. To break the tedium? And then there is probably that tribe, family or clan thing at play too.

That Pip doesn't go out much is in her favour, but even she must go to the toilet. Rita cannot be with her all the time. When her daughter wants to go others take her. I don't know what the Arabs think of the little girl. Surely she's a victim too. I don't know. Nothing makes sense.

I always thought women sought compromise rather than confrontation. Here we become primitive, aggressive like men. Preserving one's space in the horde leaves no room for compromise.

"If anything should happen to Rita..."

I wait for her to continue, before offering pitiful reassurance. "What could happen to her? She's a tower of a woman."

"I will face the woman."

"Why?" I know who she is talking about. The Arab with the bitter expression has been pointed out to me. Yet of all the Arabs, and despite her expression, she appears the most accessible. There's an openness and approachability in her face.

"I cannot keep hiding," she says. "It is better that I face my punishment -"

"Why should you be punished? You're punished enough."

"Because that is the way. I cannot live in fear." I understand her wanting to resolve the situation. She is sick of the dread. Physical pain can be dealt with, it can heal, but dread is a continuous mental pain that bruises every day.

"I can't help you, Pip."

"I know."

"Surely you can talk to them? Take Rita." Even as I ask the question I know there is no hope. She doesn't bother to answer.

I have no words of comfort. All I do is rest my hand upon hers.

* * *

As soon as Ian caught me alone he began a soul strip. On his day off he cornered me in the laundry room. I was doing the ironing.

I did our laundry, although I agreed to load and unload that of the others if it was properly sorted and ready to go. It never ceased to amaze me that the men could tinker with the farm machinery but set them before a washing machine and a pile of clothes and baffling ineptitude consumed them.

I knew he wanted to talk about the love of his life and in me he saw a sympathetic shoulder. I let him speak. His strip was indeed a tease. He was restrained and coy, and then he candidly let something slip. After the ironing we sat in the kitchen and then the lounge. His talk took us through a full wash programme. He carried the plastic basket of sodden washing outside. We hung the steaming clothes together and took them down half an hour later. For the best part of the morning he sketched rainbows in storms, spoke of candy-coated razor blades, agonies and amnesties and effectively coerced me into making inquiries. He timidly played on my sympathy, wringing our fledgling friendship for all it was worth. Then just when he thought they could get back together, something happened that irrevocably split them. This was his trump card, his finale. After which I admit I'd had enough. And then although he was done he retraced his steps. When I'd translated his timidity into vulgar prostration and tried to politely extricate myself, he shovelled more my way. We were back in the lounge when Pav looked in. He was getting lunch ready. The interruption was my escape and I left.

Thereafter I tried to keep out of Ian's way. He caught me again and enticed with new morsels that were thinly disguised things I already knew. He'd played himself out. His trump card had been total self-effacement. The light he mistook for the end of the tunnel in the turmoil of their relationship, the light he raced headlong to meet, was that of an oncoming train. His fiancée had taken his best friend as lover.

* * *

As after-dinner conversation Mike was extolling the virtues of plant oil as fuel. Even the Filipinos had remained. "Sun-flower and rape-seed would yield a suitable oil. You'd have little exhaust emissions and it'd be non-poisonous. Think about it, even a spillage at sea would be eaten by fish. And you approach it carefully with a lit match it'd probably be extinguished." Bob agreed that it was a good idea, but remained cynical. "Maybe it won't take-off in the West. The Third World countries might be the first to take it up as a viable energy solution. It'll come. It's green."

The sound of an approaching vehicle caused the conversation to stutter to a stop. Like conspirators at a secret meeting we looked to one another for deliverance. Bob got up and went into the lounge.

"It's the old Rag Head," he announced when he returned.

The uncertainty was palpable. We'd stopped work but it was as if we were shirkers and the boss was about to discover our scam. Mike and I looked to the others and they looked elsewhere.

Bob characteristically shattered the growing anxiety. "You'd better hide your pornos, Ian."

The tension had sharpened Ian's wits. "I lent them all to you." And there was a new confidence in him, borne, I thought, on the friendship her saw with me.

Of course Bob could always go one better. "You're joking. He -" he gestured outside "- borrowed the ones I had. Put them with his collection." Then to Scab: "Will you ask him for them?"

Scab grew lobster red. The poor fellow was easy meat for the quick sharks. Of all those at the farm my heart always went out to him. Bob jumped away, his arms outstretched in an effort to hold back an invisible crowd. "Back everybody, he's going to spontaneously combust."

No one was to come out unscathed. "You'd better veil-up," he said to me, surfing the crest of the atmosphere. "Tass, protect us with one of your monster farts." Tass's nether regions were apt to show their appreciation for his pistachio nut consumption. "Make it a silent one, though. Stealth, my man, stealth."

Then to Mike: "You'd better run out and put on a suit and tie."

"And you'd better watch your mouth in case he mistakes it for a tunnel, mate." For as long as I had known my husband levity and casual banter were not his strengths. But he got on well with Bob and the acquaintance had produced this fledgling comedian. Although I saw more irritation than humour in his remark.

Bob laughed loudly, too loudly. To conceal embarrassment? To send some obscure message to the approaching Saudi? Or to encourage his protégé?

The sound of the man climbing the steps gagged us and a conspiracy born out of the banter unified us against the intruder. We became partisans, albeit without a commander. Bob's mouth was not going to be our escape route. He looked sullen, almost pale. He would not be our spokesman. Up until this moment I had regarded him as being in-charge, but now he produced his exit visa that exempted him from duty.

The old Saudi appeared at the entrance and Mike rose. Nobody else moved. The floor creaked under the weight of silence. I hesitated and then got up. During the greetings and trivia such as "have you settled in?" and "you have been here before, I believe?" after making my acquaintance he glanced my way only once. He and my husband were having a conversation and I was standing up in the audience. I was conscious of my arms: extraneous limbs hanging at my sides. I thought to fold them or hold the back of a chair or even put my hands on my hips, but each position was a contrivance as uncomfortable as leaving them limply hanging. I fled my awkwardness by scrutinising our boss.

He was every bit an Arab in his tailored white *thobe* and headdress. His face was stern, yet his lips hinted at good humour. There was suspicion in his eyes. Shrewdness? His manicured Vandyke beard had started to grey and I judged him to be in his late forties. His rounded shoulders prematurely aged him. If he stood erect he would cut a dashing figure. His perfume was superior to that of the taxi driver.

"Now that you and your wife are here we are fully stocked." He gave Bob a cold glance. The statement was a bomb that shook me out of my assessment. Only when the smoke began to clear did I see its implications. Pav was to replace Eddie and I was to free up Pav. I was the cook. Call me fickle, but I hadn't planned on cooking for the farm on a daily basis.

I was stunned. During this time he gave Mike our *iqamas*.

Then he was gone. A strange feeling lingered in the wake of his departure. A need to say something, witty or otherwise tussled with a want to abscond.

Mike was buoyant and either did not notice the stillness or ignored it.

"He doesn't seem a bad chap," he remarked doing a round of the faces and settling on Bob.

"Wait till tomorrow," he said ominously. With a sardonic smile fixed on his face he too did a round of the faces.

I knew it was useless, but wisps of the strained atmosphere lingered and I wanted a little conversation. "Why?"

"You'll see."

"Honestly Bob, sometimes you're really childish." I don't know what made me say it. He was taken aback and said nothing. Presumably I was irked that nobody else appeared to want to address the subject of the bomb. I had wanted to talk to Mike privately about it, but a pang of guilt fired me onward. "I assume the 'fully stocked' remark means I'm to take over as cook." I looked at Pav. "We'll have to sort something out. I, er," I floundered on the blast's destruction and the embarrassment of my original want to cook, "wasn't planning on cooking all the time."

"I didn't come here to farm," said Pav.

I was saved. We agreed that between my helping out in the greenhouses and tending the chickens I would be almost half a farm hand. Pav would furnish the other half. Between us we'd be the lost worker.

"I'm going to hit the sack," said Ian. "We've got to get up early tomorrow." As he rose he put on a madman's smiled.

"We always get up early," exclaimed Mike, perplexed.

"That's right," said Bob, capping any elaboration.

Ian left and although the others wanted to leave they seemed to be waiting for permission.

Just as I was about to announce my departure Bob spoke. "About a year ago I was glad of the old rag-head's presence. Remember Scab? Pav was on holiday. Tass hadn't joined us then. And Sparky and Eddie were elsewhere. Ian was here." He took a breath. "We had this raging argument going, with two Arab truck drivers and two or three of their Bangladeshi lackeys."

"And?" I was still uneasy.

"They'd stacked the sacks badly. Don't ask me what it was, I can't remember. If it was just a matter of sloppy stacking I would have let it go, but they'd put them so we couldn't get to anything. One of the truck drivers - a real pillock - started gesticulating and shouting."

"And then it was a matter of who shouts loudest wins?" asked Mike.

"Something like that," Bob smiled.

"What happened?" said Mike.

"The old Saudi turned up."

"That's it," I exclaimed, disappointedly.

"Essentially. He heard the commotion and came over and gave them a guttural mouthful."

"And they went to work?"

"There was an argument. I think it was an endurance test: who could clear the back of their throat the longest. Abdul won. He's probably well connected. Who knows? He was the eldest." That was the first and only time I heard Bob refer to the old Saudi by name.

Mike nodded. "It's in their culture to respect their elders."

* * *

A guard wakes me from an afternoon nap. I am grateful. Although I've been here over seven weeks, seems like seven months, my sleep is irregular and I am plagued by a recurring dream.

Corridors and doors play an important role in this dream. I dream a lot, or more really I remember my dreams. Sleep is a double-edged sword: offering me a shadow world, cutting off the hard reality that is itself unreal and then decimating any sanctuary with nightmares. Calling it a recurring dream is misleading for the dream varies slightly. There is a recurring element. I am struggling to close a door against some impossibility. And this door is too big for the frame. Yet I push. Frenzy and fear endow me with superhuman strength. But the door catches and scrapes flagstones. I cannot keep this fearful thing out, this thing of unimaginable proportions like the deep dread that lurks under childhood's happiness. Then like a thrown switch the door swings wildly and I tumble forward. The door is now too small for the frame, affording me as much protection from the thing as the uncloseable door. I fumble with it, as if holding it still can help it fill out the frame.

This is the kind of nightmare that torments my waking hours.

We cross the courtyard.

An Indian girl, a hand holding a blood-soaked sleeve, walks urgently but silently from the toilets towards the entrance.

I see that the little shop is open. I haven't worked out its hours of business. Perhaps it opens on a whim or when the guards have confiscated fresh stuff to be put on sale. Someone told me that they take from the visitors. Their spoils end up in their homes or in this shop. No doubt the takings line their pockets.

The shop sells cigarettes, sweets, pencils, paper, magazines, toiletries and sporadically fruit and other foodstuffs. An Arab runs the shop, not always the same one. This appears to be the only work they do. Then it's probably not work, it's just another position of power. As if to demonstrate this there is an argument about a packet of cigarettes. The carton is apparently short. The Indian girl is showing the dull-eyed shopkeeper. I am unmoved by this injustice.

The guard takes me to the barred door where she hands me to an *abaaya'd* guard. The Indian girl with the bleeding arm is holding the bars. She looks as if she's about to faint. The *abaaya'd* guard takes me through and along the corridor to a male guard and a room. A waiting diplomat shakes my hand, his crispness rumpled by the poor a/c. The guard stands just inside the door: stone. The man who resembles 4B is sitting behind a desk, checking his nails, barely aware of my presence. Time is on his side. I hate his gold ring with the turquoise stone.

The diplomat is nervous. I am irritated.

"In -" he glances at his watch, a symbolic act for he glanced at it when I entered the room "- five minutes this telephone is going to ring." We both look at the telephone on the desk. "It'll be your father." My heart leaps, but he remains nervous. Then he appears to have nothing to say, but I know he wants to speak. Only when 4B looks up is he jolted. "Dawn, this is an ongoing thing. We're not out of it yet. I don't want you to say anything about what happened." His gaze steadies to check that I have completely understood him. "We're in a delicate situation here." I hate his use of the word we. "You shouldn't even say where you are."

"I don't know where I am."

He is stunned, but moves on quickly. "We're trying to arrange for your father to visit you." He has more to say, a string that tethers this carrot beyond my reach. "You're going to have to agree to a reconstruction of what happened." He meets my terrified eyes with sympathy. I know he means reliving the final events on the farm. The shock fades and I nod weakly. He acknowledges my assent with a smile and fills the ensuing impasse by placing a chair nearer the telephone. I obediently sit and wait. We all wait. Then he says: "when it rings I'll pick it up."

* * *

Next morning, just before 5 am, we discovered what Ian had meant by getting up early. We were wrenched from our sleep by the sound of prayer. I would later spot the loud speakers atop the Saudi's demountable. The taped voice carried easily on the still air.

In the kitchen I asked Bob whether he had been singing during the sermon. We had heard him from our room when he was in his bathroom.

"I was interpreting the words. If you listen carefully you'll realise he doesn't begin *Allahu Akbar* at all. The guy's speaking English. Not only that, the old rag head never plays the same tape. They all sound the same but the words are different each time. The trick is to guess what he's saying." He cleared his throat, and operatically placed one hand upon his chest and outstretched his other in a plea. "Ali Baba..." and sung nonsense thereafter.

This was typical of Bob. He would often enter the kitchen singing nonsense. I remember his version of a Sam Cooke's Wonderful World. "Don't know much about history. Don't know much biology. But I do know one and one is three." Then when I first tried to sort the men from the boys with a vindaloo I was bringing out the starters and Bob warped Abba's Chiquitita into chicken tikka. And once when he found me cutting vegetables he started an Elton John number. "Goodbye aubergine, though I never knew you at all."

Bob's "Ali Baba" harvested smiles. Mike's was a lop-sided one and my smile became a snort. This attracted a puzzled look from Mike that caused me to roar. In an attempt to stifle hysterics I snorted again. The others chuckled and I went into convulsions and tears.

Of course my husband's expression and Bob's irreverence had sparked me off. Mike was not stiff. He had less than eight weeks in which to take on full responsibility for the farm. So, unlike me he became almost clockwork. Also, next to Bob everyone was slow-witted. One of the firm-footed qualities I appreciated in Mike was his cultural interest. Not that Bob was an ignoramus. To mock one must understand. Bob's humour was a barrage of cheap shots and intelligent remarks that through quantity often hit the right spot. Nonetheless, I could never have chosen to marry someone like him. His incessant bombardment would have eventually driven me to shelter. Only a certain kind of woman would know how to bring him to Earth without shooting him down, and know when it was necessary for him to fly again. He needed someone to anchor him, patch his wounds when he fell and give him enough line soar again.

* * *

Abdul was not to come away from that first meeting completely unscathed. He would have to think again if he thought he could drop a bomb and slip away like a terrorist. Much to Mike's discomfort I charged him with ensuring the shrapnel met its target. Succinctly put, if I was to work I wanted payment. My husband could wrap the shards in a request for a note of some kind that would allow me to travel with Pav. Being alone with a male who was not an immediate relative was an offence known as *Khilwa*. I doubted that such a note existed and was surprised when one materialised a few days later. Of course we had no idea what was written on it. Was Pav suddenly my brother-in-law? Maybe Abdul was above the law, influential, or had a relative in the police force? Whatever, I treated it like a passport. The salary was another story. There was much procrastination. An official was not available, it was always difficult with women and work and so forth. "You'd be better off waiting for snow," said Bob. My husband wanted to get on with farming and hated bureaucracy. After a few weeks of heckling from me Mike was given a raise. His salary increased by a third.

I resigned myself to the fact that this was probably all I was worth out here. Besides, Mike had given blood to push the issue.

* * *

I cooked daily: dinner, lunch or both. For some reason never breakfast. Like Pav I tended to stick to the basic: a notch above bachelor fare. When I went exotic I was hampered by the myriad of likes and dislikes. Somehow I floundered my way through the labyrinth of preferences and a special dinner was made. The effect of these discussions was to turn the proposed meal into a miniature banquet. I don't really know what Pav thought of all the excitement it generated. Outwardly he didn't seem to mind.

Taking pains to present the meals fittingly were always ambushed by the utilitarian table and chairs and the fantastic structure of used implements, be it a precarious tower at the sink or a sprawling shantytown across the work-surface. One of the privileges of cooking was to be spared the washing up.

I introduced pasta to Pav's diet of rice, mash and oven chips. The Filipinos were great fruit eaters, even at breakfast, although they'd adjusted to the protein-packed start-up the Brits demanded. Fish dishes were also a favourite with them.

Pav and I had our differences. He rarely used cooking oil, preferring to save old meat fats in bowls in the refrigerator. He poured the new over the old, left it to separate into strata of lard and jelly. Digging it out with a spatula was then an archaeological excavation into meals past.

When it came to cooking something out of the ordinary Bob would often suggest the ludicrous. He'd read somewhere that the Iraqis ate locusts. "Great source of protein," he said. These insects were stupid and apparently flew into things and were easy to catch. Dipped in honey and eaten live was what Bob had read. I winded him when I suggested if he caught and killed a snake I'd sauté it for him. Luckily he never took up my offer.

I served up steak and chips as one of Bob's many last requests, and he had the gall to ask whether it was sally and chips. This harked back to one particular incident.

When wild dogs became a nuisance on the farm the lads climbed into their vehicles and drove them off. The dogs were a breed called saluki and Bob called them sallies. He once burst into the greenhouse and shouted to Tass: "Sallies at ten o'clock."

I went on one of these chases. I didn't feel sorry for these scraggly greyhounds. They were unappealing street-wise rogues. Not as cunning as foxes they could still be a bother to the chickens and when grouped their pack bravado could threaten. I was in the 4WD with Bob on that particular evening. He had his lights on full beam; elongating the shadows and making the animals appear all the more scrawny.

"It's not that I feel sorry for them," he elaborated after stating that the idea was to run them off, "because if I do hit one Pav might dish it up." He swerved to bear down on a remaining group of three. "You mustn't forget that he's from the Philippines and everyone knows they eat dog there. It wouldn't surprise me if Pav loves dog."

"Pav loves dog!" I laughed and he realised his pun and roared too.

* * *

The skyline of Riyadh never ceased to amaze me, because the run-up was relatively low-lying. The sun would haze the buildings and they'd become surreal like Las Vegas or Disneyland in the middle of nowhere. Once there I made a mental lifeline to our parked cruiser, for the bulk of the city was unknown and it was like pot holing. I'd go to tried and trusted haunts without straying. Whether it be Safeways, the Al Akariyah shopping centre, the gold *souqs* or Women's *souq* behind Dira Square (known in expat-circles as chop-chop square) or one of the several restaurants I would come to know.

The very first trip to the capital was with my husband. And to underscore the need for an *abaaya* an incident occurred as if staged.

We had just entered a shopping mall when I spotted a western couple. I was still having trouble getting used to the face tightening cold. It gave new meaning to the term face-ache. Shopping would always be a revolving door separating a refrigerator from an oven. The shoppers were mostly Filipino-looking men. There was a conspicuous lack of Arabs. When I did spot one, his robes contrasted the jeans and T-shirts and he stood out like a lord, a Jedi knight amongst the uncouth peasants. Occasionally he'd be followed by a pair of women clad from head to toe in black; pawns to their knight. One saving grace was that I did not have to dress like a pawn, although a scarf covered my head. Like the Arabs the westerners were also a noticeable minority.

"Look at that woman," I said, "she's not wearing an *abaaya*. That's the last time I come here in this cloak."

"Better safe than sorry," said Mike, glancing up from the mini stereo systems in the window display.

A man accompanied her. They seemed a little frightened and I wondered whether I looked as wide-eyed as them. They were fresh-faced with youth and must have been in their early twenties. Their pale skins said that they had not been in the country long. She was in a white sleeveless dress that reached halfway down her calves. It was far from tight fitting, for she was quite slender. Then again, the dress was not formless. A white crochet shawl barely covered her arms. Her fair hair and attire resembled my image of a Greek Goddess and I named her Helena. He too was striking with trendy slicked back hair and Clark Kent glasses.

I dearly wanted to establish contact, but didn't know what to say. Mike wanted to go into the shop. Although, Helena was younger than me some female company would have been appreciated. I was frantically searching for a plausible excuse to make their acquaintance when they jolted like spooked animals.

"Mike," I blurted.

He turned to see the two men who had startled them. Evidently they had clashed before for there was no exchange. The couple fled and the two Arabs, who were brandishing camel whips and now shouting, gave chase.

Instinctively Mike held me by the arm and whispered: "There's nothing you can do."

"Shouldn't we help?" It bothered me that I had no intention of moving. Mike need not have restrained me.

"They're *mats, matawa*, religious police."

"They're no older than the couple they're chasing." The mats sported henna-dipped beards of such a thin, straggly nature that they highlighted their youth.

"Age has nothing to do with belief. If anything it could make them more zealous."

"What will they do?"

"He's responsible for her so they'll admonish him. Whack his legs or backside. They might pinch her arms to explain." He then added: "it's more humiliating than painful."

"Really?"

"No." Mike smiled. "It probably stings. That's the lesson."

"Treated like kids."

"It's their country."

* * *

I asked visitors from the Embassy whether they could contact Ginny and big Pat. Although Pat had visited and breathed life into me, he has not been again. At first I got the standard: "I'll see what I can do." My persistence wore one of them down. He admitted that I was part of an ongoing case and was not allowed visitors. Of course, nobody could explain big Pat's visit, except to say that it had been a mistake. The problem with bureaucracy is that the individual can shed responsibility. Nobody has the authority to tell you anything. Abroad the bureaucrats can comfortably hide in the quagmire of machinations that separate governments. When cornered they will fob you off with the stock need for diplomacy.

You'd think the embassy would send the same contact person to build up a relationship. I've probably all but exhausted the department. None of them got through to me. Only this no-nonsense man will do. I don't know why. There's something beaten about him. Is it in his sagging shoulders? He's old enough to be a ranking officer, but he's not. So he's passed his prime. You can see it in his waning eyes; hear it in his stale voice. Oh, he's doing his best to hold the flag, but he's not cut out for this work. I guess the appeal of the underdog attracts me.

I have surmised that Pat's visit was not an accident, but a strategic cattle-prod jolt to bring me out of my state. They couldn't lock me up and throw away the key, which appears to be the fate of many of my companions. They couldn't do it because I'm British. Funny how something like this brings out the fervent patriot. So I'd been allowed to speak to my father.

"I'm fine."

"Good. Good. Chin up. We'll have you out of there soon."

The delay in transmission hiccups our conversation and underscores the distance. Hearing his voice blurs my vision.

"How's mum?"

"She's fine." She is not going to speak to me. She has been left at home. "You know how it is." Saying this causes my stomach to clench. She is not fine. She is in a state. Somebody must be at home with her.

"Dad." The transmission delay doesn't really allow room for superfluous words, but being prohibited from talking about my circumstances has left us with bones. "I'm innocent." I feel the officials in the room stiffen and the silence on the line tightens. Turning my back on the silence and the officials I continue. "I want to get out of here." This last sentence is a surprise. Of course I want to get out, but just how desperately I want to get out resounds in my head and I become giddy. I lock my grip on the receiver.

"We'll -" he falters and starts again. "We'll get you out of there." And to connect with me he says: "My girl's coming home."

His touch is a bear hug that squeezes the breath out of me. I can't speak. My eyes burn, my tongue tasting salty drops on my lips and my stomach lifts over a humpbacked bridge. The emotion fills me up: a balloon swelling inside my throat, pressing its walls, petrifying my mind. I search for a sharp thought to lance the emotion.

The diplomat moves. He senses the precariousness of the situation. I make the mistake of looking at him. My vision blurs but I ignore his offer of a handkerchief. He signals for me to wind up the conversation. But my father desperately wants to reach me. His voice is impervious, refusing to falter. "They're arranging for me to come out there." He races on a wave of confidence like a glorious surfer doomed to crash. "It's just formalities. I need a visa."

I can't take any more. His desperate confidence, his pain, has returned my voice. "I have to go." Once said, the emotion is punctured. I hurry to say more. "Don't worry, Dad. Tell Mum not to worry. I'm being treated okay. It's not the Hilton." My laugh is a sham. "I know you're doing all you can." I am drying up, becoming hardened like my father. "See you soon, Dad." What I next say inflates the balloon and lifts my stomach again. I compress the balloon like a snake swallowing its prey. My eyes swell with the effort. And my words are mangled by the boiled sweet stuck in my throat. "I love you. Give my love to Mum."

***

In Riyadh I dared to venture off from the usual shopping haunts, arranging to meet Pav later. I never left the beaten track and chose public places.

My trips with Pav had become polite affairs. A mutual respect stood like a wall between us. Occasionally a shaft of raw personality would shine through a flaw and we'd hit upon a theme that would keep us in conversation for a few kilometres. But we rarely ascended trivia.

He was secretive too. I had noticed that Tass's pistachios were expensive and asked where Pav bought them. He simply said that it was a business connection. I surmised that he had a deal going with a fellow countryman.

I'd been visiting a traditional house of the Najd style. It was a flat-topped block with all the adornment and effort invested in the doors and windows: lattice work, carvings and notched parapets. The windows were tiny: archers' deep-set slits. Defence against prying eyes and the ubiquitous heat. This house stood alone but at one time it had huddled with others to make narrow shaded alleyways.

I'd been aware of the well-groomed Arab inside but he made his move outside on the street.

"You are American?" Although lacking Scab's punctuating "no" it was nonetheless a question. His English was accented but good and his crisp suit said he was a businessman.

Politeness decreed an answer. "English," I said through a forced smile.

"Ah, English," he said with relish, rolling the word about his mouth like a brick of milk chocolate.

"I have an appointment," I said, quickening my step a mite.

He kept pace. "I adore your London."

Vestiges of politeness and panic squeezed a grunt of acknowledgement from me.

"There are some fine restaurants in London. Riyadh has fine ones too."

I knew where this was going and made to protest, a gesture of his hand arrested me. "It would do me great honour to have lunch with such a beautiful woman." This treacly approach might cause some women to swoon, but I scoffed and had I been elsewhere I might have shrieked. However, my smile sent the wrong signal and drawing all my aplomb to cushion his landing I told him that I was married.

"Your husband is a lucky man to possess such a jewel." He was getting worse. Merely the word possess caused me to bristle. I was becoming teeth and claws. Yet, he didn't see the signals.

"In the Arab world a man should take care of his property lest it be won away."

I stopped and hoped my smile would mask my contemptuous eyes. "Look, I think it's very nice of you to be interested in me, but I am in a hurry. I have to meet my husband."

"No you are not."

This was unexpected and my hesitance destroyed my credibility.

"Now, let us get out of this heat. You look in need of refreshment." I was thirsty.

"Please leave me alone," I said, with eyes of flint.

"Here, just in here, I can buy you a coffee." His smile was plastic. "It is a public place. I assure you that I am a man of honour." Dropping his eyes he leant close. "I have much money." Then he raised his lids like a luxury automobile's headlights.

Did he really think I was a frightened rabbit to be mesmerised by the full beam of his eyes? My expression became monstrous. "I'm not interested," I snarled viciously. He blanched with what seemed genuine shock and I strode off.

I told Mike of the experience and he was amused. I managed to draw concern out of him, but failed with jealousy. He was so damned sure of me.

* * *

"Two mates of mine are coming to stay," said Bob, to explain his reorganising of the belongings stored in the spare bedroom of our demountable. "A Bob's farewell visit." He had two weeks left. "You're invited too."

"By default," I said. He couldn't very well have a party and not invite us.

"Could you help me stack these over there?"

"Of course," said Mike, who was standing next to me. We had been on our way to dinner. "They're empty."

"Actually, I don't know why I call them mates," he continued as Mike helped him with our cases. "They're a pair of degenerates. I don't know why I'm doing this. They'd be happy enough sleeping in a cesspool."

His imminent departure had put an edge on his humour. It was as if he was acting Bob rather than being Bob. The precision wit often missed its target: an erstwhile master assassin becoming a back-alley mugger.

"They sound like attractive guys," I remarked.

"Attractiveness is not the word that springs to mind when one mentions Merv the Perv. His batman Den is no better. Still, don't let me put you off. Of one thing you can be certain, the weekend won't be uneventful."

"Very ominous. If I'm going to share a dining table with two reprobates I'd like to know more about them."

"Where are these guys coming from?" asked Mike.

"Dhahran. Aramco. Merv's a computer boffin and Den's an English teacher. A cushy number, if you ask me."

"Getting the sty ready?" asked Ian, a disembodied head peering round the corner.

"Do you know these guys?" I asked.

"Animals," he corrected. "They've been here a few times." Ian was undergoing change too. He was wrestling with his melancholic nature. At the moment he had it in a half nelson. His was an unnatural struggle, as if he was trying to be somebody he could never be. Bob was abandoning us, slowly becoming a husk of his former self and Ian was trying on his skin. The disturbing aspect of Ian's metamorphosis was that the slough he was pulling on like neoprene was still warm.

"A visit every six months is all my lads can take," Bob smiled.

"Luckily, Abdul didn't turn up last time," said Ian.

"He never does at weekends," Bob hastily interjected.

"I think we started work around midday after an evening with them."

Mike's face clouded.

"He's joking," said Bob.

But we knew he was not.

* * *

The sun was deep blue with a purple penumbra. Large drops of sweat rolled down me. They moved erratically, congregating and irritated like insects. Opening my eyes snapped the negation and for a flash the full-glare of the sun perforated my retina leaving three globes to linger before me as I fumbled for my sunglasses. I had pulled the lounger out of the shade of the oversized parasol and subjected my body to a good going over with an acetylene torch. The heat had become unbearable. Of late the temperature had not climbed beyond the mid twenties, but today there was no wind and it was in the high twenties. I wanted to pack up, my thermos of iced tea was empty, but I lacked the energy and decided to take cover instead. The effort required to drag the lounger under the parasol was colossal. The sun had broiled me in my juices. I was soft and weak. My brain was mashed potato and my limbs overcooked noodles.

The airbrushed cirrus clouds were a token gesture. They were hardly worth the effort and more flaws in the sky, as if wisps of undercoat were showing through a poor paint job. The eerie hush told me that a predatory bird was in the vicinity. I couldn't see it, but knew it would be a kite, falcon or buzzard.

Having repositioned the lounger I was just about to lie down when movement caught my eye.

I'd persuaded Mike to buy a large, beach umbrella and a white plastic lounger. On requested days one of the boys would set it up about three miles into the farm and then in sun-hat, sandals, shades, a baggy dress and a stock to ward off snakes, scorpions or inquisitive dogs, I'd stroll to the spot with a book and a Walkman for company. The large towel doubled as an instant shield should Abdul appear. My small, beach-less beach-scene cut a bizarre sight and I revelled in the English eccentricity of it. All this depended on the busyness of the farm, of course, truck drivers collecting or delivering. I was quite alone. I had asked about getting walkie-talkies. They would have been useful for the lads too, but Bob said it had already been suggested and dismissed for security reasons. Pressed he had to admit to not understanding what security and I never got Mike to question Abdul.

My favourite spot for reading and writing my journal was in the greenhouse. I'd spotted a totally over-the-top fan-backed wicker chair. Since it had been my original wish to establish a retreat in a corner of the cool green Mike and I bought it. The chair was so large I could fold my feet up on it. From a distance it looked like Elizabeth I's high-backed collar. Mike said I looked as smug as a Cheshire cat when I sat in it with a magazine the first time. Initially the main drawback was that it creaked loudly when shifting position. But when I was adrift, engrossed in a book or a letter, its protests were softened and mingled with the gentle sounds of water.

I was spellbound by the endless approach of a distant vehicle. A dust cloud marked its furious progress and yet it remained uncannily motionless, as if the billowing plume were a parachute checking a high-plains dragster's progress. The line where land met sky was fluid. Quick-flowing streamers of air, like ticker tape attached to a fan, rendered everything flat, buildings, vehicles and pivots fluttered like flags.

I had not sunbathed for quite some time. November was *shamal* season, sand storms running through to January, and a curse during this time of sowing wheat. On such days sunbathing was impossible. At first I had been "playing solar-panels", as Bob coined it, every second day, weather permitting. But the joy of constant sunshine wore off. This was partly because it was always there and partly because it was overwhelming. It didn't beat down on you; it beat you down. Oh, I enjoyed the prickly heat, masochistically luxuriating the slow chafe of sandpaper, but I could only indulge it in short bursts. I marvelled that I had paid to holiday in the sun. I was one of those unfortunate people who burnt their nose easily and whose freckles darkened first. Gauging my humour Bob hit me with the caustic warning: "You shouldn't sunbathe under a tea-strainer." After a couple of weeks the sporadic sunbathing and abandonment of various creams, I realised I was growing brown simply by moving from one building to another. For my liking there was still too much milk in my coffee-coloured skin. And I was one of the last in the tanning league. The lads were out every day. But I had plenty of time.

I stepped under the parasol but remained standing. If I lay down I would never get up. An offer of a lift back would be nice.

As it became obvious that the cruiser was coming to me I donned my hat. Then I dug into my bag for my watch. There was still an hour to go before the lads should pack up. Perhaps someone was coming to warn me that skeekos were on the farm. I cloaked myself with my towel.

"Hi," I said as casually as possible after he'd stopped, rolled down the window and killed the stereo tom-toms that had been trying to drum something into or out of him.

"Want a lift?" Ian was alone.

"You're knocking off early."

"Nature's calling." I knew that the pivot irrigation did not solely depend upon fossil water, so his answer was a surprise. "We've hit a good point to call it a day. The others are packing up." I'd accepted his sick note, but his next statement spilt ink over it. "They'll be finished within the hour." And I thought Sparky was the skiver. He'd seen his mistake and couldn't keep the exasperation out of his voice. "Do you want a lift? I'm dying for a leak."

"Yes. Can you help me?"

He jumped out and we packed my gear into the back.

Once underway the tom-toms resumed mid-crescendo but Ian quickly sent them into the hinterlands. He began blotting his mistake by choosing to tell me of the day's problems. His inference that he'd already crammed twelve hours work into eight was a botched job.

Swift words put him out of his misery. "I'm sure you work hard, and if the others say you can go then that's all right by me." Rather than soothe him my salve burnt and he drove the last stretch with a quirky smile upon his face. I had come to see him in a different light. He was the stray that Bob had taken in, but he had been playing the underdog too long. Unlike Scab who was genuinely innocent, Ian nurtured his role, continually trying to deepen his mystery, hinting at a romance of untold treasures.

He parked behind the kitchen building. "Thanks, Ian," I said retrieving my hat and bag from the back.

"You'll be hitting the shower."

"You can go first if you like?"

"No. Ladies first. I'll go to the kitchen loo." To underscore his urgency he pressed his knees together.

He began a brisk walk to the kitchen and I headed for our demountable. He'd parked the cruiser such that we headed almost in opposite directions. He would round the kitchen building before I would reach our demountable steps.

A freak gust caught my cockily perched hat and I casually gave chase. The chase was not serious for it didn't go far and fluttered like a saucer before coming to rest. Comically, just as I reached it another gust scooped it up and turned it into a wheel. Then it began to accelerate away and I dropped my bag and humour, and glanced over my shoulder for Ian. He was gone. Playing hubcap my hat took our demountable in a tight curve. I gave chase. I left nothing to chance when I saw it making a pit stop in the shadow of the building. My foot secured the brim. As I strolled back inspecting the hat I was distracted by a sliver of movement. A large flat centipede was marching furiously into the shade of the building. I watched it disappear as I brushed my hat.

I looked up to see Ian closing the rear of another cruiser. He could not have been to the toilet in such a short space of time and I was about to call out when something about his conduct stopped me. He had not seen my bag or me.

He walked was briskly, almost hurriedly, with two blue plastic jerrycans. I could tell they were empty. I watched him go into the workshop before I retrieved my bag and went to my room.

I was rinsing out my thermos in our sink when I heard a cruiser start up. I don't know why, maybe I was more puzzled than I thought, but I switched off the tap and went to the corridor. The cruiser Ian had picked me up in was gone. I stared at the space as if it would materialise. Had Ian driven away? Had he had time to go to the toilet? I began to doubt myself. Was something wrong here? Or were the long idle days getting the better of me?

I left our room and went to kitchen. Pav was alone.

"Where's Ian?"

"He's working."

"You saw him?"

"From the window."

"He didn't come here?"

Pav looked up from peeling the potatoes. "Yes." But the pause had been too long and I knew that he was lying. But why?

I didn't know what to do. Challenging somebody about something so banal was ridiculous. I was irked and went straight to the workshop.

Tass was alone.

"Was Ian just here?"

My manner put him off balance. "Yes."

I walked about slowly. The stench was as appalling as ever. I could feel it seeping into my clothes and the pores of my skin. How could they work here? Were they constantly spilling gasket fluid? "Did he bring anything with him?"

"No."

"Nothing?" I couldn't see the jerrycans.

"No." He was stressed and missed the chance to say he'd not noticed Ian carrying anything.

I walked about the entire workshop. No cans.

I spoke to Mike about it later. He said he'd sent Ian to check on a collapsed pivot they'd repaired earlier. A pivot was made up of jointed rods, broken by so-called towers, which were on wheels. A collapsed pivot was when the cut-out failed and the outer towers drove forward to double in on the inner towers, like bending the leg at the knee. "If the guy's dying for a leak then of course he can make a slight detour." When I protested that he could not have had time to relieve himself, I knew I was verging on appearing hysterical. I mentioned the jerrycans before dropping the subject.

Why did Ian lie? And why hadn't he mentioned the pivot?

* * *

Bob chuckled to himself.

"What is it?" I asked, taking my eyes off the pivots.

We were returning from the north perimeter fence that had been cut and invaded by a dozen straggly coconut-coloured camels. They'd been tucking into one of the pivots. Bob and Tass had tried to coax them off with hooting horns. An Arab had appeared and claimed that the fence was already damaged. He gave the game away when he argued that there should be no fences in Arabia and that camels should be free to roam. I heard this later from Bob. I stayed in the cruiser. I disliked camels at the best of times, but worse were the hordes of flies that accompanied them. Bob allowed things to escalate and then handed him yet another note from Abdul. The man was indignant but the note had the desired effect and he began to herd his animals off.

"I was thinking of one of the ideas Merv had when he was last here. He asked why we didn't use toilet waste as fertiliser. I was imaging Mike's reaction."

"I'm sure he'd take it in good humour."

"I didn't mean it that way."

In the short break I sensed unease in him and attached a tag of importance to what he said next. "My friends will probably bring some hooch with them." I didn't react. "How do you think Mike will take it?"

"Do you mean straight or with a mixer?"

His laugh was uncomfortable.

"Honestly Bob, I really don't know. Maybe you should speak to him?"

"Fair enough."

He had wanted an answer or at least an offer that I would ask my husband. Before I could search for an exit he began lamenting. "One of the things I thought I'd do out here was take a trip to the Tuwayq Escarpment. It's northwest of here. I wanted to shoot the Nubian ibex." He smiled. "With my camera. They're virtually extinct, you know. Fat chance of seeing one really. They're shy." Their habitat, the Tuwayq Escarpment, was a nine-hundred kilometre strip of sandstone canyon resembling the spine, a gentle S running from the fringes of the Rub' al Khali on past Riyadh. "The sands of time have run out on me, but it'd make a good day trip for you."

"It'd be a welcome change from farm, Masstock, Riyadh."

* * *

After the call with my father the room is silent. I wretchedly accept the handkerchief from the diplomat. Far from doing me good, the call has destroyed me. I want out of here. I can't take this reality any more. I'm losing myself in it. Being restricted steals my assertive self, my identity. I'm becoming like those about me: meaningless, an automaton, not even an animal. I'm willing to do anything to get out. Suicide *is* becoming an option.

Death would cheat them of the agreed reconstruction. Then again, maybe they'd welcome the easy way out. The thought of a reconstruction horrifies me. It fills me with dread, like a schoolgirl who hasn't done her revision on the eve of an examination.

But Shylock has been promised his pound of flesh. I have no choice. I have to go back to tear open old wounds.

* * *

"Where do you go at night?"

We had finished our evening meal and over tea or soft drinks, we were all waiting for Den and Merv to arrive. They were already late and Bob said that if they were not there by nine he'd drive to Masstock to phone.

I'd heard Bob and Ian leave our demountable again. I didn't get up and went back to sleep only to wake when they returned. I didn't know how long they had been out but I heard both of them go to Bob's room. The peace accentuated sound and I heard them go to the toilet one after the other. Then I heard Ian creep along the corridor to his own room.

My question was met with shock. Even my husband was surprised. But I felt I knew them well enough. I had chosen my moment carefully. I watched them all. Interrogating Bob alone would have been a mistake.

"I heard you leave last night." Tension supplanted the uneasiness.

Scab was the only one of the Filipinos to show emotion. Worry etched his features. Ian blanched.

"Have a guess," suggested Bob, ever the wise guy.

"I don't know."

"Nookie, of course." Then to the Filipinos: "Sex."

Smirks became infectious. In Scab and Ian there was also embarrassment.

"With Arab women?"

"Dawn."

"No, Mike I'm interested. I don't want details."

"You won't get them," Bob said. "A man's got to keep his tackle in working order. In answer to -"

"Nurses," Ian blurted. "From the King -"

"Don't lie," Bob snapped. "They're Arab women. Egyptians, maybe."

I nodded slowly, not knowing what or who to believe. Mike's expression said: drop it. Indeed talk was a drying well. Most didn't mind the mud. But Scab squirmed uncomfortably and Ian sat indignantly in the slime.

I knew that there was more. That same cohesion that had greeted us those first days returned. I felt like a sleuth who'd stumbled upon some awful secret. Mr. Peacock in the conservatory with the lead piping. Although I had not seen them I shot in the dark. "Why did you push the cruiser?"

Again the tension barometer overshot its scale. Under pressure only Bob seemed to function and even he was sluggish.

"We didn't want to wake you." He knew too well how to bring a conversation to an end. "Hey, Dawn, a man's gotta do what a man's gotta do."

Bob waited until half past nine, he phoned Masstock to ask whether any messages had been left and then he drove over. He returned over an hour later, as we were breaking up of bed, to tell us that no one was answering. I wondered whether they'd had an accident.

* * *

I was decidedly tipsy. The gaiety made me shamefully giggly too. Like the empty-headed bimbo June would have me be I was reduced to giggling like a schoolgirl. The shameful part was that I giggled at everything and when I was not giggling I was laughing. I didn't care. I was enjoying myself.

Alcohol had slipped me into this state. What kept me teetering on the brink of hysteria were Bob and Merv's tirade of quips. Merv had set the base tone when opening the first plastic bottle. "I'm as parched as a vulture's crotch." Dennis King, Den, too had his own brand of humour: not as madcap and thigh slapping, somehow weightier but none the less effective at the right moment. And since all timing was blurred by the *sid* I appreciated his jokes too.

"Eat, drink and be merry, for tomorrow we may diet," said Bob, raising his glass.

Sid, short for the Arabic word *sideeqi*, meaning my friend, was the name of the distillate. It was uncut and had to be diluted with two parts water before it could be drunk with a mixer. They had thought to bring tonic water and maybe it was my imagination but mixed it tasted like G and T. Later I would try it with a cola and it tasted exactly like rum and cola. *Sid* spiked orange juice was a screwdriver. I never tried the rare brown *Sid* (left to mellow with some kind of wood chips) that was said to resemble whisky.

Curiosity had driven me to try it; thought of going blind being doused by the second glass. "It's safe, pure alcohol," said Bob.

"We've been drinking it for ages and look at us," said Merv. This alone caused peels of laughter. "Depending on the quantity consumed you might feel fuzzy in the morning."

"The level of fuzziness equals amount consumed divided by personal alcohol tolerance," Den propounded.

This was the sweet sickly smell I'd noticed in the Filipinos quarters. They must have soaked their furnishings in it for it to be so strong.

All but Mike indulged. My husband rarely drank alcohol. Scab was exceedingly cautious - I think his first glass lasted the entire evening. Ian paced himself. Pav drank like a fish and his big face took on the beaming proportions of a puffed-up, but benign, piranha. I don't remember what Sparky and Tass did. They took up their customary positions in the back seats in my memory.

Inevitably we were congregated in the kitchen when the lads arrived that evening. "Fasten your seat-belts," said Ian.

Bob brought them in: "Ladies and gentlemen I give you the Merv and Den Road-show, otherwise known as the gruesome twosome." Merv was a round-faced type with the shiny pore-less skin of a young Chinese. By the end of the evening he positively glowed. He wore rounded square glasses like television screens that gave him an owl-like air. His oddball appearance hinted at a troublesome school-time. Piggy and four-eyes. Den was taller almost lanky with a head of fair curly hair and a fresh-faced innocence. He came in carrying a carton containing plastic bottles of mineral water. In my ignorance I thought they'd brought water. They would have needed some for the 200-kilometre journey. "Supplies for the outpost," said Merv, pulling a bottle from the box. Pav was already fetching some glasses. Merv broke the seal by pulling the plastic tab that encircled the cap.

"Did you inject the bottles?" I asked.

"What?" asked Bob.

I turned red and Merv put his hands up to my face. "Better than an open fire."

"What do you mean?" asked Bob.

I steadied myself. "Did you inject the bottles to get the *sid* in?"

"*Sid's* potent stuff, all right," admitted Merv, "but it's not that strong."

"Watch," said Den. He grabbed a bottle and pressed home the cap. Then he squeezed the top of the neck with the forefinger and thumbs of both hands and had the complete top in his hands. "You tip the water away and fill the bottles -"

"Tip the water away," exclaimed Bob. "You're joking -"

"Joe King?" said Merv. "No, actually he's Den King,"

"The golden oldies never tarnish," said Den.

"I'm surprised you brought a complete carton," said Bob to Merv. "But I bet you didn't throw the water away." Then to the rest of us: "He's a skinflint." I knew the insult harked back to some incident. "As tight as a camel's arse in a sandstorm."

"Thanks a lot, pal." Merv raised his glass. For a moment he seemed lost for words.

The fast and furious pace was not continuous and needed jump-starting now and then. After a short lull I asked: "Why are you called Merv the Perv?"

"Who said I was?"

I betrayed Bob with a glance.

"If you believe him you'd believe anybody."

"It's on account of his liking for ladies underwear," explained Bob. "He has a collection."

"How *did* you get out of your play-pen? Anyway, I've brought some samples," said Merv, riding the slight. He rapidly raised and lowered his eyebrows behind his heavy rimmed glasses. "Come back to my room and I'll show you." Rather than appear suggestive, he came across comically like a cartoon character. I laughed.

"It's eleven o'clock, already." Mike obviously thought things were getting out of hand.

"Captain Ahab has spoken," said Merv.

"I'd watch out if I were you," said Bob.

Merv gave him a questioning look and Bob explained: "If anyone in this room resembles the great white whale, it's you."

This was only true insofar that he was white. He was certainly no chubbier than Bob. And Pav was the chunkiest in the room, although not being white disqualified him.

"That's gratitude for you," began Merv. "Travel half way across the country, smuggling the expat's elixir to say adieu to a so-called friend, and you get called Moby Dick with a rear-end tighter than a camel's - lady present - nether regions. Thanks a bunch, pal."

"Yes, this is Bob's leaving do," Ian said.

"Bob's wake," said Bob.

"With the corpse attending," observed Den.

"It'll certainly be quiet without you," I said, caught by a moment of rash sincerity.

"Start a new year," suggested Merv. "It'd have to be zero A.B., anno Bob."

"At the moment it's 1984 B.B.," said Den.

"Maybe Nostradamus wrote of the event," said Merv.

The mischief went on until Mike, who'd assumed the mantle of sobriety, and now overacted, announced that he was going to bed. He intuitively understood that I wanted to stay. A combination of things probably prompted him to call Bob out.

Whilst they were absent, Merv asked me mock-confidentially so that the others could hear: "Is Bob going to get the cane?"

"Mike's responsible here," said Ian.

"My husband doesn't drink," I said.

"Is he a Quaker?"

"He's a good man," said Pav unexpectedly.

Merv pressed his wrists together. "Okay, I'll go quietly."

Bob returned. He looked stricken.

"What did he say?" asked Merv.

"He doesn't want alcohol on the farm."

"That's okay," said Merv. "I've heard it isn't good for the crops."

Bob was dismayed. He knew Mike was right and he did not have a witty answer to hand.

Merv got up and drowned his shout of "party-pooper" under a shattering blast of the horn. The blast slaughtered the jollity of the evening and turned me to rags. I looked to them for help. I did not want the evening to end like this.

"We'll take it back with us," said Den.

Nothing was said but I didn't miss the conspiracy between Pav and the guests.

"What really happened yesterday that was so important?" asked Ian. They'd not furnished a reason for not turning up the previous evening. Bob had phoned Masstock in the morning and heard that Merv had left a message that they were on their way.

"Unforeseen circumstances," said Den.

"Who was she?" asked Bob.

"Fluffy," said Merv.

"Again?" said Bob.

"Fluffy's a rabbit," Den said to me.

"Only a soft toy would go to bed with you. And I emphasise the word soft."

"Better than nothing."

Merv jumped up. "Gosh, I almost forgot our royal guests." He left the kitchen. My questioning looks at Den and Bob were met with resigned shakes of the head or despairing eyes rolling to the ceiling. They knew, but were not saying. Ian's shrug said that he did not know. I'd long given up trying to fathom the Filipinos. And although their customary stoicism was slipping, their faces opening with delicate smiles, inchoate eyes, slackening brows, my perception of them was not practised and they remained unreadable.

* * *

A glove puppet appeared at the entrance. It was an Arab in white *thobe* with nub of padded cloth for a head topped by a red-chequered *gutra*, held in place by a black *agal* no thicker than an elastic band. The pantomime was announced with a "salaam Alacum." No one replied. Merv repeated the greeting in a voice that was more Peter Seller's Indian than Arab.

We chorused the response and the panto was born.

"My name is Prince Ali," bowed the puppet leading the rest of

Merv into the room. "And I am Princess Jasmin," said the black sock pulled over his other hand. "You were not asked to speak," screamed Ali, head-butting her.

Merv resumed his place and began his party-piece: essentially a barrage of jokes at the expense of Arabic culture. Den had obviously seen it all before, but was mildly amused. The Filipinos brightened whilst the rest of us behaved like excited children.

"Give me Jasmin," said Den, when Merv was finished and wrapped his sock-clad hand about his glass and lifted it to his lips.

"No way."

"Let him have her," said Bob. "It's the only chance he'll get of putting his hand up a lady's dress."

"At least I now know why you're called the Merv and Den Road-show," I said.

Bob threw the double-act off stage the moment Den began to speak. "Hey, I can see your lips moving." Not that Merv had made any effort to restrict the movement of his lips.

Merv took up the gauntlet and spoke in a strangled voice. The challenge became a game when he offered Ali to Bob. "O-ay, Berb, if you thin' is so easy."

Bob took the game to new heights by choosing a tongue twister. He failed honourably.

I then realised that Bob hadn't been so animated for some time. He had been a ship whose anchor was being winched-up; the securing lines flung back. So that although he was in harbour, he had begun to drift.

"Ian, it's your turn to shine," Merv stated, having assumed the role of compere. "But you'd better take the lemon out of your mouth first."

The comment cut to the bone. Ian's natural expression was melancholic: eyebrows tinged with a look-at-this-burden-I'm-carrying anguish. His eyes betrayed him further. Their depths yearned to be plumbed. Yet, to be drawn into them was to plummet and risk ending up in the abscess that grieved within him.

Merv's scythe-like tongue was taking scalps. It swept, sliced and reaped child-cruel laughter. I stood firm as it headed my way. Despite this, when my turn came I was stunned.

Ian bravely floundered his way through an abridged rendition of the Rolling Stones' *Satisfaction*. He had been all but dumbstruck when he pulled on the puppet claiming not to know any tongue twisters. Den had suggested a song and Bob came up with the winning number. Subtlety was never Bob's forte.

Surprisingly Sparky volunteered and performed a heavily accented but surprising good *Summer Holiday* that left us in a bewildered silence. He had a good singing voice. Merv was the first to drop his eyebrows and point to Pav, who went on to do a hilarious version of *White Christmas*. A Lee Marvin *Wandering Star* would have been more appropriate.

"Okay, camel-breath it's your turn," said Merv, gesturing Pav to hand the puppet to Tass.

Tass strained out a *Wonderful World*, which may have sounded good to him under the shower but only reinforced the fact that no one could top Satchmo's version.

"It's your turn string-bean," he said to Scab, who naturally turned from anticipation pale to in-the-hot-seat scarlet. "Can you make your eyes move independently too? Or is that as far as it goes with the chameleon impression?"

Scab did Disney's Jungle Book: *I wanna be like you* which was appallingly flat. Protests from many killed him.

"Okay, fish-face, you're on," said Merv. I had expected an insult but this sent me into free-fall and to conceal the uncertainty of my laughter I told them that I had not been called that since my schooldays. I had thick, rather sour lips, and the reference to Ian's lemon sucking would have been equally apt for me. But my lips could be sensuous. My eyes were large, almost startled and my freckles gave me youth and innocence that were often infuriatingly mistaken for inexperience. I was not ugly but I wouldn't be the first to be asked to lie across a showroom car in a bikini.

There was more to the slight, though. Merv had broken the unspoken taboo of insulting a woman. Placed upon a pedestal since my arrival, I had grown accustomed to feeling unique. Naturally I openly fought any special treatment and demanded equality. But there was no getting around the fact that I was a woman among men. I too had adapted. Almost unknowingly I had made frivolity taboo, because it bordered on flirting. No matter how good-humoured, flirting could only be deemed cruel.

I struggled for a party piece and to buy time protested that Ali was a man. Merv threw it back in my face. "Why should you have it easy?"

"Do you really want to put Merv's smelly sock on?" asked Bob.

I came up with *Diamonds are a girl's best friend* which I'd done before. Mike wasn't there to sabotage my effort by saying my juicy-lip pursing resembled Mick Jagger more than Marilyn Monroe. I received a standing ovation and calls of "bravo".

"What about charades?" suggested Den. "I'll start."

Perhaps because more participation was necessary or perhaps because things were turning decidedly silly, Pav rose and announced that he was retiring. The other Filipinos followed his lead.

"Okay Pav," began Merv, "I'm not going to argue with you, but the rest of you should stay."

"Party-poopers," slipped from my lips and I consciously wondered at my drunkenness.

"I'll restrain Scab," Den offered.

But the Filipinos were determined, pleading work in the morning.

"I'll take the box," said Pav, lifting the carton of 'water'.

Merv smiled. "Sure, we've enough here to keep us going."

Silence graced the Filipinos departure.

"I wasn't going to argue with Pav," said Den, after they'd left. "That guy could do some serious pasting. I mean is he carrying medicine balls under his arms or what?"

A titter at Pav's expense was irresistible.

Although the Filipinos had not driven the evening their departure was that of an audience. The main actors continued to improvise but there was a sense of deflation. And the foolery undermined itself in its effort to ignore this emptiness. Tiredness encroached the wings and the atmosphere waned within the hour. By then it was almost midnight.

Merv asked me what Mike had against alcohol but it was Bob who answered him.

"It goes back to his father." Bob looked at me and I shrugged. If my husband had told Bob then it was no secret. Indeed I found myself elaborating.

Farmers live pinched lives. Mike's father had been in dire financial straits and his only solace had been the bottle. He'd doted on his son but in a lapse of sense committed suicide. Mike's mother eventually took in one of the part-time hands, a local lad. Again alcohol began to play a prominent role in family life. This time his mother, then the youth who didn't have the strength to challenge her, took to the bottle. As soon as he could Mike left. My husband was driven. He was not only a teetotaller, he also fought tooth and nail the stress that had killed his father: stress that had fed off penury.

"There's nobody about," started Bob, looking around anxiously, "so tell us why you couldn't come yesterday."

"Den thought he had a chance of getting into luscious Linda's knickers," said Merv.

Den gave me a lopsided grin.

"The only way that'll happen," interjected Bob, "is if he nicks them."

"Who is she?" I inquired.

Den didn't answer. Merv explained that she was a girl at Aramco. "I reckon she wasn't so bad in the past. You know, one of those good schoolgirls, always in bed by ten ... so that she could be home by midnight."

"What brings you to the arse of the world?" spurted Merv.

"Hey, I won't have that," objected Bob before I could answer. "This is not the arse of the world." He held back for a second. "But I'm told if you back there you can see this place."

Merv went one better. "This morning I was at the edge of the abyss, now I'm one step further."

Bob abruptly rose and I thought he was going to make an announcement or a toast. "I'm bushed."

"To the barracks, then," said Merv.

I wanted more and the end was too sudden but I was terribly tired too.

Bob didn't appear drunk when we walked to our demountable ahead of Merv and Den. "For a while now I've wanted to say sorry for being cold towards you in the beginning. I thought you'd be trouble and I was worried about the lads' moral. But you're okay."

"Thanks for saying so. But you're not the only one."

"Don't take any notice of Pav. That logger-headed, toad-spotted barnacle is suspicious of his own mother." Bob would use these convoluted Elizabethan put-downs to Pav's face. Only he was so daring.

But I had been thinking of Ian too.

* * *

At lunch everyone was subdued. The ventriloquist evening was destined to become legend. Mike told me that breakfast had been seen through bleary-eyes. Like our guests I had slept in and lunch for us was really brunch. He also told me that he thought the Filipinos had revelled on in private. He had to send Tass to rouse Scab for breakfast.

Afterwards only Bob, Pav and I saw our visitors off. The others were back out on the farm. Their bids of farewell were accompanied with perfunctory invitations to Aramco. It was all very deflating.

"You two have been a real tonic," I said desperately. Groans were superseded by chuckles when they realised my innocence.

When they were gone, but before the three of us split up I tried to put life into the air. Perversely I chose complicity in my husband's absence.

"They didn't leave anything," I said, having seen the Jerry cans and boxes of water in the boot when they threw their hold-alls in.

"Not much," said Bob coyly.

Pav smiled.

"It's risky carrying all that around," Bob continued.

"The Masstock boys will take some," Pav added, before turning on his heal and waddling off like plump drake on a winter's day.

* * *

The drive to the farm is blinding. I have not been buried in dungeons but the space and light make me shrivel. I sit in the back of the vehicle, manacled hand and foot. We are a convoy of three vehicles, at least eight officers and detectives and a doctor. Nobody from the Embassy. Shackled as I am is ridiculous. Could a single woman in my state get away from all these men? Where could I go?

I've been dreading this trip for days. The very idea of a reconstruction is abhorrent, but now that it is upon me, I'm strangely detached. I felt like I did when taking my driving test all those years ago: another person, another world. It had been set in the afternoon and I'd fretted and worried for days. I'd told no one. I didn't want horror stories stirring more troubles into my mind. And then it was the morning of the test and I was calm. I was strangely detached, bereft of energy with a couldn't-give-a-damn attitude. The result was that I sailed through the test in a dreamlike state.

We turn off the road and bump along a familiar track. The farm is as it was and yet brighter more unreal. Not as I remember it. Rebuilt by somebody who has not consulted my memory.

We stop outside the kitchen building. There's a lot of ordering about and men moving hastily. I look to the ground were Abdul lay. I look for tyre tracks, blood in the grit, images of violence. There is nothing.

4B tells me that I can take some clothes with me. But first we must go to the kitchen. I shuffle awkwardly to show the ludicrousness of his precautions. The shackles jingle. He is patient and waits for me at the bottom of the steps. The sand roses are gone. He takes me by the elbow. The door opens and we both look up. A face from the past looks down at us and 4B is again barking orders. Men bound noisily up the steps. Ted the head is manhandled down. "I was told you were coming tomorrow." Two others, Filipinos, in workers uniforms are brought out of the building.

"You must wait out here until we are finished," 4B tells him. Ted doesn't recognise me. Do I look so wretched? My head is shaved. He had only met me once, at the refectory for breakfast undoubtedly flustered by both a break in his routine and the presence of Smith and his po-faced wife.

The kitchen is alien to me. The horn is gone, its boom a memory. And there are other memories. Laughter and talk. Voices begin to fill my head with words like darting sparrows. Swooping and rising. Then they swirl in dark flocks. And my head begins to spin and 4B tightens his grip.

An officer stands near the window, stiffened by the presence of authority. Others follow us in.

4B tells me to put his officers in their places and then take my own place. One of them puts a tape recorder on the table; another holds a clipboard. 4B remains at the sink. Aloof, like Pav.

I sit and 4B talks Arabic to the recorder. He talks to me, urging me to describe events. And his speech takes the form of a bouquet of flowery words. His wording is so embellished that I can't see him clearly. I shift in my seat and remind myself to co-operate. Perfume assails me. His wreath of words is a girdle about my neck. And so it goes on, he speaking to me in garlands of English, and then repeating my words in Arabic into the machine.

I wonder whether the shackles are to be removed when we re-enact the fleeing. But suddenly he comes to an end. A bloody end. He abruptly switches off the recorder and tells me I can now select some things. Instead of going to the sleeping quarters an officer opens the lounge door. It has been fitted with a padlock. And here, stacked in cardboard boxes are our possessions. I assume them to be the entire crew's belongings. The officer directs me to a stack of boxes. Every one is felt-tipped in their script of indecipherable squiggles.

The first box I open contains Mike's clothes. The officer is not looking. I pick up a shirt, a favourite shirt, a shirt we bought together, a common experience, a shared experience. Too noble for a farmer, he'd said. I smother my face in it and sob. No more *huggles*.

* * *

Riyadh airport was marble and fountains. Apparently a triumph of architecture. Yet, the achievement was lost on me. I found it big, modern and soulless. Glamorous rather than beautiful. We were consumed by the less nebulous phenomena of saying goodbye to Bob. It was hard to believe that Mike and I had known him a mere seven and a half weeks. It was only Monday 17th December but he had holiday owing to him.

Ballast had been shed. Ian got last year's craze, a Rubik's cube; a puzzle Bob had mastered but one that had confounded Ian. Books were distributed. He bequeathed one of the silly printed carpets he'd hung in his room to Mike and myself. He knew we hated it. Dogs dressed up like gangsters playing pool. "Not your Bayeux Tapestry," he admitted with a wicked smile. Almost everything else he didn't want he left to the Filipinos. Scab got his alarm clock. "It won't be any more successful at getting you up than the one you've already got, but maybe the stereo effect..."

During those final days Bob had been melancholic. He had not made crass statements like: "the last Tuesday" or "the penultimate whatever". But the pressure would issue from a seam in his composure as an observation. One comment that struck me was: "Somehow I feel I've been running on the spot all this time." As if now, only in leaving, he was getting back to the real world.

He began his moribund plank-walk at the farm saying goodbye to Pav and Tass who had elected to remain with Mike. My husband's handshake and well wishing were undermined by his haste to be at some pivot that was giving problems. Bob said: "You're a good leader Mike. And I thought the last decision you made was saying: 'I do' at the alter."

At the airport Bob disappeared for a time to retrieve his passport. He shook his head with disgust as he showed us the coffee ring on the back. "The nerds used it as a coaster." Although he was in good time, we had to get back to the farm. "I guess this is it," he said as we neared the departure area after his check-in. "The end of an ear," he laughed.

Sparky revealed nothing, but Scab's eyes were soft. Ian looked shocked and embarrassed. I was not happy with a handshake and wanted to inject warmth that had been lacking in my husband's goodbye, so despite being in public I gave him a kiss on the cheek. "Keep your peckers up, punters. I'll be thinking of you when I'm drinking my port on Christmas day."

"You sod," I said, wanting connection not glibness.

"We'll all miss you," I said, catching and holding his eyes for a moment.

"Yes," agreed Ian, his voice a decibel above a whisper.

Bob's departure was dissatisfying but it could not have been otherwise.

I would have liked to have seen his face on the plane as he opened his present. He refused to do so in the kitchen.

There were always locusts on the farm. The lads kept them under control by spraying insecticide before the population was big enough to swarm. We had caught one, engulfed one in a good dollop of translucent amber-tinged cast, and plonked it in a honey jar. The label read: "100% Protein. Produce of Saudi Arabia."

* * *

Le Chatelier's Principle states: "If some stress, such as a change in temperature, pressure or concentration, is brought to bear on a system in equilibrium, a reaction occurs which displaces the equilibrium in the direction which tends to undo the effect of the stress." This was our science teacher's favourite Principle. Mr. Everest taught both Physics and Chemistry. I don't know why this was his favourite. It always seemed to me a specialisation and watered down version of Newton's: "To every action there is an equal and opposite reaction."

Why Mr. Everest should spring to mind is a mystery. I can think of more colourful schoolteachers. The Maths teacher, Mr. Sidebottom, who insisted on the pronunciation: Siddi-bot-tarm for one. He was in the habit of periodically waking everybody with a thrash of his metal pointer on his desk. There was a rumour of unfulfilled military aspirations. Chalking circles on the blackboard I remember him idly telling us: "if you could draw a perfect circle you were mad" before going on to routinely explain some geometric principle. He imparted other oddities that lodged themselves in my mind. "Parallel lines meet at infinity." One day his desk thrashing came to an abrupt end when he inadvertently brought the pointer down upon his pocket calculator, an expensive item in those days.

Mr. Everest had a quiet manner, wore pince-nez, and tweed jackets with leather elbows. His boyish inquisitiveness and greasy hair said he was not married and lived alone or with a decrepit mother. His prominence for me can only be because, despite his unassuming ways, his calm enthusiasm for his subject had an effect on most of us. Here was a person who had found his vocation. How wonderful. Because of him I'd excelled in Physics.

Bob's absence upset the farm's equilibrium. And true to Le Chatelier's Principle there were attempts to undo the stress by trying to fill Bob's place.

His absence hushed the farm. We didn't move about as ghosts, but the liveliness had disappeared. We didn't mourn either. It was as if a visiting grandchild had departed, taking all its shattering exuberance, leaving the grandparents with only domesticity to fill out the emptiness. Bob had been good for morale. More than this, he had been the marionette master, a binding choreographer, who brought us to life. We were now abandoned and left to flounder by ourselves. This was the obvious effect of his absence. Less obvious was that in animating us we had not shown our true character. As if any connection that circumvented him would be subterfuge. No longer paled by his brilliance we became acutely aware of everybody else. For Bob's bright humour had been an integral part of the farm. His commanding position obliged us to orbit and we had gladly become satellites to his glowing wit. Of course to varying degrees our personalities had twinkled, but we had never shone independently. Mike and Ian in particular had the most difficulty finding their feet.

As if it were a liability of leadership Mike tried his hand at humour. His position made him responsible for the workers' moral, but that did not mean he had to play entertainer. I recollect him calling Sparky a fartiste and going on to talk of Pujol, whose sensational wind-breaking talents (amongst other things he played tunes) were popular at the Moulin Rouge in the 1890s.

Ian also projected himself. His reasons were more difficult to fathom. I remember entering the kitchen one lunch time and hearing him telling somebody off. "You can't get sloppy about this. Between eighty-four and eighty-six. That's it. Above that and - " He stopped when I entered. He'd been in full swing and had not heard me on the steps or in the corridor. He swung wildly like a hammer thrower suddenly off balance. His anger did not vanish as quickly as he would have liked and he turned back to Sparky and Scab. They both looked subdued. "Okay?" he finally said. Sparky nodded. The heat barred me from enquiry and nobody was willing to elaborate. Pav entered and appeared unaware of the wisps of conflagration. When Tass and my husband came in they inadvertently kicked dust over any belligerent embers with idle talk. But in Ian and Sparky there was edginess. It was that same mistrust I had sensed during my first few days at the farm. So much more obvious now that Bob was not there to blind me. And although Ian was later at pains to quell the furtiveness with offers of tea and trips, I would not be fooled.

At first, as Ian and my husband thrashed about, I thought one would hurt the other. I mistook their efforts as vying for leadership. After a few days they settled down and tended to play off each other. A favourite and blatant show of who they were trying to be was the use of the introduction: "as Bob would have said". Sometimes it worked, but most of the time the laughter was not wholesome.

As the weeks relegated Bob to memory so too his legacy faded and references to him grew seldom. The lads gave up doing cover-versions and found their own voices. Attempts at humour became less frequent and the rare laughter became healthier.

* * *

There was another night excursion. This time Mike was half awake. Our a/c was broken and the silence unaccustomed.

"You heard that?" I said.

"What?" he asked thickly.

"Somebody's outside."

"Maybe it's a nookie run. Go back to sleep."

"I'm going to read for a while. Okay?"

He grunted and brusquely turned away from me as I switched on my bedside light.

When I heard them return I knew that they could not have travelled all the way to Riyadh and back. They could have reached the Masstock Dairy, but then they couldn't have stayed for more than a quarter of an hour. The only solution was that they'd gone to a nearby Bedouin encampment.

I was intrigued and wanted to wake Mike. But my hands were

tied. He didn't really care and it was none of my business.

*　*　*

Christmas festivities are for the religious or children. In the absence of both an effort was made with the motto "let's make the best it." The meal was extravagant and the kitchen and lounge decked out in ribbons and balloons. In the lounge a bush doubled as a tree and was accordingly adorned. Naturally, Christmas cards, coloured balls, lights, tinsel were not to be had. Only innocuous "Happy Holidays" cards could be purchased, but then "Seasons Greetings" would have been inappropriate. Mike and I made Christmas crackers from toilet rolls and provided the bang at the appropriate moment. They contained a self-made hat and a joke I'd copied from a magazine. More or less everyone made the effort. We'd invited four lads from Masstock, including the three Pats. Big Pat was charged with distributing the presents in a shaving foam beard.

Mike and I had exchanged gifts in our room. I wore the gold necklace and bracelet from him and he carried the dress watch from me. These were not surprises. We'd chosen our presents in Riyadh. In the case of my jewellery I had never got used to the fact that gold was weighed for sale. Irrespective of artwork, numbers were tapped out on a pocket calculator and a price suggested and then haggled.

We bought the Filipinos T-shirts. In Saudi they could be horrendously expensive. Ian received a gypsum incense burner, a *Mabkhar*, from us. My husband couldn't resist commenting that he was glad we no longer shared a toilet with him. "The *Mabkhar* might stop the fumes spreading."

Mike had suspected that there was *sid* on the farm and after saying that he hoped the amount was negligible and in a good hiding place, the location of which he did not want to know, he admitted that he had nothing against some being consumed. We indulged with reverence rather than raucous abandon.

The Filipinos were Roman Catholic, but there was nothing religious about our Christmas. Nobody seemed unduly bothered.

On New Year's Eve we closed up the farm and went to the Masstock Dairy. Mike had wanted to stay behind and hold the fort, but I insisted on his company.

The lads at the Dairy had gone to some lengths to create a party atmosphere. Their canteen was covered in streamers and balloons. Somehow they'd obtained party hats and paper trumpets. Alcohol was available. Women were lacking, but I was not alone. One man had his wife visiting and three nurses from the King Khalid hospital were also present.

I got chatting to one of the nurses and she promised to call me the next time the girls were doing something. She did call but we couldn't get transport organised, and we agreed to have another go at a later date. I telephoned once and she repeated her promise. The onus of contact then sat squarely in her lap but she never called and I was destined to remain marooned.

I enjoyed the evening. There was much abandonment and dancing: too much dancing for us women. It was impossible to turn someone down and pauses could only be taken after promises had been drawn from us.

The only thing of note was when little Pat told me that he had been caught last year trying to smuggle alcohol into the country. One of the nurses was his girlfriend and he'd wanted to get her a present, namely her favourite drink. He proudly stated that he'd had one successful run, concealing advocaat in a shampoo bottle. The trouble was that although he'd thoroughly washed out the bottle it had smelt of shampoo. The second time the contents may have been drinkable but he'd not been so lucky. He spent three days in prison, describing the conditions as bearably unpleasant. His defence was that he had not known that a shampoo could contain so much alcohol. When confronted with the fact that it could be smelt, he claimed that he'd simply bought it: it was not his custom to open bottles in the shop and smell them before buying. The company had paid for his release and his trial was set for two months later. His cockiness was given a good bashing when the company said they'd do everything to keep him on, but that he'd have to meet all costs, right down to the interpreter's fees. On top of this his 'oversight' cost him forty lashes, carried out two months after sentencing. In the telling he was quite matter-of-fact and the way he described the public flogging made it sound like a schoolboy being punished for a minor misdemeanour. He had not been required to remove his clothes and had worn a thick jumper. Like imprisonment the pain had been bearable. The five-foot cane left him bruised but not bloodied. Afterwards he had been taken to fill out some paperwork and asked if he wished to see a doctor. What he dismissed in the way he spoke was betrayed by the darkness of his brow. The four months or so of anxiety had left deep tracts in his forehead.

***

Bob's departure freed something in Ian. Everyone was adjusting but Ian was manoeuvring. Put succinctly he attempted to instigate an intimacy between us. Admittedly this had started whilst Bob was still with us. To my horror my sympathy for him since his revelation of his fiancée's rebuff and the fact that he was an orphan had been mistaken for affection. Now his advances were overt.

Ian had been brought up in an orphanage. He didn't know his parents and had no intention of seeking them out. He'd not been fostered, but we all agreed he appeared remarkably normal. All except Bob, who flew off into character smearing heights, swooped momentarily to snatch away our fabulous parentage speculations and twisted these into infamous people.

Ian's attempts to connect with me were initially the coy meeting of eyes. I did not linger on his eyes but I did not snap myself away. I assumed a blasé demeanour that vanquished him and pressed down my annoyance. Unfortunately my feigned ignorance was so complete that he became less discreet. He did not flirt at every opportunity, but Mike noticed some indiscretion.

"I think Ian fancies you."
"Rubbish," I blurted too quickly.
Mike raised an eyebrow.
"Pah, you've got nothing to worry about."
"I know."

Ian's attempts to galvanise an affair culminated on one of his days off. When he went into our shared toilet-shower unit he closed the door latch to our bedroom and was to reopen it when he vacated the room. Of course there was a latch on our side of the door to maintain privacy. At the first opportunity after Bob's departure he left our latch closed so that I couldn't use the amenities.

"Ian, you've left our door closed," I called.

Receiving no reply I went into the corridor and knocked on his door. Again nothing. I turned the knob, opened the door a crack and spoke into the room. Still nothing. Thinking he'd gone and I'd somehow not heard him leave the building I pushed the door wide to see him lying on his bed wearing headphones and underpants reading a book. He didn't jump up, but merely looked over. I spoke as he removed his headphones. Why wasn't he using his fabulous stereo system? All the lads had expensive systems, a priority of the single guys. Ian had an entire wall devoted to cassette tapes.

"You left the latch on our door," I said, noting that although he hadn't touched his player and there was no sound coming from the headphones.

"Did I?" He smiled. I was disgusted. And yet he could claim I had misconstrued everything. Maybe he'd switched the music off as I entered.

He didn't move.

"Well, don't worry about it. We're moving into Bob's room today." This was not true. We were planning to do it together when Mike had time off. When I later insisted on the move my husband was perplexed and irritated. I said that I'd do most of it. That and my "do it for me" feminine charms that bordered treacherously on the fickle broke his reluctance. I didn't tell him of the incident. I didn't want to cause a rift in their working relationship. We moved enough of our belongings to sleep in the bigger room that night.

The snub was enough to bury Ian for some time, but I knew it would not satisfactorily silence him. Another type of man would not have bothered wearing underpants. But Ian was not that confident. Yet.

* * *

The belongings I collected from the farm have been ransacked. I'd kept them in a box under my bed. Usually one of our cellmates is present to guard against theft. But nobody admits to being on duty. I go through my things and realise that some clothes and underwear have gone. My makeup mirror is also missing. No doubt this will be put to use as a weapon too.

I was called to the entrance by a guard who had handed me the box. It had been vetted. I remember feeling self-conscious carrying the box to our cell. I should have sought the inquisitive eyes. Instead I ignored them. In the cell I went through the things and was pleased to see that nothing had been confiscated.

I'd not found my rugs and wall hangings, my ethnic treasures. But they would have been of no use here.

Later that day I see one of the Arabs wearing one of my blouses. She walks by me and the entire prison population turns her walk into a challenge. I know I am being watched.

"If you do nothing, others will take things from you," Pip says to me later.

"Why haven't they robbed you?"

"I have very little. And I have Rita."

I hate my situation. A conspiracy is at work to drag me down. I don't want to become an animal. I just have to bide my time. The reconstruction has convinced them of my innocence. It's just a matter of time before I'm out of here. Let them strip me. "They're just things."

"They are all we have."

"Really?" I cannot wax lyrical. She may have years in here and belongings are prison currency. Bartering gives small meaning and comfort to life in here.

"You're not going to do anything?"

"They're only things."

Pip nods. She does not agree, but seems to accept my decision.

* * *

Part of Ian's insidious strategy entailed befriending my husband. Maybe that was not true. Naturally they spent a good part of the working day together and a working friendship was inevitable. This was why I had not told Mike the reason for the urgency in moving into Bob's room. What happened next tipped me over the edge.

Mike and I were leaving the kitchen for bed when Ian casually remarked: "Off for some *huggles*?"

I was visibly shaken and Mike noticed and stammered: "Something like that." Ian saw his mistake and looked into his cup of tea.

We left the building in silence.

"You told him?" My raging mind had no better opening.

"Yes. We got talking about relationships and -"

"You told him about us."

"Of course. Did I need clearance?"

"Don't be facetious, it doesn't become you."

We were at our demountable now.

"Come on Dawn. It was harmless. Idle talk." I knew he thought it an inconsequential anecdote.

During our courtship I had called him over to bed. Mixing my words as I'd mixed my drinks, I'd said come over for some *huggles* instead of hugs or snuggles. And this word became our word. Under certain circumstances I may have disclosed the word myself. But Ian was one of the last people to whom I would have shared such intimacy.

"I know it's tough for you, but you've got to -"

"It's okay. I know what you're going to say." I'd harnessed my emotions. "You're right." Thus disabled I added: "But with anyone but Ian." I rushed on, telling him of Ian's advances, concluding with the headphones incident.

"Why didn't you tell me?"

"Partly because it was so petty. Partly because I didn't want to bother you -" He made to speak. "You've got enough on your hands. And partly because you've got to work with him and I didn't want any ill feeling."

"You should've told me."

"I know. I thought I could handle it." Suddenly I was exhausted. I was a spinning top that had careened and mercifully come to rest. I think he saw my general unhappiness, but there was an unsaid agreement that we ignore it. He chose to have faith in me. I was going through a phase. I'd come though it.

During *huggles* I made him promise not to mention the headphones incident to Ian. It was unnecessary. And I knew he would curtail all talk of us with him.

* * *

By the end of January I seemed to be continually tired. As if my batteries were not being recharged at night I took to taking catnaps during the day.

The farm was quiet, with the boys merely tending the pivots of green wheat and grasses. When they were out working, something more than silence descended upon the buildings. Absence would be the word. There were few visitors. I threw myself into my chores to burn up the boredom and found myself with even more free time. My meals became basic after Christmas but nobody seemed to notice. If they did they chose not to comment.

One day when I was alone at the demountables I crossed the fifty-metre gap to look into Abdul's building. The last time he had been he had brought his black shrouded wife with him. She had hurried into the building like a shuffling Geisha and had only re-emerged when they left. My curiosity was aroused. Surely there was nothing against one woman meeting another? During the day of her presence I made more trips between our sleeping quarters and the kitchen than necessary to remind Abdul of my existence and so encourage a meeting. After all, I had not had a good chinwag with a woman for three months. Naturally, it was highly likely that his wife spoke no English, but at the time I just wanted something, anything.

Crossing the gap brought flutters of excitement. Abdul was not expected but I was wary. Even the lads could question me. I had no reason to be there and my peculiar actions disturbed me. Cupping a hand to the grimy window I could make out a small office. There was a desk and a sofa: all standard furniture. However, on the desk was a bottle of what appeared to be vodka or schnapps. I strained to see what it was. The liquid was clear and the partially visible label was serious but colourful. I had heard that the privileged didn't bother with moonshine. They obtained real alcohol. I was thrilled by the scandal and a day or two later I had to admit to peeking into the window to share my discovery with Mike. He didn't believe it could be alcohol, but could offer no suggestion as to what it might be.

I don't know why and I didn't say anything to anyone but I went to the workshop when it was empty and put a small pebble at the locked door. At first I checked it daily, eventually dropping to weekly. It never moved. Finally I forgot all about it.

I knew what was wrong with me. Constant tiredness was a sign of depression. I was not clinically depressed. I was growing profoundly bored. With each passing day the ratchet of boredom turned and shrunk my space. Trips to Masstock and Riyadh, even to a restaurant with Mike, became a journey along a capillary. I was suffering Bob's rut. If he had been running on the spot then I was sprinting in a hamster's wheel, expending vast amounts of energy on inactivity. My heart felt constricted by the confinement. I thought I was suffering from angina. After having trouble getting up I had trouble doing my jobs. I stretched them out to glean some satisfaction.

I did not continually lack enthusiasm. I'd bake my famous fig-cake, crushing the lonely kitchen floorboard creaks and filling the room with song and the cake's cloying aroma. Everyone loved the cake and I enjoyed treating the lads. But these were meagre victories.

I also went ethnic. To some extent I was preoccupying myself with spending sprees: treating myself to small treasures. I'm loath to admit that the purchases were inspired by June's furnishings. First came the practical. A plaited palm fibre basket with decorated leather ribbon, which I used as a laundry hamper. I bought other baskets for magazines. Soup and fruit bowls came next. Then I moved on to the decorative. I found a tribal rug for our room. Then came woven tent-hangings and weavings, initially for our room then spreading to the lounge. A donkey bag as a satchel for my magazines and books for sunbathing and my walking stock was replaced with an Arab cane, Mike stopped me buying an unwieldy shepherd's staff. I also held back from buying a camel saddle for the lounge, promising it myself at a later date. I needed more time before buying coffee pots, jugs, an incense burner, ornamental coral and shells in baskets, pottery and candleholders. I even tried to interest Mike into buying a Yemini dagger, so that the purchases would not be solely mine.

All the while I was staving off boredom with a capital B. This B was distorting into the D of depression. D came in many guises, often stealing upon me to take me unawares. Once when idly browsing a magazine I came upon a verdant English countryside scene. The lush green scorched my eyes, emphasising my emptiness and torching my flimsy world. I would combat such primitive attacks tooth and nail, but sometimes I had no strength and succumbed to the deadly lethargy. My mood would become foul. I tried to suppress my feeling, and wrestled and writhed and became tetchy.

My ailment was an illness and as such incubated. So I was able to function fairly normally. Even my relationship to my husband took on a newfound tenderness, a delicate extension charged with touch and concern. Yet, all the time I was deteriorating and denying the extent of my depression.

My illness was mine and mine alone. I was growing isolated and I sought isolation. I wanted the comfort of hibernation. B and D circled relentlessly. They were locked by the scent of blood, allowing me no peace, poking, prodding, and goading me. They waited for empty moments when I lacked energy and then pounced and tore me to shreds. Sometimes I triumphed, but complete victory could never be had. Time was their ally and attrition their strategy. I was heading for a breakdown.

Colony

"Just because you've bought a book doesn't mean you can't borrow one from the library."

I had not heard this line before, but that did not elevate it above the status of instant cliché. Add alcohol, a beach barbecue and stir. I was so shocked I didn't know what to say. Why hadn't I seen this coming? Perhaps because I had not spent the entire evening with him and I had not noticed him sounding me out.

He could at least have been a little more sophisticated. But drink had stripped away the bark of civility. Den had perfected an innocent expression: "here I am, don't hurt me". Although I didn't need an excuse, this cheap conjurer's sleight of hand was his downfall. I was tipsy and happy and couldn't muster the necessary anger or quick-witted response. The phrase "be gentle with me" shot through my head and Bob twisted it into "be genital with me." My sudden laughter chopped him down. His exaggerated innocence turned to confusion, then a question. A smile was attempted, but panic overcame him and he mustered up hurt.

"I'm sorry," I managed, wiping my eyes. "That's very sweet of you, but I couldn't." It was far from sweet of him. And tomorrow, I knew my memory of the evening would be soured by his blunt proposition, as subtle as a thumping wooden mallet. Just as he'd discarded seduction he'd dispensed with any suggestion of foreplay. What he proposed was little more than insect copulation. Didn't he know the female mantis devours the male afterwards? I'd chewed him out just for approaching.

My laughter was buckshot and he scrambled to gather up the rags of his ego. Hugging them he scurried behind the breakfast hatch. "Would you like a drink?" he boomed, opening a bottle of *sid*. Maybe he harboured vestiges of hope that I would jump into bed with him if he could lubricate a path passed my moral guardian. But his question came across as a pathetic attempt at returning fire whilst making an undignified retreat. He knew the answer before I spoke.

"No. I'm going to sleep."

On my way to the bathroom I noticed that I could not lock my bedroom door. Anger came to my side. I hoped Den would remain downstairs stitching the tatters of his confidence and cauterising his memory with drink. On the other hand Anger dared him to show himself. It wanted to kick him in his manhood.

I saw no reason to shove my holdall against the door. Although ineffectual at stopping entry, it would have acted as an early warning. When I climbed into bed I reassured myself that Den was a reasonable guy who'd simply drunk a little too much. He'd no doubt vowed celibacy to his wife and was probably chastising himself with lashings of *sid* and self-reproach. I even smiled at the thought of him at the breakfast table with his tail between his legs, listening to his collared small talk, perhaps offering me his leash with uncertain eyes. But should he approach in the night Anger was ready to offer him a verbal whipping with a cat-o'-nine-tongues. I didn't believe he would dare.

Until that night I had regarded myself as a good judge of character. I still hadn't realised I this was not the real world and my judgement was impaired.

If only my husband could see me now. Tipsy and in a house with another man, who was slowly getting sozzled in the sitting room. Of course, if he'd seen me earlier, when I'd arrived and had taken my hold-all up to the guest room, and Den had invited me into the bedroom he occupied on the pretext of seeing Fluffy his rabbit, and I found myself dangerously close to flirting, he would have been hurt.

The isolation on the farm at night was supreme. Here I had difficulty relaxing. I could not shut out the anxious buzz of human activity. I was receptive to the sheer number of people on the camp and, like a radio that couldn't be switched off I had to settle for static to rest.

He was still downstairs when I fell asleep.

I didn't hear him come in. The door was suddenly wide and the light from the landing cut a tract into the room. He was silhouetted before me and I was in his shadow. A small sound or the change in light when he opened the door must have woken me. He shifted slightly, obviously wanting to see my reaction. Slitting my eyes against the brightness, I pulled the quilt under my neck. Chad was not here.

* * *

Den and Merv had arrived at the farm on Wednesday evening and stayed for an hour. My call from the Masstock dairy must have sounded like a desperate plea. It was 27th February 1985 and I'd been in the country for just over four months. This, and the fact that I wasn't sure of the sincerity of their offer to collect me should I like to visit, made me try to play down the importance of the call. They undoubtedly understood the significance but were big enough not to test my matter-of-fact charade and raced across so that I could spend that coming weekend in Dhahran. Strangely enough, the suggestion to call them had come from Ian.

They did not come alone.

"This is my friend Rashid," said Merv. "We work together." The second statement appeared to negate the first. The man in *thobe* and *gutra* smiled and nodded. He looked younger than us and had an open yet troubled face. "We're giving him a lift to Riyadh and he wanted to see the farm." Again he smiled.

"It's a bit late for a tour," said Mike.

"That is okay," said Rashid. "I have seen the green you have here."

I challenged the threat of silence. "Would you like a drink or something to eat before we go?"

"I'll go for a coffee," said Merv jovially. "And we could take some sandwiches for underway." Without pausing he added: "There's something in the boot for you, Pav." Tass left with Pav. We all knew what was in the boot. Rashid's presence put paid to any protests from my husband.

The Arab put everyone on edge. Distrust was something I'd come to expect from expats. I felt it myself and was wary of what I said.

Merv, for all his happy-go-lucky facade, was nervous too. He was responsible for Rashid's presence and eked spasms and twitches of speech out of us. We contorted this way and that in our efforts to appear casual and inoffensive. Yet, the dynamics at play brought out no acrobats. Infrared faux pas sensors criss-crossed our talk and our progress was spastic.

"What's it like working with Merv?" I asked.

Rashid smiled before answering. "He is very clever."

"Hides it well," said Den.

It was like pressing fruit that had already been squeezed. Conversation did not flow, it did not even come in spurts: it came in isolated drops.

"Have you been programming long?" Mike asked.

"Two years."

We were grinding pith.

I was not alone in showing surprise when Merv pulled out Prince Ali and Jasmin. He looked at Mike and Ian. "When we return, we want a show." I could see that they were offended as if Merv blamed them for my state. But we were all watching for Rashid's reaction. Ian tried Ali on for size.

"I've got some black socks," said Mike picking up Jasmin.

"Good," returned Merv. "Ali can have a harem."

Pav and Tass's return became a signal to leave.

Mike collected my bag from our room.

"The boot's full," said Merv, explaining the bag in the back separating Rashid and me on the back seat. My own bag was wedged into the floor space between us. "You've got plenty of room between you." I wondered whether there was strategy in the bags between us. Did the lads mistrust Rashid? What could he do? He was hardly going to molest me. Was the boot full?

We dropped Rashid off at house in Riyadh and found our way back to the open road without incident. We didn't stop at Masstock. I thought that was the reason for the boot being full. The boys wanted to make a delivery. Instead we raced straight to Aramco.

In the Oldsmobile I asked Merv about Rashid. Conversation had been clipped until we dropped him off.

"He's always talked about coming. I couldn't very well say no."

"It was a bit risky transporting *sid*." For a moment there was a terrible silence. "I know what was in the boot." Still they were silent. "I suppose there's some left over." Their silence made me uneasy. "So I'm taking the risk too, now."

"I suppose it was a risk," Merv said. "I don't completely trust Rashid."

"Do you trust any of them?" asked Den. He was driving.

"Actually, yes. There're a couple of guys at work. They're okay. But Rashid, I don't know. He's having trouble programming. I'm not even sure the other Arabs like him that much. He's not thick; he's just not cut out to be a programmer."

"You don't have to be intelligent to program," said Den.

"True, and if you had shit for brains you'd be dangerous."

"Get stuffed."

"If any of us were intelligent we wouldn't be here," I said, ever the pacifier.

"You've drawn the shortest straw," Merv admitted. "Not only are you a woman, you're stuck on that godforsaken farm."

"I'm glad you two came. I was beginning to go nuts. I really appreciate -"

"Stop it before I upchuck," protested Merv.

Conversation was easy. At this time in the evening it wasn't necessary to set the a/c to gale-force nine. Inevitably we spoke of Bob. Like us on the farm Merv had received a throwaway postcard. We then talked of the farm before digging into each other's backgrounds. There was a wonderful liberty to our burrowing. No need for caged canaries to warn us of explosive issues. I struck a fantastic vein in Den when I discovered he was married. His wife and he had sacrificed being together to move up in the world: to buy that bigger house. He saw himself spending a year here. Merv held no such Mother Lode. He was single and worked with computers and earned even more money, or as he chose to put it: "I'm just a whore. Wherever I fill my wallet, that's my home."

"Another blister and lance," said Den, as we passed a mosque and minaret. He was an archetypal expat brim with mockery.

We raced on the open road. There was nobody on the endless ribbon of grey that tied isolated knots of humankind together. I think the entire journey of two hundred kilometres took under two hours.

Den had a housesit and could put me up. The car belonged to the occupants, who were not British. The plush, wine-coloured interior was too ostentatious for British sensibilities. The velvet seats were as expansive as sofas and the three of us could have sat up front. It was a comfortable ride, but the vehicle was still a pimpmobile. After dropping Merv off just after eleven at the all-male North Camp, where Den also normally resided, we went to the sit, drank some tea and wearily said goodnight to one another.

* * *

He's introduced himself, but all I've registered is that he's from the Ministry of the Interior. He looks like a bug-eyed Saddam Hussein: sagging features and a wedge of a moustache. He's not a well man.

There's a man sitting behind him, up against the wall. I don't recognise or remember him. I just know that he was there the whole time. Two guards stand near the door. One is a uniformed man; the other is covered in an *abaaya*.

"Are you being treated well?"

Surely he can do better than that? But I'm wary of annoying him. My father's visit may be on the line. I don't know.

When I don't answer he nods knowingly. "I do not like it here either." He fingers a carton of cigarettes, before opening it and offering me one. I take it and before he can lift his lighter I stick it behind an ear.

He smiles and lights one for himself. Leans back to enjoy his drag. Then he tips his head back and blows the smoke out upward like a whale discharging a jet of water.

He leans forward the stained fingers of his cigarette-holding hand jabbing at me. "I can give you more than that cigarette. You can take them all." He pushes the box as if it is of no consequence. "You want money? I will give you money." What does he want, this man from the secret police?

He sees that his offers are ineffectual. He takes another deep drag on his cigarette. "Dawn, I know you are innocent. You should not be here. But you must help us. We are a just people. Ah, I see you think we are cruel. No. Our justice is harsh. That is all." He pauses again. "If you help us, we can help you. Children of Arabia have been harmed."

My roar of laughter makes him drop his cigarette on the table between us. My laughter is hearty. The movement of a guard behind me makes me stifle my emotion.

"I do not understand you," he resumes when I'm quiet. Perhaps he thinks I'm mad? "The death of children is not something to laugh at."

"They weren't children," I whisper.

"What?"

"They weren't children." My voice is hoarse.

"Their families of the boys have been given blood money."

I don't know why, but his statement breaks me. So all our money went to the families of the Arabs. At first my eyes are wide. It's not the fact of the loss of the money, all that we had worked for; it's the knowledge of where it went that tears my heart out. The tears come silently at first. Naturally, justice, their justice, must be done for me to get away, but... And then sobs rack me.

His distress forces him to play his hand. "We must find the killer. The one you call Pav. Tell us where he is."

My sobs have become wailings and he hastily finishes his cigarette. He waves me away and the two guards lift me by the armpits. The cigarette falls from behind my ear. The *abaaya'd* guard picks it up. The uniformed man leaves her to take me to my cell. Once there she gives me the cigarette. This is an unexpected kindness.

Although her *abaaya* makes her anonymous I think she is the guard who sometimes has sweets for the children. There is humanity.

* * *

"Ignore them," said Den.

"Don't even look at them," Merv added.

Testosterone-high youths had overtaken us first from my far side. Then they had weaved in front of us using all three lanes of the freeway and now they were running parallel to our car on my nearside. They were hooting their horn. I didn't look but thought they were gesticulating.

They were kids, not old enough to be behind the wheel of their top-of-the-range BMW. Although without headgear I knew they were Arabs and could give us trouble if provoked. And the urge to provoke them was there, smugly asking me to see what happens. This was tantamount to peering over the parapet of a castle and wondering about the drop. Squashed tomatoes and stew. What if I waved them off? Yes, what if? And that familiar twinge of panic crackled, the show-master beckoning from the abyss of my imagination calling with megaphone distance: roll-up, roll-up, don't be afraid, it's just a bungee-jump, experience the exhilaration of free-fall.

We were in Den's housesit's second car: a Volkswagen Polo. Not as luxurious as the Oldsmobile, it was nevertheless better for parking. The tinted windows of the bigger car made their absence felt.

Another car tooted us aside and blazed on. The youths gave chase. Soon their vehicles merged into the shimmering progression to become another dapple of sunlight heading towards the melting horizon.

"They think all Western women are hussies," said Merv, revitalising the suspended speech.

"Brazen hussies. Especially blondes." Den's elaboration was not truly fitting, as I was not blonde. However, days in the sun had lightened my hair to fair.

Mike would have pointed out that Arab society did not think all women were loose but emotionally labile. Barefaced Western women obviously knew no modesty and it followed that they were unchaste and must be nymphomaniacs.

"Those kids haven't got it easy," said Den. "There was a fad a while back. Some hairdresser was doing Michael Jackson ringlet hair styling. The authorities said it was idolising and un-Islamic. They banned the look and jailed the hairdresser.

"I feel sorry for them," said Merv. "Think about their weekends. All spruced up and nowhere to go."

We cruised into the town along Dhahran Avenue at about eleven o'clock that morning. Three lanes travelled in each direction. A generous aisle of green and palm trees separated incoming and outgoing, and added to the boulevard feel and sense of cruising in. The traffic made up for the absence of life on the street. The few pedestrians who dared defy the brilliance were individualised. The sun sculptured knife-edged shadows that exposed them singularly like burrowing creatures caught above ground in the violent glare of an owl. By now I was used to this impressive banquet of clarity and contrast: a feast for the eye.

A fountain roundabout was some kind of landmark and we left the through-road for a side avenue. And the end of the cruise.

Whereas Riyadh had its eyesores and modern structures, what I saw of Al Khobar (the lads dropped the Al) was modern in that ugly, "let's throw up another concrete block" haste that had robbed the architect of imagination. Some buildings looked as if a machine had cut out doors and windows from a mammoth block of concrete or sandstone. In the stark light of day the dust on the coloured lights and advertisements, the flaking paint, the wires, seams and loose threads meant you could see the joins. A rare fine building would be let down by its neighbour. And then the pavements were raised and uneven, sometimes with a protruding twist of metal, an oversized staple used to tack the place together, ready to catch ill-protected toes. Oases of leisure were to be found in the shopping passages otherwise the schizophrenia of the place drove you on.

The town was based on a grid-pattern, but after walking for a short time I was utterly disorientated. I was sightseeing, giving over the navigation to the lads.

Of course I wore my *abaaya*, but head covering was not necessary. Dhahran and Khobar were not as conservative as Riyadh. The later was not only the capital, but deepest Saudi, unlike the more liberal Gulf cities and towns.

I soon realised that I was really along for the ride. We weren't on a sightseeing tour. There was nothing to see. We did pass some interesting shops selling carpets and antiques. When I commented that there were no price tags Merv said: "If you have to ask the price, you can't afford it." He added: "If you're interested in that kind of stuff we'll take you to the Arab Heritage Centre on Pepsi-Cola Road." Den corrected him. "Next time. It's not on today's route." The lads spent some time on a street where vendors had thrown down cloths on the sidewalk and heaped cassettes on them. The vendors hawked their ware with a call of "one riyal, one riyal, one riyal" over and over again. The speed of their delivery forced me to ask Merv what they were saying.

Many Indians, Filipinos and westerners were sifting through the plastic boxes. I was the only woman among them. At 25p a shot I mucked in too. The lads didn't call them riyals but rats, which not only rolled off the tongue easier, but suited their sense of value to us. Toytown money.

Although the sellers insisted the cassettes were original and the packaging looked authentic it was obvious they were not. A single from the Sade album Diamond Life was printed on the cover and cassette as "Your like is King" instead of "Your love is King." It made me wonder whether the word love was also taboo: very Orwellian. Den picked up a compilation with the song: "Under the baord walk" and they both tried to sing it using boa as in boa constrictor. Merv was furious that the order of the tracks of Pink Floyd's "Dark side of the moon" had been rearranged for a better fit on the tape. "The gonads, it's a concept album." Nonetheless, for one rat he bought it.

"Have you ever noticed that the Filipinos and Indians always go around in groups?" Merv asked. "Like a Hydra, break one off and he'd probably whither and die. They're always carrying a cardboard box containing a stereo." The observation touched a cord and I smiled.

I should not have been surprised that this was a mere shopping trip. A Thursday morning ritual to pass the time. Or did they think this backwater girl had not seen a town? The cassette-spree ended with a visit to Safeways to buy provisions for the evening barbecue. Here I insisted on paying for all the meat.

What truly saved the routine consumerism was the *shawarma* we bought outside Safeways and ate looking out on to the Gulf. A *shawarma* was half of a puffy Arabic flat bread opened like a pocket and filled with lettuce, tomatoes, spices, mayonnaise and strips of lamb cut from an enormous stack of thin layers on a vertically rotating rotisserie. It wasn't haute cuisine, but as the fish and chips of the Middle East it hit exactly the right spot.

* * *

Den and I picked Merv up at North Camp and drove him to

work. He'd been called to cover some program crash or as he put it: "The system's gone belly-up." Some Americanisms do work. Merv worked at one of the so-called Towers. He hoped to cadge a lift and turn up at the barbecue later. He looked at me and nodded at Den when we dropped him off. "Never mind those two," he nodded to our passengers, "watch him."

The two unlikely chaperones he was referring to were Bill and Mary. They were the obligatory family camp residents necessary to enter the family beach or the inspiringly named Half Moon Bay. Bill was a food hygiene inspector and Mary was an Irish nurse. He was the chatty bore who tried too hard to impress and she the withering nonentity. They were an odd couple: suited only in their oddness. He wore his trousers too high. His hip-wearing days were long over and he had raised his trousers to cover his spreading paunch. The rate of spread meant his belt could creep up to his armpits. She was young by comparison, late-twenties to his early forties. Her youth stopped at her appearance for on the rare occasions when a word could be pried from her she talked like an old woman, someone who denied youth's springtime, disapproving of blossoms having nipped her own in the bud. He was forever trying to be young, something which she denied.

I sat in front next to Den and for a time we listened as Bill made his bid for the bore of the year award. At the earliest opportunity Den said he'd bought a cassette in Khobar, which might interest Bill and pushed it in the player. "Meatloaf's Bat out of Hell. You've got to listen to it loud," he said pre-emptively. Without waiting for comment he increased the volume to strangle discernible conversation to within fifty centimetres. Undoubtedly because of this roughshod treatment the two of them found another lift home later.

The drive was uneventful. The usual debris. A strip of blacktop amid the wilderness. There were some undulating dunes but nothing spectacular. Many were tar-capped. Sometimes sand reclaimed edges of the road, causing us to swerve or risk skidding. There were strings of pylons, the cables stretching in long swoops as far as the eye could see, linking one oasis of habitation with another. Our perspective was panoramic and the unbroken regularity of the pylons coupled with their ever-diminishing size reached for the infinite.

We passed a "camels crossing" sign: a silhouetted dromedary on a white background in a red-bounded triangle, but we didn't see any. I heard a fine of £15,000 awaited anyone who killed a camel. Even a scrawny beast would be said to be pregnant or a prized racing camel. Of course to hit one was dangerous in itself. The weight of the beast could cave the roof of a car.

I focused on the dispersing puddle that lay on the road before of us. It was as if the road was wet, but rather than evaporating as we approached it separated like unclasping fingers. I watched the liquid draw away as if once, just once, Nature would falter and we could snatch the unattainable.

After our Khobar visit the lads had dropped me off for an hour at the camp hairdresser. I was in dire need of a haircut. I didn't mind Tass cutting my husband's hair, but he certainly wasn't touching mine.

So I felt joyful and truly light-headed as we drove to the barbecue.

We crossed a crossroads and came upon a hut and a barrier. Den lowered the volume of the stereo and pressed the electric window down. Everyone remained silent as if this were border control: a Northern Ireland checkpoint with acne'd boy-soldiers training machine-guns on us.

I had time to look at the large board planted beside the hut as Den passed Bill's and Mary's i.d.s to the dull guard. His boredom dispelled my anxiety. The only threat seemed to be that he would fall asleep whilst making his checks. He disappeared into his hut. Apparently cars were sometimes waved on and Den suspected he wanted to look at the bared-faced girls. "If he asks for your identification, let me talk."

The notice board was centrally split: on the left was English and on the right Arabic. On one side rigid, block-capital lettering to be read from left to right and on the other, what appeared to be a verbose doctor's prescription, to be read from right to left, as dissimilar as the Egyptian hieroglyphics and Greek of the Rosetta Stone.

General rules for ARAMCO beach/boat area facilities

1. Only Aramco employees eligible for family camp privileges may use this facility. I.D. cards must be shown to the security personnel on duty.

2. Two (2) adult guests are permitted per employee. (Employee dependants are not permitted to bring guests) These guests must show some form of identification when entering and when the employee leaves the facility the guests must leave with him.

3. Drive at reduced speeds in the beach area and keep vehicles on designated roadways and parking areas. Do not drive on the sand dunes.

4. Keep this facility clean by disposing of your garbage in the garbage drums.

5. Keep your children under close supervision, especially when they are in or

near the water.
6. No pets are allowed in this facility.
7. No slaughtering of sheep is allowed in this area.
Dhahran Recreation.

"The last one's a cracker," said Den, noting my gaze and retrieving the i.d.s from the unimpressed guard.

"The one in the gent's at work is also a humdinger," said Bill. "It's above the urinals which you can flush separately. Please use urinal properly."

Irritatingly he wasn't going to elaborate and was waiting for someone to prompt him: "How can you do otherwise?" I asked.

"Some Arabs were caught washing their feet before prayer time."

I wanted to protest that they would surely have used the sinks and thought this was more expat propaganda. Mercifully Den turned up the stereo and Meatloaf took the words right out of my mouth.

* * *

My memory is a sieve; not that it retains nothing. On the contrary, the big chunks remain. I can pick them out later and digest them at leisure. Even people with photographic memories don't commit everything and must consciously fix what they want to retain. For me to handle the wealth of information accrued at a party for instance, the evening generally adopts a theme or a number of themes. Chunks like the overall atmosphere or an incident or a personality are caught. I could inexplicably choose to coat a minor thing with significance and so stop it falling through. Sometimes when I am preoccupied little is registered and everything is ground to sand. But that night I was an open receptacle: a craving fledgling. I had the energy to use my full range of sieves, ones with fine meshes to pan a stream or wide ones to net rapids.

I didn't know where or how the strip of beach ended, probably at the points of the bay, a good half an hour walk apart. We drove almost to the sea and parked alongside the other cars. The low sun flung the shadows of the picnic tables and integrated benches across the fine rumpled lion-skin sand, itself trampled into a stagnant image of the palpitating waters.

Further up the beach a group were heaving a catamaran ashore, wind-surfers were coming in too. And then there were the Saudi men, content with their stiff-backed walking, their shrouded women bunching and showing an ankle as they dipped their feet in the water.

A sobriety was borne by the fresh breeze. The sun had dominated the day, and people had shouted and wallowed and disregarded it. Now evening was upon them and the sound of water was prominent, dampening all else. The spent revellers seemed mindful of this: yells jarred. So their boisterousness retreated with the sun. The sunset was not spectacular, the vast darkening sky and unyielding body of water merely compressing the crimson and peach and paella yellow daylight into yesterday.

Our party consisted of about forty people, mostly men, and all but one seemed affable.

As the evening gave out to the encroaching night, bounding the area in which we could move without a sense of breaking away, I discovered that most of them were indeed members of a club: the British Sub Aqua Club (BSAC).

I was introduced to many people and a few remained in the sieve. I was panning a torrent and a lump lodged itself early on in the evening. I tried prizing it out and then forcing it through, but I simply didn't have suitable implements to hand. Den became involved in some discussion in which I could not participate. I hadn't met anyone and found myself suddenly rudderless. This was not tragic because the bonhomie was akin to the cordial acceptance of a wedding reception. Nonetheless I found myself lumbered with Martin, the obligatory burnt-out expat.

"Hi, I'm Martin."

"Dawn."

"No, dusk." Ha. Ha. "Sorry." He smiled. "Just joined?"

I'd missed the warning *en garde* but knew he wanted to fence. And like a fencing tournament the result was determined in a flash. "Aramco or B-sac?" I asked.

"Both?" His teeth glinted.

"Neither." *Touché.*

"Oh?"

I explained.

"Take my word for it; you're better off where you are." He leaned towards me. The importance of what he was about to say was not for everyone's ears. I recoiled from the sweet smell of *sid* and cola on his breath. "There are three types of people who come to a place like Saudi: emotional cripples, materialistic hard-heads and a combination of both." Tipsiness lends such suppositions portent. He didn't look at me for reaction but looked ahead and smiled bitterly to himself. "Just look at them all."

My mood was not amenable to his conspiratorial ideas. I did not know or trust him and it could only be an uneasy pact. I was not ready to play Stalin to his Hitler.

So I lunged. "Which are you?"

"Isn't it obvious?" he had parried and sidestepped rendering me over-stretched and out-flanked.

I was saved by the Allies crashing in on our weird conversation like amphibious landing craft. "Some of us girls are going for a swim. Do you fancy coming?" She introduced herself as Ginny. Mary stood, without Bill, in the background: her favourite position. I had noticed Virginia earlier, a quietly confident redhead, although her long wispy hair was a cross between orange and strawberry blonde. As we walked to my holdall, Mary limply waiting for us, Ginny said: "You looked as if you needed rescuing."

I jumped at the allegiance. "I thought he was going to slit his wrists in front of me."

"No chance of that. He's had zips fitted."

I laughed.

"He's harmless enough," she continued, as I pulled out my swimsuit. "Mart the fart. He teaches Physics. He's not a diver, but a friend of Geoff's, the dive leader." Geoff was someone else I'd noticed. He was a large, broody type with a roguish mop of dark hair, who, married or not, made me wonder who he met at *Penistone Crags*. He had a clean-shaven youthful face that suggested a public schoolboy; all that was missing was the striped tie and blazer. Many of the men favoured the Designer stubble that to me looked slovenly rather than rugged. Whereas some chose to wear jeans in this heat, he wore canvas slacks and I could tell that before coming to Saudi he had broken away from denim. "They play squash together. Actually, he's quite interesting when you get him on an even keel; he's worked in Iran and Uganda. Most of the time his ballast is wobbly with *sid*."

"There's alcohol here?"

"No, that'd be foolhardy. He usually tanks up before he comes out."

The girls had their swimsuits on and I had to get Den's car keys so that I could change in the Oldsmobile. Thank heaven for tinted windows and plenty of space. I was beginning to regret thinking of it as a pimpmobile. What it meant was that the rest of the swimmers had gone ahead, Mary with them, leaving me exclusive time with Ginny.

We walked out to the others. The water was ankle-deep. In that short distance Ginny told me she was a secretary and the dive club treasurer. She said that Carol was also a secretary and the rest were nurses, one English and four Irish. I listened to her all the while fascinated by the bright phosphorous auroras that illuminated our wake. The milky trail was liquid electricity in the shallows and I purposefully stirred up the water to generate it.

As chance would have it this was an entirely female excursion. Starved of the company of my own sex for so long I relished the moment. Swimming turned out to be paddling as the water wasn't knee-deep and nobody seemed bothered to venture further into the lapping quicksilver. The water was cold but not icy and one quickly switched from the relative warmth of the air to that of the water. So lying on your back or front or simply sitting was pleasant. Only coming out of the water was unpleasant. "Evaporation produces cooling," preached Mr. Everest.

My situation was regarded as a hopeless predicament and incongruously I tried to embellish it with half-hearted talk of Filipino culture. I gave up with a: "yes, well I guess I am rather a Girl Friday."

"With your own harem of Crusoes," said Ginny with raised eyebrows.

I smiled wickedly. "They're not all dishy Geoffs," I admitted, letting my wickedness spill over to a grin.

"You should be thankful," Carol began, "he may be dishy but he's a complete bastard." The outburst reminded me that I was an outsider. Ginny would later tell me that Carol had been his first conquest here. Early days. She had not known that all he wanted was to notch-up another woman on his ego. He had rapidly acquired a reputation for sweeping women off their feet and onto their backs.

"I'd go nuts," said Carol. "I mean it's something of a prison here, but it's not Alcatraz." Carol was small, more girl than woman, with a flaxen pageboy-cut hair, an impish half-smile and cruel little teeth. She was cute rather than beautiful and doll-like with translucent bone china skin.

"I get to Riyadh. And you need the men to drive you to Khobar," I pointed out.

"There's a bus," said Ginny.

"And it's free," Carol added.

The rest of the conversation tended to dip in and out of Aramco happenings and what absentees were doing. At the risk of losing control they sometimes tried to give me the bigger picture. But summarising an event or character in a few brushstrokes could bring a multicoloured onslaught of elaboration and contradiction, which at once deepened and smeared the portrait. So for quite a bit of the time their familiar talk relegated me from stranger to foreigner, comprehending just enough to maintain a stupid grin.

We were out there for half an hour, the group breaking up into easier units. I had been the fleeting bonding factor, the stranger in their midst. There was no open discord, merely more empathy with some than others. Of the Irish girls Ita and Moira struck me as particularly amicable. But Ginny was the person with whom I most wanted to spend time. I was not alone. Carol enjoyed her company too and although I could be no threat to their friendship, she seemed protective of their connection. When there were just the three of us she mentioned shared irrelevancies, intimacies, experiences, etceteras, reinforcing their togetherness and so emphasising my position as interloper. Perversely, I liked Carol. I thought that in her insecurity was a susceptibility that had not adjusted to the world of grown-ups.

Everyone had wandered back and the sound of music re-ignited the lure of food and drink. We returned in an easy silence. The guitar playing and singing had subdued movement. I wanted to be part of the party ahead of us and strangely I did not want to arrive. Out here with my two companions my perspective was superior. The vitality of the party was encapsulated and dwarfed. Oh, I would become part of it, intoxicated by the levity, but out here there could be more, much more, more connection, more nourishment. My lack of female company ran deeper than I realised and I asked them to stop.

"Look at the sky," I said. The beautifully clear night was Mr. Everest's bespeckled blackboard at the start of a new term: as ancient as the cosmos, tantalising us with secrets and knowledge that had passed this way. Our party, a murmur nibbling the silence of the wide-open night, was life's frailty and brevity, huddled at a random place along a string of puny lights that traced an unsteady line between the sweep of the sky and the heaving corpulent sea. I was romantically touched by this scene of indifferent beauty and appalling transience.

"We can come out again, later," said Ginny, momentarily

appreciating my wonder. "Especially if they start playing *Streets of London*. But first I'd like to get my sweat-shirt."

We slipped something over swimming costumes and moved about the weakly lit tables of cola, mineral water, *Zit*, quiches, cheese cakes, chocolate brownies, salads, steaks, lamb chops, crisps and nuts. It was a generous free-for-all: "Oh, you must try Ita's cheese cake" or "Linda's brownies." I don't think I ate any of the meat I brought; maybe nobody ate what he or she brought. It was that kind of party. Indeed I had the feeling that offence could be taken if somebody's homemade whatever was not sampled. Taking home anything other than empty Tupperware was an insult.

By now it was dark and only the insects had the energy to fuss about the lamplights, their activity an accelerated micro-representation of our own, for we also clustered about the lights. The sun was a memory and its warmth was becoming so too.

A guitar was produced, the radio silenced and Ralph McTell's *Streets of London* was played, but we didn't leave. By then I was talking to someone else. I later discovered that Ginny did not dislike the song; she had simply heard it too often on such occasions.

Word reached me that somebody had been foolhardy and should I want any alcohol it was available. Ginny's reaction was outrage. It was a danger to everyone. "You can be kicked out for being in the presence of someone with the stuff," somebody told me. Unbeknown to me Den was among those who disappeared for a spell. If I had known I might have insisted on someone else driving me home.

I heard of a previous Dive Club being brought into disrepute or disbanded after it was discovered some members were using the bay as a pick-up point for drugs. As with many such stories it was impossible to verify.

It took some time to reach Geoff, but when he found out he let it be known that the club was jeopardised. Although he didn't scatter seeds of guilt into the gathering, he jettisoned insidious spores of ill ease. They were carried upon the chilling edge that the breeze was beginning to hone. The cold became a reason to leave and everyone slowly followed his example of breaking camp.

* * *

His face was in shadow, but there was sufficient light for me to see his impassive features. He revealed his uncertainty when he spoke.

"I -"

"Get out Den, before *I* do something *you'll* regret." I wasn't sure whether his pickled brain could handle the twist in the sentence, but I thought he absorbed the gist.

Still he hesitated. I argued that he could have come to apologise, but Anger countered: "he could do that in the morning." There was no reasoning, Anger had won and appealing to vestiges of Den's good nature could only prolong the situation.

His detached state distanced him and buckshot would spread too thinly to shock him into fleeing. So I said in a voice of brute calibre: "Get out Den." I could see the shock in his face as he realised that Anger was my bedfellow and there was no room for him. He smiled. When he moved he moved slowly, hoping to maintain a semblance of dignity.

* * *

"I'm not supposed to, but I'll leave you alone," says the Embassy official. As an afterthought he glances at the guard. "I don't think he speaks any English."

We are too absorbed to acknowledge this courtesy.

"Your mother sends her love," my father begins, turning to his bag and denying his tears. "And I've got a wad of well-wishes from your friends." He hands me envelopes bound by an elastic band. "They've already been opened, I'm afraid." He refuses to look at me.

"Dad, I don't know what you've been told, but nobody gives me a straight answer here." The guard is a piece of furniture.

"The Embassy people are doing all they can," he says, with that infuriating blind assurance his generation give to officials, be it doctors or diplomats.

"That's their standard line." I recoil from the exasperation in my voice. I don't want to be angry. I've been looking forward to this for too long. Just to talk to someone not only who loves me, but also someone who can give me straight answers. Yet, of course he can't give me answers, let alone straight ones. I will not have his blind faith in authority. More than this I don't want a confrontation with his mindset. His belief, my parents' world picture, was no longer mine. I'd left it behind. Yet, to humour them I'd often become their Peter Pan, as if I'd never grown up. But it wasn't a role I could maintain for more than an evening. For after a time I'd become the non-believer forced through the rites of Catholicism. With them I'd light a candle to my childhood, I'd even take communion, but the line was drawn at confession. Now I am not in their living room. So there is no need for hoop jumping. And I will not have it. I want the here and now. I will lacerate my hands tearing apart any falsehood. Neither will I fall into that patronising indifference. We will connect. We *will* connect.

"How's mother?"

His silence adds immeasurable weight to his words. "She's been better." He cannot bear my concern and his gaze wanders with his words. "She'll be fine again soon. The main thing is to get you home."

"How bad is she?" Now my expression is penetrating: eyes riveting his feigned listlessness. I know I'm tearing at him.

His shoulders slump and he almost folds. Guilt flows through me like a breeze from an unexpected direction. I touch his forearm as much to steady myself as him.

His faint smile seems sardonic and I withdraw to give him space.

"She'll be okay." And now I seesaw. Press him and risk alienation or give him control by subjugating my want. I acquiesce and nod longer than necessary.

But he looks straight at me and lets himself go. Tears fill his eyes and he slips under his emotion. "What have they done to my girl?" I realise what he sees. He sees a jittery wreck with a sandpaper head under a scarf. He sees wild eyes, weather-raw features and a bitter mouth-line. He sees somebody who once was his daughter.

Before I move he composes himself with an intake of breath. "I'm sorry. You're in here. Not me. The Embassy is working very hard to get you out. They're coming up with some kind of story."

He's relieved of a burden and I feel betrayed. Is he merely an emissary? "What story?"

"I don't know. But you'll probably have to sign something."

"I'm not letting them get away with this. I want the world to know the truth." Do I? Maybe not, but it seems abominable that the truth be quashed by diplomatic relations and petrodollars.

"Don't be hasty," he begins before prudently falling silent.

* * *

I woke early but didn't rise until ten. I had dozed and read and listened for movement. After I'd showered and had a breakfast of toast, cereal and two coffees there was still no movement. The thought of going to Den did not appeal. Even if he wasn't sprawled across the bed stark naked, the mere thought of the juxtaposition - me at his bedside - repelled me.

Den and Merv had planned a beach trip today. Nobody had said anything about the time. Merv said he would call. He'd not turned up at the barbecue. Perhaps he'd worked late into the night?

At a quarter to eleven I phoned Ginny.

"Jeez, you've left it late," she said, when I told her that I'd like to go on the desert picnic. She had invited me the evening before, but I had felt honour bound to Den and Merv's plans. That sense of honour had been ravaged by Den's behaviour. "I'll pick you up in twenty minutes." She knew the location of Den's housesit and she had a car.

I left a note for Den, telling him what I was doing and that I'd be back by four for him to take me to the farm.

I opened the front door as Ginny climbed out of her, er, car. She had mentioned that her tiny Honda Civic had seen better days, but I had not expected such a rattletrap. The bonnet looked as if it'd been eaten away by acid and was now pure rust. Any chrome was freckled and pitted. "The a/c's gone, but whatever you do don't open your window. It drops down and you can't open the door." Her driver side window was wound down or didn't exist. "She doesn't look much, but the motor's fine, and gets me from A to B to A without any trouble." She caught herself as she started the engine. "Okay, the time's I have had trouble with her, the guys have been queuing up to fix her. She may not be road worthy, but she's camp-worthy." Apparently it never left the camp.

She asked me why I was not doing something with Den and Merv and I thought about saying that Den was still in bed nursing a hangover and that the day was disappearing, but I told her the truth. I also told her not to tell anyone else.

"In some ways I'm not surprised. Although, I'd figured him to be pretty straight."

"Me too," I said.

"I'm not surprised because I've heard a lot of stories already. Not about Den. But others. Even though I'm going out with Colin, it doesn't stop them from flirting with me. Married or not. Believe me flirting is dangerous. It's a smaller step to consenting than it is in the real world."

"Where's Colin?"

"On leave." We passed islands of cut grass suitable for boules or croquet and finely tended plots inviting meditation and I felt a twinge of sympathy for the endless hours put in by the Asian gardeners.

We turned into a communal car park and stopped next to a scarlet Suzuki hard-top jeep which looked as sturdy as a 2CV. Standing beside it were Carol and the blond American introduced to me as Jim the previous evening.

"We're going to have to shoot," he said. Jim was a slight man and sported a hedgehog crew cut. I was surprised no one had coined him "Slim". Many people here had nicknames. I later found out that unless there was something striking that cried out nickname, you only acquired one if you remained long enough in the country. Ginny and most of the others at last night's barbecue had been in the country just three months longer than me; part of an Aramco recruitment drive.

"Okay, keep your hair on. Let me get the cool-box." Ginny went to the rear of her car, turned away from it and gave the boot handle a back-kick. "Doesn't work," she explained to my lopsided smile as the boot flew open.

We raced to another housing-estate car park and found that we weren't the last. Somebody disappeared into one of the houses to make a call. In the meantime I was introduced to another wealth of characters, some of whom said they'd met me the previous evening and I nodded agreement whether I remembered them or not. I tried to affix names to the faces and faces to names.

One of the drivers commented on the narrowness of Jim's tyres and offered him a shovel. I knew that we were going into the desert. I had not realised how we were going to traverse it.

As we waited I spotted a piece of paper sticky-taped to a lamppost. What attracted my eye to it was the company motif. It was that of the company Mike worked for. I sauntered over. Somebody was offering a reward for a missing cat. I read the name Blossom but still nothing registered. Only when I saw Smith's name alongside his office number did things snap into place. Ginny came up behind me and we spoke of the note for a moment. I spoke of June before she expressed her reservations about the existence of a pet-killer.

The caller returned to say that the latecomers were not coming.

We set off in convoy, six vehicles in all. We drove half an hour from the camp. The leading vehicle left the road and we followed. I found myself confronted by a *Beau Geste* landscape. Here were majestic dunes with their beautiful troughs and peaks, broken only by ashen tufts of hardy Tamarisk shrub. We were the fourth vehicle over a peak. I'd seen the others leap into the air and strangely believed that we would not be doing the same until Jim said: "Hold on." We came down with a crash that shuddered the jeep's sides. I joined in the squeals of delight. This was far superior to chasing sallies on the plains of the farm.

And so it went on: racing up to a peak, Jim shouting: "hold on", leaping up and crashing down. At one point Jim pointed to the roll bar to re-assure us. And as time went on I realised that we were in the best vehicle. We didn't get stuck once. Everyone else was at one time or another out pushing or shovelling. Rather than sink our slim tyres skittered over the sand. Also there was an in-built flexibility in the jeep, which I'd mistaken for flimsiness. Someone would later say: "You seemed to fly across the sand." To which Jim remarked: "Yeah, the Japs make nippy jeeps." A remark that raised smiles and tiresome brows.

Eventually we set up on the longer slope a large dune. Honey-coloured dunes surrounded us. I had no idea in which direction the road was and I didn't care.

The searing stillness was an impossibility that caused my imagination to fill my mind with a metallic rush, as if the noise of Humankind were flushing down a metal drainpipe. This was an emptiness that neighboured on true silence.

Every time a ring was pulled on a fizzy drink one had to turn well away from the group, for they were like canned fire extinguishers. The drinks literally exploded. Someone commented: "The can'll be empty if you don't get your lips to it soon."

There was no wind, just an airless heat, and the sand was too hot for bare feet. The dunes had a skin-like texture of shoreline ripples. Somebody pushed one of the nurses over the lip of the dune and down the steeper edge or slip-face - the wind shadow - and she had difficulty returning; struggling up a downward flowing escalator. Two chivalrous lads mustered energy against the prickly debilitating heat and bounded down and the three decided a photograph of them upon a neighbouring dune would be something. Perspective was lost to the uniformity and the dunes were bigger and further away than one thought. Only when the three of them had trudged up to the peak and were ant-size could you truly appreciate the dunes' magnificence. Of course their moon-boot gouges spoilt Nature's fine etching. There was satisfaction in knowing that this was not the moon and that the dunes would become whole, reclaiming the landscape and erasing all traces of disturbance. Just as they would overwhelm anything abandoned; just as the Earth would one day absorb me. And before this relentless expanse ground you down, you turned away and joined the group, spoke loudly, cracked a joke.

The feeling made me reflect on the story of *Schatzi*. We had spoken of housesitting the previous evening. Den was baby-sitting fish. Before we left for Khobar he said that the tinier ones were disappearing. I answered that he should give them more food to which he replied that he had doubled the dose already. The story of *Schatzi*, like a legend, had then been resurrected. *Schatzi* was a dog, its name from the German word *Schatz*, which meant treasure. An elderly couple, an American and his foreign-accented wife had left their house and beloved dog to Alan for a six-week holiday. The precious animal was housebound and was only allowed into the high-walled postage-stamp sized back garden for fresh air. Otherwise he slept in a doll's house between the kitchen and the dining room and ran about the house, leaping upstairs and down. Its favourite position was watching television between its owners on top of the back of the sofa. The anthropomorphizing of this surrogate child stopped just short of squeezing the poor animal into doll's clothes. Alan wanted to go on a dune picnic and decided to take the dog with him. As soon as they opened the back of the jeep the dog raced off. Alan and half the picnic crew gave chase. Everyone shouting *Schatzi* and stumbling over the sand. But the dog seemed to skip over the surface and bound up the dunes. Of course Alan was the last to give up that day, but he had not totally given up. In the weeks that followed he contacted all the authorities he could think of. At weekends he sought out Bedouins and travellers. All to no avail. He had to break the hearts of the owners when they returned. At the barbecue somebody had joked: "they'd lost their treasure in the desert", but now I could appreciate the horror of this space; a space that had sent the poor animal berserk.

The topic of conversation that remains with me at the picnic is that of Noel. He was an Irish alcoholic who'd come to dry out. This was tantamount to being hosted by the Marquis de Sade and expecting a sedate candle-lit dinner. One couldn't be blamed for thinking Saudi Arabia was the place for abstinence, but a little research, questioning those who'd been out here, could have told him that this was the land of Prohibition. There were no pinstriped suits and violin cases, the authorities definitely had the upper hand, but there was a thriving black market.

In Britain you'd offer a person a coffee, here you'd offer them a *sid*. It wasn't a status symbol or a flaunting of the rules; it was simply the done thing.

Noel had not made it to the barbecue, but had stayed behind when his drinking partner Martin decided to leave. Security found him in the early hours singing on the camp golf course. Luckily he had been too drunk to back his abuse with his fists. Noel was not a small man. Fortunately he'd remained on-camp. Off-camp he would have been treated more severely. Unfortunately being taken in meant an official warning. Company policy was one warning after that it was deportation.

Conversation flowed and I became less of a social vagrant. Small change in the form of snippets of information accumulated in my pocket. But it was a wealth of coinage and the currency appeared to vary, so I had to make do with sifting through them hoping to match them up and trade them in for easier-to-handle high-denomination notes. Time was against me and I found myself being dropped off at Den's housesit still carrying a drunk's pocket of information.

* * *

Merv insisted on conversation. For him talking was akin to breathing. Without either he would asphyxiate. Den claimed weariness, suggested Merv drive out and asked to stretch out in the back, leaving me to sit up front with Merv. Den was like an endangered species in the vicinity of a predator. His strategy was to keep still, hiding behind a headache, pleading incapacity, hoping to go undetected or appeal to my sense of mercy. Only then could he avoid extinction. But to me he had already disappeared. Even when I leaned forward and looked in the wing-mirror on the pretext of viewing something we'd passed I could not see him.

I was grateful for Merv's effortless chatter. It hastened the passing of time and thwarted any puerile thoughts of baiting Den. Of course I was reprimanded for not spending the day with them, but my reason that the day had been rapidly disappearing was accepted.

He told me how he'd spent a sober Thursday evening at work fixing a production problem.

"Were a lot of people working? All the lights were on." The lights on every floor of the two Towers had been burning.

"I don't think they switch them off," said Merv. "I suppose it's too expensive to shut everything down and start up again."

Half a kilometre later Merv spoke.

"It wasn't even my problem, but one of the rag-heads under me. You can't get them to come out. I don't know how they believe they can run the country without us. They want to get rid of all foreign labour. They'll keep the slaves: the housemaids and cleaners. They want to get rid of the expensive Westerners. It'll never work. They've got the wrong attitude."

"I've heard it called other things."

"No, they're not stupid. That's expat arrogance. I think it's laziness." He grew earnest. "More than that. It's in their culture. An easiness. They don't care about time. They think we're obsessed with it. *Inshallah*, God willing, is not a religious-coated *mañana*, it's a way of life. They're not motivated in the same way. It's probably a combination of their wealth and the belief that the foreigners are here and should work for their money.

"Sometimes it's frustrating. You can't pin them down. Try getting a date when they think a program will be ready." His words receded into thought.

"Same, same," he began suddenly as I was about to speak, "is an expression that drives me mad. They say it when they think you're splitting hairs. Sometimes it's blatantly different and they still think it's the same." He paused and again spoke before me. "We've got so many computers and systems. The latest technology. They want the best, the technically sophisticated but I think they just want to be glamorous. Management ignores the maintenance and personnel considerations. And they're not committed to doing it themselves.

"That must be some kind of record. You've been serious for almost two minutes."

"No one will believe you," he smiled. "They'll think it's something put out by Rumour Control."

On a one to one basis Merv didn't feel obliged to lark.

"Whenever there's a program crash it always seems to be Prayer time and off they go. That's if they're there. They disappear for hours on end." He shook his head; reliving some bagatelle experience not worth retelling. "I'm not impressed with some of the expats either. There's a material attitude, which says: we're only here for the *Dinero*. We're not staying. And this means they don't care." One of Martin's three kinds of people sprung to mind: "material hard-heads".

"Oh, that reminds me, here," he reached over and opened the glove compartment. "Grab that piece of paper. It's a photocopy of the one we have on the wall at work. You might like to have one."

It was an amateur Peanuts cartoon strip.

Charlie Brown: "Where are you going?"

Snoopy: "I've got a contract in Saudi Arabia."

"What are you carrying those two buckets for?"

"One is for the money and the other for the shit. When the one for the shit becomes heavier than the one for the money I'm leaving."

Five years later, Snoopy returns.

"Hey, what happened to you?"

"I cut a hole in the bucket of shit."

I smiled and shook my head. "Are you going to pick up Rashid?"

"Yeah, on the way back. Ian flipped out because we turned up with him." Merv shook his head. "I mean you have Arabs on the farm all the time, don't you?"

"Yes. I don't understand him. He phoned just to tell you off?"

"Yeah."

As we neared the farm my pulse began to race. I realised that I had been suffering, putting off a problem to which there appeared to be no solution. I saw no possibility of untying the Gordian knot that bound me to the farm. Why should Den and Merv ever invite me again? If it could be done then I needed to give Den time. The situation between us needed to be resolved. He needed at least the opportunity to express himself, if not in apology then in some show of regret. I had to get him alone so that he'd not lose face. This would be no mean feat considering the number of people on the farm, but maybe they weren't all hanging around in the kitchen. My ulterior motive of transportation to Aramco, rather than pursuing our friendship, was shameful, but what the hell.

"You'd better come in for coffee," I said.

"I'd much rather get on," said Den sitting up. "*We've* got work tomorrow." I ignored the implicit "and you can have a lie in" in his words. He was becoming diabolical. Not a whiff of an apology in sight.

"I don't want anything to happen to you. I mean *you* are weary." I lost heart as I spoke. If I did corner Den I'd get nothing.

"We've got water."

"If I may say something," began Merv. "I've been driving and I'd like a coffee." Hooray for Merv.

"We've got to pick up Rashid, remember."

"There's plenty of time."

I thought Den was going to say he'd wait in the car, but he remained silent.

All was still outside, but when we entered the kitchen we found the entire troupe waiting for us. The crowd left me no space to engineer an opportunity for reconciliation.

During our beverages Mike and Ian announced that they had a small show for us. I'd forgotten the Jasmine and Ali puppet show.

"We haven't got the time," said Den cruelly. He really was dead meat.

They looked to Merv who shrugged. "He's the driver."

"You asked them to do something," I protested. This was perverse of me for I certainly couldn't stomach the banality.

"It really is short," said Ian, deflated.

Den looked to Merv and gave up.

The show was appalling and I couldn't blame Den and Merv for tearing it to bits.

* * *

"Periscope down. Secure all hatches. Dive, dive, dive." Down I went, well passed the shelf that was boredom, onward, further into the dark uncharted waters of deep depression, where pressure dwarfed life.

Memories of the weekend in Dhahran kept me buoyant for almost a week. But the world had been turned upside down and the belly of my vessel sat in the thin medium of the farm rendering its propulsion useless, momentum ticking over to a standstill.

Again, I was alone for the best part of the day, cooking, feeding the chickens, pottering about in the greenhouses, doing the laundry and cleaning our room, all the while chewing on the cud of my time in Aramco.

I was haunted by Martin's simplification and applied it to those I had met. There was something hard in Ginny, although I preferred the word resilient. Carol was obviously crippled. She was having a relationship with Jim, whom she treated disdainfully. Funny how a weak person draws strength on the weakness of another. Jim was not truly weak; he was inexhaustibly amenable. No doubt Carol would push him to his breaking point, then he'd blow and she'd respect him until his self-reproach caused him to slip back into his cage so that she could disparage him again.

It was too early to categorise anyone else. And of course Martin's categorisation was at best questionable.

What I considered my trump card was indeed a card, a thank you card. I sent it to Merv's post box number. In it I over-enthused about the weekend and joked that if they were ever passing by to pick me up. I spent a long time writing the card, measuring my words so as not to dwell and reveal my desperation. How often could I scream for help?

The card went unanswered and with each passing day I drew into myself; shrivelling so that gargantuan spaces began to distance me from my outward self.

Mike tried to help. I confessed that going to Aramco had been a disaster. It had been will-breaking stuff. It was like a prisoner being let lose in the yard after months of solitary confinement, only to be thrown back into isolation. Over a meal in a Riyadh hotel I feigned a tête-à-tête and promised to pull myself together. For a few days thereafter I tried to expand and fill out my inner void. But the energy required was phenomenal; I had been reduced to nothing. And then Mike's understanding became irritating. I just wanted to be left alone. A wounded person doesn't want to be constantly reminded of their injury.

Days on the farm stretched before me ad tedium. March dripped into April and the farm buzzed at harvesting time; the wheat had begun turning from green to gold a month or so earlier. The lads also sowed grass seeds at this time. Then the golden fields were suddenly devastated, flattened, reduced to matchwood and chaff. Trucks came and went. They collected the grain for Riyadh. This amount of activity curtailed my sunbathing. Although the need had long gone, I missed the privilege. Bookkeeping was a welcome but undemanding responsibility.

The trucks were from the Grain Silos and Flour Mills Organisation who purchased and stored the wheat. This home-produce was eventually bought by the government at five times the world price and sold on the free market.

Wheat was Saudi Arabia's flagship when it came to agricultural accomplishment. There was a sense of national pride in the fact that nowhere else in the world had the desert been made to produce in such quantity. In the mid-1970s the arable land in Saudi Arabia was less than 150,000 hectares with an annual wheat yield 3,000 tons. In 1978 the first grain silos were built and by 1984 there was self-sufficiency in wheat. We were at the beginning of a boom when Saudi Arabia became a wheat exporter. By 1993 there would be 2 million hectares of arable land and a peak wheat yield of 4.5 million tons. The desert country would become the sixth biggest exporter of wheat.

Yet, like a mirage this visionary wonder was faulted: reality frayed its outermost edges. The agricultural adventure was drawing on a water supply that could not be replenished: underground fossil water. As early as 1985 Saudi Arabia focused on ways to regulate the use of water through the National Water Plan. By 1991 the huge financial loses absorbed by the government were slashed with wheat being bought at just twice the world level. The Gulf War and reduced oil revenues contributed to diminishing this subsidy. Shockingly, it was said that government-purchased wheat mountains were left to rot in the desert. By 1993 some 10,000 water pivots, their pumps and supporting machinery would be removed. This is not to say that Saudi Arabia no longer had a strong agriculture. On the contrary, the headlong adventure had been tempered, the gung-ho use of government funds giving way to an emphasis on water conservation and recycling.

I missed the swaying fields of wheat. The ears had been wholesome and sunshine. Of course I was being romantic. This was not always true. Sometimes bad weather had accompanied me and I could not tap into their vigour. I could find no passion. No passion at all. Nothing. Not even Van Gogh's stunted track gouged into the field and going nowhere. And I wanted crows to mock me with ear-splitting madness. Drama. Passion. But there was nothing. Nothing.

* * *

Ian, Sparky, my husband and maybe Scab were at the petrol tank outlet. Why they all should have congregated there is not clear. The three Arabs who had filled up earlier were also present. There is something amiss with the seal. It is leaking.

Pav, having just risen is unaware of the problem and saunters over, cigarette in hand. He is oblivious to their cries, for although it is morning he is drunk. Of late he has been drinking excessively. Mike has spoken to him, but essentially nobody can control him. Hand in hand with these frequent binges is his profuse smoking.

As he approaches the others instinctively back away. Pav regards them and then his cigarette. He smiles coolly and drops it to the ground. He doesn't have time to grind it out. A gossamer blue flame no taller than that of a gas hob races across the ground. The cigarette is like a pebble dropped into a medium above the ground, sending out a ripple from the point of entry. Maybe it doesn't look like this, but this is how I visualise it. In itself there is no danger. Some hot spots continue to burn and one can hop over the advancing flame if one has the presence of mind to do so. If the skirt of a *thobe* or a sock caught fire then a couple of scoops of sand would kill it.

Such accidents have a knack of appearing in slow motion. As a schoolgirl a boy threw a stone at me and I remember watching it whirling through the air - I could see the details of its rolling motion like a miniature asteroid turning over and over - until it hit me square on the forehead with a crack. Only later, when the lump attempted unicorn-horn proportions, crookedly breaking the taut skin in its effort, did I suffer the headache. So it is, here.

The flame hits the outlet and there is a small campfire. Its size could tempt one to smother it with a shirt or something. Whether anyone thinks of this or makes a move to flee is irrelevant. The top of the outlet blows and a jet of flame flies into the air. Just like an oil-strike. Then the jet billows outward at ground level, claiming vestiges of fuel, but drenching everyone in flaming petrol. The pump itself explodes. Those between it and the outlet don't have a chance. Others may stagger away and roll like fiery crocodiles. Then the tank explodes.

Being furthest away Pav is the only survivor. He disappears shortly afterwards.

* * *

I left the kitchen and made my way across the courtyard towards the workshop. I needed to check the acceptability of a spice with Sparky. He was fussy about herbs and spices. Tass was slumped over the grill of a cruiser, his head buried under the bonnet, arms stretching to check something in the engine. For fear of shocking him so that he might hurt himself or drop a tool, I walked on.

As I reached for the workshop door the hoot of a car froze me. I swung round to check Tass. I could not see him. He was at the steering, behind the raised bonnet. The workshop door was flung open and Ian filled the entrance.

"Hi, Dawn," he said loudly. "What brings you out here?"

His question was strange. It was superfluous and underscored the uneasiness in him.

Seeing I was not to be stopped he stepped aside.

"I was looking for Sparky," I said absently as I surveyed the workshop.

"I'm all on my lonesome here."

"Do you know where he is?" For some reason I began to stroll the length of the room.

"He was here. But I don't know where he is now. I'll look for him with you if you want."

His offer coincided with my noticing something and I stopped in my tracks.

"Dawn?"

"What?"

"I said I'll look for him with you."

"No. No, it's not important." I began making my way to the door.

Curiously, after trying to get me to leave, he tried to hold me back. "Are you sure?"

"Yes." It was all I could say. My mind was working overtime trying to figure out how the pebble could have disappeared from the locked door.

* * *

Because I had shrunk, the molehill, the missing pebble, became a mountain. I spoke to Mike about it.

"Maybe it got brushed or kicked away?"

"No. I put it right up against the door. They'd have to deliberately pick it up." I still had not reached him. "They must have opened the door. They have a key."

"Maybe." Either he was not convinced or not interested.

"Don't you think it strange?"

"No. It could have got swept up whilst cleaning. It does happen you know." He smiled. "Maybe they've got their sex gear stashed there."

I was scotched. He wanted to lighten me up, but his dismissal had the opposite effect and I sunk into myself, layers of algae closing over my face.

"I'll ask the lads about it if you like."

"Don't bother."

At the earliest opportunity I put another pebble at the locked door. This time I kicked it into place. As I wedged it in doubt seized me. Was I slipping? Losing a grip? Was I shadowboxing and losing points in every bout? Had depression unknowingly taken out huge chunks of me? Was I deluding myself into think I had everything under control, when all along I was punch drunk and swinging wildly? I folded my arms, clutched normality to my breast, suffocating the very life out of it. When I returned to the laundry room I saw that my lower lip was bleeding.

* * *

One day I realised that Merv and Den may no longer have access to a vehicle. Neither of them had their own. And this shock caused me to hit rock bottom. Taking a taxi had long been dismissed as ludicrously expensive and too dangerous. I began scraping the seabed, dragged along by the banal currents of daily existence. Trivialities jarred me. Nothing at all would set me off. I was heading for the kitchen when I saw my surroundings anew. Returning from the chicken coop I envisaged the trailers as a scene from one of those apocalyptic films. The future was now and this was the aftermath of some global catastrophe. For me the world was dead. Gone was the frontier spirit. Gone was the sense of home, however temporary. The curtains I had put up in the lounge mocked me: a semblance of civilisation as futile and meaningless as painting the sea. Tears overwhelmed me and I ran to our room.

Sparky's infernal pistachio nuts revolted me. Their husks and shells were always on the floor. More than this, I hated his art of silently breaking wind. When all the Filipinos but Pav had retired I demonstratively sprayed the area with the toilet air-freshener, hoping word would get back. It annoyed me too that in my absence no one bothered to mask the sulphurous evils of the toilet that wafted into the kitchen.

Somebody had taken to leaving the toilet seat up. Whoever it was triumphed. I spoke to them at dinner. I was raging and they knew it. I suspected Ian but I had no proof. And Pav or Sparky could equally have been the culprit. I knew I was being crazy. But the demountables were contained units. Oh, the kitchen had an extractor hub, but the sand and heat meant that the windows were sealed. Had we been able to open them the a/c would have packed up for good.

Whereas before my trip to Aramco I had been intermittently tormented by boredom and depression, they now ravaged me. And they were no longer mere predators. As such I had been able to prepare myself for their onslaught, even hit back. Now they were my world. They were the oceans. I was trapped in a womb from which I could not be born, being continually trampled by white horses with each rasping breath of the sea. Boredom was a subterranean current that forever pulled me down, but infinitely more damaging were the unexpected squalls of depression. They wrecked the makeshift raft I had fashioned to seek a route to my self.

I abhorred getting up in the morning and grew lethargic. I couldn't face the world. The world on offer was yet another raw day of the Jurassic period, where the appearance of a Tyrannosaurus Rex on the scorched horizon would not be out of place. But nothing so exotic would appear. Such passion had long been torched and the primitive landscape was as forsaken as that within me.

I remember looking at my journal for this time and noting the one-word entries. Even the word "Depressed" became an effort and whittled away to "Down" and finally D. Then a strange elation would take me and I'd rejoice in the mood. I learnt not to search for the source of the feeling, for to sift through the morass of depression lost me. I simply rejoiced. I came to believe that the mind could not sustain a constantly depressive level and the turgid electrochemistry needed to be regularly flushed from the system. Like a surfer startled by a sudden wave I'd try to ride it for as long as possible.

They were small bright spots. Like watching the pilot light of a new day spread at the horizon, soft and warm like lips slowly breaking into a smile. Or observing the evening light swirling between the blades of grass. Each time I felt I was a breath away from a world not normally available to our senses.

My sleep was uneasy. And insomnia frequently plagued me.

Reading, my saviour, no longer guaranteed sanctuary. The wings of the words flawed at design-stage could not carry me on flights of fantasy. The old greenhouse, that had always been my sanctum and supported my inner freedom, had frail walls. But I did spend time there, doing nothing, wanting nobody. Hatches battened.

These were my lost weeks going on centuries. If I'd had access to alcohol I would have made a damned good effort at impersonating an alcoholic. A sickly sea of liquor to contest the sea of depression. Eat your liver out Ray Milland. I knew that the Filipinos had taken the *sid* from Merv and Den, they'd appear some mornings bleary-eyed and it was obvious to all - even Mike - that they'd been hitting the bottle. Even Scab looked bad. Catching him alone after a suspicious night, I remarked that he looked tired. "Sometimes cotton wool is not enough against Pav's snoring." This served to confirm my suspicions. Whilst Scab would have drunk very little, Pav would have been affected by his consumption. Anyway, had there been any alcohol available I could not bring myself to ask for it.

Sitting in front of the television and becoming a festering couch potato was not possible either. The second channel offered English-speaking programmes. Anything a tad above harmless family entertainment was so censored that it sometimes didn't make sense. All scenes involving alcohol and intimacy were edited out. *Stars Wars* didn't suffer too much, but *48 Hours* lost almost an hour. One was left frustrated and angry. If that weren't enough, smack in the middle of a programme a test-card like transmission with the bold words "Prayer Intermission" would appear. The news too lacked essential content with many minutes of footage following the King inaugurating some building or other. Often he was shaking hands and greeting someone. There was no commentary during this *news;* there was simply music. Bizarrely it was *Monty Python's* signature tune, rendering the whole ridiculous.

* * *

The area of the brain below the cerebrum called the hypothalamus regulates temperature, appetite and mood. And just as the body's thermostat can be upset, so too mood can swing. For most of the time my mood pendulum gently sways and on rare occasions swings: manic-depressive swings. In a depressed person the axis is tilted in favour of the negative and the pendulum sways predominantly in the negative region. Most depressives fall into this category. There are sometimes reasons for this lopsided view. They are given names like reactive depression: depression induced as a reaction to some external event, bereavement for example. There is depression due to physical illness and there is the congenital pessimist: the cynic who always looks on the dark side. And then there is endogenous depression, formed within and with no apparent external cause. This was my mother's depression.

Mood swings, decline in energy, disturbance of sleep rhythm and changes in habit are all signs of depression. Oh, I knew my enemy. I'd seen his handiwork on my mother.

When I was old enough I asked her what it was like. "It's blankness, emptiness, nothingness. I'm not fraught, my dear." I remember that she once dressed me shoddily for infant school. Someone from the school must have called, for after this my father always put out the things I was to wear the night before.

I came home from school one summer's day to find the carrots half peeled in the kitchen and the lamb chops lying on the chopping board covered in flies. My mother was in the lounge sitting vacantly on the sofa. The vacuum cleaner stood before her. And I was angry with her until later that evening after the first of many explanatory talks with my father.

She tried to make light of it. "It's hereditary you know. Like epilepsy. The Huxleys suffered depression."

These attacks came and went. But my mother was a chronic patient for a long while. The doctors of the time did not recognise the illness. I read that between 1965 -1970 almost half the drugs prescribed for nervous disorders were sleeping tablets.

Only much later when a young doctor arrived on the scene and began treating her did these bouts of depression become less frequent. I learnt too to recognise the onset of one of her bouts. Her make-up would become a little heavier. Possibly sloppier. And by contrast her body became raw and knuckly. She went into the fight like a pugilist without gloves. The Marquess of Queensberry had no say here. More make-up would be slapped on to hide the bruises and stem the bloody nose and her face would sag under the weight of it. My stalwart father patched her up and prevented her from throwing in the towel.

Oh, I knew all too well what I was up against. I'd purchased my gum-shield. They say knowing your enemy is half the battle, but half can still be a far cry from winning.

* * *

May moved into June. During this time Ian was away for three weeks holiday in Britain. Mike tentatively suggested I take a break too. But I simply didn't have the energy. Home didn't appeal and anywhere else would mean being alone with the same problems and a different backdrop. I couldn't justify the expense. The company had given us a one-way ticket. The reason for doing this was that airfares from Saudi Arabia were double the London prices. Sometimes there was as much as a sixty percent mark-up. Mike had failed in his bid to purchase a return and bill them for a single, making up any difference himself.

Also Smith had said he was in the throes of getting us off the farm. It was just a matter of paperwork and time.

When Ian returned he looked refreshed, clean, as if he'd had a good wash. His hair had been professionally cut. True, the stumble was gone, but his expression itself appeared cleansed. He'd lost some tan and tension.

Differences between us were suspended. As if his short absence had closed a chapter on the past and we had agreed to start anew. He brought news of home, of television and beer and pubs and trends. He brought paperbacks; even one I had asked him to buy.

Mike tried to draw me out by involving me in general discussion. But my intellect lay fallow and I couldn't cope. I wanted frivolity. Ian assumed this role, and although he was no Bob, in moving away from Mike I appeared to near Ian. I even fooled myself into thinking I was approaching him. Perhaps Ian offered the nearest thing to the levity I had experienced at Aramco, perhaps he offered distraction or more sinisterly perhaps I wanted to shake Mike's infuriating fortitude, the very thing that attracted me to him.

Our marriage was built on tectonic plates that for the most remained firm. On the surface everything appeared to be in order and if the others noticed anything they didn't let on. But the dovetailing relationship between Mike and me was suffering from a friction that continually threatened to erupt.

I don't recall the conversation. Mike was talking about the greening of Arabia and how it was affecting the migratory patterns of birds. Ian made some derogatory comment and I laughed. "You're very witty," I said. I was not stupid enough to flirt with Ian. But when Mike dropped serious debate and attempted levity I chose sobriety. My capriciousness was not to call for new balls in a tennis match, I changed the game to table tennis, catching everyone off-guard with the new intensity and rendering their rackets useless.

The next day my unpredictability came to the fore. I was in the old greenhouse reading a magazine when Ian suddenly entered.

"Taking five after the day's excesses?" he said. He'd played his joker too early. My disenchantment with Mike was not a lasting condition.

"If I could work I would," I snapped. I felt a need to shove him away. I'd not agreed anything with Mike, although Ian may have thought otherwise, for I was no closer to my husband. I was close to no one. I was a bee trying to fly through a pane of glass, bashing myself, and woes betide anyone who neared me.

I had become Attila the honey: sometimes sweet, ultimately stinging, at odds with the Man empire. Inevitably I met my Châlons, the situation culminating one evening as we dressed for another pacifying meal in Riyadh. I unexpectedly attacked Mike for his lack of dress sense. "You look like a scarecrow." It was as if his infinite patience had become a challenge and I had to slap him with a gauntlet. This was like taking milk from a baby. He had never been a Beau Brummel, he was a farmer after all, not some turn of the eighteenth century dandy. The slap hurt me rather than him, and my bitter apology caused my eyes to burst. We hugged and I found myself letting my emotion loose, coercing him into joining me in swelling our intimacy into lovemaking. I wanted to be savaged, transported and I wanted tender connection. We left it too late to go to the restaurant and much later ate toasted sandwiches in the kitchen.

We realised that we had neglected each other. We had slipped into complacency. Work had been our excuse. Of course Mike had often been too exhausted and I had been too easy to forgive him. So we'd neglected one another and our selves.

Making love was then fashion, but after a couple of weeks of rediscovery this too began to go the way of reading.

During this time Mike took me into the Tuwayq Escarpment in search of the notoriously shy Nubian ibex. We didn't see any, but found something else. We stopped arbitrarily and carrying binoculars and a small rucksack climbed the rocks of a sandstone canyon. Finding a flat shaded spot with a commanding view not far from our cruiser we settled down to a picnic lunch. We talked a little, but didn't quite connect. This wilderness steered us into reflection, relegating talk to a back seat. So we were comfortable in thoughtful silence.

The sandstone was bright, the shadowed places inky. Most of the rock was cliff-like. Although we didn't see any, Mike said that there are caves and pools here. I asked him about wild animals and he admitted that there could be wolves. Maybe the stick he carried wasn't only an aid to climbing.

After eating and not seeing anything other than an eagle, which we followed through the binoculars, we decided to ramble. So we packed up and locked everything away. Mike slung the rucksack over his back and hung the binoculars over his neck and we set off. The rucksack contained a bottle of water and his camera. For fear of getting lost we kept the sun in approximately the same position and tried to avoid straying from a straight line from our cruiser. When we began climbing Mike was forced to put the swinging binoculars in the rucksack. We paused frequently to admire the view and drink water. After about an hour we agreed to return via a slightly different route. To avoid climbing and negotiating rock, we descended. Mike led. I lost sight of him for a moment near the base of a canyon. When I came round the large rock he was crouched. I asked him what it was, but saw for myself, before he answered. He didn't answer and got up. We stood side by side staring at the scattering of spent cartridges.

"Hunters?" I suggested.

"I don't know." He looked around and a twinge of panic gripped me. I too searched the rocks. We'd not heard any shots and these shells could have been months old. There were at least twenty of them. Mike suddenly strode off. "There're more here."

I went over to check. He took out his binoculars. "There're scars on the rock over there." He let me look through them and I spotted dried out melon skins or paper.

"Let's go," I said. Mike nodded but took out his camera instead. He took three photographs. And before we left he pocketed a handful.

"Something to talk about," he said. By the time we'd reached the farm we had decided that youths or the army had been playing or practising.

***

It is still dark when they open the door. I stir. There are four of them. Instinctively I pretend to be asleep. Rita sits up as if she has been awake all the time. They watch her swing her feet over the edge of the bed. Is anyone else awake? Despite being a large woman she is amazingly agile. She drops silently to the floor. The guards back away as she stands and looks from bed to bed. I close my eyes as her head turns my way. When I open them again she is at the entrance. The two remaining guards follow her out.

One of the other women sits up. I remain still. She looks around before lying down again. I know she's not going to sleep because she's on her back, her knees making a tent of the blanket.

I close my eyes and eventually doze off.

Pip wakes me. "Where's Rita?"

"What?" I sit up and glance at her bed. "She's not back?" Two other girls stand behind Pip. The bed of the woman who was also awake when they came is empty. A baby is crying and a child is pleading for something. Otherwise the prison is not quite out of slumber.

"Where did she go?"

I don't know what to say.

"We'll go with you," says one of the others. Without her

bodyguard Pip won't go to the toilet.

"I'll come too," I say, throwing back my blanket. I don't know what I'll do if anything happens. I can't get involved. Any day now my exit visa is going to be stamped on my passport. But any day now has been any day now for weeks, months even.

Three of us escort Pip and her daughter. When we're standing in the queue I tell Pip about Rita. Tears fill her eyes.

"She's probably gone for questioning," I offer. "She'll be back."

Pip and the others look at me in disbelief.

"What? What is it?"

"Today's Friday," says one of the others.

* * *

I thought I had come through the storm until one evening in the kitchen. Then I realised I had simply become anaesthetised. The others were no less shocked than I. They did not have the presence of mind to grab pitch-forks, lanterns and flaming torches to drive the monster I had become from their midst.

All I remember was that the conversation had been harmless and that this screaming ordinariness waged war with my restlessness. Maybe Ian had wanted to empathise or sympathise, maybe some of my boredom had rubbed off on him; whatever, I flared like a cobra and spat words into his eye.

"Don't be so bloody sick." I hurtled onward. "What for?"

"The experience," he whispered, the blood continuing to drain from his face and put fire in mine. So the monster that had risen from the depths was a vampire: undead and snarling.

"That's a typical masculine answer." I was putting all men in the stand. For his statement: "I'm thinking about going to an execution" clawed some fundamental brutality I associated with men. My haste dispensed with step-by-step logic. They were expected fill in the dotted lines themselves. I just began ranting. "For the experience we have wars. We have millions spent on the military and dubious scientific experiments. Instead of the needy and starving. For the experience we -"

"I'll go with you," said Pav, raising the Jolly Roger.

This broadside almost keeled me and I turned fierce eyes upon him. But the changing position caused the wind to abandon my sails and I was only left with childishness. His smile too was the infuriatingly smug verification that women were trouble. "I didn't expect anything else from you. You're the most insensitive man I've ever met."

I returned on Ian. "Why not save him the trouble?" He remained expressionless. "Do a *Death of a Princess*. Video it." This documentary had been about a princess who had committed adultery. An expat had recorded her execution using a camera hidden in a cigarette packet. She was shot in the head and he beheaded. I saw a twinkle at the suggestion, but he dare not speak.

"Dawn -" Mike began.

"Oh, go to hell." My gavel had come down and I wanted silence. All men stood accused. Utterances from them could only mean disorder. I knew I was using semaphore on the blind. Hoping to topple my chair I jumped up, but it merely screeched backward. "Go to hell, go to hell all of you." And I was outside, ready to kick the sand roses asunder, slapped by evening's impossible silence. Then I was running to our room, letting the tears cascade from my eyes, not brushing them away, just as I'd wanted the chair to topple, I wanted these tears; I wanted them for their child's look-at-me-world utter desperation.

So I'd been scraping rock bottom all along and now the full extent of the grazing broke the surface like glowing embers. I'd missed the seismic tremors. I had exploded nonetheless, pouring larva into the monotony they had come to accept as harmony.

There seemed little point in apologising. That would be back peddling and I still thought the idea of going to an execution totally inane. Of course, I could have apologised for the manner of my opinion's delivery or my puerile attack on Pav or my general truculence, but I felt they did not deserve it. Anyway to extricate these apologies from my standpoint on the execution was too much of an effort. Finally I simply did not have the energy to break through the iced marble that had formed between us.

All this I had decided before Mike entered our room.

I could count the times I had seen Mike lose his temper on one hand and have fingers to spare. This was one of those times.

I caught his severe face as he came in but I felt my raging was stronger. He acted as if I was not in the room and went about his toilet. He was Van Helsing: all confidence and solemn precision. I should have heard the jingle of heavy machinery, but I was listening for Ian in the creak of the floorboards under the linoleum. Apparently he had prudently chosen to remain in the kitchen building.

I was indulging my toenails. I had grown used to the igloo

setting of the a/c, finding quenching almost tangible liquid in the cool. But the dry air had cracked Mike's lips and my nails had lost their translucence.

I waited for Mike to finish brushing his teeth before petulantly spewing a gob of brimstone and sulphur his way. "I'm not apologising." It was a foolish move. I'd given my position away. I was not merely a vampire. I was a demon too. A fabulous monster.

"I didn't expect anything else." The gob, successfully deflected, congealed and sizzled ineffectually in a corner.

"Don't you think it's immature wanting to go to an execution?"

"My personal opinion is an opinion and -"

I knew where this was going. He was driving me into a cul-de-sac. "You haven't got any opinions," I lashed.

"Is nobody to be spared your horrid tongue?"

"No. If I have to put up with such conversations after every meal -"

"We're out here together, but still there only seems to be three people you think about: me, myself and I."

"Ha. Ha."

His use of strategically placed explosives to stem my flow was working and I did not know what to say.

"Nobody asks you to stay on. In fact I think most of the lads would prefer it if you left after eating." This was acidic holy water on my skin. The vampire in me was scorched.

I was trapped and drying up fast.

"If you can't hack it then I'll resign and we'll get out of here."

But this wasn't all. He'd cruelly saved the capping charge for last.

"I didn't tell you, because it didn't come to anything and you'd have been disappointed." I hardened against him. "You know I can't really leave the farm, but I'd contacted the Aramco hydroponics centre to see whether I could pay them a visit and take you along. After all, we've been here six months and it couldn't hurt to talk to Smith directly. The reply was promising but then it all fell through. Pav made a couple of calls for me from Masstock."

So Pav had been an integral part in trying to alleviate my depression. It was too much, still I did not cry. However, I remained dumbfounded. Half of me wanted to embrace him, the other half wanted to strike him for such subterfuge.

He had an olive branch to pull me free. "Of course, it may have meant an evening in June's company."

I shrieked with horror and collapsed in tears of pain and laughter.

* * *

My sleep was not good during these days and one morning I rose shortly after Mike. By the time I had showered the lads had gone to work.

I was heading for the kitchen when I saw Ian coming out of the workshop. Because he was pulling the air compressor I could tell he was going to do the generator's daily maintenance. The oil was checked every morning and the outer oil filter cleaned out with the high-pressure air hose. This would me no power for a short time.

On the spur of the moment I swung round and made for the generator. He'd already reduced the revs of the 275 horsepower diesel engine by the time I arrived. Unfortunately this was not the fortnightly oil and oil filter change that meant shutting it down completely. But one could get by talking loudly.

"Morning," I said.

He returned the greeting and bore down on his unease by concentrating on the chore at hand.

I didn't know how to continue and came straight out with it.

"I'm sorry I blew up about the execution." He glanced at me and had such difficulty suppressing his smile that he could only nod and look away. I smiled back, but mine was stretched with cynicism tinged with disgust. "But -" his smile vanished and the job deepened his brow. "I wanted to appeal to you not to video it." Still he said nothing. "Mike's not happy about it at all. And before you think otherwise, he didn't ask me to talk to you." I was in full swing, but his entrenchment was so effective that I became desperate. "You know his position with alcohol on the farm. What do you think he'd feel about such a video lying around?"

"It won't be lying around," he said mechanically.

I had one last trump to play. "Even if you do video it, I don't think you'll find a buyer. When *Death of a Princess* was broadcast it caused an outcry. I think Britain and Saudi Arabia broke off diplomatic relations for a number of months. I can't see that happening again."

He waited for me to say more. Then he switched on the air compressor, hissing away any further conversation. I moved back and stood limply.

Until this moment I thought he might have sought escape from his self-imposed sentence. He knew there was no use appealing for clemency from Pav. But what if someone offered him an escape route? Now I knew he had condemned himself to go.

I watched him for a moment or two before marching off.

* * *

"Not more wackos from Aramco," exclaimed Ian.

"I don't know Colin," I admitted, "but I don't think we'll be subjected to a Merv and Den vaudeville act." Strangely I didn't want to share Ginny and her boyfriend with the farm. I wanted to keep the worlds separate. Colin was an unknown entity and I could not predict the chemistry of their stay. However, I expected much from a boyfriend of Ginny.

I'd last seen her almost eighteen weeks ago or to count up the gates scratched upon the wall 124 days.

My "go to hell all of you" outburst was antiquity. By no means forgotten, but written-off: an automobile accident that meant a change of vehicle. Of course there was more behind it than protesting the execution. There was Ian's cat and mouse game and my feeling that the crew were suspicious of me. As if my presence was a threat.

I didn't knuckle down or buck up; I acquiesced. I didn't apologise. I merely grew humble, at most rueful. I went on a spree of cooking elaborate meals and I think this was accepted as a form of peace offering. The lads were unbearably kind and wary. Time would mend the damage. Nothing more was said of executions, although this was not the end of it.

So the weeks passed. I settled back in the sleepy province and decided to regard Aramco as Disneyland: an incongruous man-made phenomenon, dazzling and immature by comparison.

Then a week and a half ago I received a missive from Ginny. She wanted to visit and could I give her a ring at work to make arrangements? Just a few sentences scribbled hurriedly in a card. Yet, to me it was a Godsend, practically a miracle. The heavens had opened and dropped a message on a shaft of glorious light as ostentatious as anything Cecil B. had accomplished.

I had something upon which to focus. I could throw away the sextant Mike had given me. It was a contraption he used when ill winds blew him off course. Not exactly a patented wonder solution. The instructions were user-defined. That is, the user decided how it was used.

I was baffled by something so contrived, so hard and fast, so absolutely man-made. It was undoubtedly clever, yet however complex it could never satisfactorily deal with the variegations of human emotion. Were his emotions so simple? Had he analysed his emotions so completely that he could circumnavigate any emotional problem with this thing? I worked with inherent warmth, an indefinable nebulous thing, befitting the meteorological swirls called mood. They were unpredictable.

And now I had a lighthouse. A triumphant tower that warned and beckoned and hailed: "Land ahoy!"

Yet, my bursting joy was held in check by fear. This solitary wretch had grown used to thin soup and the timeless abyss. The prisoner had become institutionalised. And I had just over a week in which to reinvent myself.

Of course I was exposed to betrayal on all sides. The stretched membrane of my former personality masking my inner emptiness was taut like a drum and one poke with a sharp word or pointed remark would pop the masquerade. I would be finished. So what did I do? I told them of my delight; reasoning that in sharing my happiness they would be less likely to threaten it.

Had I had the opportunity I would have reassured Ian that I would not bait him about his plan to video an execution. Despite his preparations his plan did not seem in earnest. Even he did not seem to believe it would not happen.

And I waited in dread for the last minute call via the Masstock Dairy to say that Ginny and Colin could not make it. As each day dripped uneventfully by, so the scales tipped towards their coming. On the day of their arrival I could hardly breathe, as if I'd forgotten and had been holding my breath all along. Or had left the seabed and reached an erratic surface offering painfully quenching gulps of vitality? Whatever, the rarefied medium was dizzying.

Ginny and I greeted one another that Thursday morning with lost-friend hugs. The bemused looks of our partners cemented our smiles. This joy was not so outrageous when considering the distance and sense of insecurity when travelling off-camp. Apart from the usual pitfalls of driving, Ginny and Colin were not married.

Any fears I had of the lads not accepting them were vanquished within the first ten minutes. Ian and Mike took a fancy to Ginny and although I can't speak for the Filipinos, certainly Tass shone more than usual. Ginny - damn her - was half a head taller and leggier than me. She was so striking she could get away with wearing anything. Men's clothes for instance, a suit and tie would be farcical on me but sexy on her. Furthermore, all my worries were unnecessary, for to strike me down would be to set her upon them.

Colin was not conventionally handsome and at first sight he was a disappointment. He had an intriguing face: somehow ruggedly angry. His hair was a dirty straw colour. As I got to know him his charisma lent him the good looks that had nabbed a girl like Ginny.

The evening was not a lurching, unpredictable flapjack that the company of Bob or Merv and Den would have produced. Neither was it a dud. The blue touch-paper was lit when everyone was where they wanted to be: at a safe distance and sure of footing. Everyone participated and observed. The evening created no culprits or victims and was tranquil and continuous and sparkling like a Roman candle.

The Filipinos may have been disappointed that no *sid* materialised, but they didn't show it. And possibly because the conversation was not of the firecracker ilk they left early.

Introductions and potted histories paved the way. News from the outside world was skimpy. Like being on holiday only the sharpest event pierced our cocoon. Thursday July 4th 1985. Understandably reports on the Iran-Iraq war and the Beirut situation or Israel (never directly named, at most Tel Aviv) were more prominent than news from Europe. Conversely, the European press pushed Middle East reports to the inside pages, condensed or analysed in special editions, but rarely daily bread. On the farm our seclusion was complete. During all the time I was in Saudi I only remember one piece of news reaching us and even that was early on, a few days after our arrival. It was Indiri Ghandi being killed by her bodyguards on 31st Oct 1984. Only something of such extreme nature got through to us.

Ginny and Colin had relished the afternoon tour of the farm, remarking continually on the peace. Colin couldn't get over the prolific growth. His jaw dropped when I told him that in the summer Rhodes grass grew one metre in twenty-two days. I was able to answer most of their questions. Ginny asked about lizards. For some reason she thought they bit. In confidence Mike asked me whether she thought Komodo dragons were loose on the farm. I told her that we had nukes and geckos before saying that they weren't dangerous unless you happened to be a gerbil. "Plenty of game," Colin remarked. I said many migratory birds visited us. Water foul such as duck and heron stayed a few weeks before moving on. "We had quail when I first arrived." What an idyll we painted. There was an unwritten farm code when showing visitors around: don't mention snakes.

After talking about the farm we moved onto Aramco. This talk yielded a reason, other than to see me, for their visit.

"It's the superficiality," said Ginny. "It's hard to maintain high-spirits. You've just got to get away."

"Yes, you can't keep up the pace," added Colin. "You become moody."

"Staving off boredom with events and parties," proposed Mike.

"To some extent," Colin agreed.

"It's all artificial," said Mike triumphantly.

"Of course," began Ginny, "but do you think your farm is any different?"

I smiled. "At least you've got the choice."

"True, but it is hard to get away." Ginny pondered for a moment. "There's more. Col's nutrition analogy sums it up."

Colin nodded as he tagged prompt to memory. "I was talking about the entire set up: our environment. If we consume all about us, then we've been gorging ourselves and we're still suffering a vitamin deficiency."

I remember wanting to mention Martin's theory, but there were too many negative things being said about Aramco for my liking. I felt Mike and Ian could think me simple for yearning to return. "Well, I'd love to visit again."

"Return to the den of iniquity?" queried Colin ominously.

The word den so obviously popped the same person into our minds that Ginny and I glanced at one another and burst into laughter.

Ian, Mike and Colin exchanged perplexed looks.

"It wasn't that funny," said Mike, the statement almost a question.

This was petrol upon fire and we roared.

"I'll have some of what they're on," said Ian, whose safe distance made him the quietest. He seemed mesmerised by Ginny's nimble fingers. Earlier I sensed he was trying to contain his enchantment when he remarked that Ginny looked more Irish than English. There was some truth in this, what with her red hair and fine dusting of freckles - another reason for my taking to her - and her erect Maureen O'Hara posture. She admitted that her grandmother on her father's side had been born in Cork.

We recovered in sobs and whimpers. I knew that she had not told Colin of my brush with irresistible Den Juan.

"But that's it," exclaimed Colin. "It's a holiday. One big, endless beach party. To visit for a couple of weeks is great." He looked at me. "Ultimately it's wearing. Trampling over the same ground. I'm waiting for the mud-slinging to start."

When we retired sadness lapped at the edges of my well-being: they would be leaving tomorrow afternoon and I would be at sea again. I knew that I would sink rapidly.

They slept in our old room, sharing amenities with Ian. The one next to us still acted as storeroom.

Over breakfast next morning they suggested taking me with them, saying they didn't mind bringing me back the following weekend. They'd worked out the logistics of putting me up. I looked to Mike and although we both knew there was no discussion we went through the motions: the logging of the comings and goings on the farm could be done by anyone, the laundry could wait and maybe Pav wouldn't mind the extra cooking and the chickens...

We left after lunch that Friday.

* * *

My conversation with Ginny during the drive to Dhahran was an overture containing the signature tune and medley for what was to come. Even the horror stories were an appetiser for what I was to hear at Ita's poker evening. Colin played chauffeur up front, rarely interjecting like the musician solely responsible for the cymbals, whilst Ginny and I were conspiring choirgirls speaking under the rush of the a/c and the music of the stereo. Ginny explained that Colin had rediscovered *The Doors* and was partial to *The Rolling Stones*.

We talked of anything and everything. Our conversation was flowing, with a patchwork-quilt diversity whose colours seeped into one another with the natural ease of a rainbow. I confessed to having scraped rock bottom. "You know, the feeling that this is not life but existence," I said as lightly as possible. I then sought justification. "You saw that video player Ian bought?"

"The one in the lounge? Yes."

"Seven-systems," interjected Colin, "you can play American -"

"I expect you're going to tell me he's got porno-films," said Ginny.

"Maybe. He gets them from the Masstock dairy." I suspected they obtained these uncut videos through an Embassy or Air-base connection. "But that's not the reason for mentioning it. He's also bought a video camera." I wanted to let this sink in, but she spoke into my pause.

"He's suggested making a porno? And he wants you to take the leading role. Or do I mean *roll*?"

I refused to disintegrate.

"Ginny, don't you see?" I had mentioned this to her on the telephone. Not the wisest of things. "He's going to video the execution."

"You're joking," exclaimed Colin.

Silence was my answer.

"He could land in prison if he tries a stunt like that." My answer remained the same.

"He'll never get away with it," said Ginny. "These cameras aren't small, are they?"

"No. It's a hefty thing."

"How do you know he's going to do it?"

"I don't. He hasn't said anything to me. And he's not likely to; he knows what I think. But I've seen him outside with it hidden in a duffel bag. He's been practising."

"A duffel bag?" queried Colin.

"Yes, he's covered it in large ink-spots to disguise the hole."

"I don't believe it," said Ginny.

"He didn't strike me as having the bottle to go to chop-chop square, let alone video it," said Colin. "Do you think he'll do it?"

"I think so." Ian had assumed a stance. I sensed reluctance in him. But his tongue had tied his hands. And Pav had cemented his position. He was encased in the concrete shoes that could only take him down. I couldn't help him. And now I wouldn't help him. I just hoped he'd find a way out.

"What does Mike think?" asked Ginny.

"He told Ian he would be putting everyone on the farm at risk. Ian said he'd put it somewhere where no one would find it. I don't think he could stop him. The funny thing is: I probably put the idea into his head." I played down my outburst and told them of the *Death of a Princess* comment.

"You know they say that the princess wasn't executed," said Ginny. "They say a Bedouin was bought and sacrificed in her place." She smiled knowingly. "The video's on camp. I don't know who's got it, though." That a copy of the film was circulating out here was incredible.

We talked a little more before Ginny spoke of Aramco. Unlike the previous evening my objectivity was not clouded by emotional convictions and I was more receptive to her qualms. "There didn't seem much point in mentioning people only we know," she began. "But Carol and Jim are driving me crazy with their bickering. I always blamed Carol but it takes two. And Noel is getting worse. You didn't meet him, did you? He's the resident alcoholic. You heard about the golf course incident? Yes, of course, at the picnic. Well, Martin and Geoff and some of the others caught him spray-painting "Allah is dead" on the side of a house. He was out of his head, of course. And it took all the lads to overpower him. He hates Arabs."

"What's he doing out here?"

"Drying out."

"Actually, I meant if he doesn't like Arabs why is he out here?"

"Money."

"What could be worse than a guy coming out here to dry out?"

"A female alcoholic," interjected Colin, loudly.

"Oh?" I queried.

"She'd be invited to all the parties and have *sid* thrust in her hand," he said. "To have a party there are two prerequisites, alcohol and women. Women get invited to every do."

"Jealous?"

He laughed.

On top of this Ramadan had just finished. The month of fasting whilst the sun was up meant frayed nerves all round. Fasting meant no bodily intake. Obviously food was out, but so was smoking and most harmful of all drinking. Even swimming was frowned upon for fear of accidentally taking in water. The nurses had borne the brunt. Hasty late night and early morning cooking by weary souls had resulted in a welter accidents and burns. Colin mentioned that at work a room had been designated for the expats to go to eat, drink and smoke. The windows had been newspapered up. Only the very old and young and the ill were exempt. On the farm we'd not been affected. I'd only noticed the special discounts in Riyadh. Ramadan meant sales.

"Then there are the perverts," Ginny continued. "Somebody stole Linda's lingerie from the washing line and Ita spotted a peeping tom. We've got resident Arabs, but I don't think it's them. Perhaps they're outsiders getting passed security. Perhaps they're invited."

"Aren't these things reported?"

"Sometimes. But what can security do? We're just warned to be careful."

I shook my head in dismay.

"And if that's not enough there're rogue taxi drivers." She explained that there were official camp taxi drivers, but occasionally someone would hire a vehicle off-camp and enter. This taxi would then cruise the streets looking for mischief.

"What about the pet-killer?"

"I haven't heard anything."

"Do you remember our desert picnic and seeing that notice about a missing cat?"

"Vaguely. You said you knew the woman."

"Yes. The wife of Mike's boss." I paused. "Well, they found the cat." Mike had told me this after my outburst. He had found out about it during one of his talks with Smith about a possible Aramco visit.

"Dead?"

"Decapitated."

"So it's not something put out by Rumour Control."

"No."

We were interrupted by Colin and Jim Morrison wanting us to light their fires. We joined in, wanting the release, singing, shouting out the chorus, putting passion and smiles into each other's faces. As if someone had died we bawled out for dear life.

Encapsulated in our diminutive vehicle, we devoured the black top and chased the puddle. The forsaken wasteland tried to defy our progress: presenting us with more and more of its parched self, but for a tiny moment we were Titans.

*　*　*

A tiny darkening mote that would first smoulder and then flare: a flame spreading like that from Pav's alleged cigarette, this one peeling back the remaining fabric that is left of my world. And yet it is a light at which to clutch. They want to release the official version of what happened: Pav, drunk at the beginning of the day carelessly dropping a cigarette and dispatching all to a fiery end. And for a time I am amenable to their persuasion. I want to believe it. I want the madness to stop.

"So you agree that is the way it happened." The young

diplomat cannot believe his luck. His achievement lights his face. As expected he grows cautious when I nod again. Even if I am not being honest he wants the accolades of his superiors. Where others have failed he has triumphed. "This'll hasten your departure from this Godforsaken country." He smiles and then bucks-up, realising he may have overstepped his mark. Regardless, he wants the prize confirmed and lowers his voice conspiratorially: "We'll have you out of here before they change their minds."

Things have changed. Rita was Pip's minder. But she is gone. And she left us on a Friday. Thursday and Friday were execution days. Of course she could have been freed and the day was mere coincidence. Many had voiced the possibility, but few if any believed in it. So now Pip is vulnerable. And the Arabs could turn on me out of pure meanness.

I ask whether Abdul was an accident victim too, but like the others this official claims not to know. And now he wants away. He wants to get out of the room before he loses the prize. His charming smile says "I think we are finished" and he makes ready to rise from the desk.

"Just one thing," I say, returning him to the tightrope. "If this is what happened, how are you going to explain why I've been held for over five months?"

The smile falls from his face, as the tightrope becomes a quivering knife-edge. His inexperience comes to the fore and he uses his arms to maintain his balance, half standing, half leaning towards me, his fingertips on the desk. Then he straightens. "Bureaucracy," he manages and before he picks up his briefcase, which has remained unopened, he notices me watching him unknowingly wiping a palm on his trouser leg. He musters a smile and I feel something akin to sorrow. His sweaty hand is familiar, an identifiable European emotion and not alien and clammy and spicy and grabbing for me.

"I'll arrange for a signing." His enthusiasm is doubtful. He is not sure whether I will sign. I too am not sure.

* * *

That first night I slept alone in Ginny's apartment. She slept at Colin's place. Colin had left all-male North Camp as soon as he was eligible for a place on Main Camp. All men started at the former and could opt for the latter after a number of months. The longer the duration on North Camp, the more points one accrued and the better the choice of accommodation on Main. He'd got the most basic of buildings, which nevertheless was twice the size of Ginny's. Nationality played a role too. On arrival you were loaded with points. Americans got the most; they didn't need to roll a six to start. The rent was heavily subsidised but North Camp was free and many chose to stay. "For me it was a choice between money and quality of life," Colin explained.

Unlike my previous visit this was the working week, the working day ending at 16:00. The nurses work structure did not follow conventional rules and I was constantly in the company of one or more of the nurses during the day. They worked shifts of five-day blocks with earlies starting at 7:00, lates at 15:00 and nights at 23:00. After each block they had two days off, three days after a block of nights. So I went shopping, swimming at the pool and even went to aerobics just to prove how unfit I was. I even travelled to the beach by bus on someone else's i.d. card, an impostor among the beachcombers, despite the lack of resemblance between the card owner and me.

All these things had their moments: small refrains punctuating the bigger compositions. And what were the symphonies? There were three of them: the poker evening, the party and the day trip. Unfortunately the whole was brought to an abrupt end. As if my recording of events had run out of tape, the playback would always be cut-off. On Saturday morning my husband would be rushed to hospital having made, as I would later put it, a concerted effort to kill himself.

I spent one afternoon at the beach with Ita and an English nurse called Gillian. My name was Racquel, a radiographer. The real Racquel had gone on leave and leant me her i.d. card. Nobody ever scrutinised it. We left the bus and carried our small cool-box to the edge of the sea. Then we undressed, folding our clothes on one of the benches. Although we were on an Aramco beach and one-piece swimsuits were the norm, I did see a couple of bikinis. The Arabs didn't seem to mind.

We stretched out upon our towels and I coated myself with suntan cream. There we lay, sometimes speaking, occasionally reading, eating and drinking, then simply wallowing with closed eyes or contemplating the unmoving cloud streaked sky that was azure marble. Funny, how the clouds never seemed to inhibit the sun. The heat enfeebled us and the effort to turn over became gargantuan. Gillian suggested they train an Indian to patrol the beach, decide when one side was done and flip us over with a large spatula.

She swelled when we laughed at her suggestion and I saw that she had been cowering all the time. Gillian was a wounded creature and I swooned with a smile urging her to rise again. "All this eating and lolling he'd have to be Samson," I said. "I'll need to be carried back in a wheel-barrow." But Gillian slumped back into herself.

We fell silent.

Ita was the first to rise. She was one of those beanpole people who couldn't keep still for too long. Although she was a bundle of energy that bordered on nervousness she was not scatty. She went off alone when Gillian and I said: "Later" to her suggestion of a swim. I was on holiday, I said to myself. A quarter of an hour later she returned. "Anyone for a stroll?" she asked snatching up her towel to dry herself. A storm of sand covered me and I shrieked.

"I think I'll go for that dip now," I said, sitting up and looking over my fine covering of sand.

"Oh, sorry," said Ita.

"I look like a Kentucky Fried Chicken."

"For the length of time you've been cooking you probably taste like one," said Ita.

I didn't feel like swimming and said that I'd wash myself off and then go for a walk with her. "I want to take some photos." Gillian opted to remain with our things.

I'd used the camera on camp, photographing deserted streets just in case it wasn't allowed, but mainly taking snaps of my companions indoors. There was too much risk involved in photographing Al Khobar or Riyadh.

"Do you work with Gillian?" I asked when we were out of earshot.

"No. She's in radiography and I'm on the general ward."

"She seems a nice person."

"Yes, she's fine."

"Although, I get the feeling she lacks confidence."

"I don't know her that well. I do know that she's had a rough time of it."

To my disappointment she didn't elaborate and we went on to talk of other things.

We walked until we reached a large hump of a dune, which I decided could offer a terrific view. Ita decided to go back and I ascended the virgin mound alone. As I framed-up the shot, my bare feet, which had been cooled by the damp sand at the shoreline, began to register the heat. I had hadn't taken much notice of the brittleness of the sand as I'd climbed. This rapidly turned to searing pain. My soles were burning. Thoughts of nimbly or gingerly going back the way I came were dismissed. I had to get off the sand as quickly as possible. So at the risk of slipping or getting stuck I chose the steeper edge that dropped straight into the sea. As I crashed downward I heard and felt glass crackling underfoot: the surface had melted and was like a gossamer sheet of burning salt.

The effect of the sea was instant and arrested my tears. By the time I'd walked back to the others I had recovered. Brushing away oatmeal socks I explained what had happened. Ita inspected my soles.

Miraculously no damage was done, but I'd learnt my lesson. How easy it was to forget the power of the sun. Of course it was hot, but not unbearably so. I put the temperature at middle to upper thirties. There was a sea breeze and the air was dry. The days of 50°C plus temperatures and then those of unbearable humidity were still to come. Ginny told me that last August they had three weeks of humidity that made her gag for breath. And Colin said that he thought his place had a leak until he went outside and saw condensation drops coming from his roof like melting ice.

* * *

Of course it was Ita who introduced me to the gruelling aerobics sessions: one and a half hours jumping around and sweating. This was when aerobics was jogging on the spot with interruptions for kicks, swings, dainty-looking hand and foot dance routines and jumping jacks. The sessions incorporated hand weights that the American trainer called heavy hands and skipping ropes she called jump ropes. There was isometrics, basic Army training, stretching, boxing, and other exercises, the whole choreographed at a furious pace by this Barbie Doll, whom I regarded with awe and hate. My flippant wheelbarrow comment at the beach had a lot to answer for.

Linda was there that first time. I knew her only fleetingly from the barbecue evening and had labelled her with Merv's good schoolgirl comment. She extended her arms to embrace my friendship. I willingly complied but I was wary of her hunger. She was in her element at aerobics; driving herself fanatically, hooked on her own natural opiate. She was an endorphin junkie.

"Did you know they tried to ban it?" she said breezily, after the session, popping a piece of gum into her mouth. Whereas I felt flushed, she looked vibrant, fresh, vitalised and bright. The true athlete recovering quickly.

"For heaven's sake, why?" I asked, mindful of the gymnasium echo in the school hall. Ita was talking to someone else.

She was surprised by my question and missed a beat in her relentless mastication. "It's mixed, isn't it? And leotards don't exactly hide the figure." Again I'd forgotten where I was and protested that we were behind closed doors.

"It is ridiculous. But Arabs do live on camp, although I've rarely seen them." Her eyes were splendid. "If they did ban it, we'd start it up as a debating society or something. It was a welcome break a few weeks ago, when we had self-defence lessons. But there's nothing like a good workout. Well, maybe one thing..."

I smiled with her, before asking about the self-defence lessons.

"It was exclusively for women. But by the end of the week I was rather sick of it."

I nodded sympathetically. She measured her tone when she next spoke. She was laying down the conditions of her friendship. "I'm my own person, Dawn. I'm not part of the clique." I knew that she was not a member of the dive club, but didn't think she was excluded from other gatherings. "I do what I want." She looked at me. "Don't you think people should do what they want?"

"What do you mean?"

"Be true to themselves."

"Of course, as long as it doesn't hurt others."

My answer did not please her and a tiny light went off in her eyes as I dropped a notch in her estimation. In that single moment my suspicion was confirmed. Her hunger was a ferocious loneliness.

"Life's tough enough out here for us women as it is," she went on. "There's nothing wrong with preferring the company of men." I was not of her breed. I was being shoved with the pack and the lone wolf was turning away.

"There're plenty to chose from," I smiled. Her smile was a respectful acceptance of our difference.

* * *

If Linda was ferociously lonely then Gillian was desolate. Ita had accepted me and somehow Gillian came up in our effortless conversation.

"She is a sad character," Ita began as we made our way to the on-camp golf course. Ginny would replace the word sad with flaky. "She's had a lot of bad luck with men out here. She's not like Linda. Linda wants fun." Linda was said to change her boyfriends as often as her underwear. "Gillian's had three or four relationships. She wants a real boyfriend, but I think she smothers them when they come along. And you can't tell her that's her problem. Well, I suppose you could, but it wouldn't do any good. It's her nature. She finds a man and throws herself at him, giving him her all." Gillian threw herself at their feet and eventually they walked over her. Instead of "please wipe your feet" stamped across her forehead "please abuse me" could have been the legend.

We were taking a roundabout route to the golf course. The streets were pristine and the gardens of the private houses burst with purple bougainvillaea and candy-pink oleanders. Communal buildings: schools, offices, halls and health and recreation centres were fronted by more ambitious, permanent offerings: grasses and cacti. The National Commercial Bank was present too, although in a disappointing trailer-like building. Stout gravel islands of cacti broke any remaining monotony. The trees were parched green, the leaves covered in a film of dust; but green nonetheless, thanks to the tireless work of the Asian gardeners. The camp was indeed a town, with distinct areas and architecture such as old town and the Hills, and warranted a map and a bus service of its own.

"The right man will come along," I said.

She nodded, but didn't appear convinced. "I hope so. But let me tell you what happened with her last boyfriend. I don't like gossiping, which means that's what I'm about to do." She didn't wait for my smile. "He lived with her and then went on leave. That's what he told her. He actually left good and proper and she found out later."

"Bastard." I couldn't help myself.

The sun was in one part of the big sky indignantly glaring at an insouciant moon. This sight was common: both of them inhabiting the sky at the same time. And depending upon the time of the day, the moon could be hard like a freshly cut thumbnail or faint and almost translucent like a cuticle.

"Yes. She didn't see it coming. I'm not saying we did, but we suspected. I can't help feeling that most of it was her fault. Nobody deserves such treatment, but it was as if she denied the obvious. She lied to herself. That's the perverse thing. I think she knew she was lying to herself. She knew it was wrong."

The golf course was a large open space not unlike off-camp: as if they'd forgotten to use this area. Admittedly it was not wild with brush, but neither was it green, just hard compacted ground. Ita hadn't seen anyone playing but had heard that the players carried a patch of turf with them. I suspected that the most time was spent at the 19th hole. An Indian dressed in a white overall - street sweepers wore florescent orange - sat under a tree next to a patch of sand he'd meticulously raked. Beside him was a large can of water - his day's supply.

"Look at that TCN and his rake. Spot the difference," Ita challenged. The man had a boy's frame and runner beans would have had a difficult choice between him and his rake. TCN stood for third country national, Ita explained, the lowest in the Aramco employee hierarchy.

The Asians were subordinated, elevated spitting distance above slavery. There was something of the war movie loaded-choice in their decision to come here: the prisoner's chance of financial freedom in a mission with a ninety-nine percent chance of mentally perishing. I would hear stories of bribing connected agencies for the chance to work out here: dealing and bidding sizeable portions of their prospective earnings away.

* * *

In Ita I had a good friend, but in Ginny I had a soul sister. The evenings were hers. We went to the women's *souqs* in Al Khobar one evening, on another Carol cooked for us; there were a couple of quiet evenings in which we did nothing. Then there was a Trivial Pursuits evening where I was teamed with Jim, Carol with Colin and Ginny with Jim's friend and countryman Huck. Carol and Colin won and we went on to play charades.

Before the lads arrived, we three girls prepared some snacks. Carol had accepted me, having realised that the brevity and rarity of my presence posed no threat. Ginny was not present when Carol was suddenly candid: "Jim loves me, you know." She said it with flippancy; as if his love were a trophy to be brought out of its glass cabinet to be polished and shined and held high.

I wanted to step back from this intimacy. "You met out here, I suppose?"

"Yes." She was blunted, but eventually said: "How did you meet

Mike?"

I was surprised by her enquiry. She had never shown any interest in me. "At university. I was in the final year of Business Administration. Mike had returned from Saudi and was completing a Bachelor of Agricultural Science Degree." I wanted to say more and waited for her interest to prompt me. But the prompt never came and Ginny returned.

At dinner only Huck was a stranger to me. The girls assured me during preparations that he was there to even the numbers and it was not a blind date.

Before clearing the table the subject of the pet killer arose and a possible link to the self-defence lessons.

"It's all a waste of time," said Jim.

"Why?" Carol asked.

"Because you don't know how you'll react when attacked. You'll probably just freeze."

"I doubt it. What we learnt became reflex."

"For that week."

"Show us something," I said.

"Okay." Carol rose. "Pick up that knife." she said to me.

She moved away from the table.

"Watch it," said Colin. "You've had a couple of *sids*."

"Come at me. No. Raise the knife as if you want to strike me. Yes. That's it, come on." She blocked my attack and bent and twisted my arm so that I lost my balance and dropped the knife. "Block and twist," she said holding my arm and breaking my fall. "If I want to I could punch you in the back."

"Try me," said Jim.

"Okay."

When Jim attacked he brought his free arm round to grab and eventually overpower her. She was furious.

"You knew what I was going to do," she protested. "Normally you'd be off-balance and worried about falling."

"Really?" he smiled.

She fumed. I broke in again. "That was easy. Show me something else."

"Is Ian getting that dangerous?" Ginny asked.

I reddened and teased. "Not yet."

Carol showed me another move but her heart was no longer in it. Afterwards Colin insisted on getting the Trivial Pursuits out before we got too pickled or one of us got hurt.

* * *

"It's about time we had another scandal."

This enigmatic statement came from Aine towards the end of the poker session. Only Marie, pronounced Marry, and Alan were playing for the seventy riyal pot, in itself not a great deal of money, but in a game were one riyal was the minimum stake, this was an astronomical win. Alan was in fact Alana and like Paula might be shortened to Paul so she preferred the abbreviation. Names were often reduced to one or maximum two syllables. Margaret became Mags, Hilary became aitch and so on. I was lucky with my name.

And what the name Pat was for the Irish men so Mary was for the women. Nothing as base as physical attributes were used to distinguish them and this Mary told me she was Mary O. There was Mary, Mary F., Mary Mc (pronounced Meck) any others having opted to use a second Christian name.

I'd dropped out early. The Irish were hardened players. Even two of the three men present took a beating. Pat was one of them. He was the Irishman who met us at Dhahran airport all those centuries ago.

The players who'd retired followed the game to the end, but their attention was slowly turning to the conversation Aine had kindled with her incendiary statement.

"Wasn't Ramadan enough for you?" asked Ita. Ramadan aside, I knew that a nurse's working life to be unusually exacerbating out here. The maternity ward, for example, gave rise to fathers disputing the sex of their baby; his wife had definitely given birth to a boy. The final humiliation was demanding to speak to a male doctor. And then there were the women brought in time and again with some sexually transmitted disease. Efforts at getting their husbands treated, husbands who travelled internationally and brought it into the family, inevitably failed.

"That was strenuous but there were no scandals."

I heard of problems that routinely leapt normality. Ita told tell me of sickle cell anaemia, the altered haemoglobin causing an enlargement of the heart and abdomen, disturbing the blood circulation and leading to painful swelling of hands and feet. A terrible affliction that thrived in an environment that approved of first cousin marriages to enhance the strength of the tribe.

"These things come periodically, then?" I enquired.

"There are levels. You've got the trivial but still scandalous things. Like the thieves who stole Linda's knickers from the line -"

"I heard about that," I said, "and the rogue taxi drivers."

"One tried to force his way into Frances's room." I didn't know her. She was another nurse. "She got the taxi at the airport and he offered to help her with her bags. When she came to pay him he grabbed her. She screamed and luckily he ran off."

"Four nines," said Alan, defiantly placing her cards upon the table.

"Four tens," returned Marie and there was laughter and statements of disbelief.

"There's the pet killer," said Mary O.

"Cat killer," Pat corrected. "If he exists, he's worse than any of these taxi drivers. He's psychotic. I heard that he collects the paws."

"I thought it was a dog last time," said Mary O.

"Yes I heard that too," said Alan. "Maybe cats are easier to get because they're usually alone."

"It could always be an Aramco brat," said Pat. This was the unflattering name given to kids born in Saudi Aramco. His next statement ended the subject with an ominous silence. "Whoever it is has the makings of a serial killer."

"Perhaps that's why there were those self-defence lessons a couple of weeks ago," I offered.

"I doubt it. This place is continually having theme weeks," one of the lads said. "There are motto weeks all through the year. I remember a safety week where an inspector was at the Towers - you know the multi-storey buildings? Yes, well this inspector went up with the Filipino window-cleaners in one of those cabled platforms. Now, this guy's there to check on safety procedures. And guess what happens? About three storeys up a cable snaps and the two Filipinos are hanging from their safety harnesses. And this inspector breaks both legs and an arm. He wasn't attached." He laughed. "One saving grace was that he had his hard-hat on."

"I was talking of a real scandal," said Aine, setting us firmly on track again. "Like that Saudi girl."

Mary O. told me the story of the girl who'd been brought into hospital after cutting her wrists. She was unmarried and pregnant. After an abortion the *mullahs* took her away. She refused to name the father and was sentenced to death. Her own father was imprisoned for failing in his daughter's upbringing. She was stoned to death. The modern method, apparently, was to bury them under boulders using a tip-up truck. The girls could only say that the story was true up to being removed from hospital. The rest was hearsay and unverifiable rumour.

"What about the shooting two Christmases ago?" asked Mary O.

"Most of us haven't been here that long," said Alan.

"Does anybody know what happened to the Arab?"

"He's probably out on bail," said Aine.

"What happened?" I asked.

Mary O. turned to me. "A Saudi ran amok in an office somewhere -"

"In housing allocation."

"I heard it was in the Administration building."

"It doesn't matter," interrupted Mary O., before a further location was proposed. Then to me again: "All that is certain is that there was a shooting. An Indian was killed - at least that's what they said - and an American got shot in the stomach. Somebody else may have been wounded."

"He just flipped or what?"

"The American was his boss and the Arab had lost face over some parking allocation."

"He must have been a little touched to go shooting about. Or there was more to it?"

"Most likely both."

"There's always Superman," Alan offered.

I checked faces for interest. "I haven't heard it," I said.

Alan smiled. "A doctor and nurse were taken by Security to the Hills." This was the name of an area on camp where the best housing was situated. "A neighbour had called after he'd heard cries for help. Security broke in. In the upstairs bedroom Superman was pinned between a wardrobe and a King-sized bed. His lover was wearing only a necklace. She was gagged and tied down spread-eagled on the bed. His blue underpants were open at the front." She paused. "He'd obviously climbed upon the wardrobe to leap on her or the bed and it'd crashed down trapping him and breaking his arm." I laughed. When I settled Alan added cream. "It was his house but not his wife."

I told Mike this story on the phone and he said he'd not heard it before but it smacked of a yarn. Such as the old American lady drying her beloved poodle in the microwave and then successfully suing the makers of the machine. Or the woman going to the doctors with a boil on her cheek after an African holiday and being vainly treated with creams until she caught the growth with her comb and out crawled tiny spiders. Maybe there was an element of truth in these stories. But embellishments turned them to legend and then they did the rounds until they became clichés. At the time I took the Superman story at face value.

In the confines of the trailer we could have been in a luxury, heated cabin in the Klondike. We were not quite the lawless, motley crew of those Gold Rush days, but we were every bit as isolated. The company-issued furniture was utilitarian: teak tables, chairs and settees the latter upholstered with large cushions in stripes of different browns. Emerald posters of Ireland helped the pot-plants in greening the wooden panelling.

"I guess it qualifies as a scandal," began Pat. "One of the Indian cleaners found a dead man in bed in his room at North camp. He was an American and had died of a heart attack." He reflected. "In some ways it doesn't surprise me. The way the canteen works you're encouraged to overeat. The other day was steak evening. The word macabre doesn't describe it. There were rump steaks and because of the possibility of gristle or fat everyone, and I mean everyone, had at least two steaks on their plate, three was the norm and some had four or five. Instead of knives and forks chain-saws would have been more appropriate."

"And how many did you have?" I smiled.

He grinned. "Three. Two were on the plate before you spoke and a third on offer."

"You seem to have digressed," Aine observed.

"True. The point of the story was that they imprisoned the Indian."

"That's their policy. Slap everyone in prison. Witness a car accident, it's prison until they sort it out."

I related little Pat's New Year's Eve tale of smuggling.

"A few years ago," began Noel, "they discovered a distillery on camp." Noel was the alcoholic I had heard about, but tonight he wasn't drinking. He loved poker and had been invited on condition he behaved. For him there was no in-between so tonight was abstinence night. Most of my companions were relatively young, middle to late twenties. Noel was over thirty and a seasoned expat. He spoke in a careful way, giving his words a solemnity. He did this not for effect, but because he was insecure. Like an actor can find confidence under the mantle of a character, so Noel needed the shroud of alcohol to be complete. Before us he was disrobed. The quandary was that you didn't want this diminished man; you wanted the full-blown character and then not his drunkenness. "The still was in the attic of an apartment occupied by a guy called Dave. He claimed he didn't know anything about it, but they could see it was in use. He was an Aramcon and the company always tries to help, but this was outside their scope. He was in deep shit. The punishment was a £15,000 fine, two years in prison and 250 lashes. I spoke to someone who visited him. He said Dave was in a communal cell and said that his cellmates had spoken of how long they'd been there, what their crime was and what they expected to get. When it came to an Indian in the corner he said he'd been there three months, but that he'd get nothing because he was a witness."

"Three months," gasped Ita.

"It's like a police state," said Mary O.

"Amazing how much we adapt," said Pat.

"If the readies are right..." Noel smiled, ominously. His hoary bush of a beard seemed to swell. I was reminded of George Bernard Shaw.

"What happened to Dave?" asked Marie.

"He managed to get himself deported."

We all agreed that the best philosophy was to keep your head down. If you got mixed up with the law you would find yourself in a quirky bureaucratic morass, a can of worms that would devour your reason. It was agreed that even the British Embassy had trouble fishing you out.

I had heard this talk before, not so blatant or undiluted as on this evening. There was that same incredulity and fascination. But underlying it all was fear. Fear. I had experienced it myself, in the car with Merv and Den on our way to Khobar. The attitude was not so much keep your head down as bury your head. Don't get involved. On camp, behind closed doors, you could make merry, but out there you were sober because, especially as a woman, you could find yourself walking a high wire.

* * *

After calling us to gather about his raised desk, and we were sitting upon high wooden stools, he lit the candle and placing it in a saucer of water, overturned a glass upon it. With dramatic understatement that keened our attention he said simply, almost soothingly: "Observe."

Even the rapidly diminishing flame, extinguishing in a thread of grey smoke, the water level rising in the glass, was fascinating under Mr. Everest's direction.

* * *

I'm rereading that English magazine again. I'm stumped at the competition page: trying to remember my original sentences. I think the first was that Saudi Arabia destroyed my life. The sentence taunts me. But I can't concentrate. I feel something swelling inside me. All the dread of this place, all the frustration, all the hate, coming together to fill me up until it bursts from me.

It's four in the afternoon. Pip has just left the room. She's gone to the toilet. She says she is going to try to talk to the Arabs. Two of the girls have gone with her. I can't go. I can't help her. What good could I do? One of the first things she said to me was keep your head down. That's what I've been doing since I've arrived in this damned country. That was her philosophy and it hasn't helped. She's in trouble. More trouble. As if such a thing should be possible.

I could accompany her. She is my friend. But like the others I would be of no use. Moral support is a luxury that has no place here. Support must be real. And what could I do? Block and twist? My mind takes my arms through the motions. I try to go back to the magazine.

Saudi Arabia destroyed my life. True. And now all I've go to do is lie low and crawl out of here. It's just a matter of time. Everything's being prepared for the signing. Any day now the embassy will come back with the papers. But Pip is my friend. By staying here I'm running away. Am I going to regret this too? Will I be too late, again? Of course it's too late now. Isn't it? I can hear Pip's daughter crying next door. She senses something is wrong. Pip left her with another woman. If I'd had her I'd have had an excuse to stay put. But Pip didn't want to involve me in any way.

I sit up and swing my legs onto the floor. I strain to hear a commotion. There is nothing. Maybe nothing is happening. Maybe they've decided to forgive and forget. I'm procrastinating. There is little sound. That's it. There's a lack of commotion. The level of activity is subdued. Anticipation is in the air.

For the morning toilet I was with Pip. There is always a queue.

So many women. Many try to go earlier or hold on. The Arabs would never try to get her then. And Pip has always held herself till the next morning. But today Pip has to go. The soup wasn't good or she's got another bug. Whatever, stomach cramps have got the better of her.

I look over to Rita's empty bed. It's remained unoccupied out of respect. But I'm looking beyond her bed at the window and thinking of the shutters and the sharpened spoon.

Pip had said: "You'd better stay away from me. If you get involved you'll be punished. You'll be kept here longer."

The old Indian had spoken to me. "Nobody can do anything. Others may want to help her, but they're afraid."

"The Arabs are only a handful. If you all got together..."

"You do not understand the Asian mentality." She regarded me before speaking. "Even you did nothing when they took your belongings." I look away. Of course nobody wants more trouble. Everyone wants out. Only the Arabs know the true hopelessness of their situation. They're women; they've known a form of imprisonment all their lives. They can come to terms with their predicament. Why, maybe this was a form of freedom for some of them.

I don't know what I'm thinking but I'm on Rita's bed reaching through the window, fingering the slats of the shutters for the spoon. I can't find it. I ease each shutter closed. The spoon is gone. I know Pip has taken it. I don't know why, but panic throws me from the bed. Now I can't think. I'm outside striding towards the toilets. There are others out here, but I might as well be crossing a barren savannah. All I see is the Arab woman at the toilet entrance. She's seen me. She's looking into the toilets. I can't hear her, but no doubt warning those inside.

The woman at the door doesn't attempt to stop me. Her smirk is offset by the hardness in her coal black eyes.

When I enter the toilets and see them everything leaves me. As if my will was linked to my momentum. I suddenly realise where I am. I don't know what to do. I don't know what to think. Light and shadow tell me that the Arab behind me fills the entrance. I take in the scene for clues as to what to do. Pip is on her hands and knees. A beaten dog. The big brute of a woman, the henchwoman of the Arabs stands over her. Half a dozen Arab women stand about. One is the shrouded old woman who spat at me. She's the person in authority here. It seems little has happened. The lecture has been verbal so far.

All eyes are turned to me. The henchwoman is the first to move. She looks to the old woman for instruction. I can't read the signals but the big woman slowly bends down and I see that she has a foot upon the spoon. She picks it up. Again I'm wondering what I'm doing here. I don't look into Pip's eyes. She's as surprised to see me as the others. I don't know what the woman wants to do but I part my lips to speak. Can I reason with them? Will they understand me? I see the answer in their closed faces. Sallies at ten o'clock. I see my husband's angry face and hear his shout. This time I reply. My voice is a whisper and I clear my throat and speak firmly. "No."

It's a word they understand. The old woman speaks. Her Arabic is clipped and I hear the contempt in her words. The henchwoman turns on me. The spoon is raised above her and I'm about to be attacked. It's madness. I don't think. I freeze. No. She's going to hurt me. She's slow. Such is her confidence. I move. Block and twist. And it's done. The spoon clatters to the floor, she follows, but I break her fall by holding onto her twisted arm. She's reaching for the spoon. I'm not having it. Beaten is beaten. Stay down, you bitch. I slam the flat of my free hand in her back. There's a crack and her face hits the floor.

I pick up the spoon. The henchwoman remains on the ground. She's stunned, blood coming from under her face. I have the spoon in my right hand. I'm an animal bent aggressively ready to take any one of them on, pointing the spoon erratically from one to the other. Their eyes are as wide as mine; but I have wildness, they have disbelief or fear.

* * *

The following evening was Wednesday, the end of the working week and the night of the "What you were wearing when the ship went down" party. Although it was not a failure it was a surreal series of sketches that summarised all that I had come to know of the characters on the camp. As if all that had gone before had been rehearsals for tonight's performance. Somebody had said "free interpretation, please" and this is what I observed. I had been there a week, still not long enough to be a player.

The trappings of a party were present: the talk and laughter and dancing and drinking and a liberal dose of intrigues. At the time I enjoyed it as a party. Only later did I see the subterranean forces at play.

There were no bad people amongst the expats. Yes, they were flawed, hurt, damaged, whatever, but not one of them wanted to harm another. This was campus life and another student bash.

Four guys had formed the band *Dhahran Dhahran*. With songs like *Hotel California, Wonderful Tonight, Radar Love, Jump, Ain't seen nothing yet* and the difficult to dance to *Stairway to Heaven* they lent to the student shindig feel. I don't think I have ever continually danced so much and I was grateful for their brief tune-up pauses.

The party was in the birthday boy's flat. One of the standard bachelor types: the ground floor being a large lounge-kitchenette, upstairs bedroom and toilet-bathroom. This meant that the band not only shoved conversation to the pauses and outside, it forced people to dance, line the walls or get out. Smokers were obliged to sit in the gravelled, walled-up porch, where most of the furniture had been hauled. So although there were only forty or fifty people the place was crowded and vibrant and spilled outside. We were deep in the bachelor housing section and I don't think any Arabs lived in the area. Nonetheless the band had to stop at midnight and let a stereo take over.

Surprisingly there were only two men for every woman, but I didn't feel any predatory discotheque intimidation. Typically, few men were dancing. There were some of the bigoted sort best described as beached louts looking over beer bellies and criticising the breasts and bums of passing bikini'd women. Most were intense, grave types that reminded me of Ian. Ginny agreed that men didn't make good wallflowers. "About as engaging as Triffids," she said. Only three men were jumping about with the throng of women. I danced with no one and everyone.

One of the men, the most individual in dance and dress, bumped into me and mouthed a sorry. At the end of the song he spoke.

"Anything other than pogoing is an act of violence here. Sorry."

He was right; there was no room to dance. "They're good, aren't they?"

Cords were struck before he could speak and he turned away, folded into himself and jiggled about. He wore black jeans, white open-necked collar-less shirt and, despite the heat, a black leather jacket. The jacket had tassels and fringes on the sleeves and about his neck dangled a thonged pouch containing his roll-your-own gear. He looked like an ageing rock musician. He was not a rock star. He was one of the behind the scenes stalwarts: the session musician. He was the type of guy who would have passionately played an invisible guitar during *Stairway to Heaven* had the music not been live.

At the next pause we conversed again. And so it went: speaking between numbers and occasionally shouting in each other's ear.

"Were you mending your Harley when the ship went down?"

"Nothing else to wear. My stuff's packed." He didn't comment on my attire. I was in Colin's pyjamas.

His name was Chris and after just eight months he was leaving the Kingdom in the morning. He didn't want to leave, but in Aramco-speak he had been surplussed. Not quite a euphemism but nevertheless a nice way of saying fired or sacked. The ultimate goal of the Saudis was to be foreigner-free. The company periodically, perhaps symbolically, had these purges. "In a few months they'll be recruiting again," someone said.

The party was both to celebrate the occupier's birthday and commiserate Chris's departure.

He was hoping the party would take him through to his morning flight. His epitaph was a statement he repeated when bidding goodbye: "leave a space for me on the dance floor."

I didn't dance continuously, although my legs truly ached as I walked to Ginny's car later. She had kindly lent it to Ita and me. But I was on the floor for nearly all the band's songs.

In a break at ten-thirty somebody best described as a pinball accosted me. I'd noticed him earlier. It was hard not to notice him for he seemed to be everywhere, or better still: all over the place. He was catapulted by the event, hurtling from person to person, lighting them up with joy or indignation; nonetheless enlivening the party. He was a manic version of Bob and Merv. The type of person who'd talk to you embarrassingly loudly on an early commuter train and you'd shrink and become monosyllabic, diminishing the volume of your words to set an unheeded example. And here he was meeting those same insufferable commuters. So he'd ricochet from these encounters, his chromed confidence coming away a little more tarnished. Although he had no brakes and discretion was no more than a word he was not short of sensitivity. He had that exhausting eagerness for life that can make wonders, but more frequently underscored a growing disappointment in human nature. For he had chosen the Herculean task of bringing life to the living. His intricate sensitivity was not calibrated for this thin medium and he could not adapt. Survival was too little for him; he had an abounding desire to celebrate life. Carol called him a basket case.

I too was probably a disappointment to him. I could not match his verve. I was given my five minutes of allotted wit and failed to show due appreciation. Partial successes were probably honoured with ten minutes of ear-boxing. There were no complete successes.

"I know you're Den and Merv's *friend*," he said suddenly, after I had told him of the farm. I was stunned and had no time to question whether he was insinuating I was their mistress. "That's okay by me." Had Den spun some story? "But tell me, have you got it?" His eyes had started to glaze over. In their desperate sparkle I glimpsed an acute case of Colin's vitamin deficiency.

"What?" I reacted, arrested by the sight of his mouth working up into a lather.

"Why the happiness baton, of course."

"Sorry?" I blustered. "Look -"

He clasped his hands in front of himself and assumed a sagely stance. Relaxing his brow and half closing his eyes, his expression became abandonment, his frenetic self cast aside. I could imagine his bathrobe as a kimono as he put on a Chinese accent and went into the character. "Ah, Confusion says: 'Only one can hold the happiness baton.'" I had an inkling of what he was driving at and was wondering whether he was an extrovert Martin, when he spotted another candidate and with a "oops, there goes gravity" rushed off in the direction of the entrance. Although I was irked by his *friend* comment I was glad to be rid of him and smiled philosophically to myself. The bright lights of a newcomer with prospective bigger points had drawn him away. I wondered what his end total would be, for the accumulated points would be his measure of the success of the party.

* * *

This evening was inextricably tied with the AEA (Aramco Employees Association) cultural trip the following day. Or rather the day trip is swamped with memories of the party. For it was during this trip that bursts of the party would flare in my mind, sometimes inexplicably but always suddenly like a subliminal film cut. They would singe thought and then linger, tingling and hissing like the cooling flash bulbs of cameras of old. Placed before me, I was forced to scrutinise them to set them in some order in the album of my mind.

Having slept very little I was running on empty. We went to a camel and Bedouin market, to Hofuf and the Al-Qara caves. Despite the full programme we were by and large left to roam and go at our own pace. So it was a pleasant day, contrasting the fury of the party.

There was camel hair and sheep wool for sale and gut water bags resembling kidney-like bagpipes, but this Bedouin market was more akin to a flea market. Everything was laid out upon worn carpets. The sellers, mostly shrouded women sitting with their wares, gossiped in their alien tongue as we wandered in pairs. On offer was everything under the sun, gaudy plastic flip-flops, plimsolls, cheap biros, throwaway razors. There were sun-drenched packets of *Omo* and *Daz*, things I'd not seen since my childhood. Their faded state made them appear as if they'd been around that long. And without the passion of colour they appeared like imitations, as if this alien society had tried to copy our civilisation. The only difference between the sellers and us was our uncovered heads, our *abaayas* cloaking rather than enshrouding. Yet, despite our dress we might as well have been from another planet. Indeed, Carol had produced three fans that we fluttered like monstrous, petrified butterflies.

One woman sat behind a small holocaust of spectacles. As Ginny, Carol and myself neared, her henna-yellow hand waved us over, burrowed into the folds of her *abaaya* and guardedly took out a beautiful gold brooch. The incongruity of this jewel in her hand shocked us. For some reason we knew that the piece was genuine, but even if one of us was tempted we could not gauge the price or fully understand her method of sale. She presented it to us like an Egyptian sidling up to a tourist and flashing a scarab in a cupped hand. Was she merely being secretive for fear of being robbed or was she breaking some law? We smiled and shook our heads and moved on.

Merv and Den turned up at the party. Rashid was with them. I didn't recognise him at first. His attire was western: jeans and T-shirt and somehow wrong for him, as if he were in disguise. Tarzan in a suit. He looked as if he had come to the wrong party too. He had alcohol watery eyes and a permanent smirk. He was not disapproving. He was bemused, even enchanted and seemed content to ogle and drink and smirk.

Merv admonished me for not telling him I was there and insisted on a dance. Den approached me much later, having graced me earlier with a nod. If he'd been wearing a raincoat he would have turned up the collars and said something oblique: "The rain in Spain is warm." To which I was supposed to dovetail. In the event he spoke, waited a moment in which I said nothing and then slipped away. "I hope there are no hard feelings, Dawn. You can't blame a bloke for trying." It wasn't that I didn't want to forgive him; it was the manner of his apology. He was darkly tipsy, surfing a wave of elation and I wasn't sure who was apologising: Den or some alcohol-induced self-effacement of him.

"I can't believe those guys hang around with that Arab," said Carol.

"I get the impression he hangs around with them," I said.

"I think they've tried to shake him off," said Colin. "Damned dangerous."

My look prompted elaboration. "They're middlemen," said Colin. "They supply *sid*."

"Yes," I began. "I know." Did I? Colin was saying that Merv and Den had a direct contact to a supplier. I was curious to know the set up, the identity of the supplier. Then sense took over and I didn't want to know. Or was it fear again? I didn't believe some torturer was going to tear the secret out of my fingernails. I simply didn't want to know.

There was another encounter with *sid*'s influence, the memory of which is linked to the camel market. We'd met up with Colin and Jim and were wandering about bunches of animals and groups of white-clad Saudi men. There didn't seem to be much going on, but I guess their conversing could have been haggling. I had expected more drama, throwing of hands in the air, that sort of thing.

The Bedouins were not untouched by modernisation. They transported their water in tankers freeing themselves from their reliance on wells. They also carried their prized camels in trucks. Tied up with rope, trussed up like chickens, their legs tucked under themselves, the animals would be hoisted to or from a lorry by the small crane of a pick-up truck.

I've always thought the camel an ugly creature. With its mouthful of black and ivory bamboo shards. The way its lower jaw rolls like a cow chewing cud. Their sleepy eyes bespeaking a lumbering dumbness. With bodies that were all hard lumps and bumps, knobbly bone and gristle, they were like mugged horses, animals beaten senseless and condemned to being hunchbacks.

Some Arab boys asked us whether we wanted to ride. They didn't pester us or cry baksheesh, baksheesh, baksheesh. We declined a ride but agreed to be photographed atop one of the beasts. Naturally all this was for a price. I had reluctantly agreed so that Colin could cut a better deal. So each of us took a turn at being photographed upon the bristly mats and rough carpets heaped upon hairy chocolate humps. Like flying, getting up and coming down involved the most danger.

Mentioning my dislike set Jim off. He said that the camel was a remarkable animal, perfectly adapted to desert life. He told me that the hump was mainly fat for food storage rather than water. Whereas Man would die with a 12% water loss, camels could withstand as much as a 40% loss. They could see almost as well at night as during the day and their eyelids were translucent, allowing them to "see" in a sand storm. I was not impressed and petulantly dismissed them as ugly animals nonetheless.

On the one occasion I dropped a dance and was pouring myself a cola I found myself standing next to Noel. He was in his element: the fog of liquor. His face loomed out of its mist and fumbled for connection. The name Mr. Bumble sprung to mind for he had chosen to attire his corpulent figure in a voluminous nightshirt and cap. He looked decidedly Dickensian. I was pinned in a corner by his hulk and although I could have brusquely moved passed him I felt honour bound to give him some time. We didn't have a conversation as such. I concentrated on his words hoping my nods and monosyllabic concurrence were appropriately timed. His alcohol-swollen tongue lolled in front of his words, sloshing their inflexion high and low like goldfish in a tank on the high seas. His "I'm still here, take me seriously" plea in his brow was betrayed by his languishing eyes. They were heavy lidded to hoodwink me. There was no wickedness in them, but they peered from the thicket of his beard: the gloating eyes of a village peeping tom. His jaw was loose, unhinged, and his bottom lip enlarged and glistening. His very face seemed slack. His bulk was imposing and although he was not ugly booze made him so. And like the camel was battered into ugliness, drink had battered him into a poorer version of himself. Bernard Shaw was absent. He stopped mid-sentence and looked at me quizzically, as if realising for the first time who he was talking to and then with a large glass in hand he weaved unsteadily away. His goal was the front door and head down he dribbled an invisible football towards it. He experienced no challenges and the only tackles that occurred were accidental collisions he instigated.

I smiled. He was harmless, especially to women, but he was a danger too. In no way suicidal, he was more the type of person who'd wreck a place in a rage.

A cake with a single candle was presented to the birthday boy, generating hushes and brash comments. Ita recited an Irish toast. "May you have food and raiment, a soft pillow for your head, may you be forty years in Heaven, before the Devil knows you're dead."

* * *

"It stinks here," Carol said.

Huck who had arrived to ask us whether we were on our way to the fort smiled sheepishly. So far he had been quite anti-social. He had an expensive camera with an imposing telescopic lens and was everywhere to get that best shot from the best angle. One side of his hair was matted and he looked as if he'd been sweating profusely.

"You bought a T-shirt," Ginny observed.

"Pooh," I said, "what is that smell?"

"It's me," said Huck calmly. "I knelt down to get a shot. A camel behind me decided to take a leak. Maybe I edged backwards to frame up or maybe it moved towards me, I don't know. But it was like a hosepipe. The rag-heads couldn't stop laughing. I threw my shirt away and bought this."

Outside the fort, Qasr Abrahim, an Arab boy had spread his goods over carpets: all manner of copper, bronze, pewter and brass. There were the curve spouted *Ghawah* coffee pots, jugs, pots, pans, etched trays, mortar and pestle and shallow bowls. He also had some chunky *Khanjar* daggers in their bead and stone encrusted L-shaped scabbards. They were phallic and said to represent an Arab's virility and so worn in front rather than at the hip. He even had a *Narjeelah* or what we call a hookah or hubble-bubble pipe. At the risk of sounding plebeian I found these wares more interesting than the fort itself. After gaining permission I photographed the boy and his wares rather than the fort. The fort was classic in structure: a crenellated parapet atop a block of a building. It appeared to be built out of sand. "Must've been one helluva big bucket," said Jim. Had some expert explained its history or an overlooked anomaly I could possibly have shown some appreciation. I think we were all disappointed. In any case our collective exuberance paled the background. We were ignorant tourists. Without guides our observation was accompanied by thin wit.

This building was recent history and somehow shallow. Saudi Arabia was bereft of any visible history and despite the skyscrapers there was an inherent absence of progress. There was the ultra-modern and the ramshackle shantytown existence. Both relatively recent. There were no ruins to be revered, to present the idea of history and sense of advancement. But progress was subjective. I would read of the lives of Bedouin sheep on the Jordanian-Saudi border being jeopardised through eating plastic bags - such an epitomising symbol of modern society - snagged on the sparse vegetation. Maybe Mecca offered a sense of the past. As a non-Muslim I would never know. Indeed, if progress is measured by Man's command over Nature, then here there was stagnation. Nature would not be governed. Man had to adapt.

The trip was not totally barren on the cultural front. One of the AEA organisers enriched our outward journey. He rode the second coach on the homeward one. He talked non-stop. Telling us that the place was a geological wonder, with fossils dating 15 - 17 million years BC. And they were not merely sea creatures but animals such as giraffes. There were numerous sites with abundant fossils and crystals. We were drenched in his enthusiasm and glimpsed another Arabia. He insisted that when it rained the desert bloomed, becoming green from horizon to horizon and butterflies would materialise from nowhere. Everything was otherwise dormant. He pointed to grey buildings that looked like land-locked battleships, telling us that they were cement or asphalt factories. What little there was he subjected to his amplifying eye. But he was not all lofty reverence and awe. He brought us down with a bumpy landing. "The change has been too swift for the layman. They'll have a good vehicle, but you'll see the canvas of bald tyres." Their meeting the twentieth century was not accompanied by such baubles as beads, mirrors and the trinkets that the Africans received. They got cars and highways.

Hofuf was a living town with ample mosques. Contrasting Riyadh, which was international and cosmopolitan, this place was run-down. There was no striking architecture, but it was living and breathing on a daily basis. Babies were carried sidesaddle in gut or hide bags. Kids went about arm in arm or holding hands. Carefree thoughts were marred by seated figures with disease-ravaged faces. Others had that dull-eyed social-security official look. I remember hearing from an Aramco chemist that he'd analysed a piece of the hard-soil children were encouraged to suck for its health-giving properties or to generate saliva. It contained a high percentage of lead.

The gold souqs were said to be good, but we skipped them, favouring the covered fruit and vegetable market.

We were treated to the oriental. Sheltered stores were fronted by a mountain range of colourful spices. Intoxicating aromas assaulted us. A hand worker in a tool market allowed us to photograph him. Someone was selling the small twigs, *darum*, which the Arabs chewed to clean their teeth. This brought back the dentist's comment. "When I first came here they had the finest teeth I'd ever seen." He had been outside talking to a small group. The band had finished and I'd seen Ginny, Carol, Colin and Jim off. I stopped outside near the door and didn't really eavesdrop as much as catch a snatch of conversation. "You notice the difference all the colas and sweets have made."

Ita called me over. She was talking to Aine who was smoking.

"Great party," I said.

"Ah, but you missed my gender-bender party," said Aine.

"Now that was good *craic*," Ita added.

"You missed Colin in drag. His melons kept falling onto the floor."

I spied Linda and saw Ita and Aine anew. Despite the ratio of men to women they didn't have steady boyfriends. Being nurses they were used to wearing little make-up. In public the Arabs insisted upon modesty. Therefore whilst there were no clowns, a party was a great opportunity to doll oneself up. The girls were not ugly, although Aine was sturdy and matronly. She lacked femininity and walked like a farming woman. I think the main reason these girls were alone was because they did not flirt. Only serious offers would be considered. And I think the nurses drew strength from one another as much as from any catholic faith. Like the Filipinos they were not easy to read. They had the cultural cover of numbers that almost rendered them individually inaccessible. And if there was any hanky-panky it was carried out with the utmost discretion. Not an easy feat out here.

Linda was their antithesis. She oozed sexuality. When she entered the room wrapped in a bed-sheet like an off-the-shoulder toga I felt the band miss a note. A bed-sheet would normally be formless, but she'd pinned it to flaunt the long sheen of an athletic leg as she strode. Only bubble-wrap could have been more provocative. Gillian's negligee covering bikini appeared vulgar by comparison, Ita's T-shirt and night robe were sexless, Aine's nightshirt formless and my own pyjamas lost their appeal.

To see Linda in action was to watch a professional. Her smile was perfectly coquettish and you could see it beguile the men. I knew she scorned the pious nurses. More, she believed that they were no better than her, simply not as obvious, and therefore more scheming than righteous. But she was a Lucrezia Borgia and this was her world and how she saw people. Hurt, laughter, everything was a tool to be used. Under extreme circumstances tears would also be wielded. That was how one kept in control. She was a marathon runner putting as many men between her and her loneliness. And as a runner she snatched up the plastic cups extended her way, gulped down some of the contents, experiencing fleeting refreshment, moving on, preparing to reach for the next. If she could, she would crush the cup, wanting to test its strength, before discarding it. All the time she was on the move: a fugitive from her self.

* * *

We boarded one of the two air-conditioned coaches at midday to take us to the Al-Qara caves. (Also known as Ghar al-Nashshab: "The cave where the arrow maker worked.") This was our lunchtime pause. We'd stopped for an hour at 6:00 am at Abqaiq to breakfast and pickup sandwiches and newcomers, so by then we were starving.

We had an hour here before being transported to the Potter's Caves. I remember wondering at the lush palm trees I assumed to be date. Their density was overwhelming and when I looked carefully I could see regularity. "Saudi is self-sufficient in wheat and by next year it'll be eggs, milk, meat and poultry," Bob had once said. Saudi Arabia would become a major exporter of fruit and vegetables. Such variety meant the date was no longer the staple of the Saudi diet. Nevertheless, the country would command one tenth of the world's production in date palms. A substantial amount would go to international aid.

We entered the caves and for a time I found myself alone with Jim. The way Carol handled him I thought a ring through the nose more suitable than the stud in his ear. Like Ginny I didn't totally blame her. She would snap at him: "Jim, if you are going to be pseudo sophisticated at least pronounce it properly and not in that lazy American drawl." And when he said: "have a nice day," she said: "Sometimes you're so irritating. You know I hate that." Jim was not timid; he was just not as brash or confident as the Brits. Jim wore brightly coloured socks. They'd glow at his ankles, adding an iconoclastic dimension to his otherwise conventional dress. For that short time in the caves I grew to appreciate that he was not a weak person. As if he knew exactly what he was doing with Carol, generously sacrificing himself for her confidence. And his altruism was truly generous. Being American made him socially opaque to me. He required more time. Perhaps the Irish, the Filipinos and these Americans demanded more time because one is better at gauging character within the parameters of one's own society.

"I'm not going in there," Carol had said at the entrance.

Jim had answered: "the best way to beat a phobia is to meet it head-on."

"Don't talk crap."

Ginny and Colin broke away with a suddenness that rooted me to the spot.

"I'll protect you," Jim offered.

"I feel safe already."

So Carol waited for us outside. Contrasting this abrasion, on the journey back to Dhahran she lay her head in his lap and he stroked her hair.

"There goes the slag, sorting out her screws for the week." This was the vile comment I caught as I was returning to the party. The two men were watching Linda. I didn't know either of them but that didn't stop me giving the speaker my best withering look.

Geoff had the same attitude as Linda and differed only in gender, yet he was a stud, a romantic figure, a Giacomo Casanova and she a slag, an abused figure, a nameless prostitute.

I would have loved to have known what had taken place between Linda and Geoff. In such confines their rapacious magnetisms could not have avoided an encounter. Presumably it had been a challenge, each seeking the demise of the other. At best they would have established that like poles repel and gone their separate ways.

The serpentine caves were like mountains cut vertically, prized apart and allowed to fall back together again. On the sketched map the dead-ends and place-names such as rat passage and bat passage did not entice me, but I was not claustrophobic and wanted to see the large area called the Majalis and get passed Fat Man's Squeeze.

"You shouldn't blame Carol too much." I didn't know I had, but presumably he'd sensed my reserve. "She's just insecure. I think she had a rough time as a kid."

"I don't dislike her, Jim. I think she doesn't like me." He made to protest. "Oh, she accepts me, but that's not quite the same thing, is it?"

* * *

The doom-merchant was standing alone at the bottom of the

stairs. Above the music of the stereo I asked him whether he recognised me. It had gone twelve and Ita had proposed leaving in fifteen minutes. "Martin's desperately interesting when you get him on his own," she had said. Ginny had agreed and I was flabbergasted. I'd neither avoided nor actively sought him out. The opportunity to catch him alone simply presented itself.

"Of course I recognise you." He didn't appear too drunk. "Let's face it; there are not too many female faces to commit to memory."

His attire was a token effort: a mask and snorkel dangling under his chin appeared to be there for the practical reason of catching any runaway drops of alcohol rather than for the party's theme. He was predominantly in brown. I unconsciously noted that whereas most had a multicoloured wardrobe his contained only autumnal shades, as if his summertime had passed. There were no screaming scarlets or loud lemons; his was not a passionate autumn.

"I even recall our conversation," he said.

"Three types of people?"

"Yes." He looked critically at the dancers, forcing me to do the same, as if willing me to see through his dark eyes. "Baying hounds anxiously craving morsels of affection."

I wanted to laugh, but anger came instead. "Were you always so negative or did you grow like that?"

"Buddhism says existence is pain." Then he laughed heartily. "No, it's the evil brew that makes me like that." He had opted out of the game and in so doing knew there was no chance of scoring. He was wrestling with a self-imposed celibacy and he was suffering. I knew that he and Noel flew to Bangkok on a regular basis. I had heard of some of these lads marrying Thai girls to get Aramco married status, receive better housing and qualify for more company-paid flights. Bachelors were entitled to only one paid flight a year.

What I was then about to say was lost to the yelp. Linda had given a short scream and although I spun round all I saw was a bunch of men at the entrance. Word quickly went round that somebody called Kieran had grabbed her by the hair. For whatever reason it sounded to me as if he wanted to drag her off caveman style. He didn't get very far. Men were upon him. They pushed and manhandled him. One of the most assertive was the one who had made the vile "there she goes" comment. Ita and Mary O. tried to avert a lynching.

The music continued and thwarted muted conversation.

Nevertheless talk was sober, the aftermath of shock, as if the eye of the roaring hurricane, an eye of clarity, were passing over us. What really returned the party on course was Pinball's sudden raucous laugh. Not quite a laugh at a funeral, but almost as ripping.

Linda and Kieran never returned, only the half dozen gallant Galahads filtered back.

I learned on the drive home with Ita that Kieran regarded himself as Linda's boyfriend. Linda seemed unsure of his presumed status but played along. He was "a really nice guy" and his action was completely out of character. He was shadowing the marathon runner: traversing a parallel course or taking back-street short cuts. For her part, she was amused and drank from his insistent cup again and again. The intimate flavour appealed but the drink did not slake. Either she could not bring herself to crush him or he would not be put down and continually sprung back into shape.

Martin could have gloated, instead he commented: "Somerset Maugham said: 'the tropics is a first rate place for second rate people.' The same could be said of here. Except this place is not first rate. These people have lost the plot. That's why they've dropped out. They're looking to each other for guidance. To compound their problems they've come to an environment that doesn't have a map." This was a glimpse into Martin's treasure of knowledge. He was a tabloid reader who secretly felt more comfortable with the broadsheets. More than this he was the Ancient Mariner, sitting on the fringes of life, grabbing the unwitting guest when it suited him. The albatross had long fallen from his neck and he had condemned himself to travelling the expat scene, trying to show them the errors of their ways. One would have had to spend a lot of time with him to hear of his albatross, in itself probably banal, the journey providing the interest. "Don't think I'm putting myself above them. I'm here for the money too. But I know one thing that a lot of them don't." He paused. "Aristotle Onassis encapsulated it." He stopped again, this time to recall the wording. "'A rich man is very often a poor man with lots of money.'" I wasn't given time to react to this quotation.

"Stop bleating." This was Geoff's banishing line and the effect was immediate: Martin mumbled something to the effect of refreshing his cup and was gone. Strange to think that these two were friends. Behind closed doors they probably had a lot in common. The same could not be said of their dress. The naval disaster had caught Geoff at the roulette or flapjack tables. He was in a black tuxedo with a bow tie upon white shirt. The bow tie was now undone and the shirt open at the neck, making him look untidy and half-dressed. Yet, in style he remained the most suave and over-dressed person in the room. Again, I was reminded of a dapper public schoolboy, this time impersonating the Las Vegas singer condescendingly mingling with the crowd.

"So, how are you doing Racquel?" My Aramco i.d. was a camp-wide secret. The bush drums worked exceptionally well here.

He was a head taller than me and I had to look at his throat. His Adam's apple was a bulge that slid like a mouse under a carpet.

"How long are you staying this time?"

"Another week." I had squared it earlier that evening with Mike, during our once every second evening telephone call.

"There are a few places on the dive trip to Jana Island."

"I'm not a member of BSAC." The mouse moved up and then down.

He leant against the wall and took his weight from a leg, extending one and bending the other. The effect was to bring his eye-level to a nose above mine. Untypical for a man he looked me in the eye. Geoff's eyes were piercing, almost hypnotic like a cat's. They betrayed his slouching indifference and their inchoate brightness tried to evoke a fire. He sipped his drink and the mouse was a prisoner, confined to a few paces.

"I think we could make an exception," he smiled.

I couldn't help smiling too. Most of my friends were going on next Thursday's adventure. My smile gave me away and I needed to balance my joy.

"I can't dive," I said foolishly. He was the almighty director and I was a vulnerable hopeful on the casting couch. The role he was casting tonight was that of bed companion.

In retrospect I should have been big enough to give him a verbal pasting. But appearance does have an effect. I was not wobbly at the knees, but I was intimidated by his killing looks as much as his reputation for devouring women. His presentation alone was the difference between a fine and a poor calling card. Everyone has a tick and my final visual judgement rested on shoes. Martin wore trainers, as did most of the lads, if not open-toed sandals. Surprisingly Noel wore brogues. Geoff was in shiny, black, hand-made Italian shoes. But then anything else with his attire would have been ridiculous.

"You can snorkel," he said, pausing to reassess me.

I nodded and wondered how I could redeem myself. He was toying with me like a ball of wool, nonchalantly looking for a loose end, or simply waiting for me to unravel on my own accord.

Time was my ally. He was nowhere near pulling out his price tag when Ita said that it was time to leave.

"You're leaving?" he managed.

"Afraid so. I have to be up at 4:30 for Hofuf -"

I had to board the bus at the rear of the main dining hall before its 5:00 am departure.

"Oh, that's a waste of time." Handling loss was not part of his repertoire.

"I've not been."

"Hardly seems worth going to bed." I admired his tenacity.

"I need my beauty sleep." Considering it was almost one o'clock it would be a meagre dosage of beauty. He would have an answer to this too, but I did not wait to hear it. "You can put me down for the Jana trip, though."

Anoud

I have never liked hospitals. The deliberate inconspicuousness of the patients gingerly walking on verrucas or using immobility as camouflage always puts me on edge. It is as though they think meekness can give complications the slip. And in stark contrast: the staff with their no nonsense step and brusque healthiness. Finally there is the inoffensive decoration that fails in its attempt to alleviate the sterility of the place and one is left with an insipid supermarket feel.

Mike's hospitalisation meant I didn't go on the Jana dive trip. Wednesday's party and Thursday's cultural trip left Friday relatively quiet. I spent the day with Ginny and Colin. We got up late and idled the day away. For the evening I insisted on treating them to a meal at a restaurant of their choice. We ended up at the Oberoi in Khobar. The quality of restaurants varied, but the absence of alcohol reduced competition to food and most hotels offered impeccable cuisines.

We talked of Linda's yelp and the psychological effect of being cooped up. I'd heard from numerous sources that Kieran was a decent chap, as if what had happened rested entirely with Linda, leading into speculation on her carryings-on. I remember Jim once commenting: "Somebody forgot to tell her that the set for the rich-bitch soap is next door."

On-camp life offered an exhilarating state of flux that I'd only experienced at university. However, experience was a defining factor. These singles creeping to end of their twenties had had relationships or The Relationship. And the pressure of life out here was causing seepages. Colin encapsulated the feeling when he said he wanted to write a book. He was a science fiction fan, and during our diagnosis of the party we spoke of Gillian, he said: "I wouldn't say she's clinging but have you seen the film *Alien*?" He raised a hand, put his thumb in mouth and spread his fingers over his face. Ginny elbowed him. Colin's off-world novel would have humans mining some mineral or other. Because of the suffocating humidity they would be confined to buildings. Only the native aliens could move about freely. They were aqua-creatures with gills like flowing sails at the sides of their heads resembling Siamese fighting-fish and were known as flag-heads by the humans. Multinational efforts held abuse in check and the aliens were rewarded and treated amicably. Colin had thought out the inter-human possibilities and extra-terrestrial relationships. "Extremes bond," he explained, "like soldiers under fire." He admitted the video series *Vietnam* in the camp library had tempered his ideas. "Even the sprinklers here remind me of the phut-phut of helicopters over the jungles of Vietnam." The sprinklers were of the rocker-type used at tennis courts. Ginny chipped in: "You understand his love of *The Stones* and *The Doors*."

On Saturday I spent some time in the library. I met Ginny after work and we returned to her apartment to get our gear for aerobics. The phone was ringing before she opened the door.

Her face was stricken as she handed the receiver to me.

In keeping with our calling every other day I had not planned on speaking with my husband this evening. We had talked yesterday before I left for the restaurant. Our conversation had irritated me. Mike had appeared strangled like a hostage under kidnappers. I mentioned it and his hesitation gave him away, but he just said: "I'm just tired."

"Hi Dawn." It was Ian. "Look, Mike's had an accident. He's okay, but he's in hospital." He went on to explain what had happened and although I listened I did not fully take in what he said.

My lack of comprehension was obvious when I tried to relate the accident to Ginny. She phoned Colin and an hour later we were on the open road. Colin deposited me at the farm just over an hour and a half later and an hour after that, Ian waited for me in the car park of Riyadh's King Faisal Specialist Hospital. On the way to the hospital he was strange. His eyes were sparkling and manic. He repeated that he'd been trying to reach me since yesterday. I sensed guilt and moved away. Returning to the car park after visiting my husband I knew of his culpability in the accident and I was irritated by his gentleness. Before sinking into an awkward silence, he tried to tackle my irritation with banalities.

I found my husband propped up in bed in bland hospital pyjamas. His face was unmarked, but bandage was visible below his neck. We pecked lips. He smiled but he knew better than to claim that it was nothing. Nonetheless he apologised for pulling me back to the farm and I reproached him. I'd been away a good week, so it wasn't like breaking a leg on the first day of a skiing holiday. I held his hand, feeling for limpness and not finding any. I'd already heard about the accident but I wanted to hear about it from him.

Ian and Mike were at the infamous number seventeen with its built-in rice paddy. Sparky, Tass and Ian had earlier run into trouble carrying out some routine maintenance. Ian and Mike now had it ready to run but it shorted and died. Mike sent Ian to fetch Sparky. At this point everything became about as clear as mud to me. Between the engine gearbox and the pump gearbox was a connecting shaft the lads referred to as the PTO, the power take-off. Mike saw the problem and got the power going again, but he decided to await Ian's return before attempting to engage the gear drive. He said something about differing revolutions per minute. When he saw the dust of an approaching vehicle, he assumed it to be Ian and against his better judgement, he decided to have it up and running before he arrived. Sparky's wiring wasn't quite up to the mark and Mike got a shock. His chest slammed against the machinery before flinging him some seven metres. If he'd got entangled in the shaft he would have sustained more severe injuries. As it was he landed face down in the pool and was still unconscious when he was dragged from it a short time later.

The person coming out to him was not Ian. He'd popped into the kitchen with Sparky for a non-alcoholic beer. It was Abdul. The old Saudi saved my husband's life.

Mike wanted diversion and asked me about Aramco. But this was one of those times when all else paled and I mumbled something about having a good time. He'd already heard a lot during our telephone conversations. He was interested in the cultural trip but we never really left the subject of the accident. He didn't want my anger or sorrow and at one time I found myself joking.

"You certainly had a good go at trying to top yourself. Electrocution, trying to grind yourself in a mincer and then drowning."

"Don't make me laugh," he retorted, holding his sides in cramped laughter. He was badly bruised and had two broken ribs. The doctor had said he was lucky not to have punctured a lung. Nonetheless they wanted to keep him for another night. They feared he would go back to work if discharged.

We were silent for a moment but he had more to say.
"There's something else I have to tell you. Ian swapped his day off with Scab." It was a false start and he repositioned himself. "Ian and Pav went to an execution on Friday. And before you ask, yes, Ian recorded it."

* * *

"I thought the next time we'd meet, it'd be at Heathrow," my father begins as we disengage.

I smile weakly. But he is weaker. My God, I am the one

suffering. I'm in isolation. Then I'm ashamed of myself. His humour is of course a smoke screen I'd long ago learnt to circumvent.

"So did I." I exhale, dispersing the smoke.

"Why?"

"If you're caged in a zoo you're liable to act like an animal." It was a line I have been practising in my head. Since the fight I've been held in isolation. Lots of time to think. And that's the best I can come up with. What a state. I realise something else is troubling him. "What's wrong?"

He dare not turn away or put up obstacles. Instead he pretends not to hear.

"Dad? Is it Mum?"

He crumbles and suddenly looks old. My silence is insistent. "She's not good. All this worry. You can understand that."

I nod. My mind's eye visualising her forlorn silences. Reels and reels of old incidents are mounted and made ready to run.

"You've got to get out of here. This place is destroying you. Look what you've become. Sign what they want." He interprets my silence as stubbornness. "Does it matter what's true?"

I should have anticipated the question and I am caught off-guard. "What about Mike?" Saying his name after all this time is like pointing torchlight into the recesses of my mind. And although my aim is true, simply through familiarity, I waver and the light falls upon hideous attachments that come swarming from the deep. The reels play, but they're not from my childhood. A sleight of hand has swapped them with more recent material. A horrific face, bloated with anger. "Run, run. Dawn, run." I am overwhelmed and close my eyes and scramble for the shutdown lever before meltdown occurs.

Dad pulls me clear. "Wouldn't your safety be more important to him? He'd put that before the truth."

I know that I am not in danger or that the only danger to me is myself. But I cannot argue against him. My only thought is outrage that Mike be used in such a way. He is dead. Let him be. And yet, it was I who brought up his name.

I fall apart and tumble into my father's arms. I'm nodding, although deep down I'm still unsure of my convictions.

* * *

I knew Ginny had phoned Masstock a few days after my return, but it was almost a week later before I was ready to speak to her. By then my husband was back on the farm and pulling almost his full weight. Of course the day after his release he didn't sit still, he was out driving a harvester or whatever. Thankfully he didn't lift anything. We spoke about Mike and then Ginny told me of the Jana dive trip.

"You can look at Colin's photos when you next come."

"You could photograph?"

"No." I felt her smile. "Geoff wrote no cameras on the trip sheet. Harbour control and all that. Colin wrapped his in silver foil with his sandwiches in his Tupperware lunch-box."

"The old fox," I laughed.

She expected me to speak when I quietened down. When I didn't she asked: "You're not getting down, are you?"

"No, not really." I considered before going on. "Do you remember before we went to the Oberio I spoke to Mike? Good. Well, there was a reason for his behaviour. Ian and Pav had been to an execution that lunchtime. And yes, he recorded it." I was in anticipation mode. "And no, I haven't seen it. Of course Mike's worried. I think the boys here - Masstock - have it. I don't know. Ian's assured Mike he's got a good hiding place. It's put a terrible strain on the farm. There's a horrible distrust." I couldn't convey atmosphere on the farm. "We were originally told we'd be out here for six months, we're into our tenth. I told Mike that I wouldn't spend another Christmas on the farm. I'd go home."

* * *

Naturally the two men were affected in different ways. Ian most visibly. He drew into himself. The depression at the cradle of his brow, eased after his vacation, deepened under the weight of his troubled mind. His eyes darkened. I could almost understand his talk of going to an execution. Putting it down to boredom. But to actually go was another thing. Curiosity could have driven Pav, but Ian was the sensitive type. Was this the same person who'd swapped paperbacks with me, who'd read *One thousand and one nights*, who'd been jilted and hurt by a girl? He could only have wanted to prove something to himself.

When I first saw him when he took me to hospital to see Mike his eyes were manic. He was having trouble digesting what he had seen. Now his eyes were dull coals that lacked lustre. His preoccupation was over but he was devastated.

Pav absorbed the experience into his stoic bulk. His change was not as obvious. If anything his crab-like armour thickened. The benign frog became a smirking toad.

Of course, these were the long-term effects. In Ian's case an inner devastation grew ever more thinly disguised. Initially he put on an ill-fitting brave face. He'd glue it with jokes and an opinionated interest in the farm that according to Mike was lent voice before reason. Ian's decisions and commands were frequently flawed. And the harder he tried the more he erred. His duress showed in his slipping face.

He was also smug. Smug in the belief that I was yearning to know what had happened and that he was not going to tell me. As time passed he realised I was not going to inquire and through ever more blatant enquiries of his own, he discovered that Mike had not told me what had happened. He found my lack of interest incomprehensible. He was burning to share the burden with me. Especially me. For I should care about his suffering. And he kept pushing his Pandora's box under my nose. My statements about not being interested grew ever more caustic. In time his smile became a grimace: his smug expression a stricken one.

Yet, part of me felt sorry for him. My stance was on the reasonably firm ground of ignorance. If I had truly wanted to help him I would have had to understand what he went through. But I was repelled by the effect it had upon him and wanted no part of it. So I could not help him.

* * *

We ignored the strain by becoming exaggeratedly independent. The British stiff upper lip set in. I got back into my stride. My Aramco time had rejuvenated me. My husband's recovery and a new-found intimacy born out of his brush with death, and our united front against Ian's video empowered and sustained us.

I went jogging in the evenings, my Walkman pacing and accompanying me. The isolation allowed me to lip-synch the singer aloud. My accompaniment rarely reached my imaginative heights, but that didn't deter me from trying.

I rediscovered my journal and my sanctuary in the old greenhouse. Almost everything that transpired at Aramco I put to paper and in so doing subjected it to further analysis. I did not enter my feelings about Geoff. Like Mike at the pivot head, sometimes one acts contrary to one's better judgement. When I left Geoff, affected by the *sid* and my triumphant escape, I had to muster all my energy to resist giving him a consolatory kiss.

* * *

Out of the blue Mike and I were invited to Abdul's demountable. The relationship between the old Saudi and us had, until then, been a strictly working one. He and Mike had conversed when necessary. I think he kept us at arm's length because of his experience with Bob. But rescuing Mike had brought the two men closer.

I was excited and expectant all day. I should have known that I would be separated from my husband. He greeted Mike and ushered him into what I took to be the lounge. I was treated only to a glimpse of the room. He led me to the other end of the building into the room he used as an office. Apart from his clean-swept desk and leather swivel chair there were two couches sandwiching a coffee table: his conference area. On the couch against the wall sat a black enshrouded woman.

"My wife, Anoud," said Abdul.

"*Merhaba*," I managed, still in a state of shock. I think she nodded.

The moment he closed the door on us, she removed her *abaaya*. Her intoxicating beauty stole my breath and riveted me to the spot. Apart from the kohl about her eyes she appeared to be wearing no make-up. Her youth should have made her pretty but she was more than this; she had a potential beauty, a voluptuousness like a young Sophia Loren. And she could have been a gypsy. She had strong Chinese-black hair, but full of bounce, almost unruly. I put her in her early twenties, certainly younger than me, making her at least half her husband's age. Whilst he was no hunchback she could certainly be Esmerelda. I later noticed her man-like hands and was no longer sure of her age. Her dress was plain and low cut and tailored. All her jewellery was silver. A Koranic amulet sat at her cleavage and simple bangles adorned her wrists. I spied an ankle bracelet too.

She beckoned me to sit opposite her, and swung her legs off the ground and folded them under herself.

I came out of shock and exhausted my Arabic vocabulary by using the second word I knew. "*Shukran.*"

She was doubtlessly bemused that I should thank her for proffering a seat.

I promptly established that she didn't speak any English. All my expectations at gaining an insight into their culture were dashed. Our conversation was as barren as the landscape in which we found ourselves. A Tarzan-and-Jane introduction killed a good two minutes, but that was early on.

I accepted coffee from the pot on the table and dared to try one of the cold meat pastries. They were delicious, but I'd already eaten and I treated a second piece like a radioactive isotope: consuming it half-bites.

I was being self-centred for it was as much an ordeal for her too. There were many silences filled with embarrassed smiles. Then one of us would hit upon possible connection and become Italian, excitedly gesturing; charades without the rules. We'd repeatedly strike key words in our native tongues as if hammering away would aid comprehension. We'd give up, exhausted, grateful of the deserved silence, hoping it would last before giving way to emptiness again. Then we'd once more scour our minds, mindful of the language barrier, foraging the cultural ravine between us for something to share.

There was plenty of time to scrutinise my surroundings. That said, it was an act of betrayal to let the eyes wander, as if admitting to having given up foraging, having given up on each other.

Unsurprisingly Abdul's tipple was not in evidence. The bottle of liquor or whatever I had seen was nowhere in sight.

A picture of the King had a wall to itself and a calendar hung elsewhere. The room resembled the makeshift office of a used-car sales lot. There was not the chaos, but the same utilitarian feel.

I noticed the expensive shoes she'd removed. They were stilettos. After seeing them I would be forever drawn to the shoes of the veiled women in Riyadh. Many hinted at rebellion. At least my western viewpoint took it to be rebellion.

Her Koranic amulet was of simple design and I wanted to ask her about it. Was it to ward off evil spirits? To bring good luck? I had no idea. We hadn't even established an alphabet and asking about it would be to ask for a thesis in joined-up writing.

Seeing how beautiful Anoud was, for some reason brought back Ginny's *Death of a Princess* comment: "You know they say that the princess wasn't executed. They say a Bedouin was bought and sacrificed in her place."

I thought I'd kept the distance out of my eyes when I saw her looking at me. Caught out, I could only smile.

There was no escape for either of us. We were there because our menfolk wanted an evening together. Why hadn't Abdul left Anoud at home? Maybe it was Anoud's idea? A break from sitting at home. As I saw it, it was a case of out of the frying pan and into the fire.

At one point we heard movement outside and in a flash Anoud was veiled up. Far from leaving one of the men had gone to the toilet. The flush of the cistern gave us again cause to smile.

Somehow we endured two and a half hours together.

* * *

"The Arabs have that hillbilly attitude to women," said Ian, after I'd spoken of my ordeal. Our attentiveness was his spur. "Keep 'em ignorant, barefoot and pregnant."

Pav grunted and Sparky smiled to himself. Tass and Scab had already retired.

"She must be half his age," I went on. "Maybe as young as sixteen."

"She's probably older than you think," said Mike. He would tell me that she was twenty-five. "He probably didn't marry her because of love."

"Lust," said Ian.

Mike shook his head. "Not even that. The tribal mentality is ingrained in their culture. Marriage is an alliance. A business arrangement."

I was not convinced. "I'm sure if she'd not been a sweet young thing he'd not have married."

"I didn't dispute the fact that it's a patriarchal society. I just said tribalism lends itself to arranged marriages. The group before the individual. I believe you can say no, today."

"Really?" I asked.

"I think so. But it's rare. Nobody wants to lose face. There's probably a lot of sounding out." He'd run into some kind of cul-de-sac and chose a side-alley. "There are advantages to arranged marriages, you know." He paused. "You don't have to go through all the heartache of failed relationships -"

"You just have heartache with the big one," said Ian.

"Maybe," Mike smiled and threw me a glance before continuing. "But in the big one you make a bit more of an effort. You compromise." He waited a moment. "There's also the fact that because of the importance of the family the parents know their children and have a better understanding of the suitability of a partner. Let's face it, they want their children to be happy."

"Does it work like that?" I questioned. "I mean when they're older? Or are they married off as babies?"

"Possibly a bit of both."

Then he looked at me. "You hit it on the head when you said it's like a landed gentry type marrying a gypsy. If she is a Bedouin there's a cultural disparity between them."

"Is she his only wife?" asked Ian. Until this question Ian had not really been with us. He'd talked to us, but not with us. As if his presence could be interpreted as allegiance, he talked from behind a shell that was mainly composed of arrogance. I denied him the benefit of seeing how much his attitude infuriated me. I think he knew. But this was part of the game. The loser was the first one to admit unease.

"Yes," said Mike. "Most Arabs can't afford more."

"Having up to four is discriminatory," I said.

"Historical," said Ian. "Mohammed wanted the war widows taken care of."

"It's not applicable today," I said.

"Take the Iran-Iraq war," Mike offered.

* * *

"Has anybody a key to the locked storeroom in the workshop?" My husband had waited until everyone had finished eating before asking. I'm sure Ian noticed that Mike and I were solemn during dinner. Not so much quiet as holding something back. Mike was working up a necessary anger to broach the subject. I was the silent partner. I knew his irritation and being the instigator of the imminent ill will I was meek.

At first nobody answered. Then Ian decided to play spokesman. "No. I think Eddie was the -"

"The door has been opened recently," Mike said flatly and he strained not to look at me. But the others suspected and their glances warmed my neck.

"How do you know?" asked Pav. It was not a challenge.

"I just know."

This was not enough and they relaxed.

"Then I'll break it down," he said rising. Everyone blanched. Even I had not thought he would go so far. He saw our shock. "We can use the room and we can always get a new lock fitted."

Ian brightened. "Maybe we should wait and get a locksmith to open it?"

This made sense but I had warned Mike of their need to stall. Logic dictated that he take up Ian's suggestion, but this went against his pact with me. My husband could find no words and simply left the room.

All eyes turned on me and I was surprised to discover that words failed me too. Sparky got up and went to the kitchen window.

"He's going to the workshop."

They all looked at each other and I knew my presence held them in check.

Emboldened by their confusion I found words. "You'd save him a lot of trouble if you found the key."

I wanted to tell them that I had seen the gouging arc the pebble had made in the concrete floor. Shoe prints in the grime and dirt showed that somebody had tried stamp the line away. Although Mike was sceptical he had agreed to look into it for me.

Still nobody spoke and because I wanted to see what was behind the door I left.

In the courtyard on the way to the workshop I was tempted to turn around and it took all my will to keep my eyes fixed ahead.

Mike was trying to wedge the tongue of a crowbar at the door as I entered. "I know they've got a key." He looked over. "Don't you think it's odd that we're the only one's who are curious about this room?"

He nodded slowly. He was growing angry. He was angry with himself for what he was doing. Angry with me for putting him in this position. Most of all he was angry with them. "You're right." And he pulled on the crowbar and there was a terrible ripping noise. Now he had something upon which to vent his anger.

"Can I help?"

"Bring me that hammer."

We were still prying the door when the others arrived. We glanced at them, giving them a moment to offer the key before going back to the task. They stood helplessly just inside the workshop.

Wood splintered and I grew angry. Mike was red with exertion and wrath. If the others had come to reason, my husband's appearance gagged them.

Suddenly the door was broken and gave up the room. Mike pushed it aside and something glinted in the light from the workshop. He obstructed my view as he searched for the light switch on the inside wall. I stepped closer. A strip-light flickered alarmingly and eventually exposed the room's secret. I gasped.

* * *

I stand at the entrance to our cell. For three weeks I have been in solitary, but even there I felt the terror. Nobody seemed to know what to do. I knew the Arabs would regroup. They would not give up their status so easily. They'd have to make an example of somebody and there was only one person who would do. Me. Anyone else would win them nothing. The guards seemed to know this and that is why I was in solitary longer than necessary.

There was a stalemate in the toilets. Me with the spoon. Raging, ready to take tongues. Scalps weren't possible. Boiled down to a person I don't recognise. Pip on the floor. Before the skirmish could break out into a full-blooded battle or slaughter, depending upon the participation of the Asian population, the guards burst in. I was escorted by two of them to one of the solitary cells near the entrance. My door wasn't locked and I could go to the toilet as and when I wished. Of course there was an ever-present guard at the desk in the corridor. So it wasn't really solitary. I wasn't being punished. I was put out of circulation until they'd defused the situation.

The last time I saw someone in authority, they said they'd put me back with the others as soon as possible. Despite the danger I wanted to be back among my friends. Not to fight with them against the Arabs, but to be with them. I also craved company.

And so now I'm out to a heroine's welcome. No laurels and garlands but honours. I'm being directed to Rita's bunk. It's the top dog position I don't want or deserve. But there is no arguing against their overwhelming insistence.

Enough of the Arabs have been transferred to present no threat. Even Pip is safe. But I have been put in a charlatan's position: a revolver heroine claiming to have hung up her holster. Yet, it is only a matter of time before other gunslingers call me out.

* * *

Mike and I were dazed. Although, my husband was also on the brink of bursting. A countdown had begun during the breaking of the door. He had channelled his anger into the task. Now he was quivering on the brink of ignition. The others were still at the door and if anything they looked depressed. Houston, I think we have a problem.

Why hadn't they given up the key?

This explained everything. It explained their night excursions. It explained various enigmatic incidents such as Sparky hiding when I came from the greenhouse to ask a question. It explained Ian taking the jerrycans to the workshop. "I'm dying for a leak," he had said. And over time it would explain much more.

The still was the copper cylinder of a boiler. Of course it had been adapted. The lower heat supply and return pipes had been plugged and I would learn that the immersion heater had been removed from the top and soldered or welded near the base of the 50 litre cylinder. The lower cold water supply had been fitted with a tap for cleaning. The opening that accommodated the immersion heater was stoppered and used for filling. The outlet at the top, normally to supply hot water, had a copper pipe attached to it. This was diverted through a 25 litre metal chemical container. This too had been modified. Short copper pipes had been soldered to it. Both had rubber pipe attachments. One pipe led to a water tap and the other disappeared into the ground. The copper pipe from the still ended just beyond the length of the chemical container: the condenser. At this end there would have been the receptacles. I saw two demijohns and four boxes of water - maybe it was already *sid*. There were bags of sugar and yeast, rubber tubing and a couple of funnels on some shelving. Also on this shelf was a videocassette.

The hush was cathedral, ghosts of monumental, but now dead convictions murmured from the alcoves. Although the echoes of their thoughts were almost audible the lads did not dare to speak. They were afraid of being incinerated. I wanted to reach out to Mike, to touch his shoulder, but I did not dare. I had rarely seen him angry, but I'd never seen him rocket. Should he do so, it would take an age for him to come back down.

To let off some of his fury, a jet of steam jerked his arm and the crowbar came crashing down to buckle a joining pipe. The sound was physical pain: my husband's frustrated cry. I could feel him trying to find a solution to the problem. The problem was what to do now, what to do with the infernal thing. There was no hiding its use. The workshop offered all manner of cutting tools. But possible remnants of alcohol put that out of the question. I left the solution to my husband. My mind had begun working on the subsequent atmosphere on the farm. The situation was polarised enough by the execution and the accident. Now this.

My husband eloquently solved the problem. He turned to the ragged crew. "Get rid of it."

"Mike," Ian began, "can't we -"

"No."

"Mike," Pav's voice was more authoritative. "I think -"

And then my husband was a frothing monster. "I don't care what you think. You're all bloody idiots. Arrogant, pig-headed idiots. You've endangered us all." He was struggling to express himself and the terror in his voice suddenly ebbed. "I'm disappointed." This could have been a laughable statement, coming from a teacher directed at his pupils, but it struck home. My husband was held in high esteem. He had treated them fairly, even generously, and they had let him down.

He returned his attention to the still. When he spoke his voice was normal but weary. "I want it gone." He did not look at them.

"Mike," Ian began again, his voice as reasonable as possible, yet edged with a plea. "Can't we sleep on it? I mean; it's getting late."

My husband was quiet for a while, but I could see the veins on his neck: the beast rising. "It was never too late to make your deliveries." The contempt in his calmness did not go amiss. There had never been any Bedouin prostitutes. "Get it off the farm. Bury it."

He marched out of the workshop, taking the crowbar with him. The lads didn't part. They were too stunned. All they could do was awkwardly shift out of his way.

I was still for a moment. Then I followed him. Ignoring them as I left.

I don't know whether Mike feared for our safety. I never asked him. But I think he put the crowbar under our bed.

* * *

After the discovery of the still we all sunk into ourselves. As if someone had died, the magnitude of the incident silenced us. And maybe somebody had; maybe friendship had died. Each of us had to come to terms with the consequences. Had all hope of harmony finally died? Or was it trust? Were the others mourning the loss of their extra income more than our friendship? There seemed to be no hope. We all wanted to put the thing behind us. Only time could give us the distance we needed. Perversely, as with our feelings about Ian's video, Mike and I tried to continue as if nothing had happened.

Our position with the Filipinos was relatively unchanged. It had always been a working relationship. For me Ian had become treacherously unpredictable. My husband had no problem keeping up the affable facade, a simple extrapolation of their working relationship. I spent the best part of the day alone or in Pav's company, with little to distinguish between the two. Mealtimes had always been more than times for eating for me. Just as bedtime afforded the chance of private discussion with my husband, so lunch and dinner had been the social high points in my day.

The farm afforded little elbowroom and petty, niggling things would quickly wear me down. Unlike before when they could be aired and so dispensed with, now the atmosphere was too rare to broach them. So I had to absorb the pettiness, itself contributing to the frustration.

The subtle changes in Ian's behaviour taken individually could be ignored, but they had a cumulative effect on me.

We were not churlish, but our actions were childish. For instance Ian suddenly had no time to read the paperback I'd borrowed from Ginny for him. Or I would chose to purchase a cassette tape myself, rather than ask to listen to his copy. Borrowed articles were returned, like expelled diplomats.

There was a rota for washing the dishes, but not for making tea. If I was making myself a cup, I'd offer to make someone else one. Whereas before Ian may have declined and said that he'd love a coffee instead, he simply declined. Then a few minutes later he'd get up and make a coffee or even a tea. If necessary he'd explain that he'd changed his mind. I continued to offer for a while. When he offered to make drinks I accepted. Then I stooped to his level and said I'd make it myself later.

He took to soaking the dishes overnight even when it was not necessary. Rubber gloves and piping hot water were too feminine for him. Then he was sloppy in the washing early next morning and I began to show him his sloppiness. He offered to clean it and sometimes I let him.

More than anything else the toilet seat infuriated me. He'd regressed to leaving the seat up. The smell clamped my jaw. And yet again, I could be accused of being petite bourgeois. All I could do was loudly close it down and use the air freshener.

It was all pathetic, childish, petty, niggling.

* * *

The glacial atmosphere on the farm was ether. And I had no urge to phone Ginny. Perhaps it was shock? We were floundering and dazed in the emotional fallout. The atmosphere was too enormous and too puerile to convey. I didn't have the energy to explain.

Then a short letter from her forced me to plan a trip Masstock to call her.

Reading her missives betrayed the fact that she was a secretary. They were hurriedly written at work, the letterhead giving her away, in organised bullet paragraphs with little embellishment. Shorthand. Their incisive nature was subtly devastating. In their unassuming way the dramas between the lines were kernels that, infuriatingly, could only be furred by my imagination.

She had written that one of the lads had thrown a toga party. She strongly suspected a conspiracy to see Linda in a bed sheet again. Despite having seen Linda only that one time in a sheet, this was how I would always imagine her. In her element, rising out of bed to open her sheet, like Bela Lugosi opening his cloak, to take somebody under it to satisfy her hunger.

Word had gone round too that Kieran had asked her to marry him. She hadn't made up her mind.

Then she wrote that Noel, and this was her buried headline, was being deported. Mr. Hyde had not concealed himself. Reading Ginny's letter made me wonder whether he wanted deportation. He had booked into a Khobar hotel with two litre bottles of cut *sid* for company. Of course he'd not remained in his room. More than six police officers were needed to subdue him.

When I later expressed some sympathy for Noel Colin surprised me with his venom. "He's a chauvinistic yob." Although Colin was also a Martin fan, he had never liked Noel. He told me that when Noel heard of Kieran's marriage proposal he remarked: "Why marry the cow when you can get the milk free?" Possibly Noel was not the big character he would have us believe him be. Perhaps he was a sham and there was no Dr. Jekyll, just a person he'd invented.

Tantalisingly she wrote that when I phone her she would to tell me about a scandal Martin had caused at school.

* * *

It would be perverse to say that I was hurt when Mike alone was invited to Abdul's demountable. I felt, albeit romantically, that our ordeal had established a mutual sympathy between Anoud and I. If Anoud was on the farm - I'd not seen her - then she was realistic rather than romantic and I was relieved and insulted.

We were all in the kitchen, between dinner and bed.

"I wish I had the conversations you do," I said.

"It takes a while to reach this level." In explaining his conversation with Abdul to us, my husband no doubt cut away the time spent reaching an acceptable wavelength.

"I'm afraid our dear Bob upset Abdul in other ways," he continued. Talk of Bob was talk of the holy. One could carefully mock, but not be irreverent. With respect to the atmosphere my husband was treading very thin ice. "One of the first times they spoke to each other was in the lounge."

Sparky nodded.

"Bob put his feet on the coffee table, showing Abdul his soles. It's a great insult in the Arab world."

"He wasn't to know," protested Ian.

"Probably not," Mike smiled. "But he didn't get off on the right foot, did he?"

My husband's humour jarred and Ian spoke impulsively.

"You're pulling our legs."

Groans and smiles from the Filipinos were followed by queries as to the truth of sole showing. There was always something naïve about their humour. They were quick to laugh, easily humoured. It was at once delightful and irritating for its simplicity. Despite the appearance of levity Mike had unwittingly sledge hammered the bruise between himself and the lads. In showing an understanding of Abdul he effectively drew away from them. When speaking of Arabs, jibes and complaints were in, distant fascination tolerated, but understanding was tantamount to changing sides.

Everyone was trying too hard to be normal.

Until this evening and this conversation our talk had been strictly business. There had been little humour and this evening was a first stab at loosening the tension. I felt it going terribly wrong. My husband's talk with Abdul gave us neutral material for conversation. But the lines he delivered were ill chosen.

"I'm not bothered if I never have to converse with another rag head," Ian said suddenly. "They're a crazy bunch." His brashness was uncharacteristic and he blanched under the shock of it. "On the one hand they're all politeness and generosity and on the other scheming and tribal. Then they're upset if you insult or drive them into a corner. You try nailing one down to a firm decision. And then they can be all macho. I tell you they're schizos, the lot of them." Listening to him I felt he was imitating Bob. There were echoes of Merv there too.

"Tribalism lays down hard and fast rules," said Mike.

"If you use that word again I think I'll scream," I said, hoping to ease the strain, but knowing I was making it worse.

"What?" he asked. "Tribalism?"

I made to scream and he put his hand over my mouth. This was another thing that separated Mike from the others. Necessarily, touch was reserved for our room and his handling me rubbed their noses in our intimacy. I pushed him brusquely away as if he'd smeared my makeup. I wasn't wearing any.

He smiled uncertainly and carried on regardless. "You can't pin them down because they don't work like us."

"Leave out: like us," Ian suggested, "and I'll agree with you."

Merv's words came to mind. "They don't think like us. They don't agree to deadlines because they might not meet them. And they don't want an awkward situation."

I began looking for a mercy killing.

"Shirkers," said Sparky, Bob's word sounding strange coming from him. Mike had lost the Filipinos too.

"No," said Mike. "They'll get it done, but in their own time."

"They don't want to take on responsibility," said Ian. "Because if they did, they'd be answerable and made to feel guilty."

"Worse than that, they'd risk shame." My husband was undeterred. "They'd lose face or *Wajh* and that's something they try to avoid." He paused. "Their language, the basis for thinking, does not fit with the western business world."

"Well if they still believe in Scheherazade, Sinbad and Saladin, then God - or maybe a genie - help them."

Mike smiled. He'd given up. I wanted to hear more, but understood that Ian insurgency would sabotage all structure at foundation level. He'd assumed the role of sapper, bearing the standard of western thought and although not waging open war he was subversive. To be heard above the sound of his prejudice, he'd have to be taken alone, strapped down and made to listen. To do this would be a declaration of war on our part. Funny, a few months ago I would have taken his blithe demolition for wit.

"I'm bushed," said my husband and I was tempted to say bushwhacked. My relief was palpable and we exchanged smiles that defeated the others.

We were the first to leave.

From then on our meetings with the Arabs were never discussed with the others. Enquires, however made, were deflected with a few dismissive words. Kitchen discussion rarely strayed into the controversial and as such lacked essential substance. It often slipped into the banal: the levity we'd nurtured through familiarity.

Such conversation was then the preserve of our room. We covered so much ground I even shied from speaking of it to Ginny. It was too rich a topic for the poor medium of the telephone line.

"Okay," began Mike after I prompted him. "I'll substitute Bedouin values for that 'T' word."

"They're not Bedouins anymore," I said, making myself comfortable on the bed.

"Not physically."

And we spoke of the Bedouin legacy, relating it to what we had personally experienced. Slowly, ever so slowly, we prized an opening in the clamped crustacean-like shell of the Arab world.

Merv worked with computers. The very nature of his work demanded precision: one or zero, yes or no, on or off. He worked at the heart of the industrialised world: far from Nature, far from the land, far from familial concerns and tribal responsibilities, far from emotions too. His work, work with machines, automated him. He linked up to the machine to become a node. I remembering him saying that it sounded dangerously like nerd.

He said he too thought the Arabs were not lazy. He said they weren't bothered. Driven would have been a better word. As if they had all the time in the world the concept of a deadline was foreign. Why should one overtax oneself? "What will be will be." Their concept of time was other than ours and its roots lay in the past.

Our Gregorian calendar is not absolute in its precision, being one day out in 3000 years, but to all intents and purposes our sense of time is anchored to Mother Nature. December is always winter. Conversely the Arab calendar is lunar and gallops through the seasons. Against our calendar it is eleven days earlier each year. The Arab sense of time floats freely. This coupled with their language and tendency to hyperbole does not easily admit absolutes.

"When do you think you'll have the program ready?" Merv had asked his Arab colleague. "You can't pin them down," he told me. "And when you force a date on them, they pale as if you've insulted them." He'd not insulted them, but he was being antagonistic, boxing their honour with jabs straight to the face.

He had been wrong to think they weren't motivated because

they were rich or that the expats were there to do the work. Of course these two things didn't help. But there were deeper reasons.

"I'll see you tomorrow afternoon to discuss such and such," Abdul had told Bob. Bob had sacrificed his day off to meet him and Abdul hadn't turned up. Of course Bob didn't lose his day off; he took it later. "Unreliable," he said to me. "Typical Arab." But when an Arab says he'll see you tomorrow afternoon he doesn't necessarily mean the next day, but in the next couple of days. If he'd given a date and a time, written it down, told you again in no uncertain terms, he may have turned up. Abdul's arrangement had not been specific or binding, it had been a suggestion, equating to "Perhaps I'll see you tomorrow afternoon."

Arabic is an art form. And the Arabs are enamoured by their language. It is elaborate and poetic and renders English a series of blunt utterances. Even Arab statesmen, those who have had much to do with the West, have tried to delight by presenting an English communiqué in verse.

"You are an American?" This was the time I was caught alone on the street after visiting a traditional Najd house in Riyadh. His English was accented but good and his crisp suit said he was an Arab businessman.

And then he began his bombardment of compliments that drove me to rudeness. "I'm not interested," I snarled viciously. He seemed genuinely shocked. Yet, at the time I didn't believe it.

Now, through Mike's insight I saw that he *was* shocked. In giving him short answers to his advances I had not discouraged him. One could say I had encouraged him. For what I considered politeness, he mistook for interest. Had I said: "I am married and I am not in the least bit interested in having coffee with you, today, tomorrow or in the next ten years" I may have been understood. This circus ringmaster exaggeration would be interpreted as neurosis in my world, but in theirs such emphasis was necessary to be understood. A simple yes or no would not do, for yes and no were not emphatic and could be interpreted as imprecise.

Finally, the lack of variety in the landscape, the downright hardship, was made up for in tales. Incidents became legends. Storytelling and anecdote were cornerstones to the immediate and extended family. People ware adorned with personalities of panoramic proportions.

Exaggeration, poetic or otherwise, was their form of communication.

Language was to blame.

* * *

Ginny and I talked of the still. "I don't know whether they buried it, but by morning it was gone. Only the shelving and empty bottles and buckets remained."

When my husband had returned to Earth we mused over the logistics of running it. He said that the temperature would have been strictly controlled and I remembered Ian admonishing Sparky. "You can't get sloppy about this. Between eighty-four and eighty-six. That's it." All the clues had been there. "I've made my million anyway," Bob had said. Of course he had spoken figuratively. Their modest operation had supplied Merv and Den and Masstock. And Ian said that since our arrival they had drastically reduced production.

"You said in your letter that Martin caused trouble."

Ginny explained that during his Physics lesson Martin had explained that shooting stars were meteorites entering the Earth's atmosphere. He had contradicted the Koran, which states that the cosmos is protected and that meteorites are emblematic of Satanic forces being shot down. "The school heads posted a declaration on the notice board. It said that the explanation of shooting stars was a Christian interpretation. Everyone was supposed to sign it."

"Did they?"

"All but Martin. The others admitted that it was diplomatic but ambiguously written. Who knows what the translation said." Martin's resignation was not the lonely social suicide Noel had chosen. Having made the mistake of challenging Islam, whether inadvertently or not, he had decided not to sign the declaration or apologise. Suicide all the same. "Oh, Kieran didn't sign it either. He wanted an excuse to resign."

"Dropping like flies."

"A year of this life is enough for most people."

"What about Linda?"

"She never says anything. She just pushes herself harder at aerobics." Maybe she'd not given Kieran an answer to his marriage proposal, but his leaving meant that he had his reply. I could imagine her burning herself up: sweating into the open wound to accentuate the pain in the hope of accelerating the healing.

"There's more news." She waited a moment. "Jim's resigned."

I was lost for words. "Oh."

"Carol's putting on a brave face, but I think she's terribly hurt. Who could blame him? He told Colin that if she loves him she'd come after him."

"He didn't resign for a reason? I mean, it's nothing to do with this Martin business, is it?"

"No. He's had enough. Told me he wanted to get back to the real U-S of A." She sighed. "I'll tell you, Dawn. Colin and I are ripe for another trip to your farm."

"Come any time," I said.

"The way Carol is, it might be better if I stay."

"Is she that bad?" I blurted, my disappointment hurdling my sense.

"Yes."

* * *

Around the middle of September Mike served the subpoena. Four weeks after our first meeting, Anoud had requested my company. Or maybe it was Abdul? In any case I had no choice, I had been as good as summoned. There was more than decorum at stake here. A refusal would be a snub. Unlike the previous time when we met in the evening, we were to meet during the day. Abdul wanted to take Mike to Riyadh to look at some farm equipment.

"Don't be too long," I said to my husband. I was not looking forward to spending an entire afternoon shifting from cheek to cheek smiling in a glum silence.

I decided against going shopping with Pav after lunch for I felt duty bound to meet Anoud on time. Pav arrived before I went over and handed me a card from Ginny. It read simply: call me urgently.

This was unusual and I wondered whether she had tried to call me. I was still thinking of the letter as I crossed the gap between our demountables.

This second meeting was a pleasant surprise; there was fruit in the barren landscape. Anoud had taken it upon herself to bridge the chasm. The structure was rickety and could not support heavy conversation. But light loads could be carried across. For when I entered the demountable on the dot of two Anoud was not alone. I was not received in the spartan office, but in the more ambient setting of their lounge.

After a slightly vexed prompting from Anoud, the third person in the room meekly introduced herself.

"My name is Marina. I'm here to translate." Contrary to her name there was nothing aquatic about her. She was a slight girl with a mousy face. Her large eyes rescued her from being rodent-like, but her nose and sallow cheeks and small lips conspired to make her poker-faced.

I brightened and Anoud beamed and nodded.

And then of all things there was silence. Who should be the first to cross the bridge? Then we both spoke and hands offered the lead and we laughed. Marina smiled, but was well practised in keeping her feelings in check.

Anoud was insistent, Marina explaining that the decision was the prerogative of the hostess.

Marina was a Filipina and it became obvious that Marina could not speak English or Arabic well. So our bridge was of frayed vine and cracked wooden slats. I formulated my questions simply. We could span small talk but not reach the heights of elaborate discourse. My opening remark was rendered all the more mundane by this to-ing and fro-ing.

"It's wonderful that we can talk to one another."

"Yes."

I felt responsible for stumping her and let the pause grow, thinking she'd want to fill it with what she had intended to say. Her opening was equally superficial. "Would you like a drink? Or something to eat?"

I declined and we smiled awkwardly into the impending silence.

Apart from the wooden incense burner or *Mabkhar*, whose worn simplicity hinted at antiquity, there were two objects in the room that interested me. I pointed to one and asked her what it was. She spoke and Marina brought the bottle to me. She held it like a waitress presenting the label of a prized vintage. "It is a bottle of rose water from Taif." I remained seated but unaccustomed to such service I felt I ought to rise. I leant forward instead and took the bottle in my hands. So this was what I'd mistaken for alcohol.

"Smell it."

I had seen a shopkeeper in Riyadh daubing the *ghutra* of a customer from a vial.

After a false start we were galloping. Between Anoud and myself there was a connection born out of common disability. There was laughter and ease between us. I tried to involve Marina but she chose not to participate. I wanted to ask Marina about her life, but the opportunity did not arise. She did not seem unhappy, merely tired. Towards the end of our time Anoud made the observation that I lived in an upside-down world. Most of her life was in the company of women, whereas I was surrounded by men. "It would drive me crazy," she concluded. Asking her why produced astonishment. "Because they are men." I wanted to delve, but Mike and Abdul returned. Marina fetched Anoud's *abaaya* and Anoud went over to a shelf. I rose too, straightening my attire. Then she was before me smiling and I thought she was going to embrace me, instead she held up a small package. My reaction was to say no, but she pushed it towards me and I had to take it. My smile was embarrassed. Marina helped Anoud disappear under the cloth.

The men came in.

* * *

4B is waiting for me. He appears angry. There are others in the room. They are facing the blank screen of a television in three loose rows. The guard leads me to the best seat in the first row, next to 4B. Nobody has said anything.

4B turns to me. "Tell me about these," he says, handing me a few photographs. Normally he would have opened using my name. "Tell me about them." There is nothing in his tone, but omitting my name confirms his anger.

Until now I didn't think things could get any worse. Now, after all I have been through, my freedom is in question.

They are the photographs of the empty cartridges Mike and I discovered on our day trip to the Tuwayq Escarpment. Mike had not had the film developed. It was too dangerous. Instead he had slipped it in a pocket of one of our cases.

I tell 4B the truth. He nods impassively and I get the impression that he doesn't believe me. When he takes the photographs back I don't bother to seek out his eyes to show him my honesty.

He says something in Arabic.

The blinds are pulled and we watch a video begin to play. Abruptly scenes from a farm appear. It's our farm. The film is unedited and there are wild swings or strange focusing on a corner of a building. Noise is also unedited: sometimes a muffled voice, sometimes breathing, but mostly gritty footsteps. I know what this is and wonder why I have to see it.

As abruptly as it begins, so too, some ten minutes later the setting abruptly changes. It's dark with a sliver of light. The sliver jumps and takes up most of the picture, but there's a black area. Suddenly Ian's face appears. It's distorted by his proximity and horrified by the black area. Then he's gone and the screen blackens. Suddenly it is full of light. Ian's big face fills the screen again. He looks worried. Then he's gone. I make out part of an alleyway. Then we're swinging wildly. Bright and dark, shadows and sky, buildings. The swinging assumes a rhythm. Bring and dark, bright and dark. There are sounds of traffic and a distant crowd. I shield my eyes. 4B eases my arm down and points to the screen.

I'm struck by the mundanity, the vivid ordinariness of the scene. There are snippets of pedestrian life in downtown Riyadh. I glimpse a street vendor. Then clothes consume us and their density increases and causes the screen to darken. The screen becomes darker and darker until it is black. And we are left with noise.
Then there is light: bright uncompromising light. The white buildings are blinding too.

I recognise the white central mosque also known as the *Jami*, or Friday mosque, at Dira Square. I squint at the pristine marble steps and terrace, minaret, dome and arches gleaming under the swollen sun: a sun that shrivels the shadows. Icarus has passed the point of no return. I see the National Commercial Bank skyscraper and the Red Sea Palace Hotel. And the sound of traffic reminds me that life not only went on, it was going on.

Like my front row seat Ian also commanded a privileged view.

I know it's Friday, punishment day, just after mid-day, after the *az-zur* prayer.

I know much more and I see more than the film presents.

Ian is the only European present in the gathering of about fifteen hundred people. Most are Arabs, men in their white *thobes*, women characteristically shrouded: living furniture under black dust covers. There is a sprinkling of colour in the clothes of the Filipinos, Sri Lankans and Pakistanis.

I know this from the bits and pieces I've heard or overheard. The camera doesn't show Ian or Pav but I see them.

The crowd surges and I know that Ian and Pav are at the shoreline. Pushed and shoved. This is a form of greed. I spy a guard with a rope whip. Or is there a rope cordon?

In the audience there is a hum of expectation. For this crowd of spectators is to witness a spectacle. Ian is mute with horror. Pav almost bored.

Officials arrive. The executioner stands alone and nobody speaks to him. Either they don't want to disturb his psyche or there is nothing to say. He is a giant black man, also in a white *thobe* but with a *Taqiya* or white skullcap for head covering. He stands at military ease: hands clasped behind his back, feet astride. But in his hands is a four-foot long sword.

Surge and recede. Ebb and flow. Rock and tilt.

Minutes later a police motorcyclist leads a blue and white van and some police cars through the crowd. A doctor alights, his profession betrayed by his white coat, stethoscope necklace and black bag. Ian wonders what he could confirm at a beheading, until he begins taking implements out of his bag and placing them on a table at the rear of the terrace. Some are tools for amputations.

One of the officials, a mullah or *sharia* judge, has started to read from the Koran.

Two high-ranking police officers in crisp khaki and medals join the other officials. An officer unrolls a scroll and reads, presumably the crime and the punishment.

And then the prisoners are brought from the van, supported by a policeman on either side. Ian had the impression they were held by the policemen not because of the fear that they'd make a dash for it, their hands were manacled behind their backs, but because they appeared to be drugged. I remember him telling me this during one of his efforts to entice me to watch his video.

Now there is silence. All are still. Respect for the poor soul? The camera quivers.

The bareheaded prisoner is helped into a kneeling position in front of a heap of sand. Does he face Mecca? Ian marvels at the man's docility. No scream for life? Here is an unimpressed drunkard about to receive a knighthood. His soiled *thobe* resembles a nightshirt and the comic image that this person has lost his nightcap and candle, twisted into a macabre goodnight wish.

The executioner brings out the heavy, curved sword and it glints in the midday sun, a signal for fifteen hundred people to hold their breaths. He measures his aim, focused on the back of the neck, not quite a golfer. The executioner's artistry comes to the fore when he suddenly prods the base of the unfortunate's spine with the tip of the sword, causing him to arch and raise his head slightly. Before he can slump down again the sword has been raised and is already cutting through the air. There is a thok, like chopping wood, but the sound is wet. The head thuds into the sand and arterial blood shoots out. The body seems suspended, but topples. Crimson splashes the hard white marble. The body's legs and arms twitch vigorously in frog-like spasms. Breath returns in an "*ah*" not unlike that at a fireworks display.

Before the blood stops spurting, Ian has thrown out a jet of his own. Luckily he is near the front and misses nearby shoulders. It had been his day off and he'd slept in and eaten a late breakfast shortly before leaving.

The camera becomes seasick. Ian's legs are disappearing from under him and before a real commotion can take hold, Pav and another grab him and take him away.

* * *

"It rained on the day she was born," I told Mike when we were on the open road. He was driving me to Masstock so that I could call Ginny. "A good omen, here. Supposed to bring good luck." And Anoud considered herself fortunate for having been chosen by Abdul. He was an important, well-to-do man: a good man. Yes, she was a Bedouin and it had been an alliance marriage. She was sad that she had not given him any children. She had suffered a miscarriage in the first year of their three-year-old marriage.

The second object in the room that had interested me was a Koran. Anoud had said that an unbeliever was not allowed to pick it up. To ease any feeling of censure she added that she could not touch it during menstruation. Also, it should never be carried below the hip. She placed it on the table and turned the pages in front of me.

Of course it was unreadable, but I knew the Koran to be a mixture of Old Testament brutalities and New Testament wisdom. Like the Bible it was open to interpretation, giving birth to sects and splits. Along with the *Sunna*, Prophet Mohammed's actions and words as recorded by his followers and the *Hadith* his recorded pronouncements; the Koran was a blueprint for Islamic society. Out of the *Sunna* and the Koran, the law, the *sharia*, was formed. All this was made to answer all the questions of modern society. And together they would answer all future questions too.

And, of course, if the Koran answered all questions, then it was at odds with history and science. There was only the now and the future.

There was no need to draw on anything else. No need for past experiences. Everything was written. What would be would be.

Mike had also had his cultural dose. There had been conversation on their journey to Riyadh, the essence of which revolved around the corrupting influence of the West. According to Abdul tradition was being violated by the forbidden or *haram*. The mini-skirt was *haram* dress; the US dollar was *haram* money. He did not fear for himself. He feared for the youth. "He feels the youth are not wise enough to see what he calls pollution," said Mike. "He meant moral pollution."

"You can't have your cake and eat it," I said, the image of the cola-and-teeth dentist at the party coming to mind. "They want what the West has to offer. They have to take the rough with the smooth. Pollution and all."

They even touched on punishment. Yes, they lopped off hands, feet, heads, but according to Abdul, brutal though it may be, it was certainly punishment. And the law was absolute and clear to all. Everyone knew the difference between right and wrong. In the West this sense wasn't as clear-cut. And even if it was, lawyers could turn cases around. And finally the fickle man-made laws were destined to always be one step behind evolving crime.

I again thought about the Koranic amulet; the present Anoud had given me on parting. To protest that all I did was absently look at it on our first meeting was futile. I knew not to admire but I'd been caught staring at it. Had she admired anything of mine? Had I worn anything to admire? Aside from the fact that I'd not thought to take anything for her, I had not wanted to go in the first place.

I would only ever know Abdul through my husband. And through their conversations I realised that Abdul had set us in front of a loom. At first I had recoiled. Ski mittens of western prejudice hampered my husband and me. But we were curious enough to take the threads he offered, and over time an ancient pattern began to emerge. A different picture or perhaps a picture we knew but had never seen from this perspective.

"I think he's trying to turn me into a Muslim," Mike said suddenly.

I knee-jerked: "I'm not veiling-up." We smiled. "He probably sees a receptive person in you."

"Probably. But he has some good arguments." I shot him a

concerned look and he deflected it with a smile. "I didn't say persuasive."

"Like what?"

"Like the importance of the extended family, their sense of duty and loyalty to one another, respect for their elders. A feeling of belonging and security."

I hadn't expected bullets and was wary of childishly deflecting them. Admittedly his last comment made me want to spit out about female confinement. "I value my freedom and individuality."

"Yes, but their society offers a sense of place. There are roles. Husband and wife have a division of labour." He was standing firm. Attacks on the fairness of these roles were too easy and broke unspoken rules. Should I bring the full weight of western thought to bear he would step back and say he wasn't speaking for himself. "The failing of the church, the growth of the new religion called independence, consumerism and materialism - greed I suppose - are leading to the breakdown of the family in the West."

"The Saudis don't seem averse to a touch of consumerism and materialism themselves."

"Pollution," he smiled.

I would not be dismissed so easily. "Abdul is not running this venture for fun."

"He's a businessman of course. But first and foremost he's a Muslim. Islam comes first. In fact he'd tell you that not only does it come first, it governs his business dealings too."

"Islam is a way of life," I said wearily.

"Exactly. And he believes it's the fastest growing religion in the world because it addresses the dearest and natural elements of human life: the family, the village, the tribe."

"Especially impoverished people steeped in tradition."

"You could look at it like that. He'd say that these people are more in touch with Nature." He pondered. "You know, it just occurred to me that in the Middle-East that 'T'-word lends itself to tyranny. Which itself does not sit easily with democracy."

"So Western ways can't work here?"

"Only on a tyrannical - tribal - basis."

"How does he explain away the radicals and terrorism?"

"He doesn't. In every ideology there are the extremists." He paused. "I'll be generous. He does see a flaw with today's Islam."

"Oh?" Being a woman I could see many, but I was intrigued to know what Abdul regarded as a flaw in his own belief.

"Islam's failing is its clergy: the *Ulama* and Mullahs. People rely on them to interpret the Koran for them. Rather than learning for themselves, they pay these people to recite the Koran at various ceremonies."

"I thought they learnt it."

"Yes, but they rarely know it or understand it all."

"You'd have chaos if we got up and started regurgitating the Bible in church. Nobody's that devout."

"True. In the West. But Islam is supposed to be a guideline for life. In every aspect." We were quiet for a moment. "Abdul said something else that I found interesting. He said that life's journey was the purpose not the destination. Sound familiar? Yes. But he said destiny is Allah's province."

"Amen."

* * *

"I won't keep you in suspense," Ginny began after she phoned me back at Masstock. "But I can't just burst out."

"What?" I snapped impatiently. "What is it?"

"Merv's been shot."

"What?" I repeated inanely.

"He's been shot."

"You mean with a gun?"

"Yes, crossbows are rather hard to conceal." Her glibness only slightly alleviated the tension slightly.

"He's okay, though?"

"Yes." Then, "he could have bled to death I suppose."

"Go on. Was it an accident? What happened?"

"One of his rag head colleagues blew his top, I think his name is Rashid. The one he and Den sometimes took to parties. He caught Merv nosing about in his desk. That's about all I know."

"There must be more than that."

"There probably is, but nobody's been allowed to see him. And it's not because he's so badly hurt."

"What do you mean?"

"I mean there's been an info blackout. That's how it works here. Nobody knows anything. Even Merv's colleagues have conflicting versions. I mean, what was he nosing about in the rag head's desk for?

And a shooting usually has witnesses. Somebody must have overpowered him. When you reach someone in authority they just tell you that Merv's okay and needs rest. He can't have visitors just yet. We may be able to see him next week. Maybe then we'll get the full story."

"Why maybe?"

"I don't want to sound pessimistic but Colin thinks they could be debriefing him. You know, giving him some friendly persuasion. Somebody phoned the British consulate, but they said they couldn't give a press release before the facts were known. In other words they've put a lid on it."

The hiss of the open line underscored our distance.

"There's another thing. Not as spectacular I must admit, but worth mentioning. Carol went to bed with Geoff last weekend."

My mind numbed. "I thought she loathed him."

"She did. Now she thinks even worse of him." Ginny's tone wearied. "I'm pretty sick of her at the moment. Time for another trip to your farm."

"Any time."

"I'm afraid that we don't have the energy."

"Talking of energy that reminds me," I began. I wanted a drama of my own. "Do you remember me telling you of that guy insinuating that I was having an affair with Den and or Merv. The guy acting like a pinball? I was wrong about him. His words were: 'so you're Den and Merv's *friend*.' And it was the way he said friend that stuck out. Don't you see? He was referring to *sid*: friend. He knew the farm supplied them."

"I see," she said, although I could tell she did not see or want to see. Aramco dramas were enough for her. She said we'd never know. He'd left after the hair-pulling party.

"Actually I'm trying to persuade Mike to visit. He's been in contact with his boss there. We were supposed to be out here for six months. It's nearly a year now. I've told him he has to be face to face with his boss."

"Quite right. When will you be here?"

I smiled. "Maybe towards the end of October. The farm will be quieter then. He knows that something'll have to happen before November, otherwise he'll be stuck here sowing the new wheat."

"Could what's-his-name take over? The other Englishman?"

"Ian you mean? No, I don't think so. Mike doesn't think he's quite ready."

"Then somebody would have to come and take over. And that'll mean a hand-over period."

"I suppose so."

"So you're looking to be out of there some time in eighty-six."

"Thanks a lot."

"Sorry."

"You're right, though."

"Get the thumb-screws out, Dawn."

"They'd be useless on Mike. He's an ox to that sort of thing. No. It'd have to be a pretty good argument. I think I'll go for the holiday number." I paused before explaining that we had agreed to go on holiday between the jobs. I was sure that we weren't expected to work a solid year without a break. There would be something in the contract that we could wave at Smith.

"There's one problem with coming with Mike. I might have trouble avoiding his boss's wife." During my visits to Aramco, the possibility of bumping into June had remained at the back of my mind. I felt certain that we'd not meet socially. Invariably one came across the same faces at these Aramco gatherings and she belonged to a different set. She was of the older generation, those who had made a home out of this life: one thousand and one soirees. Most of us were in our late twenties, stopping over, not certain enough to put down roots, not committed enough to move on. We fermented in the heady fumes of high-octane superficiality, on ebullience and frivolity, on transience.

"If you don't want to meet this woman, don't let on you're here."

* * *

The tea is now beyond drinking temperature, it's almost too cold; nonetheless the older consulate sips it tentatively as if it is scalding. He looks to me, but I make no move towards my cup.

I remain unresponsive and the consulate clucks his tongue as he returns his cup to his desk. He pulls a fountain pen from his breast pocket and unscrews the top. "You must sign this paper."

There is a lifetime of authority in his voice. He is distinguished, all silver sideburns and oil. It's this latter trait than turns my stomach. He cannot see that what once passed as suave has become slick. He's been hanging on by his school ties for too long and they've become frayed. The colours have changed and he's lost touch. I'm not impressed.

The younger diplomat is accessible, but he's on his knees. And someone crawling doesn't impress me either.

"What is it?" Up to this point I'd reflected their convivial demeanour. They'd not realised that the depth of my sincerity was that of cold glass. Throwing me a morsel had not impressed me. They told me that when the police arrived at the farm, chased and caught me, they'd already picked up an Arab. He had apparently led them to another. Dismissing my inquiry as to what has happened to them with a "that's in the hands of the Saudi authorities" had soiled the morsel.

"I've already told you," says the underling full of understanding, but sounding condescending. He leans forward in his chair beside me and returns his empty cup and saucer to the desk. He is the legal council to the British Ambassador. "We can have a translation sent on to you."

I shake my head.

"Surely you can understand that it must be in Arabic?" he asks.

"I'll sign what you want if it's in both languages on the same sheet."

The consulate loses his temper. He's been out here too long. He is used to obedience, especially from women. "Young lady, you are in no position to make demands." The underling shifts uneasily. The speaker snatches up the paper and shakes it ineffectually like Chamberlain. "This says that there was an explosion, an accident. That's all."

Theatrics are wasted on me. "Both languages on one sheet."

He subjects me to his best glare. His face is such a caricature of indignation that I smile; a reaction that spurs him on. "Madam, we are on your side. We've gone to a lot of trouble to get this far. You haven't made it easier for us. Brawling and then that video. You should be thankful they're willing to believe you. Do you know that there was a suggestion that this accident could have included you?" I pale and the underling clears his throat to speak. The consulate has gone too far. "Not from us, mind you."

Now I know why I am here. I know why I was not taken to al-Malaz prison. All this time in this shit-hole my life was in jeopardy. But would my government have allowed it? Would they have abandoned one of their citizens? The sickening thought that they would only have dared do this with a woman scars my soul.

"Just sign it," says the underling, not knowing where to look.

***

"I was looking for a program-listing," Merv had told his story so many times that it had the polished sheen of his face. "He hadn't come in yet and it was already ten." He was talking of Rashid. "I thought he may have locked it in his drawer. There's a trick to opening them, you see." He glanced at Mike who sat a little behind me; otherwise he spoke to me. "You lift them up from underneath and pull. Start with the lowest and work your way up. So much for security." He smiled and his stomach tightened and he winced. I thought about reaching across the hospital bed to his hand. "And what do I find in the middle drawer?" His smooth delivery showed in the ease with which he sidetracked. "Look, the canteen in the building is crap. Most of us bring sandwiches and take them outside for the half hour lunch break. One dingbat eats pot-noodles every day." He pondered. "And nobody's told you anything?"

"No." I assured him. "We've come straight from the farm."

"Didn't you talk to Ginny?"

"Tell us what happened, Merv."

"What Rashid had in his desk took the biscuit - the dog biscuit - so to speak." He pressed back a smile. There was nothing visible to suggest Merv was hurt and when I remarked that he looked well, far better than Mike had, he said that he had been positively anaemic a week ago. "He didn't have biscuits. He had tins of pet food in his drawer." My heart went out to him for his humour. "And one of those trapper's nooses. You know, a loop of wire. It doesn't take Columbo to work out what that meant." He checked we were with him. "I was wondering who to go to with this stuff when just like in the flicks, he appears. Of course he's shocked and we stare at one another. I don't know who was more shocked."

"Didn't anyone else see you?"

"We were standing so people could see our heads. It's not open-plan. Everything's partitioned off. We've all got our own cubby-hole."

"Sounds like cattle pens."

"Exactly that," Merv smiled, plainly liking the analogy, filing it away for future use, the next time he related this story, perhaps. "I don't know why, I just said that I was looking for the listing. This put him off guard. But I was an idiot. I looked down at the pet food and wire. It was only for a second, but when I looked up he knew I knew.

He pulled out a lower drawer and I thought he was going to get the listing. I just stood there. And he pulls out a gun. I mean; this guy's got a loaded gun in his drawer. Can you believe this shit?"

"What did you do?" I asked.

"I did what I always do. I smiled. I mean; I couldn't believe it. I didn't have the hiccups so there was no reason for such drastic measures. It was wacky. I think I thought it was a toy. I don't know."

"Then you struggled and it went off," said Mike.

"Not even that. I said: don't be a moron. He'd mixed with us long enough to guess what I meant. Anyway, he was. Boy was it loud and there I am crashing to the floor. I remember hurting my hip against the side of the desk. And then I'm kind of half under the desk and my hand is wet. I look up and he's gone. There's a lot of shouting and another gunshot. That made me jump. The funny thing was, it didn't really hurt. When I woke up here, man, was I in pain. Think of your worst stomach ache and multiply it a thousand fold."

Then he slammed us with a punch line that left us winded. "Of course, all that I've said is a lie." He savoured our bafflement. "What really happened is that I went hunting wild rabbits and there was a terrible accident." I almost thumped him for his expression. He was disappointed when we showed no desire to play his game.

"They bought you out," said Mike.

"Some guys from the embassy brought a lawyer and a magnifying glass for the small print in my contract. But yes, to be honest I let a golden arm twist sign the truth away." Shame was his expression, and he grew philosophical rather than defiant. "Next stop the green, green pastures of England."

We were silent for a while.

"Where's Rashid now?" I asked.

"Good question. I was told they caught him in the building. But a colleague said he saw him get away. My bet is that they arrested him and they're holding him somewhere. He's probably got detention and a thousand lines: I must not shoot expats."

In the short silence that followed Merv looked at us and then away. He concentrated on our faces when he next spoke. "I heard about the still." Shame stole his bearing again. "It's no consolation, but I was never keen on those off-camp runs. They were too damned dangerous."

"You still did them," said Mike.

"The farm produce was cheaper than the camp stuff." That first time we met Den and Merv, when they came to see Bob for the last time, they had not brought alcohol, they had come to collect it. Hence the increased clandestine activity before their visit. "The truth is we negotiated a discount, because of the danger." Then I saw a new meaning to Bob's as-tight-as-a-camel's-arse-in-a-sandstorm comment.

"When you came to see Bob off," said Mike, "you were hoping I'd join in."

"Yes, that side of it was Bob's idea. He thought a leaving do would be a good excuse to introduce you to the alcohol."

"Loosen us up," I said.

Merv gave his best you-can't-blame-us-for-trying look.

"And that time I was low," I began. "You didn't come to rescue me."

"That's not entirely true."

There was a cool silence that none of us wanted. I warmed my expression and touched Merv's hand. "I don't know that we'll see you again." As soon as he was well enough to leave the hospital he was leaving the country.

"Open that drawer," he said. "Don't worry there's no gun." Mike and I melted and Merv glowed. "Write your home address in that book."

***

"Mike looked good. No lasting injuries?"

"Nothing. At the time he looked worse than Merv." We'd already spoken of Merv. "It's four months ago now."

"That long? It seems like yesterday."

"It seems like forty months."

There were smiles. We skirted the subject of Carol with polite enquiries, moving along the bank of it as if along a massive lake, looking for a mutually agreeable place to take the plunge.

Ginny put the kettle on. "So you've escaped meeting the boss's wife?"

"Yes," I smiled, restlessly standing in the middle of the room. I was glad of this time alone with her. I wasn't sure what plans she'd made with Colin or Carol. Mike said he'd aim to be back by nine, though I thought he'd be lucky to get away before ten.

We'd left the farm just after eleven that Wednesday morning. Not the best time to travel, but Mike was to meet Smith at two that afternoon. Afterwards we drove to see Merv. My husband's meeting with his boss had gone as well as could be expected. He'd extracted a positive maybe in the form of a promise that we'd be in Dhahran before the end of January. He then threatened me with Smith's invitation to an evening soiree. I said it would be more like a foray. "I told him you'd made other arrangements, but that I'd ask you." We met Ginny at the main refectory and she mapped the route to her place before he left.

"Tea?"

"No, let's go for coffee." Intuition told me I'd need it.

"I haven't got any cardamom," she smiled.

I'd touched on my meetings with Anoud, but humbled them in anticipation of her tales.

"Instant'll do."

She placed the cups on the coffee table between us.

I braced myself when I thought she was about to launch herself, but she sidestepped.

"Noel's gone. I told you already."

Her active life shrivelled her memory of our missives and phone calls. "Martin too. The end of last month."

"I told you about Den, didn't I?"

"No."

"His wife wrote that she was leaving him for someone else. She had the spunk - Colin's word - to write the Dear John letter on toilet paper. Get it? Dear John. Toilet paper."

We smiled.

"It's not funny, is it?" I said soberly.

She continued to smile, but was philosophical. "Makes you wonder why he was out here in the first place. All that talk of sacrifice was a facade."

"Maybe he couldn't face the relationship?" She looked at me as she remembered his advances on me.

"At least we've discovered where all Lennon and McCartney's lonely people belong." It was a sentiment I was sure infringed Martin's copyright.

We sipped our coffees. And our silence was more reflective than awkward.

"Do you fancy going to the party?" I asked.

"There's one tomorrow, but it might be a bit much after the camel racing. We could do. Let's see what Colin and Mike have to say."

"What time's the camel racing?"

"Four."

"That'll be too late. We'll be long gone by then."

"You're leaving tomorrow?"

I nodded.

"Was it worth coming?"

"Of course," I smiled. "If you think this is a whistle-stop tour then you should know that Mike originally wanted to return tonight."

"Well, you don't have to go back with him. We could take you back Friday afternoon."

"I'll speak to Mike."

"Maybe we should go to tonight's party," she began thoughtfully. "Jim is going to tomorrow's and Carol won't go." Saying her name she had absently touched the surface of the subject with a tip of a toe. A chill shuddered the length of her body and quickened her eyes. "She wants to go to tonight's."

I waited.

"I don't know whether I can take Carol another evening." She meant that she was not sure she could handle her presence. "I suppose I should tell you that about a week ago she went to bed with Geoff. Or should I say he went to bed with her." I didn't interrupt to tell her that she'd told me this on the phone. "That guy's heartless. Really. He told me she practically seduced him and he felt sorry for her. I mean, as if he expected me to swallow that."

"I can't believe she seduced him."

She laughed unconvincingly. "When you see her you'll see she couldn't seduce a sailor after a ten year stint on the high-seas. She's broken. If he didn't seduce her then her seduction was accomplished in a single sentence like let's go to bed. She was drunk, for Heaven's sake."

Ginny was spent. Even talking to me was an effort: as if she was giving testimony for the umpteenth time. I understood her but was deflated. I thought my very presence would lift her. Yet, I was forcing her to churn up all the tiresome intrigues again.

And it struck me that I was invincible. I may not have been happy. But atmosphere on the farm had made me impervious. And maybe I drew satisfaction from the vindication of my instincts about the farm crew. How I had doubted myself. Or maybe the new unification of my husband and I, somehow making us stronger than before, offered untold reservoirs of energy. Even Merv's accident paled Carol's state.

Finally, contributing to my demeanour were my enlightening meetings with Anoud. I don't know. Whatever, my perspective was superior and I could not lower myself to a petty vantage point.

Despite Carol's demise Ginny was sick of her. I saw then how little I knew my friend. I didn't know how to help her. And she was aware of this too. Rot was warping our friendship. Until this moment it had always dovetailed. We weren't connecting and she was as irked as I.

"I'd better call Carol if we're going. Colin could pick her up on the way over."

"Yes. Then I'll tell you about Anoud." Compared to events here, the theme seemed insipid. And to tell her of Anoud could increase the rift in our friendship, but we needed distraction.

She phoned Carol, her voice picking up immediately, not because of me, but because this was whom she presented to Carol: enthusiasm in the face of hopelessness.

She then spoke to Colin before resuming her place. I skimmed over my meetings with Anoud emphasising their lack of content, but successfully kindled talk of Arab culture.

"Islam preaches that true freedom lies in realising the transience of everything that is physical."

"That can be," she said. "But it means that all the Arabs I've met aren't very devout."

"Pollution," I answered, explaining that Abdul had meant moral pollution. "Before oil the Saudis income was through dates and horses and a tax on the *Hajj*. Abdul believes that Allah gave them such wealth to bless and curse them. To test them."

Ginny regarded me and I could feel her stepping away. I persevered as if shock could arrest her departure. "Anoud does not seem suppressed. She seems quite serene."

"Oh, come on Dawn," she laughed. "You said yourself she's a Bedouin, she probably doesn't know any better."

Sadly my friend was talking like a typical expat. Conversation on the level I enjoyed with Mike was not going to be possible. Unlike Ian, convincing Ginny was worth the effort but time was against me and our conversation petered out.

We spoke of the still and the alcohol runs. We spoke of Rashid and came back full circle to the shooting.

Carol and Colin arrived.

Colin was a more robust version of himself, almost brutish, as if making up for Carol's lack of presence. For the feisty person I knew was gone. Carol's mask of social acceptability had been battered thin from within. The emotional turmoil shifted under its wafer surface, almost physically: purple and bruised, hopeless self-abuse at its finest. She was not broken, more stripped of her social veneer.

A strained normality embarrassed us. At nine o'clock Colin suggested giving Mike till nine-thirty. A note with directions to the party could be put on the door.

With this limit we managed to fill the time with stuttering talk of on-camp happenings that had nothing to do with our social circle. One story was that of an American who stole his neighbour's bicycle. At first he admitted the theft and then denied it. There was an argument and security was called. A doctor came with them. They searched his house, ostensibly for the bicycle and found US$100,000 covering his bedroom walls, his suitcases packed with empty cola cans, rolls of Riyals in a life-jacket and in the garage the missing bicycle and a box full of condiments and cutlery taken from the refectory and various Al Khobar restaurants.

Colin would make reference to this story at the party. We were alone in a corner, watching the throng, Carol having stormed off, Ginny in the toilet. He had not made his comment when telling the story: Carol could have misconstrued it.

"I think everyone goes crazy out here. Pop goes the expat." He was tipsy but not drunk. On camp he could still drive. "We're all bits of popcorn. Tip the little pieces - they all look similar in the beginning - in a pan with a smattering of hot oil. Put a lid on it and heat. They pop and twist and warp and turn inside-out." He sounded so much like Martin. "This heat and blandness exposes people. Pop goes the expat."

* * *

"It's good to see you again," said Linda above the music, giving me her delicious smile and a cheek-to-cheek hug. She gave her gum a couple of chews. "How come I didn't see you at aerobics today?"

This was not a fancy dress party and she was in jeans and T-shirt. Even so, they were sprayed on.

"Because I wasn't there," I smiled, noting that it could be taken as a rebuff and quickly following it up with a fib. "I only arrived a couple of hours ago." Sometimes I didn't understand myself. I then embellished the lie by exaggerating the frequency with which I jogged on the farm.

"That's great," she exclaimed, not dropping her mastication or breathless optimism. "Any form of body styling is okay by me. Perhaps we could go together? How long are you here for?"

"I'm leaving tomorrow morning." I was becoming a compulsive liar. I didn't dare glance at Ginny.

"Hardly worth bothering, was it?"

"My husband is here on business. He'll be here later. You can meet him."

"If I'm still here." The sparkle in her face continued but appeared somehow forced. "I find these parties a bore. My voice is hoarse from shouting and this smoke gets me down." It wasn't that smoky, most of the revellers followed the custom of smoking outside. "I'll get myself a water." Then as if not seeing the full plastic beaker in my hand: "Do you want something? Oh, no I guess not. Catch you later."

Ginny talked about her after Carol said that she couldn't stand the woman. My companions had been reticent, feigning distraction, as I'd spoken to her. The gist of Ginny's short discourse was that Linda had abandoned all decorum. Her recurrent suitor, Kieran, had left and she'd given up marathon running for cycling. Now she could cover more distance and openly snatch cups on her tour de French letters.

The throb of bodies in the room generated a voodoo heat. Someone even sported a top hat nested upon cascading blond hair that should have been dark and in dreadlocks.

Geoff's unexpected arrival at ten-thirty caused Carol to storm off. When he entered he acknowledged us from a distance. "I'm not staying in the same room as him," Carol hissed and went outside. Ginny and I trotted after her, Colin shook his head and sought company elsewhere.

Outside in the enclosed porch there was a clump of four people on a settee: three men, one with a girl on his lap. Carol passed them, lifted the latch of the wooden door and went into the open. When we caught up with her, her face was contorted with despair.

"You can't avoid him forever," said Ginny. I stood by limply. "Running out just shows he's won."

"I'm not running out. I'm just sick of the party. If I stay there's a good chance I'll end up in bed with him again." This shed another kind of light on Carol as the victim. She was still a victim but to herself, a victim to her own cruelty. "Nobody really cares, you know." She chose to turn her drowning eyes to me when she wasn't looking out over the parked cars. "Sensitivity is out. You've got to protect yourself."

Ginny inspected the car park too.

"It's all so, so " - she floundered for her words - "so meaningless."

"What's so meaningless?" Ginny challenged. She'd heard it all before and I could feel her rolling her eyes. If we were to be an interrogation team then I was being left the role of sympathiser.

Carol glared at her with equivalent irritation. "Why life. Life, of course."

"Life may be meaningless," I began, "but it should at least mean something to you."

She looked at me quizzically as if I'd spoken in Swahili.

"I'm going home," she said flatly. There was no arguing.

"Colin'll give you a lift."

"I want to walk."

"I'll get Colin." Ginny turned on her heel. Carol began to walk and I walked with her.

"You might as well let Colin take you." No answer. "Why not stay?" Her pace did not alter. "You haven't met Mike. Then we could give you a lift." She walked on and I began to falter. The corner would take us out of sight of the house. Her cruel self-denial irked me. I'd run out of reason. So I went for the jugular, striking with the short, sharp name that was taboo in front of her. "If you love Jim so much, why don't you go to him? I'm sure -" The cut froze her. She choked and couldn't speak, and stood shock-still, a wound silently gushing. I lost my grip on my switchblade tongue. Disbelief was in her face, horror in mine.

"What do you know?" she spat.

My tongue was blunted. Yes, what did I know? Who did I think I was? I wanted to apologise, to reach her. I wanted to slap her, tell her to piss off, tell her that we were sick of her self-pity, embrace her.

She walked on and it was my turn to stare into nothingness. What did I know? I was an outsider. Yes, I was an outsider here and a superfluous member of the crew on the farm. Oh, I cooked, but they could do just as well without me. This was not my social world. I was a visitor. And on the farm there was no social world. "It's all so meaningless," she had said. Was she completely wrong? Or did she mean to say that it was all so lifeless? Bob talked of running on the spot and Colin spoke of a vitamin deficiency. Whether the on farm or riding this heady jovial carousel, there was an essential ingredient missing.

Here time was an irrelevance. Transience and superficiality harboured no sense of progress. Without a deeper richer medium in which to dip, one swung carelessly in the gaseous enthusiasm. All the time up without coming down, hang-gliding the rarefied atmosphere under the communal umbrella of merry cumulus clouds. Revelling in witticisms and pseudo-insightful quips until one faltered, exhausted and fell to earth. Living twice as hard to stay up lent to mood swings. Remove the financial motivation and there was nothing left. Imprisoned by your own greed you risked becoming institutionalised. The subject of money had come up from time to time and it seemed to me that rather than rejoice over the wealth, many acted greedily and were apt to whinging. They were in possession of a growing pearl. For they were like oysters, their shells gnarled and thickening against the onslaught of superficiality. Meanwhile the pearl grew and slowly pressed at their innards, squeezing and wringing out the substance within. Material wealth juxtaposing their cultural destitution.

To say that no women spoke to Linda would be a gross exaggeration. The social system was too fragile for blatant rudeness. Of those who conversed with Carol most were blasé and uneasy and moved on before slipping. All were aloof, talking from a safe distance. Even Geoff burnt bridges. The boat analogy was not completely fitting. Everyone was in the same boat and one should not rock it, were true enough statements. But a submarine was a more suitable vessel to describe this community. Everyone was in a self-contained unit. All linked for survival. Kieran pulling Linda's hair was a fissure in the fabric of the simulated world. People struggled with a door, turning the heavy wheel to seal off the flooding compartment. Carol was leaking. Martin had sealed himself in and used explosives, but he'd caused damage beyond his unit. Noel had not upset the others. He'd crawled through the torpedo tubes and jettisoned himself away. And the analogy worked if the depth gauge was the bank balance, increasing the deeper one went, until nerves broke or one went beyond the point of return. Pop goes the expat.

Ginny was calling me back. I turned and waved and plodded to the house, testing my face for composure, wondering when Mike would arrive. I was shaken and that familiar depression was threatening to spoil my humour.

When I reached Ginny outside the walled porch, I hid my mood behind concern: "I'm worried about her."

"Don't be. These histrionics are a passing phase. She has to work it out of her system."

"You don't think she might do something silly?"

Ginny forced a laugh. "Lord no. Not Carol, she's not the type." She reflected and when she next spoke she was speaking as much about herself as Carol. "I think the way she's acting is symptomatic of a greater problem. A kind of unseen attrition. As if all this levity, the need to retain a superficial level, eventually wears you down and you crack, go on holiday or talk head."

"Talk head?"

"A phrase Colin and I use. Confide in someone." I was acutely aware that Ginny and I never talked head. Then again, I'd not had a heart to heart with Mike for a long time. It just didn't seem necessary; we knew each other so well. "Carol has lost her head-talker. If ever they were that close. Who knows behind closed doors? Shall we go in? I could do with something loaded."

"I hope you mean a drink and not a magnum."

We laughed loudly, too loudly and I hoped that Carol was out of earshot.

I recognised the girl in the lap of the man on the settee. They were now the only ones in the porch area.

"Hi, Gillian," I began, nodding Ginny on. "I didn't recognise you." I meant I hadn't seen her earlier.

"Hallo," she returned. I'd never seen her so happy. She was practically delirious. Far from the melancholic person who'd accompanied Ita and myself on the beach all those aeons ago.

Perhaps she didn't remember my name. "Dawn here, from the backwaters."

She looked at the man pinned under her. "She's from a farm hundreds of kilometres from here. This is Eric." She continued to look at him. "Isn't he a darling?" The unfortunate man managed a smile before she cupped his face and kissed him full on the lips. I watched, embarrassed.

They both turned to me and my embarrassment became chagrin. I expected Eric to speak. When he looked at me his eyes were glazed with alcohol, love, subjugation, I don't know what. Mostly he tended to look at his drink or her shoulder or her breasts.

"It's a great party," she exclaimed. I wasn't sure she had noticed that a party was taking place. "Did you come with your husband this time?" I knew then that she was not deliriously happy, more jittery and terrified. The alien that Colin suggested she was, was not gestating snugly in Eric's stomach; only her digits clasped his face.

"He should be arriving soon."

"Introduce us when he comes." This was a see you later if you must.

"Catch you later," I said, mimicking Linda. I gave her a smile and a nod and then a glance at what was her current victim, a worm of a man proud at capturing a female out here, not realising that he was in her clutches. He was another she would take indoors, ignoring her friends like she was ignoring this party and with a grip brim with tenderness and intimacy suffocate the life out of any connection with him. She would choose the music to which they should dance whether it suited him or not. Sexual perks would make him deaf in one ear. And this same record would run its course, get stuck at the same flaw, repeating, repeating, repeating, repeating until either he gave because he was baited by its jarring repetitiveness or she gave because the flaw was not being breached. Predictably he, the worm, would eventually turn, wriggle free, go underground, seek safety in a medium she did not understand and the ultimate victim would be her. Wrong? Too cynical? I thought not.

* * *

I entered the crowded room again, seeing only Ginny as if looking down the telescopic sights of a rifle. I made a bullet line towards her. So I was shocked when a voice lambasted me from the side as sure as if an obstacle deliberately set itself in front of me. I was even more upset when I saw who it was.

"Hi Dawn."

"Hallo Geoff." Ginny wasn't looking my way.

"Back in the fairground?" He was again against the wall, as if he didn't like anyone or anything behind him. This time he was in a loose T-shirt and beige slacks. Other men lined the wall, mostly in pairs, standard Triffid wallpaper. Of course, Geoff stood apart. The throb of people was behind me, their bodies muffling the stereo, innards absorbing the bass of the speakers.

I sought conversational neutrality. "Have you heard anything from Martin?"

"I think he's still in Bangkok," he smiled. "Let's face it, he was about as useful as a corkscrew out here." Speaking so of his friend sent me on a quest of his face in search of a blemish, a blot upon his handsome features on to which I could latch and find him less attractive. There was a mole on his neck. Not enough. Ah there, his earlobes, weren't they too large? Yes, I could dislike him for his oversized earlobes. "I guess Ita would disagree." He said this secretively with a knowing look. Ita was not there she was on nights. Before I could ask him what he meant we were interrupted.

"Hi."

"Oh, hallo." I was taken aback and instinctively kissed him.

"This is my husband, Mike. And this is Geoff. He's the BSAC boss." Fierce heat burnt away any residue of conversation.

"You're the farmer?"

"Yes," said Mike, still wondering at my rash affection.

"I'll get you a drink," I said.

"I can get one," my husband returned. He wanted to extract himself from this situation as much as I.

"I was going anyway," I persisted.

"Spot the married couple," Geoff chuckled. "I'll tell you what, I'll go. What do you want?" He was a slick one.

When he was gone Mike teased me. "I can see why you like these parties."

I could not be angry with him. Any rebuke would have been an exaggerated reaction requiring immediate explanation. "Him? He's not my type. Have you seen the size of his earlobes?"

Mike was perplexed and I gave him my dimpled whimsical look. He laughed.

"How was it?"

"June asked after you." I threw out my tongue. "Otherwise it was okay. More sedate than this." Our space was being continually encroached by the dancers.

Colin greeted Mike and they talked.

Mary O. came over and introduced me to a new arrival, another Irish nurse, called Oonagh. "Come on, let's dance," said Mary O. to me. "Lift that cloud from your brow." The three of us merged into the oscillating whole. Perhaps Mary O. had seen what was always in my face. Perhaps she saw the contrast in Oonagh's face. Like a college sprog or fresher the new girl's face was open. A purer version of Ian after his holiday. She was a green horn to us veterans, and we were enchanted by her bright-faced look, wanting her company, inadvertently draining its light as we related this world to her. Tourists fascinated by an untouched place, relentlessly trampling over it all the same.

I spent a lot of time introducing my husband to people: Aine, Marie, Alan and Racquel, my double who looked nothing like me, but whose i.d. card I had used. Even Linda got a look in. Watching my husband closely, unconsciously looking for fodder should he mention Geoff again. Ita, Huck, Carol, Jim and, of course, Martin and Noel he would never know. Den appeared. He vainly tried to shield his lost eyes behind talk of Merv, before moving on to another party. His presence resurrected memories of his advances and the ventriloquist evening and Bob. Riding on borrowed phrases he half-heartedly suggested we go with him to the other party. "Armageddon, they say. A real scorcher. Knock the pips of this one. Bring your own blindfold and last cigarette, they say." But he couldn't galvanise our group. After he'd gone Ginny said: "If you think the foliage here is thick, where he's going you'd need a machete to get through it. Talk about Triffids."

I asked her about Ita. "Yes, something started between Martin and her."

"Do you think that's why he left?"

"It's possible. Their liaison was an unlikely one."

Camp life was a place of ever-diminishing circles. I was skimming the surface of the intrigues but my assessment was not far off the mark. Carol's demise was incest-like. Pairing Ita and Martin was peculiar by normal standards. This was a quarantine syndrome: confine people long enough and there'd be collisions, compromises, odd liaisons. Familiarity breeds contempt or attempt.

I was no longer a social pauper. I had mastered their currency; it was not complicated. I could tell when I was being short-changed and knew the counterfeiters, the gossip peddlers. Why, I could even launder someone else's ideas so they came out with the legitimacy of my diction. Of course my knowledge was limited and I was dangerous. The people I knew were reduced to cardboard cut-outs painted in primary colours: for Linda not always on heat, chewing a wad of man, Martin not continually depressive, Noel not always drunk, Carol not always full of cruelty and so on, but this world frequently brought out these traits in them. Like students there was some play-acting. But unlike students they were not hampered by self-discovery. Age had crystallised their personalities and rendered them less malleable. And this was how I knew them. Therefore although my currency was never up-to-date it was acceptable.

If Carol's outburst forced me to glance over my rose-tinted glasses and see the darker side of this social world, then Mike's presence effectively tore them from my face. Through his eyes I could not rise above an empty enthusiasm for the place. The shadowy Triffids that lined the walls and crouched in corners, desperately interesting and yearning, seemed more prominent then ever. All the intrigues took on a B-movie feel: the plot thinning as time went on. I couldn't find the bouncy cumulus clouds to lift me up. Dancing elevated me a little, but the press became irritating.

"I know why you're ripe for another visit," I said to Ginny, referring to the farm.

"Thank God I've got Colin." Outside the walls of their relationship was a harsh land. Looking upon it cemented their dependence and so their friendship.

I wanted head talk with Ginny, but this was neither the time nor the place. I had always thought of us as not only inhabiting the same planet, but also living on the same street, even as next-door neighbours. But in the space of these last few hours she had moved to another city.

I had Mike just as she had Colin. I wanted to know her again. Ultimately I wanted to ease her worries, mine too, and return to our easy rapport. I didn't know what we needed to say. I just knew that it was necessary for us to talk alone. The opportunity never arose.

**

"Astronauts undergo stress tests," Colin stated generalising our talk of Carol.

"It's the histrionics I can't abide," said Ginny, sipping her coffee.

"Maybe the human condition requires strife," Mike began. "There're not too many problems out here. Everything's available. So people generate problems."

Our breakfast post-mortem of the party had become a general analysis of camp life. How many times had we discussed variations of this same theme? It was an unfathomable preoccupation that defied logic, like hospital patients discussing the symptoms but not the cure. Here the cure was obvious to everyone.

My mind wandered to the poster of Irish doors on Colin's bedroom door. Revealing frontages to what possibly lay behind them. Mock Georgian, all frosted-glass, shed-like in green-gloss, panelled. And I saw too only the public faces of these people. And if they were houses, then Pinball had crazy paving leading to his; Geoff's had a well-tended inviting garden, but the house appeared to have no entrance; Linda's was modern, clean, efficient, plastic; Carol's appeared sweet, but some plants were poisonous and Merv's would appear pedestrian until you spotted the bright pointed hat of a garden gnome.

Enter and one would be led to summery attics with shafts of honey-dusted childhood memories: the acceptable anecdotes, away from the cellar of secrets, the false wall, or even the crypt containing an image-destroying corpse. The abodes themselves were not suffering normal wear and tear: most had structural faults. These had not been apparent earlier, as if everyone arrived freshly decorated. Some had used ivy, others bushes and trees, still others colourful tarpaulins to hide any obvious damage and ongoing repairs. Like mine they had their secret annexes, antechambers, favourite alcoves and other places of sanctuary. Cracks and idiosyncrasies had begun to surface on the facades. Subsidence and dry rot were in evidence. Most obviously Carol had taken to vandalising hers after allowing hobnailed boots in.

Of course bitterness makes me pessimistic. Were Mike, Ginny, Colin, Bob, Scab, Tass, Sparky warped? And what of Ita, Aine, Paul, Mary O. and the others? Even Ian's wound was nothing extraordinary and certainly healable. No, there were normal people who'd strayed here.

I made Ginny promise to visit, emphasising it by making Colin bear witness, but stopped short of setting a date. Only on the farm could we have the time to get close again.

I think she understood why I was not staying on. The effervescence had dissipated. Had I known that I would not see her for many years I would have remained.

On the way back to the farm Mike and I sat in an easy silence. I was drowsy for a while. We touched on camp life once. He appreciated my submarine analogy but offered his own.

"They're like oarsmen, toiling to the bang of a drum, having a panoramic view of where they've been and a restricted one of where they're going. They're a jolly lot, sugaring their lives with *sid* and partying. Galley slaves nonetheless."

"Shackled by money?" I added. What happened Snoopy?

He nodded.

"Who's banging the drum?" I asked.

"That dive leader chap?"

"Geoff? No, I don't think so."

"Then it's nobody," he said. "It's the illusory pulse of camp life that keeps them pulling on the oars."

"And us?"

"We've a clear view of where we're going." He was piqued as much as surprised.

"You have." I didn't want this; it was heading for a confrontation. The party had been a calamity and I could not tell him that it wasn't like that earlier, that things had grown more strained. "I'd like to get off the farm soon."

"January."

"Good." I would have to bear another Christmas on the farm, after all.

I looked out across the empty vista, having just passed through another shantytown clustered about a pristine mosque. Saudi Arabia was a land of extremes: extreme heat and extreme nothingness. Where water was scarce and everything was cooked down to its elemental state. The land was reflected in the Arab people in their extreme wealth and extreme want. They had adapted their ways to suit the environment. Elaborate talk and rituals, perfumes and ceremonies, unity and family.

This inviolate land affected the expats too. They were apt to emotional extremities. The imported society suffered. Most sense of homegrown culture was gradually and inexorably burnt off. Ground down to the essential.

* * *

Muslim prayer begins with the muezzin's call declaring: "There is no God but God; Mohammed is the Prophet of God." I would stop after the first four words. For I don't believe in Him, Buddha, The Beatles, Beethoven, money or Microsoft. Neither do I claim to be an existentialist, atheist or agnostic. Tragedy knocks the material into touch and the spiritual takes a hammering too. Everything, absolutely everything, is thrown into question and mundane relief. You're left with primitive religion or banal philosophy or emptiness.

I had emptiness. My inherited propensity for depression allowed me nothing else. And my mother's death a few months after leaving Saudi didn't help. My ordeal probably hastened her death.

I remember the pills I was supposed to take and thinking of what I had once said to my mother during one of her lows. Her daily consumption was on the kitchen table before her and I jokingly suggested she play Solitaire with them.

My departure from prison was hasty and surprising. There was no time for lengthy goodbyes. I didn't leave like Rita, but I only just had time to scribble my parents' address on a scrap of paper. I pressed it into Pip's hand and we hugged. I never heard from her. And despite numerous attempts I failed to find out what happened to her. Within the country one had trouble getting information, what chance did one have outside? It pains when I think of her and her daughter.

At some point a priest came to talk to me. I was still in Saudi, at the air base, I think. I wasn't in prison, but under house arrest. His casual attire enhanced the progressive image he was at pains to project. Although not quite backslapping, he was everybody's buddy. One of the boys. I found his diabolical boy-scout serenity irritating. He talked and talked, rapidly exhausting his repertoire of approaches, falling from his favourite originals to bland textbook ones. The more he talked the more glazed my eyes became the more his brow knotted. Perplexed and constricted he offered me silence and even this went unacknowledged. The quiet space was gratifying and I dreaded the thought of him shovelling words into it. After a long pause and when I feared he was about to speak again I uttered my first and only sentence to him. I dabbed my words with a sweet syrupy kindness I thought would appeal and simultaneously mock, so satisfying my need to convey threat. "Go with your God, but please go."

* * *

What had I expected? A stretch limousine? True, the windows were tinted. Many of the private cars had tinted or mirrored windows. Nevertheless this was an ordinary saloon. Abdul did not use this chauffeur. He drove his cruiser himself. Undoubtedly this man was the women's chauffeur. In any case they were not so disgustingly rich that they could dispatch a private jet to collect their favourite ice cream from Italy.

The chauffeur opened a rear door and I climbed in. I discovered that the person in the back was Marina. Naturally she was covered. This was the only opportunity I was to have to talk to her, but she was her usual reticent self, maybe because of the chauffeur, I don't know, and I was too excited about the party. So, after some brief shots in the dark, silence like our *abaayas* shrouded us.

Day was giving itself up to night.

I suspended my excitement during the uneventful drive. Long ago I had learnt how to dull myself. I'd practised on my journeys to Riyadh with Pav.

When we stopped at the solid wooden gates that broke the high wall and the chauffeur tooted the horn twice I was jolted to life. The garage-sized gates were pulled back and we rounded the circular fountain in a large courtyard. The building surrounded us and I was reminded of a fort. Although there appeared to be no-one standing at the parapet, the crenellated finish aided the image.

A European builds a private house on a plot of land, effectively surrounding it with a garden. An Arab builds his structure to the limits of the land thus surrounding the garden. So it was with Abdul's place. Subconsciously, I no longer regarded it as Anoud's property. This was not something I had come to accept. This was how it was in this country.

Marina opened her door. "Wait," she said when she saw me going for my door handle. A figure appeared and opened my side.

"Thank you," I said to the man, who did not look at me. I felt foolish for speaking English, but it was too late to say "*Shukran.*"

"Come with me," said Marina, heading towards one of the arches. Everything that was not solid white-washed concrete, was veined marble: cool like frozen slabs of pond water. Dipped spots neck-laced the fountain and strategically placed soft lights illuminated the courtyard. Light burnt at shuttered windows.

We entered the two-storey building under the arch and turned left. I guessed that this corridor ran round the courtyard, with all the rooms leading off. We reached a corner and ascended stone steps that spiralled once. I assumed there to be a stairwell in each of the four corners. We walked a corridor that mirrored the ground floor: walls broken by Roman-arch crescents where the rooms had windows facing the courtyard.

Marina opened a door to a small room with a sin and a mirror. We went in and removed *abaayas*. She waited and I realised this was my moment to check my appearance. I followed her along the corridor.

A woman stood. She had been sitting on a stool outside a closed door. Marina said nothing as we approached. I had resolved to speak when spoken to. The woman knocked on the door and opened it.

I was stupefied not by the light and sound spilling into the hushed corridor but by the abundance of colour. I must have stood and gaped for I didn't see Anoud until she was almost upon me.

There were about thirty women in the room. I knew that I had been invited to a party but had no idea of numbers. Just the intoxicating presence of so many women was bewildering. I had not been in such exclusively female company since straying from the beach with the others at the BSAC beach barbecue some eight months ago and then we'd only been half a dozen or so. These Arab women of all ages, shapes and sizes were wearing extravagant dresses the likes of which you'd see at a pageant or on bridesmaids. Swishing dresses of satin, chiffon, lace, even velvet fanned out. There were large bows and tight bodices. Admittedly the older women were not so brash, but their evening dresses were no less feminine. I too had chosen an evening dress, but by comparison I was a Cinderella whose Fairy Godmother had forgotten her. And to think I had gone to great pains selecting inoffensively long sleeves, a high-neck and shapelessness.

I was dismayed that Marina had not entered the room.

"*Salaam 'alaykum* (Peace be upon you)," I blurted.

"*Alaykum is-salaam* (And upon you be peace)," Anoud returned and smiled, and I knew that I was her honoured guest.

Others approached but I wanted to give her the gift I carried. At the risk of veering from some unwritten convention I thrust my laden hand in her direction, my face deciding to do its best furnace impression.

The choice of gift had caused me some headaches. I had decided to go for the easy party option of bringing a bottle. In this case a bottle of rose water. However, this party presented me with the opportunity of giving her something for her amulet. At the shop I found rose oil, which I considered suitably expensive compliment until I saw the hand-held silver sprinklers, not unlike those Christian priests use to disperse holy water. She seemed delighted by the sprinkler.

A small crowd had descended upon me and I was greeted by each and every one of them. I felt silly repeating the same phrase, this was Japanese bowing and I'd become a nodding dog. Yet, there were smiles and everything was amicable. I occasionally threw my name in to break the monotony. Even a *Merhaba* or two slipped in.

All this came to an abrupt end with an angry shriek. Harsh words parted the crowd. Anoud blanched and led me to a group of older women sitting together in a heap of shiny cushions. Some hierarchical impropriety had taken place. My presence or giving Anoud her gift had caused things to go awry.

I walked down a loose avenue of guests slightly behind Anoud. Her high heels clack-clacked on the marble floor. I felt considerably flat-footed in my moccasins. I'd come to the ball in carpet slippers. I had expected to remove my shoes at the doorway or thereabouts. Another surprise. All the women wore glossy high heels, even stilettos. I'd not expected bare floors either. Later, when a guest brushed the hanging edge of the tablecloth of the food-laden tables that lined one wall, I spotted the large carpet rolled-up underneath.

These women, one of whom was Anoud's mother, gave the others stern looks. I received smiles and smiles tempered with critical looks. They did not rise and as with the others there was no shaking of hands or touch of any kind, merely the ritual greeting.

Anoud had picked up a few words and was saying "mother", "aunt", "sister." I noted Anoud's and Abdul's mothers. In the introductory furore I missed the connection with someone who was later to become the real honoured guest. This woman, an Egyptian, was either Abdul's brother's wife, Abdul's cousin's wife, or the wife of some other relative of Abdul's or finally a business colleague's wife.

If there was a simultaneous gathering of the men in another part of the house or elsewhere Mike had not been invited.

Despite the painstaking introductions I don't remember a single name from the party. They were not names with which I could associate.

I had some stilted conversation with Abdul's sister who spoke appalling English before a new arrival appeared. I observed their greeting which certainly wasn't in any guidebook I'd read. They touched fingertips and afterwards brought the touched index finger to their lips and kissed it. I'd started swotting-up on the unfamiliar social etiquette as soon as I received the invitation. I'd read that the length of the verbal greeting reflected the respect or depth of friendship. If it was respect, how did they greet their King without going on for half an hour or more?

Anoud came over and said something to Abdul's sister who turned to me and said: "Eating time."

Trolleys of steaming food had been brought in and the dishes placed on the tables.

For want of something to say I gloated: "Oh good." Then hoping to bury any faux pas I added: "The food looks good." I had only fleetingly seen the spread and knew that what looked like sausage rolls were not. I still believed I was the honoured guest and was in mortal fear of being presented with a sheep's eye.

The older women were already at the food and I was horrified to see some of them trying something and if it was not to their liking putting it back. There was no queue, neither was it a free-for-all. It was all relaxed and orderly. Abdul's sister did her best at trying to tell me what things were, until she called a girl in her late teens over. She was one of the youngest present. There were no children. Her English was far superior to my companion's, yet I felt forces at play and did not draw the girl into too much conversation. Through her, Abdul's sister said that a meal without bread was not a meal and I was obliged to take a piece. With what was on the table, bread seemed extraneous. There was so much to try that I never ate the same thing twice and didn't manage some things at all.

I would have liked recipes, but the austerity of our language made this nigh on impossible. And although some of these women were Bedouin, there was wealth here and servants had prepared the meal, so maybe they didn't have the same recipes.

The bread was not a grave error, although crackers would have sufficed, for there were numerous dips: hummus or mashed garbanzos (chick peas) in one bowl, sesame paste covered in oil in another and then one containing avocado seasoned with garlic, parsley, cumin and salt, also under oil. There were pastries too: spinach, goat cheese and meat with pine nuts, cracked wheat and meat patties, puffy crispy fried shrimp crackers, black and green olives, a fiery hot pepper relish, flaky cheese puffs, raw beet and spicy pickled lemon halves, lemony salads of cress diced cucumbers, tomatoes, carrots, parsley and croutons. Stuffed vegetables and fish were on offer. Mounds of white rice laced with raisins and pine nuts towered in colourful porcelain bowls, there was saffron rice too and plates of okra. There was a whole roasted lamb bursting with macaroni and hard-boiled eggs and slivered almonds. There were cheeses, macaroni, custards, cakes, melons, dates and date cookies, short fat bananas, grapes and the smells of cardamom, saffron, cumin, cinnamon and pepper. The amount of food was staggering. I knew we would not eat it all and that the leftovers would go to servants.

Iced water and fruit juice cocktails sat in pitchers.

I fixed the plate in my left hand to make sure that I only used my right hand and cause no offence. I had begun to wonder how to sit. With so many in the room it would be difficult not to present someone with the soles of my feet. The women already seated on the cushions strewn in piles about the edges of the room, with or without shoes, had tucked their feet behind them so that their soles faced the wall. I wasn't sure I could maintain this position. As a foreigner I could be forgiven such coarseness, but ignorance was a trait I did not want to project.

The problem was solved when Anoud appeared with a small ottoman. I refused but she insisted and I was left to feel conspicuous: perched above the others. All that was missing were my shield, trident and helmet to complete the picture of Britannia.

I sat at the wall facing the entrance and the food. To my left were the older women and the dark carved latticework that covered the window onto the courtyard. I assumed it could be removed. The opposite wall, looking outside was broken by archer's slits covered with fine mosquito mesh: dark as an old tea strainer. Simple wall hangings adorned the walls.

Everyone in the room had that blue-black hair making me the fairest of the all, but that was as far as it went with the Cinderella comparison. I was not the most striking. Not all were like Anoud: voluptuous or beautiful. Some were plain, plump, leathery, hawkish. But all bespoke character.

At first I returned to the food when my companions did but eventually I went alone. I regarded this as a compliment. I made an effort to bring up a belch at the end. The women about me appeared pleased.

There was much stiff talk until Abdul's sister was called away and I turned to the girl who spoke passable English. Feeling condescending I left my perched and sat on the floor.

She told me that she was married and happy. The latter assurance seemed an unnecessary challenge, perhaps to an assumed bigotry on my part. So her assertion was immediately suspect and had the opposite effect to what she intended. Had the circumstances been otherwise I would have asked her why she had felt the necessity for emphasis.

* * *

There was some commotion and I followed everyone's eyes to the woman who shook her head in submission and rose. Silence fell upon the gathering and she began to sing. Her voice was good enough to stand alone. What she sang was incomprehensible, but when she finished there was much jubilation and ululating. My companion told me it was a love song.

Anoud and three others came over and sat with us. Before we could converse we were distracted by another woman being coaxed into performing. She didn't rise and began speaking measuredly. I was told she was telling a well-loved folk tale. When she was in her stride, the smile never left her face. There was much laughter. She good-humouredly put down those who interrupted her with contributions or heckling. My companions became so enraptured that they broke off translating.

During the story I reflected on what Mike had said of their language being like poetry. I knew that like the Danes, for instance, with their many words for describing snow, so the Arabs had a hundred words for the horse or the sword.

I was beginning to fear that I would be called to do a party-piece. The thought of pulling Prince Ali and Jasmine out of my bag put a smile on my lips. Singing *Diamonds are a girl's best friend* was not out of the question. Many of them could know of Marilyn Monroe. I didn't relish the thought of prancing up and down with outstretched arms, but sitting seemed restrained. Then it occurred to me that they could think I was mocking their wealth.

My fear was realised when the teenager, their spokeswoman, asked me whether I would do anything. *God save the Queen* sprung to mind, but I shook my head. Other cultural rules were at play here and I was terrified of damaging thousands of years of civilisation in one fell swoop. Mercifully I was not pressed.

One woman spoke to me in French, but I was stumped by the years that lay between now and school.

Before we found conversation through my interpreter we were ushered towards the older women for a group photograph. I saw a servant return the camera to a guest after taking the picture and after we resumed our places I asked Anoud whether I could have a copy.

Conversation was again thwarted when another woman began to sing. I had no idea of the time, there were no clocks and I wasn't wearing a watch. When yet another woman started to sing I wondered whether I could last the entire evening. I could not simply leave. Apart from being interpreted as an insult, I was dependent on them taking me home.

The stuttering and frustrating dialogue was generally channelled through the teenager. Her translation blunted subtleties but the essence remained.

When we had time for conversation I began to wish for the interruption of song. One of Anoud's companions asked whether I had children and then whether I would have children. I answered probably.

This uncertainty was met with incredulity and I found myself listening to them explaining the role of women.

They were not trapped between two cultures as I had thought. These women were content. I could have said resigned, but they did not paint pictures of desperate women. On the contrary they appeared genuinely happy. Ginny was wrong.

Another thought that struck me was the sheer joy here. It was liberating.

The gist of what they conveyed was that there were physical and emotional differences between men and women. Arab women had an important role in their society. Motherhood. Something of a dirty word in the West. With respect to a woman's place in society both Christianity and Islam concurred. Religion in the West had declined in importance and coupled with women's drive for equality, basic values had been lost. Their worldview held that equality was flawed by gender differences. True freedom lay in fulfilling your God-given role and attaining His and therefore your own aspirations. In the West women ignored this and tried to compete with men. If not that, then they'd sold themselves to the empty transience of fashion; fooled into thinking that beauty was the ticket to happiness. In Islamic society women had the security of purpose in which to mature and grow. Why, the veil was proof of this, as security and protection and allegiance to their men.

I did not necessarily agree. But neither did I protest or challenge. I was inquisitive: trying to grasp what they were telling me to the full, to increase the quality of the grist so that I could not mill it to powder with a few biased clichés.

To this end for every mental dismissal of mine, I could now conjure up a counter argument. Their world was sound if one embraced Islam. Time and again their religion came to the fore.

My openness and overt interest spurred them on or they wanted to know me better and they led me to a woman. I thought they were bringing me to someone who spoke fluent English. On the contrary the person they presented spoke no English at all. But then communication with this person transcended language.

I'd noticed her earlier. Not because she was one of the oldest. Not even because she seemed the most downtrodden. But because there was an aura about her. Before the food arrived, from across the room she had caught my eye, as if she had sensed me observing her and in that moment I felt her draw something from me. Only when she turned to the person talking to her was I released.

When Anoud presented me I gathered that she was a great aunt.

Her crab-apple face was severe rather than benign. Even her range of facial expressions seemed limited and reptilian. Her callused hands bespoke a hard life. Yet, there was an irresistibility about her that instilled, or almost hypnotically drew out, trust. She could not be denied. Her eyes had little white, so it was almost impossible to tell where she was looking. Women shuffled and she patted the sudden place beside her. The others sat in front of us, making a loose circle.

When she unexpectedly took my right hand in her hands I did not flinch. Normally I would have shied away. Being British I expected my space to be respected by strangers. It seemed self-understood that she be allowed to do this. Her smile was a crack of knowledge, as crooked as an alligator's grimace. Her leathery hands clamped about mine. I was under the spell of her dark, rheumy eyes. I could not break away and did not want to break away. She continued to look at me. Words were spoken to her, not as requests or suggestions, but respectful like offerings. But her listening to them took second place to absorbing me.

Panic was about to buckle my smile when she spoke. Anoud reached over and tapped the back of my left hand and I looked at her with relief and a questioning shake of the head.

"Your hand," said the teenager.

I lifted my left hand and saw the gnarled fingers of the old woman open. I smiled awkwardly and gave up my free hand too. Yet, the woman continued to look into my face.

She spoke again, and others spoke, and from their tone I felt they were imploring her. I asked what she had said, but the teenager just smiled and the others continued to speak to her. I was searching faces when my hands were turned. She lifted my palms close and went over their lines and contours with a thumb as if reading them through touch and for a second I wondered whether she was blind. The others fell silent, straining to hear her occasional mutterings. Then she looked me full in the face again and I felt something cold and frightening in her. Her smile was the unyielding grip of an alligator.

She arrested my growing fear anew by speaking. The others babbled and she curtly admonished them.

By now I was growing peeved by what I wanted to believe was ominous play-acting, but I was rooted in the terror that there was nothing phoney in her behaviour.

"What's she saying?" I asked, unable to look away.

Perfect English like pure oxygen cut though my scrambled thoughts.

The crystal words came from the Egyptian sitting beyond the woman. "She said that it is a shame that you are not a strong believer." That I could be a non-believer was incomprehensible to the old woman. Atheist was not a word in their vocabulary. Before I could ask why it was a shame the old woman spoke. I looked to the Egyptian for a translation. A gesture said wait. Others nodded silently as the woman spoke. When she appeared to have finished I received my translation.

"For something to exist, somebody must have believed in it. Look at that wall hanging. Is it not beautiful? Observe the intricate pattern the artist chose and deeper: look at the substance, the way it is woven. Now look at the skin on your hand. Or take that camera. It is truly a magnificent piece of equipment. It can zoom and self-focus and choose when to flash. Only a person could have made something so complex. And now consider your eye. Do you really think it could all be chance? Trial and error?" She smiled triumphantly. "Are you, yourself, not living proof of the existence of a Maker, a God?"

Resisting being drawn into argument I dived into a side-alley. "Yes, but why did she say it was a shame I was not a strong believer?"

The Egyptian spoke to the old woman who replied with a shrug. I had the feeling she was asking for guidance rather than elaboration. She looked at me when she spoke and her hesitation said there was more. "She said she saw pain and sadness in you."

I was aghast.

Glances were exchanged.

Abdul's mother clapped her hands sharply and I jumped. Anoud's mother then told a tale to a silent room. I was left to stew. Anoud smiled sympathetically from time to time, which was disconcerting rather than comforting. When the tale was finished the old woman spoke to the teenager who helped her to her feet. She left the room. Anoud's mother's tale precipitated great discussion. I looked to the Egyptian who knew I was suffering.

She smiled, but it was a wry, cruel smile. "You want to know more?"

I waited and eventually she looked away. I fetched myself a drink and resumed my place next to the Egyptian.

She smiled. She didn't like me.

"She saw something, didn't she?"

"She said you are not a strong believer -"

"That's not what I meant."

"I know. And I know that you are a non-believer."

She was being deliberately evasive, so I went on the hunt. "It must be nice to have God to support you."

"Then you do not know religion or God. Religion is a guide to living not a preparation for dying. God is an ideal, not a super-being to be proved. He is a hard, cruel master. Look at the world. Surely the thought of a God is more frightening than the thought of his non-existence?"

She was being indirect so I became perverse. "And do you also believe in the prescribed role of women?" Apparently vestiges of pent-up arguments were seething beneath the surface.

"You are asking whether I believe in Islam? Yes. Naturally. Women should be educated. But being a wife and mother comes first. Later, with the advantage of experience, they should work."

"Your country is westernised and at the same time Islamic. Here they won't tolerate another religion."

"The marriage of the western ways and Islam is not a stable one. You think they are afraid that Christianity could take over if they let it in. No, no. You are very wrong. They fear the threat of your cola-culture. To the young it is very persuasive. They fear that religion could take second place. Like it has in the West."

I nodded understandingly. Strangely I sought this woman's friendship. Presumably because I could converse with her. "I'd love to visit your country." What I thought was a compliment had adverse effects.

"You have not understood what I have been telling you." I took the swipe without wincing. "Travelling for pleasure is relatively unknown in the Islamic world. Many of these women have never been outside their country. We travel on business. Hajj is an exception, but then it is a journey to God and to one's inner self. Travel for us has no other purpose. Tourism is decadent. It is Western."

"Your country encourages tourism."

"Yes. Tourism brings money. I don't have to approve. But it touches wounds." She paused. "Extravagant shows and concerts are held in Luxor and in the shadows there is poverty."

"Mismanagement," I offered, not wanting to say corruption.

"We are proud of our monuments. But they come from an un-Islamic time. The pharaohs enslaved the populace and declared themselves gods. You will find it hard to believe but many of us are not proud of the ancient Egyptians. In the eyes of the West our history ends about 1,000 BC., after which we just declined. But Cairo has the oldest university in the world. The Al Azhar. It is over 500 years old and was the basis for high schools in the middle Ages. But few westerners visit it. Many do not know of its existence. You are drawn to the great blocks of stone. They are magnificent, aren't they?" Then, as if she'd forgotten something she hastily went on. "Ah, and mummies. Yes, you come to our museums to see them. For us they are not works of art, but the dead exhumed. And we turn our heads in shame. So again you touch a wound. The Koran explicitly damns the death-cult of these Egyptians as idolising."

"I see the uneasiness this must cause in your land." I could see too that Islamic fanatics could use poverty to their advantage, tear at these wounds, scream indignation at the heathen decadence, move the people against the West.

"Do you?"

"Yes. All I wanted to do was visit."

"Yes. But you should no longer be surprised by the attitude of these people. They are -"

A servant stood over us with a large brass tray of coffee cups. A second servant poured coffee from a long-spouted ornate brass pot. Anoud presented the Egyptian with a cup. I knew that formally the giver should take the first cup. These well-placed leaves of text I had committed to memory had been blown by the mind-dilating events of the evening. In any case the idea seemed ludicrous as there were so many people and if everyone starting playing nodding dogs the coffee would be cold. Perhaps the ritual did not apply under such circumstances. However, at least three cups should be drunk. Not such a gargantuan feat: the vessels were the size of eggcups. There was one other thing I had read. Coffee was served at the conclusion of an evening.

The liquid was slick and pale green and spiced with Guatemalan cardamom. *Gawaha Arabi* (sometimes *gahwa*) was an acquired taste. After the third cup I rocked it gently as I gave it back to the server. This was how one said "no more, thank you." To say it would have had no effect.

Anoud had given out the first round; a companion of hers had then taken over, so my friend had joined us.

She saw that I was not as troubled as before. Neither was I joyful. I told the Egyptian to tell her that I had had a very enjoyable evening.

The teenager came over and beseeched the Egyptian.

"What does she want?"

"She wants me to dance. I was once a belly-dancer."

"A great belly-dancer," said the teenager, crouching before us.

"Well-known," the Egyptian corrected.

Anoud interrupted and the teenager translated. "She says she was a great belly-dancer. She still decks the tables of many Cairo restaurants at Ramadan." I mentioned this to Mike and he said during Ramadan the well-off paid for tables to be laden for the disadvantaged.

The Egyptian closed her eyes and shook her head from faraway. A distant hand was wearily raised to signify that all was bagatelle. Then her eyes snapped open and she returned to us. "I have not danced in public for many years." I wanted to ask why but she spoke to the teenager.

She then sat up and stood the cup on her outstretched palm. The liquid quivered as she waited for complete attention. Slowly she moved her arm, bent at the elbow, towards her body, travelling under her armpit and on. She completed a full circle without spilling a drop. She was double-jointed.

The teenager squealed with delight and the woman did it again with her other arm.

* * *

Anoud's party and the monstrous final evening pressed the weeks before the end into insignificance. Thus these weeks were rendered a series of banalities.

A new cycle had begun. This was where we had come in. There were a few late deliveries of seed and the like, but generally the comings and goings tailed off and there were few strangers on the farm.

Tass left for a well-deserved break. The lads were made acutely aware of his absence every day they went out. I only noticed it in the lack of pistachio nuts and farts.

I spoke to Ginny, but we didn't connect. Seeing *The Hollies* on camp was an excuse for getting together, although we didn't need one. I thought this group no longer existed, but they were doing Sun City and the Saudi circuit. In the end I couldn't work up the enthusiasm and piled my hopes into her visit. Something that would never be.

* * *

We have turned onto the airstrip where parallel lines meet. And I am drawing such perfect circles in my mind. Circles that would make Mr. Sidebottom proud.

I'm in the belly of a military plane; sitting alongside a perky American woman whose name I don't remember. She is a nurse. The aircraft is bereft of comfort, depressing and dark. There are some soldiers grouped near the front. I know they have been told not to talk to us. We sit like paratroopers, along the length of the fuselage. I've asked why I am not being taken out on a commercial flight and they tell me that they're all booked up. Expedience is another excuse. I know the truth is to do with security through isolation. They don't want an incident. I don't care. I just want to get out.

Before boarding, a female officer painted my face. Said she wanted to put a bit of colour in my cheeks. I put up no resistance. I was listening to a fly incessantly demonstrating the Doppler Effect.

Only much later would I sit in front of a mirror, begin routinely combing my returning hair, and suddenly catch the appearance of the person before me. I'd sat before mirrors before, although there was a long period when I hadn't. This time I saw my face anew. My metamorphosis had been a gradual thing, but no less shocking than that of Gregor Samsa. I was a car-crash patient having undergone plastic surgery, viewing a familiar face that was not quite my own. The disfigurement I had suffered lay beneath the surface, but I saw it in my appearance.

The plane banks and I glimpse something out of one of the few windows. Strange sewage-work-sized disks on the endless landscape. More perfect circles. Birthmarks blemishing the skin. The pivots of a farm.

Being out of Saudi should help remedy my depression. But I am suffering a new kind of depression, a location-resistant one. Combating it seems futile, like encouraging someone hooked up on a life-support machine with no will to live.

Oil and Water

The *Enola Gay* was a battered white Chevrolet.

The dishes were still soaking when it arrived. The suds were gone, the water lukewarm.

In an effort to remain in company Ian often let the dishes soak, washing them as late as possible. Sometimes he got too tired and left them for the next day. I'd noticed that since the execution he couldn't abide being alone. The slightest pretext was enough to keep him from retiring. Weight training with the Filipinos was a short-lived fad for him. His efforts at winning my sympathy had long dissipated.

Tonight Mike had asked for contributions to his list of farm requirements. Abdul and my husband were to make necessary purchases. "Abdul's coming early tomorrow morning."

"Early?" Ian repeated ironically. Pav and Ian stayed on. Scab and Sparky had gone to their rooms. Tass was not due back for another week.

Mike was steadfast. "He knows we're short-staffed."

Mike, Ian, Pav and I were not edging towards reconciliation. What started out as a discussion on what needed purchasing, replacing or repairing, had slipped into terrain we'd once frequented and facilely grazed: Bob's kingdom. As if returning to work after a vacation we were hit by the fresh familiarity and under scrutiny the deflating mundanity. The rift between us was tragic and, although we were not stumbling towards embraces, handshakes were possible. A camp had materialised in the valley between us, common ground, persuading us to leave our own. A Camp David.

When the visitors came we were still walking uncertainly, tracing old routes on autopilot. We even broached the taboo subject of the still. Ian taking wary delight in telling us of their nocturnal excursions. Driving to Masstock or supplying an insatiable black-market through Pav's Filipino contacts. They'd stop on the road with their bonnet up and wait for their contact to arrive. There was confessional relief in Ian's speech: as if sharing the experience excused it.

Sitting about our nightcaps we peeked under dust covers until we found something suitably innocuous. An old discussion was polished up and we smiled anew. As with the Aramco stories these too could not be verified. They lay firmly in Bob's kingdom, in the deep expat hinterland of Saudi-bashing.

To overcome the water problem many ideas had been proposed. Cloud seeding was one and adapting tankers to carry water one way and oil the other had been another. This latter idea had proven technically impossible. The most bizarre I had heard was that of towing an iceberg. I could not free myself of the image of a colossus of titanic proportions arriving as an ice-cube for the King.

In retrospect it seems strange that none of us rose to see who would arrive at such a late hour. It was after nine-thirty. Nobody wanted to jeopardise the armistice that appeared to be a mere arm's length away.

The four of them -

* * *

Stop. "Just a minute," he glances at me. "May I?" He already has. He excitedly presses rewind, then play. "*and they were in the -* " Stop. "Sorry," he smiles. I hate his smile. Rewind, play. "*There were five of them in all and they were in the hall -*" Stop. He is triumphant. "See, you say there were four of them. Yet, under hypnosis you claim there to be five. Dawn, I feel -"

I cut him off with a mumble.

My mind, my personality is again being picked with talons of steel. His clumsiness is metal jabbing tenderness. Of all the psychiatrists, nearly all of whom preferred being referred to as therapist, this supposed hypno-therapist is the most annoying. His very profession puts him at a disadvantage. He is an intruder who has connived his way into me through a back door. He's broken a pane of glass, reached in and turned the knob. And I loathe listening to the distant voice that I barely recognise as my own; the tape flattening the wholesome resonance that sinus and cranial cavities lend the speech I hear in my head.

This government-appointed quack isn't doing his job properly. His bias is showing. Aren't doctors meant to establish your strengths as well as your weaknesses?

"Sorry?" he smiles again and something physically squirms, flexes, inside me.

"There were five of them," I snap irritably. "Four came in and one stayed outside."

The smile. He won't meet my eye and I wonder who is assessing whom. "I see." He makes a minuscule note in my file. "Shall we continue?"

* * *

The four of them were in the corridor before anyone reacted. The men stood. I remained seated, petrified by the jarring of their scraping chairs. Pav and Ian, nearest the entrance, were the first to get up, their backs to the sink and kitchen appliances. Mike stood through reflex. Ludicrous though it may sound, my first thought was that the visitors were going to ask for directions. Ludicrous, because one had to leave the main road at a simple unlit sign. My next thought was better: along the lines of requiring petrol, oil or a tow. Yet, any one of these shrivelled under the fact of the farm's obscurity.

I only partially saw the first Arab for he remained in the doorway as if he'd drifted into the wrong room. His dirty *thobe* aside, he looked slovenly. He was slack-jawed, his bottom lip hanging; only drool was missing. He scanned the kitchen emotionlessly, as if he relied on another to endow him with sense. And so it would prove to be. If others smiled, he did too. If they frowned, a moment later his brow would furrow. His empty gaze riveted me to my seat. His eyes were not glassy but he looked like someone with influenza.

I heard his voice before I saw the speaker. He was talking to Ian or Pav or both of them. "Sit, my friend." To allow the speaker in slack-mouth was forced to edge uncertainly into the kitchen. "We mean no harm." He was smiling and the Mouth grinned and nodded slightly. The comment struck me as peculiar. Why make such a statement?

In general the speaker's appearance, even looks, were more acceptable than that of his companion.

"What do you want?" asked Mike.

The speaker turned, the smile remaining. "Why so aggressive?" He spread his hands and leaned back as if he was about to give Mike a friendly bear hug. My husband was unimpressed and the speaker switched on an expression of astonishment, before reverting to his trusty smile. He stepped back. "Ah, my friend here." He put an arm around the shoulders of Mouth, who was robbed of sense by the proximity of the spokesman, and looked ahead concentrating on the words for a clue as to what expression to adopt. I could see a further two *thobes* at the entrance. "He has frightened you? He is a poor beggar. Harmless." Mouth didn't know how to look and remained dull.

Despite the speaker's assertions no one moved. "Sit," he pleaded.

"What do you want?" asked Mike again, this time pouring calm reason over the words.

The Arab gave a stage laugh. Mouth grinned broadly and I was frightened. His smile frightened me. It was wily, like the leer one sees on a skull. He was indeed poor. His teeth were bad. He was thin maybe undernourished. Or maybe he'd sucked a lot of stones.

The two further Arabs at the door filled the entrance. They couldn't enter without forcing the speaker and Mouth deeper into the kitchen, which in turn would mean the boys retreating. They looked into the room and I only glanced in their direction once. One of them was big, a head taller than anyone else present. The other was the size of the speaker and looked oddly familiar.

"Ah, you Westerners," he shook his head in wonder, "you have no sense of hospitality."

Appalling moments were marked-off by the clack of the clock.

I felt Ian about to protest, but Mike spoke first. "Do you want tea?" The tone of his voice was neutral and so successful that the speaker could not fault it or find insult in it. He barely mouthed the word tea before a broad smile stretched his lips.

To understand our position is to understand our bondage, our fear. Months of virtual vegetarianism had not rendered us passive. From our arrival onwards we were aware that the country did not follow our rules and we had next to no rights. There was an inherent fear of the unknown. We were quite content to stick our heads in the sand. Fear kept us ignorant and conversely ignorance was fear. We were second-class citizens. To tangle with an Arab was to risk the frightening vagaries of the authorities.

"Yes, yes," he began with exaggerated enthusiasm.

I was relieved that the Arab hadn't reacted differently. He could have grown angry. Equally, Ian, who was slightly closer to the man than my husband, could have said something provocative.

With hindsight it may have been better to challenge them, since such a confrontation was merely postponed. There were a number of things in our favour. Sparky and Scab were not present and could help us if we called for them. Pav was instilling a decent level of respect in the leader. But more than anything else this early in the encounter, there was a sense of uncertainty in them as much as in us, an uncertainty that was open to negotiation, one with which to could reason, even persuade.

At the time I was grateful for my husband's diplomacy.

Pav moved before anyone and for a moment I think the leader thought he was going to be attacked. Mouth's emaciated body stiffened.

The wall-cupboard was opened and Pav was reaching inside by the time the leader looked to his companions.

There was an awful silence filled by the blunt sound of cups being removed from the cupboard, tea-bags dully extracted from the carton, the crash of water into the electric kettle and the final click of the switch.

The leader watched the entire operation as if for the first time. I think he looked on in horror at this utilitarian procedure. Western brutality: everything stripped down to necessity. Maybe he was checking Pav's every move. Such was his absorption that he spoke only after Pav had resumed his earlier position at the window.

"Five cups," he said. Then as an afterthought: "please." Pav gave nothing away and fetched a further cup. During these moments I had time to assess what this meant. The obvious point was that there was a fifth member to their group. Less obvious, and not without sinister connotations, was that this person was outside. Why would they post somebody outside unless their intentions were dubious? This was the first glint of danger. Before there had been the possibility of innocence, chance. Now there was design: a mote on the face of rational circumstance.

"Come, let us sit," said the leader, looking to Pav rather than his companions. Pav expressionlessly filled the mugs, returned the kettle to its place and took up his corner position. His attitude worried me. He appeared to want to aggravate the situation.

I sat. My fears of sinister motives were somewhat allayed by their dress. Their faces were exposed. No masks. All but the big one wore the standard red and white check *gutra* held in place by a jet-black double-looped *agal*. The white skullcap, which sat under this affair, was all the big one carried upon his head.

The smaller one at the door strode into the room. He was only small compared to the giant next to him. The kitchen floor creaked, tightening against the burden of their intrusion. I tried to find the familiarity in his mean face. He had tucked the tails of his *gutra* under themselves, turban-like, exposing locks of glossy blue-black hair. His features were too distinctive. He had hooded eyes that also spoke of that stone-sucking dullness. His brown irises were so dark that the pupils were lost. His face was pockmarked too, ravaged by some childhood disease, possibly smallpox. When I realised he was going to sit to my left I snapped my eyes to the big one.

Mike sat, but not in his original seat to my right. He moved closer to the doorway. Ian seated himself in his original place. The leader chose to fill the place between them. The big one took Pav's seat, directly opposite me to Ian's right. The leader said something in Arabic as he sat and Mouth left the room to return a few seconds later with the fifth member of the group.

The newcomer was also familiar but I couldn't place him. His clothes threw me. They were wrong. He took the seat between Pockmark and the big one. Only Pav and Mouth remained standing. Then I saw through the newcomer's unshaven face. I knew him. The last time I had seen him he'd been wearing western clothes. Now his Arab attire looked strange. I saw the hopeless drugged eyes. Like his companions he looked wretched. But he'd spent months stranded on the wreckage of his deed, not moving forward, having no future and left to scavenge on his past. My thoughts were spinning. Had the others recognised him too?

If it was true that corpulence was a measure of affluence in the Arab world, then these men were impoverished. Even the big one looked unhealthy. That said, apart from Mouth it was difficult to tell whether they were skinny or sinewy.

Whilst I was wondering how to communicate to the others what I knew, the leader looked about with a theatrical question mark on his face. Mike was about to speak, but the leader gave an order and Mouth picked up a mug of tea. He placed one before the leader before fetching another and going round the table, passed Ian, the big one and the newcomer to Pockmark. I stared into my empty cup, noting the implicit hierarchy through my horror. Pockmark was the second in command. My horror lay in the fact that Mouth had carried one cup at a time. His left hand was missing. I had not noticed this before. He was probably adept at hiding his affliction. He served the big one and the newcomer before returning to his mug at the entrance end of the work-surface.

We watched the leader pick up the tab on the thread and lift the tea bag to the edge of the cup. He pressed it against the cup with his thumb. Ian's teaspoon lay nearby and dipping the tip of his thumb into the scalding liquid sent a shiver down me. He knew he was being observed and moved the bag up and down. Without speaking he lifted the bag, moved it up and down in the air, teasing the last drops out and took it across the table to Ian's empty cup. Two fawn drops plopped upon the white laminate. He smiled at Ian as he dropped it into the cup.

His companions followed suit. My eyes were upon my hands but I was aware of Pockmark as he dropped his bag into my cup.

The leader stretched over for the jug of milk; one of the items of crockery that I'd discovered at the back of a wall-unit one day. Before this the lads had been content with the carton. "You are not drinking?" Without moving my head I glanced up. He was speaking to Mike, saying it more as an observation than a question.

My husband spoke for us all. "We've had ours."

The big one took the jug next, but only because he could reach it. Pockmark came next and then Rashid. Mouth came over and was left with a thin trickle. I was the only one who seemed to notice and I looked away as he glanced about the room for someone to act or articulate for him.

The leader's performance was not yet over. He slid the sugar bowl noisily over to himself. His hands were not dirty, but they seemed so as he fingered the sugar-cubes. I shifted slightly to hide my cringe. I made a mental note to throw any remaining sugar-cubes away. As it turned out by the time Mouth had the bowl there were only two left. I remember thinking that the inevitable post-analysis after they'd gone would be perfect neutral ground. The experience was unifying too. At last we had something to put the still and video behind us.

The leader lethargically plopped five cubes into his cup. Only then did he pick up a teaspoon and stir. He turned the spoon one way for a while and then reversed the direction, before lifting it out and without shaking off the drops, placing it loudly on the table, as if it had a home into which it had to be clipped into place.

He relished the silence as his companions dropped sugar cubes into their cups, looking from face to face, smiling benignly in an effort to spread his meditative spirit. He was not ugly and had what one could call an intelligent face, lit in street-wise way. If he'd been English his face would have been expressing an "isn't this grand?" look.

* * *

"You've got to find your own peace, Dawn," he says. "I'm no shrink, but maybe you should confront the past? Write about it. You always said writing was therapy." My father is right. What happened in Saudi has eclipsed my life for years. My mind has become a cemetery: full of the past and the dead. It is high time I lay ghosts to rest.

So I begin to reconstruct my journal. I search for a ruminative voice, but my voice is uneven. The therapy is over and I have a mental health certificate. But I am not healed enough to examine the wound. The effort chokes me, and I splutter and cough before I learn how to use the utensils at my disposal.

Writing is a form of therapy. A way of coming to terms with what had happened. I did not want to write a book. In fact like the Koran I had handfuls of leaves, snippets that I kept in a shoebox.

"There's a book trying to get out of this box," said one boyfriend, reading a note. I told him I had begun putting one together. Funny, that I should reveal myself so readily to him. I guess with each successive relationship I've wanted to be understood. Of course, like the others this too ended in failure. This one accused me of being self-centred.

He was right. I have become obsessed with telling my story. It has filled me up, that all I can do is regurgitate. Plumps, there's a book.

Writing it took time. A lot of time. I had not intended to write a book, but when I began floodgates were opened and it all came gushing out. I took up the pen with a vengeance, reading up on Islam and the Arab world to help me understand the driving elements behind what had happened. At the time I had not taken everything in and the dynamics of many things became apparent in the book.

My research meant reading many of the books purportedly written by Saudis or people who'd been there. Most were of such meagre substance; they were obviously pasted together. The contrivance is most telling when the Western-thinking person's point of view showed through. These books are knitted webs of hearsay and fabrication. I abhor them for they are money-spinners and dangerous propaganda.

The editor sorted out the turgid mass that was my story and chiselled out a novel. He tore out some of the routine day to day running of the farm saying that it slowed the plot. My life a plot! He rendered the occasional indigestible stream of consciousness intelligible. He cut out some of the personal touch, which often involved my husband and I commented that the end result seems indifferent to him. He softly replied that if anything the book had been therapy for me not a monument to Mike. Ultimately, and he has forgiven me, I feel the editor sensationalised and in some way cheapened my story. I can say this now, because it is truly in the past. The effort required to get it published distanced me from the contents. The goals were shifted from being therapy to something to get published, from an object of passion to an object.

Perhaps it is coincidence that when the government got wind of the book through my indiscreet research there appeared to be no problem with the much-talked-of compensation. The condition was that I dropped publication. I was being paid off. When I showed no signs of relenting they hinted that they would pooh-pooh the story as that of a crank. They went so far as to say they'd drag my therapy into the open. But my story was no threat to National security, no *Spycatcher*. You would think they would have learnt from that fiasco.

The government's opposition was an obstacle I was able to circumvent. I had signed away the truth and agreed that my story would come out as a novel. Even then circumstance conspired against me and the road to publication was pitted and stony.

* * *

Moving counter clockwise from the leader was Ian. Next to him in Pav's seat was the big one. He looked boyish, there were remnants of puppy fat in his cheeks and his beard was more bum-fluff. I wanted to read gentle-giant in him, but bitterness turned down his mouth-line and he was more oafish. Although bigger than Pav he didn't look as muscular. Then came Rashid whose face shed a misshapen light. Was he still being hunted for the shooting? His haunted eyes made him appear less dangerous. Between us sat Pockmark who was mean and ugly and weasel-like. His was a face that would have no qualms about casting the first stone. And of course lastly, standing near the doorway opposite Pav was Mouth: the simpleton. They were all younger than us, in their late teens early twenties, at most Ian's age.

When all was still, Mouth having returned the empty sugar bowl to the table, the silence clenched. Nobody wanted to speak and that was how the leader wanted it. He nodded slightly, approvingly. Silence was an encore for him and a hand went under the folds of his *thobe*. I froze when I saw the encrusted hilt of one those L-shaped *Khanjar* daggers. Essentially ornamental it was a small machete nonetheless. I looked to Mike, but because he was sitting alongside the man I wasn't sure whether he'd seen the weapon. Without fully understanding my concern he acknowledged me with reassuring eyes. The leader pulled out a crumpled packet of cigarettes. He extracted a cheap lighter and a cigarette and lit up.

I was still contemplating the knife when I noticed the affected way the man smoked. He held up the cigarette almost in askance, his fingertips and thumb were pressed together, holding it so that it was virtually perched. He used Mike's cup for an ashtray.

The silence stretched.

My eyes flew up from my clasped hands to ricochet off individual faces before casting downwards. I didn't look at Pockmark or Rashid. They were too close. Their presence cut Pav out too. Movement was at a premium and my head remained still during these lightning reconnaissances, as if humbling oneself in the presence of a deity, daring fleeting excursions to check expressions. During one of these I met Ian's eyes. My speed was such that nothing was transmitted.

Moments later he thumped the silence. "Were you just passing through?" I think that whereas my husband genuinely wanted to keep things under control, Ian wanted confrontation. He wanted to kick them out.

I looked at the leader. His eyes were closed, allowing me a longer gaze. His eyes would be my starting pistols: as soon as they would open I would snap mine away.

The clock played metronome. As it ticked off the moments its sound appeared to be incremental: each movement seeming louder than its predecessor. This would happen again later, although I may have sought its sound and so amplified its significance. A consequence of this was that subsequently in doctors' waiting rooms, train stations, any public place where large full-moon faces resoundingly hacked off the minutes I would get an anxiety attack. Even now I only allow digital or silent sweep clocks in my home.

I was appalled to see that it was just after ten. They'd been here merely twenty minutes. It seemed longer.

"No," he answered, his eyes remaining closed. Curiosity opened them moments later. He stared at Ian, who returned his gaze. I'd missed the starting-shot.

They impassively stared at each other, a simmering aggression.

Mike was about to intervene when Ian spoke again. "Then what do you want?"

Everyone was watching them.

The leader was mulling this over when Rashid pulled out worry beads and began a ceaseless finger exercise. Six beads out, six beads in, back and forth, the tassel dangling below. He was smirking. He understood English.

Pockmark spat something in Arabic. The leader did not look

away, but spat something back.

Impatiently the leader sighed. "We are your guests."

"No," Ian protested. He toned down his clarification. "*We* are the guests."

The Arab was puzzled and then smiled broadly. Couldn't Ian see the menace in that smile? "Ah yes, of course." He nodded slowly. When he spoke his words were measured. "And my friend here," he gestured towards Mouth: an arm sweeping passed Ian, a palm to his emaciated companion, "he has no job." The cigarette smoke constricted me. A nerve had been touched.

Arab unemployment caused a lot of resentment. But I had also heard that the general attitude to work, all work, be it menial, manual or managerial, was not honourable.

Pockmark placed a battered packet of cigarettes on the table and lit up too. He also had an affected way of holding the cigarette. He held it in his left hand wedged between his middle and ring finger.

The issue was carefully discussed at length. With some diplomacy Mike was able to bring across that we were not to blame, that the employers were mostly Arabs.

The leader appeared to enjoy the talk and I was relieved by it. There was reason in it. More than this, the personal touch, like that between kidnapper and hostage, built connection. But the subject was exhausted, wrung of all aspects, and Ian and my husband were reluctant to stray.

Not only did I have no wish to speak I did not dare speak.

* * *

Mike asked the leader about his English and I held my breath again. During the unemployment conversation Pockmark and Rashid spoke in Arabic. The leader had answered them and I guessed that they were following the talk. As the discussion progressed the leader grew irritable with them, as if they were badgering him. Conversation had been an uphill chugging train. Dropping to a crawl and then to an exhausted standstill. Only then did Mike ask about his English.

It was a tremendous gamble on my husband's part. He sensed that the leader was under pressure from the others, but he wanted more conversation. My husband could only deal with understanding.

Pockmark spoke again and the leader nodded and glanced at Pav. Mike's question was going to go unanswered.

Pockmark's legs flopped apart as he slouched, trying to find comfort in the plastic chair. His right knee touched my left leg. I slowly moved my leg away until the edge of my chair bit the tenderness behind my knee. Brazen hussies. His leg did not follow. He kept his hands on the cant of the table where he picked the dirt from under his nails.

I knew that Rashid had no power within this gang. They'd taken him into their fold. Yet, I was tempted to appeal to him. He, a killer of house pets, the person who'd blown his top and shot Merv, offered tenuous reason. But again I was acutely aware of my debilitating gender. Had the others recognised him? They had only seen him once when he'd visited the farm.

"Your friend should sit," said the leader to Mike. Receiving no reaction the leader continued. "Then we can tell you why we have come." It was an offering.

"Sit down, Pav," said Mike.

Pav was stone, an oversized garden frog squirting water in our faces through a split in his wide mouth.

At first I didn't understand why the leader was keen to get Pav to sit. Neither did I understand Pav's reluctance to come away from the window. But of course it was not his position in the corner that was at issue. It was his nearness to the knives in the wooden block on the work-surface.

"Yes, Pav," said the leader, "sit with us, my friend."

Pav, his hands remaining clasped before him, neither spoke nor moved. He was a bulwark.

"Don't aggravate these people," Mike said, the tautness in his lips stiffening his words. Ian looked over. Only Rashid and Pockmark were preoccupied. The former looking at his cup, the latter indulging his fingernails taking deep drags on his cigarette. Yet, these two appeared the most attentive.

"Pav?" queried my husband. Pav was dead. Petrified by a spear in his back and we were waiting for the trickle of blood to escape his lips.

Pockmark gave Pav a glance, looked at the leader and showed his disgruntlement by sighing loudly. His sigh released and then increased the tension. He made a quiet remark that obviously twisted the leader's insides for he blanched. Maybe Pockmark didn't want blatant confrontation for he took diversionary action. Despite what had gone before what he did took me completely by surprise. His knee moved purposefully to mine. And to leave no doubt about his intentions he turned to stare me full in the face. I was instantly on my feet. There was a lot of movement, but he remained seated, leering at me. Mike was up. Pav unclasped his hands. Mouth shifted his weight off the work-surface. The leader snapped his head from me to Mike. Ian flinched, but like the big one and Rashid he missed the moment to rise.

Then there was no movement. New positions had been taken and we had to come to terms with them. We all stopped breathing. I couldn't hear the clock. And in this hiccup in time the refrigerator juddered to another equally mundane susurration level.

Pockmark snorted. And the leader rose slowly. Even he respected the strain. He raised his left hand and placed it upon Mike's shoulder. "Sit, my friend," he said calmly.

"Seet, seet," mimicked Pockmark.

And then the leader was shouting. Pockmark replied derisively and he too rose. I took the opportunity to edge back to the wall. My chair was askew, between Pockmark and myself.

The shouting continued, Pockmark letting fly. He gesticulated. I thought he was going to knock over his cup or throw it at the leader.

With European languages I can sometimes imagine what is being said, but with these two I didn't have the remotest idea what they were saying. Perhaps my husband got the gist, or a smattering, but to me they might as well have been speaking *Klingon*. There was obviously more to it than Pockmark making an advance on me. This was a power struggle.

The leader broke off and swiftly took the horn from the refrigerator behind him. I steeled myself against the impending blare, but when he swung it round, aiming it from the hip like an automatic weapon, the sound was so deafening I had trouble containing a scream. Everyone flinched. The man was not content with one blast and attempted to squeeze out an ever-increasing boom.

He was smiling. The others too. Now it was Pockmark's turn to blanch. Seeing the others amusement he tried to speak, but the leader drowned his words each time. Spent and glowering he returned to his seat. The leader looked from face to face like an excited child. He was laughing now. I was brim with anger and terror. I was disintegrating.

When the leader had been sitting, making his tea, I had elevated him above the others. To mock one must appreciate and I'd attributed him intelligence and a sense of humour, however cruel. I'd given him pride, pride that sought majestic silence. His companions were the slobbering hyenas, destined to continually disappoint him. I had not wanted to acknowledge that they were his friends: that there was the appeal of the hyena in him. This had been too frightening to contemplate. Now he'd thrown off his exalted mantle to humour them, to butter them under his will. And I could no longer deny that he was the same as them. They were just raw versions of him. His coat had a better sheen. That was all.

He gestured Mike into his chair and motioned for me to sit too. I took the empty seat next to my husband and belligerently took the time to make myself comfortable. Pav took up bouncer-stance and Mouth leaned back against the work surface again.

* * *

The tea was passed drinking temperature, but the leader sipped it as if it were scalding. He slurped noisily and the others followed suit. More cigarettes were lit and the building cringed. Smoke scorched my eyes, assaulted my nostrils, irritated my skin, clogged my lungs and strangled my stomach.

The cigarettes were brake lights in the mist. And we were hurtling through the unknown, danger just ahead of us, flaring with appalling frequency. I wanted to disappear in the smoke. I wanted them to disappear. For the moment the problem of Pockmark was solved. But I had a new problem. My earlier nightcap swelled my bladder and my bowels didn't feel good either.

When the leader returned his drained cup to the table Mike spoke.

"We have to be up early," he said. My husband hadn't realised or did not want to realise that he couldn't negotiate with malice.

The leader contemplated the statement, but was never called up to react, for the front door opened. The Arabs flinched and Mouth went into the corridor. The others stood.

Sparky strode in. "What is all the noise?" he began. He'd heard the horn. "Who are..." His voice trailed off and he was puzzled when Mouth held his arm.

Orders were snapped and the leader urgently turned to Mike. "Are there others on the farm?"

I could feel Mike weighing up his answer.

"Another ten," said Ian.

The leader swung round and for a second I thought he would hit Ian. They stared at one another. "I've been on a farm like this. There is no need of so many." But he was not sure. "There are not enough buildings here." He glared at Rashid before turning to Mike again.

"There are no more."

The leader looked at Sparky. "Go over there." He pointed to the seat next to me, my old place next to Pockmark. Sparky glanced at Mike and Ian before moving.

I looked at Sparky as he moved round behind Rashid and Pockmark. His expression was filled with questions that he did not see my question. Was Scab awake? I knew he sometimes wore earplugs. If he were asleep he would surely have been seen.

The leader stepped slowly towards Pav. Pav separated his hands, placing his left on the work-surface. The leader moved dangerously close. When he was alongside him he turned away and shielding his eyes looked out of the window. It was too dark to see. He turned his back to Pav to look into the kitchen, all the time he was deep in thought, mulling over the options.

My bladder was painful and I felt my control slipping. Impatience and frustration were pushing me to the same goal. "You -" my voice dried up. All eyes were upon me. I started again. "You want something. Why don't you tell us what it is?" Maybe a woman addressing him had not been wise.

I met the leader's gaze before looking to the wall-unit near Pav.

"Real hospitality," he said suddenly, as if this should have been obvious from the beginning.

I shook my head to show that I didn't understand, petrified by the thought that they wanted me. He looked to Mike and then Ian. They too were lost.

"*Sideeqi*," he hissed angrily, a gob of spit landing on the big one's shoulder. I saw him catch the exchange of looks between Ian and Pav.

So this was what this was all about. Redskins looking for firewater. I was safe. For now.

"We don't have alcohol here," said Mike when the silence had run its course.

"Liar," he yelled, taking two strides towards Mike.

I think Ian saw imminent danger, but he spoke with the utmost calmness. "And if we give you some, will you leave?"

"Ian," protested Mike. "We -"

"Mike, please."

"But we haven't -"

"Mike."

Ian had raised his voice but Mike went higher still. "Don't -"

"Mike. Mike, please."

We awaited the leader's answer. He smiled broadly. "Why of course, of course." He was triumphant and shared his triumph by saying something in Arabic. The others approved and Pockmark muttered what I imagine was something along the lines of "at last."

The leader stared at Ian greedily. Ian looked passed him at Pav and Pav looked at Sparky giving a tight-lipped nod that was so slight I waited for a confirming replay.

Mike was shaking his head. I read his thoughts. Having discovered that there was alcohol on the farm, we had opened ourselves to all sorts of trouble, now and in the future.

"I'll get it," said Sparky.

The leader eyed him, his brain working overtime. He raised a finger and pointed at me. "You go."

"I don't know where it is," I said victoriously.

He took time digesting this new variable and I was compelled to continue. "The Filipinos have it." This could have been a mistake for he glanced at Ian.

I knew Ian had been over for the occasional tipple. I think this started after the execution.

With downward-cast eyes Ian said he didn't know either.

Again the leader spent time trying the figure out whether he was being fooled in some way. His next words were in Arabic. Rashid pocketed his beads and got up. "Okay," he said to Sparky, "you go with him." Sparky hesitated before rising. This time he chose to go behind Mike and me. He was between the refrigerator and the leader's chair when the leader ordered him to wait.

Sparky could not hide his astonishment. His eyes were lured by the leader's gaze, and they helplessly followed as he led them to Pockmark. All eyes were on this mean-faced man as he placed an unsheathed *Khanjar* dagger on the table before him. His smirk was terrible. He was in his milieu, this was his world at its most exhilarating, and he couldn't help his expression.

"Just get the *sid*."

To my amazement my husband exploded. He jumped up. "That's enough. You talk about hospitality and then you threaten us." I don't quite know why, but I reached up and held my husband's hand.

Was I trying to encourage him or calm him? I don't know. He returned my squeeze, but did not look at me.

Pockmark picked up his knife and everyone in the room became rigid. One of Rashid's hands disappeared to grasp the hilt of his own dagger. Maybe the others did the same. The leader strode between Rashid and Sparky to stand face to face with Mike. Now he had Sparky and Ian behind him. I was watching his hands. Mike remained firm. Fearlessly? Fearfully?

What happened next appeared in slow motion. Yet, I didn't have the time or the presence of mind to hinder the action. The leader's right hand came up and slapped Mike on the face. I saw the blood leave my husband's cheek, the skin, despite its tan, yellow with the hand's departure before rushing back like a tide, a red deluged spreading from his cheek and engulfing his entire head. Even his neck became scarlet.

There should have been silence but Pockmark giggled and Mouth made a similar noise.

Mike didn't move. The slap had turned his body to stone.

"You care about this woman?" The leader had seen that we were holding hands but his question was rhetorical. "I am a reasonable man." This seemed a laughable statement. The frightening aspect was the earnest way in which it was said. His next sentence was not so controlled. "I am not a fool. Why do you treat me as one?" Mike made to speak. "Why do you lie to me? You said there was no *sideeqi* here. This is all we want. My friend there wants more." He was referring to Pockmark. "You know what I mean." Mike squeezed my hand. The man changed his tone in mock allegiance. "I think it best if you give us the drink, don't you?" Then he was back to his reasonable self and his favourite command. "Sit, sit."

Mike obeyed. He didn't look at me for a long time. And through my hand I implored him to turn to me. Later, when the redness had localised, glowing only at his cheek, he looked over. In the meantime Sparky and Rashid left. Mouth left the room too. We could hear him in the corridor and outside on the steps. The leader took up Mouth's place near the entrance.

The blow had not hurt Mike, but it had been shattering. Flat-handed, it had been truly a slap and the burn was a belly flop of embarrassment rather than pain. What it meant was that my husband was stripped of leadership. He had no authority under the new regime. His dignity had taken a smack. He could only stand idiotically firm. He was heroic, stiff, broken and stupid: Sir Alec Guinness at the *River Kwai*. The realisation that these intruders defied domestication smashed him. I'm sure he had hoped to harness the leader, and by default the others. Then he could steer them and bring their wildness under control. But the leader had thrown him. And my husband lay bruised and forlorn.

* * *

I'm standing at the crossroads. The cars at the traffic lights are steaming the area with dry ice. I like the cold. It's not the deepest winter juxtaposing high summer, chilly rather than cool, damp instead of dry. Even the trees are inverted: gnarled roots reaching into the slate sky.

Like the spider in the housing of my wing mirror I've found my niche. It's a lonely place, but a place in which I can reflect life, giving the illusion of living. I can deflect life too. Sometimes the winds of reality threaten to damage my house, but I can hide for days, weeks. There are intruders too, but my cold existence tests their perseverance and eventually sends them on their way. Oh, I save the highs of such intrusions, wrapping them up and savouring them at leisure. Melancholy is my constant companion.

My answer-phone is a firewall. No alien bodies are going to invade my sanctuary. But I receive few calls anyway. Only my father phones and although I can fool others I cannot fool him.

I work at an estate agent in the property services section. I am conscientious and private. I don't care what the others think of me. Frigid, depressed, morose.

Another year has gone by. I can count them off in cuckoo calls. And again the question of change looms. For how many New Year's Eves have I gazed from my flat window and thought of change? How many times have I indifferently observed fireworks popping and scratching the fabric of the sky like a cat tears at cloth.

Recently there has been a change. In reassessing my past I have unconsciously begun to reassess the present and tentatively the future. As if confronting the past is a re-bleeding a badly healed wound. Maybe it can heal properly now?

The book is almost finished in the classical sense. There's a beginning, a middle and an end. But there are gaps. Not Swiss cheese holes, but blackouts, that need filling. I have been edging along a flimsy network that does not have the structure or strength of a web. My progress is in darkness, but my heart quickens at the thought that the end of this particular strand is Ginny.

The strand has become a road that ends at a house in Croydon. Ginny and Colin have married.

Hugs and joy dissolve like a soluble tablet plonked in the sea. Talk is wary. We stalk one another, testing each other's strength with little shoves and pushes, even strategically placed pinches. Talk of expats gives us testing time. Colin tells me that Noel is in Brunei, Martin in Thailand, Den, Linda and Gillian are still in Saudi. Linda chewed Den up. Carol met another American and now lives in Chicago. Many were reduced to defining incidents or foibles. All the nurses have returned to Ireland or moved on. I'd tracked down Ita myself. She was in Donegal. She was her fast-talking self, sweeping away people namelessly with himself, herself, your man. Everyone knew Merv if only by name, but Ita had his telephone number. He was in Amsterdam. I'd had one telephone conversation with him. He'd heard of the tragedy but hadn't known of Rashid's involvement. He let slip that he suspected the Arab came to the farm when they picked me up because he was on to them. Their car boot had been so full that Rashid and I had our bags on the seat between us. I had taken a real risk travelling in their *sid*-laden car. My remark that he had no compunction about going ahead with the collection brought the call to an end.

The wine with the meal begins to reassure us and we come closer. Sniffing one another like inquisitive animals. We want joy, but to reach it we must first have confrontation.

We've spoken long enough about what we've done since Saudi. We drop into a laboured analysis of the Saudi experience. Our conclusion is that most of the expats had been reality-fugitives. And the Saudi experience had made refugees of many of them. Not quite of the life-mutating proportions I'd experienced. But refugees just the same.

"It's a shame," says Colin. "One would think it was a great opportunity to get to know a foreign culture." He has forgotten that I knew Anoud. But true enough; westerners were actively discouraged from making contact. The Saudi society was an impenetrable building. Glimpses could be had through the slit windows; otherwise one is left outside to build one's own rickety structure to make up for the cultural deficit. A structure built out on routines, habits, distractions, scorn, all held together with the adhesive of humour.

Finally we talk of what happened to me. I can't palm them off with "read the book." So I give them bones. There are no tears, but they read between my words. See the pain in my silences. At one point Ginny places her hand upon mine.

If the others from Aramco were houses, even mansions, then I became a fortress. To outsiders, strangers, new acquaintances or work colleagues it would appear as if I'd locked myself in the belfry. Up with the bats. Early acquaintances were baffled even amused by my idiosyncrasies. They inevitably turned away, whether knowing or not knowing of my hurt and my therapy. The untrained eye would not see the inner chaos that revealed itself as flaws on the outer wall. I had taken pains to conceal them behind bushes and trellises of vines. I'd disguised and camouflaged or distracted with an eye-catching sham. These were the anomalies that intrigued. Externally I was fortified, even prickly. Inside I appeared to be a normal house, albeit a badly shaken house. The window-frames broken or coming away, doors not fitting the frames, either too large and unable to close, or too small: western saloon doors, swinging wildly. Somehow I was upstairs, horrified, looking at the bed precariously balancing on the edge of half a floor, the stairs missing, sheer drops, incomplete ceilings, carpenter's unfinished work.

The victorious psychiatrist was the last one. An obvious statement, but others had laid the way for her. And time had healed; in some places not properly. This last psychiatrist, a woman, strolled about the moat studying my defences. I wasn't unnerved by her cool strategy, more by the ruthless ally she had at her side. I was under siege and checked and rechecked the dungeons, which kept love, culture, faith, life. Only hope had slipped through the bars and although terribly wounded by my archers, swam the moat. She had to be resuscitated after the arduous journey and then brought up to a decent level of fitness for the assault. So from my bitter position I could see their tent of high command, the psychiatrist and her ace, a formidable opponent: me.

My walls were breached and I was devastated. A week off work was barely enough to build a stockade. Luckily nobody prodded or even remarked upon the gaping holes in my structure. Time was mortar and eventually I had a structure with which I could weather the storm of everyday life.

"It's all a long time ago," says Colin. But his pick does not dent the ice after I have finished speaking. Only I can break it.

"I'm on the mend. In fact I'm toying with the idea of going out with someone at work. He's a bit of an odd-ball." The ice shatters with the fact that I should call someone else odd. They laugh and I find myself laughing too.

The lights change and I cross the road. When I enter the office I see the odd ball at his desk hunched over his thoughts. He has shown an interest in me on a number of occasions. I have always put him off. I ask him whether he's interested in seeing a particular play. For I have decided to say yes. Yes to life.

* * *

It was rash of me to speak after such a massive event as the slap, but in me rebelliousness was born out of my husband's demise. More importantly I knew I could not wait until they left.

"I need to go to the toilet."

The leader looked at me, wondering whether my words could have hidden meaning.

"It's at the end of the corridor," I said.

His old smile returned. Of course, he was our friend. Just passing through. Wanted to pick up supplies. That's all. Slap? What slap?

"Then go," he said, as if nothing was stopping me, a hand gesturing towards the corridor.

I rose.

"I'd like to go too," said Ian.

"When she comes back." He looked at Mike who nodded: "You?" Then to Pav: "What about you, Pav?"

The Filipino returned his stare. His skin was rhino hide; only a snort was needed from his monstrous nostrils.

"Can he speak?" the leader asked me when I was almost passed him.

I chose not to answer.

Every footfall was a step in the right direction and I wanted the cubicle to be five kilometres away rather than five metres.

My toilet was a painful gush of relief. I cried quietly, wiping my eyes and blowing my nose on toilet paper. I didn't want to go back. The tiny window offered no escape. The thought of using my body to barricade myself in crossed my mind. Bizarrely I thought I could burrow through the floor like some animal. All I did was straighten my clothes, flush the toilet, wash my hands and check my eyes in the mirror. I looked pitiable.

I didn't want to open the door, but watched my hand rise to the latch. I knew I would see the leader at the end of the corridor and I tried to will him away. I wished that my eyes would see what I wanted. I pulled back the door and the corridor was empty. Could it be true? Had they silently left? Were they ever here? I walked towards the kitchen. About half way his head popped out and I jumped.

I noted that it was twenty to one as I returned to my seat. My smile at Mike was weak. He knew I had been crying.

I wondered whether Scab was going to return with Sparky and Rashid. Or was he awake and hiding? Had Sparky got a message to him?

Mouth said something from outside.

Ian looked for permission to get up; when it was not forthcoming he made to rise.

"You wait," said the leader.

Moments later Sparky was back carrying two plastic bottles. He put them on the work-surface beside the leader. Rashid carried another bottle and a satisfied expression. There was an exchange of words and the leader remarked on our cleverness. "Bottles of mineral water," he smiled again. Sparky was ushered to his seat and Mouth appeared at the entrance.

I wanted to ask Sparky about Scab. His face told me nothing.

"You've got what you want," said Ian, pain and weariness etched upon his face. "Why don't you go?"

The leader blew up. Before anyone could flinch he'd hit Ian across the back of the head. Ian glared at him, but remained seated. The Arab spoke to his companions without taking his eyes off Ian. The leader had dropped his courteous attitude when he hit my husband. That act had unleashed him. He seemed unhinged, acting before thinking. Disobedience would not to be tolerated. We were cowering children, ignorant of the rules and he was an unpredictable teacher. His mood swings, from deep calculating thought to the ravings of a petulant child, were psychotic.

"You wanted to go to the toilet. Why don't you go?" This was said in a voice that was a mockery of Ian's own.

Ian went to the toilet and we watched the leader search for glasses in the wall-units. He didn't ask us. He placed more than five tumblers next to the bottles. He spoke and Rashid helped him splash the clear liquid into the glasses.

Whilst they poured Pav lifted himself into a sitting position on the work-surface next to the sink and the block of knives. Ian returned as tumblers were placed on the table. Pockmark was in his element when he put his dagger on the table. But in doing so he had shown his cards. There was no reason to be poker-faced. Positions had been stated and Pav had read the situation correctly. Traits that I had suspected now surfaced within him. I didn't care about their dark source. I was simply glad of them. The rest of us were rational beings, optimists, naive fools. Tiredness twisted my thoughts. I fantasised. If Sparky was quick enough he could pick up Pockmark's dagger. Mike and Ian could take on the leader and Mouth, leaving Pav with Rashid and the big one. Mike and Sparky hemmed me in, but I could jump up onto the table and kick Khalid in the face and... and... and ... This was the stuff of Hollywood.

Mike went to the toilet and returned.

Everyone was back in place. Mouth mimicking Pav, sitting at his end of the work-surface near the door, partly obscured from my line of vision by the refrigerator.

"We will all drink," said the leader.

It was then that I had an attack. All these bodies in the kitchen, pressing me into a corner. The stale air and the lingering smoke constricting me. A camel kneeling upon my chest. Curving its neck to look at me with its drooping jaw, a crowbar-bashed horse, mouth dislocated from the head. A grimace of dirty bucked teeth. Long-lashed lids and glaucoma bulging globes bearing down on me. I began to involuntarily hyperventilate. There was a drainpipe roar of the beast in my ears and then it spat upon me. The saliva was shockingly cold and as I blinked into focus I saw the leader staring at me.

Mike's concern had spurred the leader into splashing a glass of water in my face.

"Are you okay?" Mike asked. I nodded. Although I wasn't sure. He turned to the leader who no longer leaned over him and was standing in front of the refrigerator. "You have what you want, you should leave."

Pockmark spoke. He was pressing the tip of his dagger into the table.

"Soon," he promised, sitting and taking a pull on a cigarette. Then, as an afterthought, he spoke to me. His smile was askew. "My friend thinks you are very clever. He thinks you were pretending." I closed my eyes on him. I closed my eyes on all of them.

* * *

So began the most macabre part of our night.

None of us touched our drinks. Even Pav wasn't tempted. A number of times the leader enthused and tried to get us to drink. But he did not insist. I'm sure some of the lads thought that when the Arabs were incapacitated they would be easier to handle. Maybe they'd taken this into account for Rashid didn't drink much. And the big one never finished his first glass.

Mike and Ian made an effort to humour these people. I marvelled at my husband's reservoir of energy. I was spent and could not speak. Sparky and Pav were silent.

Memory has crushed the conversation of these hours into momentary fragments. Like the short-term memory of age, were you forget what you had for breakfast, but vividly recall some childhood experience, so it was with these hours.

We learned that the leader's name was Khalid and that he regretted the manner in which he had called upon our hospitality. He introduced the others to affect some bonhomie, but I wasn't paying attention. I remember the conversation bristling at talk of Christian brutality. Mentioning the Iran-Iraq war brought up the fact that Christians had dropped the Bomb and the Holocaust sat squarely in the Christian lap. Arab cruelty was not touched upon.

I drew into myself. An action that was a precursor for weeks to come. All of us retreated as the alcohol advanced in the Arabs. We didn't relax but the level of alertness dropped a notch and so too did the level of anxiety. Maybe that's how Ian and Mike maintained their buoyancy, bobbing just above the surface of an abyss.

I surreptitiously glanced at the clock a number of times. The instrument showed-off its dominion over time: what I took for a few minutes could be a half hour chunk and conversely, what I thought bordered on aeons was mere minutes. I hated the elasticity of time. And I hated the clock and wanted to tear it down from the wall, to jump up and down and smash its bland face to smithereens. I was jealous of its indifference. For I too did not want to be. I wanted the clock's safety, its impervious insentience.

I probably appeared unaware of what was said. On the contrary I followed everything. I absorbed the expressions. A dual consciousness established itself in me and allowed part of me to wander, to be free. Walks that took me down banal paths like composing entries for my journal, that this would make a good plot for a story, how tired we were all going to be during the day. Didn't these Arabs sleep? I imagined talking to the Aramcons about our ordeal. I pictured Ginny and Ita's reactions. I wondered what they were doing now. I wondered what we were doing here. Why were we out here? We were all chasing the dollar. But it was like chasing the puddle: trying to reach a mirage. For money can buy things, the so-called creature comforts, to ease your path through life. But money and things were not enough. Life demanded more. The soul needed food.

Around three o'clock Mike dared to quote from the Koran. I don't remember what he said. I don't remember whether he wanted to jolt or support them with something they understood. I was astounded that he still sought to tap into some vein of intelligence. To me it was obvious that these Arabs were not zealous *matawa*. They were some frustrated hybrid: social half-castes, perhaps outcasts. Not surprisingly the effect was to infuriate Khalid and then the entire group. Miraculously Mike picked his way through the verbal minefield into which he'd stumbled.

The influence of alcohol showed itself as a fickle creature. Khalid became boisterous, unbelievably Mouth's jaw became looser and he did dribble. Rashid who had drunk very little grew agitated, ready to chastise his companions, or flee. The big one, drinking even less than Rashid, nurtured an air of Buddha contentment. They didn't unsettle me. Pockmark did. He grew sullen: his dark eyes smouldering with pent-up ferocity. His companions seemed oblivious to his dark force. He joined in the conversation, but wasn't part of it and I could feel his mounting frustration.

His dagger remained on the table. Now between him and Rashid, out of Sparky's reach.

Talk of them leaving was taboo. But this party had to run its course. Next time we farmers would be ready. We'd hire Yul Brynner to gather six others to prepare and protect us.

* * *

Although it was still dark outside a new working day was about to begin. It was five-fifteen. I wondered about Scab's internal clock. Had he really slept through all this? A number of times I had imagined him waking, seeing what was happening and going for help. Had that been the case help would have arrived by now. Or would it? He couldn't drive, taking a vehicle would have alerted them; therefore he would have had to run the twenty odd kilometres to the Masstock dairy. I had no real idea how long this would take but unsafe mental calculations came up with a depressing round trip of three hours.

The party was winding down. The end in sight. Boxers mustering last reserves of energy to swing wildly and lose their balance. The Arabs were not drunk; they were slowing. Half a bottle of *sid* stood on the table. Conversation was carried not by itself but by the perverse need to show stamina.

At one point they hinted that they'd like to take some of the *sid* with them. A consequence of this could be that they would sell it. Whatever, I knew they'd be back for more.

The presence of tipsy Arabs was an obvious danger. This was becoming augmented by an additional lesser danger. Abdul could arrive within the hour and then it would be jail for us all. Time was running out. I sensed a feeling akin to enough was enough. We had a farm to run. These men had got what they wanted. It was time they moved on.

Conversation was treacle, burdened by fatigue, slurred by alcohol, frayed by nerves. Into one of the ever more frequent silences Pav suddenly shouted. He was still sitting at the window. Apart from Mouth who had been sent outside, positions had been maintained throughout the night. Pav had not spoken since the Arabs arrival and his voice seemed strange.

"Help," he shouted. Everyone started. He continued quickly, almost equally as loud: "Is what you need." Had he wanted to shout? I decided that the strain had split his granite stance. Pockmark fingered his knife.

We were all puzzled by this outburst, none more than Khalid to whom he spoke.

"What do you mean?"

His tone became more reasonable. "You need help to your car."

Mike exhaled. There was challenge in Pav's tone, but it was not the challenge we feared. And we were weary too, becoming careless, wanting something to happen. Willing something to happen.

"You are telling us that it is time to leave?" questioned the leader with unnerving calmness.

Pockmark spoke, Khalid answered. The former began muttering, but he didn't appear to have the energy for frenzy.

Khalid had the energy. He yelled at Pav: "You don't say when we can leave." His companions sobered. "I say when we leave." And then childishly: "I was thinking we should leave, but not now. Not now that you have spoken."

Pav was stoic. Expressionless was an art form he'd mastered. I was furious with him.

Silence consumed us.

The abominable clock axed off more time: each clack truncating our thoughts, leaving us with inconclusive stumps.

"Go!" Pav shouted. And for a second time everyone was shaken.

"Christ, Pav," blurted Ian.

The room settled but still rocked.

"What?" asked Khalid, coldly.

"I said you should go." Pav had flipped. His voice had settled; but his words, toned down as they were, could only be a challenge.

"Is my English not good enough?" asked the leader. "Or are you stupid?" He laughed falsely. To Mike. "Is he stupid?" I caught the glint of fear in Khalid's eyes.

Mike gave an answer that communicated to Pav too. "Not normally."

Pockmark spoke again. He was gouging at the table with the tip of his dagger.

On my list of people ordered by social acumen I would not have put Pav at the top, but there was no excuse for this, it was not only stupid it was downright dangerous.

"Then he thinks we are stupid. Are we stupid?"

"No," said Mike too close to look at the man. Khalid looked at me and I shook my head. His lips thinned and he nodded.

He spoke calmly to his companions.

"No, we are not stupid." Then he looked at each of us to be sure of our attention. "But you think we are stupid. What is it you call us?" I didn't like where this was going. "Rag heads?" I closed my eyes as if his words were blows. "You think you are superior to us." His questions may not have been rhetorical, but his aggressive tone allayed any thought of replying. "We are the backward rag heads, too ignorant to run our country. That's what you think." He jabbed Ian with his hand.

"No," he snapped.

I had always been aware of this prejudice. They sensed or imagined a superior stance in us and were affronted by this feeling. The onus was on them to dispel this perceived prejudice by trying to prove themselves. Prove themselves as equals or above. Theirs was a male-dominated society and the accompanying machismo aggravated this standpoint.

Ian looked at me. I looked away.

The leader continued. "You people have no manhood, no pride," he said scornfully. He'd forgotten about me. I made no sound. He spoke in Arabic, the contempt remaining. Pockmark laughed and Khalid laughed with him. They conversed excitedly. Pockmark suddenly glanced at me and I looked at my lap. Mike and I were no longer holding hands and I desperately wanted his touch. Miraculously his hand moved and held mine. Khalid spoke, Pockmark and Rashid too. They shifted in their seats. Were they making ready to leave? Oh, Pav please, please remain still. Relief was but a tear away.

By now it was so late we'd have to forfeit sleep.

With my head still bowed, I spied Mike and Khalid. I avoided looking in Pockmark's direction. Mike was staring at a point on the table and Khalid was taking a cigarette from his packet. Ian was gazing at me and to evade communication I turned my eyes downward again.

We were in a lull once more. These were more excruciating than speech. With speech I could at least gauge the situation. Even if they spoke Arabic I now had an intuitive feel for their language and even though I had no idea what was said I could tell whether they spoke in anger. With silence I couldn't tell whether they were resting, having achieved some level of contentment, or fuming, working themselves up. Had Pockmark suggested what I most feared? I was too tired to speculate.

**

There was movement. Somebody coming up the steps, opening the door, in the corridor. I looked up as Mouth entered and spoke. I'd not heard his voice before and was surprised that it sounded hollowed out. There was substance but it didn't come from his vocal cords. They were filtered or coated. Had it been nasally I would have put it down to a sinus problem, but there was more mucous here and something like perpetual catarrh twanged his voice.

Khalid stubbed out an unfinished cigarette on the inside of Mike's cup. There were six or seven butts in there. My eyes stung. He followed Mouth into the corridor. We heard the clunk of a car door shut. My heart leapt. It could only be Abdul. Ian was staring at me and looked relieved too. He dared to lift one edge of his mouth-line to affect a lopsided smile. I looked at the clock. Twenty-five past six. Who else could it be? Scab with the cavalry?

Mike had said Abdul would not let him down, but even I had had my doubts. That Abdul should appreciate punctuality I attributed to a number of factors. The first was an improved understanding of the farm. Then Abdul and my husband were friends. Mike had a better appreciation of Islam through him, conversely Abdul could have picked up a bit of the West.

Khalid returned, Mouth in the entrance behind him, accentuating his leader's panicked expression.

What happened next cannot be briefly explained. Too much happened. Weariness and time have messed with my memory. I've gone over it in my mind and under analysis so many times that it's hard to distinguish between what happened and what I thought must have happened. And I have replayed it and sometimes had it triggered into replay. Involuntary embellishments have adhered themselves to these moments like lichen and some have become unrecognisably barnacle encrusted.

"Mike," Abdul called from outside. He would have seen the Chevrolet. That it was him was a relief that choked me. I could see myself tipping the half-bottle of *sid* down the sink as soon as the Arabs were out of the room. Because Ian was sitting directly opposite me I smiled weakly. He smiled too, but his was a sardonic smile. My face soured when I saw his smile was there for all the wrong reasons.

The Arabs were on their feet. Khalid did not know what to do. There was no back door. He said something to Mouth who left. Was he to delay Abdul? I couldn't see it myself. More likely he was told to go and start the car.

Was Abdul climbing the steps? I didn't know. My eyes were on Ian. We were not locked in some mute communication, for although this contact was more than a glance, the duration was mere seconds. His look frightened me. Maybe it was a Morse code series of glances. Arabic was spoken hastily. Mike had turned from me to Ian. Pockmark was looking my way, restricting my facial muscles. I have no idea what Pav and Sparky thought or did. My eyes were beseeching Ian not to do anything, but perhaps he interpreted this as the opposite. Fatigue and the brink of exultation confused us. I should have shaken my head. My imagination also puts a scream in the constrained atmosphere. A scream that comes to a piercing silence into which Ian spoke.

Even before the words left his mouth I knew he was about to

make a serious mistake. All my antennae were pointing outwards and my level of alertness was definitely more discerning than his. Men tend to deny their emotions and generally lose out when it comes to intuition or sixth sense. This is not a magical or mysterious power, rather awareness. Being more attune to the overt minutiae of feeling, be it expressed in a gesture, tautness of the facial muscles, even a smell, I smelt danger in the situation. And my lips parted to whisper the word no, although I never made a sound.

"Time to run rag head." The words were spoken with horrid spitefulness. I wanted to believe he didn't know that this would shame the man. In retrospect I know he knew what he was doing and of its effect. He knew Arabs. We'd spoken of losing face or *Wajh*. Could he have had so little an appreciation of the precariousness of the situation? Then perhaps *Wajh* itself had driven him. He had been shamed by his behaviour at the execution; he had taken himself to the brink and was not proud of the way he had reacted. This was his chance to redeem himself, to swell his chest. Perhaps he was building on our earlier steps towards reconciliation and thought this would firmly set him up.

Khalid and Rashid exchanged looks. Khalid blanched. I did too. Mine was in disbelief. His embarrassment became anger. Others may have gone pale. He pulled out his blade. So shiny and ruthlessly clean. It should have glinted but it didn't. There should have been a scream, but there wasn't. I thought he was going to threaten Ian and nothing more. Perhaps he was. Much later I would marvel at my optimism. Founded in denial. Some optimistic part of me could not and would not believe in the worst. This was the denial that caused hesitation. In the movies I had always wondered at a character's hesitation in the face of imminent danger, be it a split in the earth or an oncoming train, reasoning that fear would surely be overridden by the instinct to survive. But I now know, that it is not fear that rivets one to the spot it is disbelief.

If everyone had remained still the outcome could have been different. Khalid may have threatened Ian or given him a cut. And they all could have fled. Pushing passed Abdul...

There are many ifs.

The order of events was not sequential, but simultaneous from all corners of the room. Pav jumped off the work-surface onto his feet. Mike and I stood. Khalid brought his knife to bear on Ian. He could have shouted an order. The big one and Rashid were turning to Pav. Pockmark's dagger was swinging round towards Sparky who tipped backward rather than get up.

Pockmark was pulling back his blade, high in the air. Drops flew from it and splattered the big one's dirty white *thobe* and a single drop splashed Ian's cheek. A small brilliant red slash, instantly brushed on him.

I think I was shouting: "No, no."

Ian's expression was wide-eyed shock and Sparky was crashing awkwardly to the floor. His chair clattering, the table screeching as his legs stretched out. He was an exhausted log, giving up with a sigh and slumping in a shower of lights. Guy Fawkes gutted. Pav had two knives, large and small. Ian's shock turned to slanted-mouthed pain. He was still looking at me, but I don't think he saw me. He must have been standing too. Mike was reaching for the blooded knife in Khalid's hand. After an age Ian looked down at his left side, his hand coming up to press where his gaze stopped. His swollen face looked at me. His left leg buckled as if he'd taken a sharp kick in the back of a knee and I was reminded of a wobbly newborn giraffe. To break his fall his blooded hand grabbed Khalid.

Pav was hunched and jabbing forward. Pockmark was stuck behind Rashid and his route to me was blocked by Sparky sitting on the floor like an old wino. The big one and Rashid were stepping back.

Ian was on his knees pulling Khalid down, Mike trying to wrest the knife from his hand. The big one was half turning. To flee? To help Khalid? Rashid was moving back and Pockmark was coming out. Pav was driving them all to the entrance.

Had I moved forward? Somehow I was near Mike who was locked in mortal struggle with Khalid. Ian had climbed the work-surface and was falling upon the big one.

I was shouting. I hadn't recognised my husband's horrific face: a crimson and pained Picasso caricature. Or I hadn't realised that he was looking and shouting at me. He was saying the same thing over and over. "Run, run. Dawn, run." I'd never seen him so angry with me and I was hurt. The empty doorway was to my right. I hesitated. Mike's urgency was more than insistent, it was fierce and if he could he would have pushed me. In these moments I didn't think. I didn't have time to scrutinise the wisdom of my husband's decision; I just obeyed. Blindly obeyed. Even now I am taunted by self-recrimination.

* * *

I threw open the front door. Abdul looking up from the foot of the steps, Mouth turning from him. It's ludicrous to think that they were talking to one another out here given the noise behind me, jarring furniture, scuffles, grunts, but that was how it appeared. Mouth went for his knife. My goal was to flee and nothing was going to stop me. Whether he pulled his knife before I bounded down the steps is questionable. He must have changed his mind for he reached for me hoping to clasp the arm that was pushing him aside and launching me away. On contact his grasping fingers stung, but I winded him with surprising force. He fell backwards, missing Abdul and banging against the Chevrolet. His attempt to hold me had not hurt, but as he fell backward he tried to tighten his uncertain grip and his nails scratched my upper arm. I was not hurt, but later I would rub my arm as at the burn of stinging nettles.

I turned left to run round the building. Mouth was chasing me. I felt him behind me. And all the corners, the length and width of the building, the expanse of the square that was bounded by this building, the greenhouse and our accommodation buildings, all these things stretched out in a conspiracy to distance me from my destination. Familiar distances and objects pooled together against the commuter late for her train, asserting her awareness of them as she tried to sweep past them.

I don't know when I noticed that Mouth was no longer behind me, certainly at the greenhouse. I assumed he'd been called back. I was blind in my frenzied determination to get away. And I was highly aware. As I had thrown open the door, the fragile daylight was as much a slap as the clear air. The morning air flared the embers of cigarette smoke and gritty tiredness in my eyes. Crossing the courtyard area I could hear them in the building behind me. The jarring sound of scraping furniture had ceased, now there were shouts. Some stalemate had been reached and combatants were yelling one another on.

I was confronted with *Schatzi's* dilemma. The horizon was a lifetime away. I was free to run in any direction and for the moment I just wanted to put distance between Man and myself. I ran and ran, past the greenhouses, the workshop, the sheds and petrol pump. Somewhere coins clattered on the kitchen table. A large Y. Why? Why? I ran far out into the fields of grass. Where Man had sprayed an environment upon which Nature could cling. Like overseeing skin as the largest organ of the body, so too it was easy to forget that grass is a plant. But not out here. Out here this Nature was artificial. The edges of the pivots were well defined. Unnatural.

Insects were indifferent to my plight. There was no shade, no hiding place out here. Shadows were weak: as young as the new day. One could press oneself into the ground to get below the level of the taller grass. Such rational thought came later, when the physical strain of running buckled and protested my frenzied demands. Another consciousness began to tell me to seek shelter rather than distance. I couldn't see any vehicles and looked back towards the distant buildings, almost invisible in this virgin light. I stepped towards them. Glitter between a greenhouse and the storage building reminded me of the vehicles in the courtyard. My manic determination had blotted them out and I had seen only the way through them.

Panic gripped me and I began to run back.

I like to think I was driven by the urge to assist my husband, but my actions don't support me. The closer I got the slower I went. My ears strained to hear above the searing silence. My thoughts were in tatters. Why was I returning? To jump in a cruiser to get help? Of course I would drive. To hide? To charge into the kitchen? The silence unnerved me.

I was at the corner of the Filipinos demountable, staring over the courtyard vehicles at the kitchen window that the morning had rendered opaque. The building afforded some shelter, some shade. The clatter of the kitchen door on the other side of the building seized my breath. Silence threatened to engulf its sound and I had to remain vigilant to keep it from slipping into imagination. I had heard the door crash. Why hadn't I heard someone on the steps? Or someone in the building? Then a shuffling. Yes, someone was coming round the building. Vulnerability sent me forth and I ran into my favourite greenhouse. Once there I knew the stupidity of the move. Outside I could have hidden behind the vehicles, moved about the buildings, spied upon the person. Not only was there no shelter in the old greenhouse, the rows of vegetables on the ground were no taller than the grass fields and from outside shadows of movement could be seen through the milky Perspex. I was not thinking rationally. I was thinking emotionally or not at all. I went straight to my wicker fan-backed chair. I had the presence of mind not to sit in it: to sit in it and hum or sing? No, I was not that far gone - not yet. Instead I crouched behind it.

Shivering threatened my crouching position. My legs trembled, like they did during some of those aerobic floor exercises. Yet my forehead was damp. I wiped large droplets of sweat from my eyebrows.

Reason was a multi-headed creature, a Hydra, each head rearing up to argue the others into submission. Stay here, you're safe. Don't stay here, you're not safe. Choose a better hiding place. A narrow trowel, a weapon of sorts, supported the current speaker in the argument that I should help my husband. If not that, then at least seek revenge. It was this last thought that made me scramble for the dirty trowel and leap towards the door. No, not the direct wish to seek revenge, but the wish that I should have no need of revenge. The thought that everything may not be all right urged my hand to clasp the trowel. Dread was a very real force. And way back that old optimist, that desperate fellow was stroking my forehead and repeating his quiet litany of "it'll be okay." It was his litany and its soothing monotony that made me desperate. I could have trampled through the lines of vegetables to make a damning B-line for the door, but ingrained conditioning had a say. Or I could not think and my actions relied upon routine. In any case I moved deftly.

I hesitated at the greenhouse door, listening for activity, for anything. The Hydra hissed and my grip upon the trowel tightened. I tore back the door and moved swiftly across the courtyard. There was stealth in my movement. I was crouched and would have preferred a lighter step, but terror burdened me. I would have preferred less sound, soundless steps, my heart was thumping in my throat, making my breathing irregular, driving it to loud spasmodic gasps.

I was turning the corner of the kitchen demountable, taking in the scene before me, the absence of the white Chevrolet, when I heard the door of a vehicle in the courtyard click open. Abdul's cruiser was outside his building, but he was nowhere to be seen. In actual fact the scene was as bereft of visible life as that out in the fields. My silent call for life was answered in a flock of birds. Their appearance overhead startled me and I cursed them. They were fleeing too.

There was nothing to say that something appalling had taken place. Nonetheless I was filled with Hitchcock trepidation. This and the sound of someone in the courtyard propelled me. At the top of the wooden steps - how horridly they creaked - I noticed that the sand roses were damaged. They looked as if they'd been kicked. Either broken or smashed in, remnants of their structure were visible only on one side. An accident victim's smashed skull, perfectly intact when viewed from the right angle. An apt metaphor for my state during therapy. I was shaken and had to lean a hand against the opposite wall to steady myself as I entered the building. The corridor was empty. Nothing to see. No arm ominously stretching out from the kitchen across the corridor floor. No, no arm. Nothing to say anything was amiss. And although the heads of the Hydra were turned away, I felt that I could peer into the kitchen and see that it was empty. It was too frightening to see the boys and Arabs all sitting amicably together, smiling in my direction. Ghosts of what could have been.

A voice was calling from outside. I was stepping down the corridor. Legs giving way, hands flat on both walls, a lilting ship at sea. Water blurring my vision. Looking into the kitchen. Not able to look directly. Slumped bodies and blood. Stains and glistening wounds like torn oranges. The trowel clattered to the floor. Dirt breaking off. I was still standing, held up by hands gripping the doorframe, breathless rasping: a short crucifixion. I was retching when the door opened behind me. Pav called again. He has come to take me away. Knowing this I was compelled to look at my husband.

I should have been screaming, but I don't think I was. And if I was it was absorbed by my husband's body. Sucked in between his parted lips. An inward flowing scream. And from between his lips a scream may have escaped, certainly a last breath, a sigh. Now there was a hole into which my life was pouring. Coldness sucking in warmth. The emptiness greedily demanding light, life from its surroundings.

Even now I associate Mike's parted lips with Mr. Everest claiming that there is no such thing a cold. "Cold is merely the absence of warmth." Darkness was the absence of light. This was scientific fact, not human fact. I wanted to scream that death was not the absence of life. Death was more. Something terrible. Worse than the absence of life. It was a cold that was a rejection of warmth. It packed an avalanche about the heart that would take aeons to thaw. And even then clumps of organ tissue would be left irreparably damaged.

The Bedouin believe that among other traits being an Arab is synonymous with being a storyteller and it is said that when an Arab dies a library is lost. Similarly then, the death of my husband was the destruction of a universe: the void filling the space that he had occupied. The surroundings in taking him unto itself had simultaneously supplanted his existence. Books burning. And with his loss so my universe was irreparably damaged, a sizeable, indeed life-threatening part of it collapsing and sweeping into his open mouth, chasing the existence that had been squeezed out like air from a sinking bottle.

I did not throw myself upon him for it was no longer him. But I should have. Did I? I had been robbed of gruelling last words. A semblance of touch, yes even this dissatisfying touch would have been better than nothing. I had only that last horrible look of his in my mind. An image that would fade with time, but now it was all I saw. An expression braced in anger, stripped of tenderness and subtlety, pure and elemental like a baby's, already no longer my husband's face. For no matter how angry he had ever been "Is nobody to be spared your horrid tongue?" he had always been uncomfortable with anger and its purity had never lasted. Now it was his death mask.

Pav was holding my arm, trying to tell me something, pulling me away. And I was falling away from him into the lounge. He followed with words. I had no idea what he was saying. I would later ask him and he'd dismiss their significance with a wave of his hand. He didn't remember either. At the time his expression weighted them with importance. In my mind Pav was also against me. Hadn't he been instrumental in this disaster? I backed into the lounge. My eyes were wild and he made an effort to show me empty hands. As he did so I saw my chance. He too had entered the room. If I was fast enough I could slip passed him. I relaxed my body feigning submission and he dropped his arms and stepped forward. He only had time to brush the fingers of his right hand against Mouth's psychological bruise.

I burst out of the building and bounded down the steps. He was behind me, but no match for me. He was built for field rather than track events. Of course he was shouting, but I don't think he left the courtyard.

And there I was out between the fields again. The grass twitching as if waking. Whereas before I was struck by the emptiness, my head turning this way and that with choice, this time my thoughts were cluttered with images. Images from the kitchen, images that extinguished the background and rendered choice obsolete and transported me to tortured places.

The trowel clattered to the floor. Dark soil broke off. What would a Said Holmes make of a trowel at the entrance to such a scene of carnage?

On the table the tumblers and a bottle of clear *sid*, a translucent tower, a snub-nosed rocket. A party gone horribly wrong. Aramco, my Jupiter, my Bringer of Jollity, was as distant as the planet itself. Yet, because of the tumblers and *sid* and because other than the Masstock

Dairy I had no other sanctuary, I fell to my knees and hoped telepathy would open a way for me to contact Ginny or anybody. The party scene haunted me. Devastation taken to its extreme. For me all the laughter of being in Saudi, all the fun at Aramco, the sham, all flashed passed as a film coming to an end, summing up all that had gone before in an orgy of images, before flapping endlessly in a white flag of nothingness. Given up and gone.

If my fortress puts the Aramco crowd's buildings in puerile doll's-house relief then the party dream that surfaced from time to time twisted a blade into their sense of self-importance. These people were not cardboard cutouts. But the public stage upon which they performed offered only a frontal view. Wounds were normally the preserve of accelerated intimacy. But at this party, the party taken to its conclusion, months had passed and it was still going. For some, notably Noel, the party was years rather than months old. Familiarity lent to carelessness. So that a head would toss, the hair would part and a disfigurement would flash. Or a T-shirt would lift as someone stretched upward and the bottom of a scar would show. In a stride a piece of leg would betray a blemish. And it was monstrous, obscene. All these nice people of the community as I knew it. Was June's world any different? There were atrocious wounds from life's front-line, tended and nurtured, buffed for perverse brinkmanship evenings. Many were self-inflicted or small cuts, scratched and hacked into real wounds. One could remove the shroud from Colin's Vietnam analogy. The Aramco atmosphere was full of humour. There had been lots of laughter. But the humour had been a mobile army surgical hospital (M*A*S*H) at its savage best. The Arab could be the elusive Vietcong, however the real enemy was displacement. Everyone repairing themselves, plastering themselves, anaesthetising themselves. The worst wounds were those that were not self-inflicted. They offered embellishments of injustice and incomprehension. And when competition time came round, everyone would cringe and groan submission and beg not to see the biggest wound of all. And they'd look nonetheless as I lifted my clothes. Sometimes Pinball would laugh into the monumental silence: "I can see you haven't got the happiness baton."

The trowel clatters to the floor, hard earth breaks off. I don't look near the kitchen area in front of me. This is where Mike lies. Sparky is where he was when I left. Sitting against the wall, legs akimbo, head dropped, chin upon his chest. Except for the red stain on his shirt he could have been asleep; a sombrero was all that was missing. He sits alone at that end of the kitchen, behind the table. Everyone else is in front of me. Pockmark lies face up, his arms up as if interrupted during some floor exercise, sit-ups perhaps. His *thobe* is slit length ways, open and revealing and glistening and I think of filleted fish. He seems to be staring above his head, his eyes rolled up to look at me. Ian is slumped over the big one. They present only their backs and a drunken-stupor could have brought them into this position. Mouth lies on his side in front of me. He's in the foetal position, his very own position, knees to chest, eyes closed cramped up in a puddle of blood. My husband lolls against the standing cupboards under the work-surface alongside Ian and the big one. His poise is practically a reflection of Sparky's own. They sit almost opposite one another. However, my husband legs are twisted and he can't sit unsupported, so he's leaning against Khalid or Rashid. I don't remember. His head is almost upon the Arab's shoulder. Another two buddies who'd succumbed to the influence of alcohol and passed-out. His head is below the man's shoulder, tipped back, looking up, his lips parted about to issue an "ah" for the dentist.

  I was still crying when I heard the cruiser. I scrambled into the grass and hid and watched Pav drive by.

* * *

  I am well into the writing, and although it may still be therapy, the yearning for answers has became obsessive. I have begun a search for Scab. What began as a background activity moved centre-stage as obstacle after obstacle was placed before me. The Saudi and British governments stonewalled me. The former out of policy, the latter when they got wind of the book. I approached the Philippine government who half-heartedly pursued my request. They did not officially know the incident. And knowing him simply as Scab didn't help. The fall of Marcos didn't help. A lot of things didn't help. To cut a long and tedious story short I located him after a year and a half of pestering. Two further months went by before I talked to him on the phone in March 1990.

  Speaking to him and hearing his punctuating "no" brought painful tears of joy. Some holes were filled through telephone conversations, but my obsession was so advanced that I had to see him. I was even more anxious to meet when he said he'd found Pav.

  When we meet in a seedy bar in Manila, which I know to be of Pav's choosing I am shocked by Scab's appearance. The telephone had allowed me to excuse his cracked voice. But the cracks don't stop at his voice. They are in his face: deep trench-lines of worry. A clay mask racked over and gouged by a combined-harvester. He is also prematurely grey in places. Scab spent eleven months in prison before being deported. He admits he was not mishandled, but the horrendous fear of it had worn him down. Stories of minor misdemeanours or nothing at all being trumped up to a capital sentence were rife.

By comparison I like to think I have successfully internalised my suffering.

Tass and Pav are also present. All three are pleased to see me. There is no animosity and Pav makes sure I am safely in a taxi before saying goodbye.

One bizarre fact baffles me. When Rashid went with Sparky to fetch the *sid* Scab had not been discovered. He'd slept through their visit. Had they looked in the room and seen a mere ruffle of bedding? Or had Rashid decided to leave him? Scab didn't know.

We agree that Ian terribly misjudged the situation. Abdul's presence may have given him reckless confidence. My presence too. For had I not been there he may have held his tongue. Maybe I'm being vain, but his ego may have felt questioned. But we come to no conclusion as to why he said what he said. Personally I think he was riding on the back of Pav's bravado. What he - what we all - had taken for idiocy on Pav's part had reason. He had not wanted to provoke the Arabs, but under the circumstances it had been a risk he had chosen to accept.

Pav had stood at the window and seen Scab emerge from their demountable. There had been nothing wrong with his body clock. "Help," had been Pav's shout to him when he was near the building. Scab had stopped, but by then Pav had been forced to turn his attention to the room. Scab had been puzzled but carried on round to the front of the building. There he'd seen the Chevrolet and Mouth sitting on the steps. He'd moved back out of sight and returned to the window, hoping to communicate with Pav or possibly catch some of the conversation. This was when Pav shouted for him to go.

In an emergency Scab could have driven. He thought the noise would be too risky and chose to run to Masstock. He ran between the pivots to come out on the road where the farm was bounded by the North fence. He ran for about half an hour before a car stopped and gave him a lift. Although he refused to speak in the car, the Arabs curiosity was sufficiently aroused for them to accompany him into the Masstock main building. He told his story to one of the expats, but it was one of the Arabs who convinced them to call the police. Typically the expat shied from such drastic action and wanted to shift responsibility by calling his overseer. I would have done the same. This Arab called the police. Afterwards everyone was interrogated. The dairy was closed for a day. All those who had not been in Scab's presence were released and work resumed. The others were released the following day.

Pav's story is a touch more adventurous. Funny, but he's the one person I would have nominated not to perish in a Saudi prison and he was the one who evaded it. Had I left with him he said he would have attempted to leave the country. No mean feat without a passport. We could not have stayed: I would have been too conspicuous.

He had plenty of cash. Money he'd accrued through selling *sid*. All the lads had their stashes hidden on the farm. The police never mentioned the money.

Pav lay low in Riyadh. He stayed with friends, living and working in the industrial district for three years. He knew of Scab's imprisonment but could do little. He left well before the Saudi government, wanting to stem the flow of money leaving the country and open job positions for its nationals, initiated the first mass expulsions of illegals in 1995. He escaped by buying a passport during the Hajj. He wasn't forthcoming as to whether the owner or some third party sold it to him. I didn't enquire. It's feasible that the owner sold it to him, for of the two to three million pilgrims observing this tenet of Islam some tens of thousands stay on illegally and find work.

* * *

What brought me to the kitchen a second time is not easily explained. I'd not looked at Mike the first time, but I'd seen him. I'd seen the limpness of his hand, the loll of his head, his terrible mouth through which his life had escaped, the way his body seemed to have caved-in as if the substance was a sham and he were a shell. All that life, good-hearted naive wit, intelligence, more than anything his accumulated intelligence, all of it snuffed out like a candle between a forefinger and a thumb. Just as the silence of the desert poured the cacophony of humankind down the drain, so too my husband's hastily whispered stream of knowledge fell upon Neanderthal ears. With photographic precision I recorded the image. He was gone. There was nothing I could do. Why did I go back? It was not rational, but succinctly put, if a reason is needed, then I needed to say goodbye.

I can't say whether I ran, crawled, strolled, took a direct route, or was watchful. I was somehow again climbing the steps. Again seeing the broken sand roses. When had I last been there? Was it hours ago or twenty minutes? I could not recall. I was very thirsty. The sun had not risen to bear its full acid heat, but my skin prickled.

When I entered the building I sensed something was wrong. I couldn't say what at first, but I moved cautiously. There appeared to be no life here, but I was alerted. Strangely, I was a step away from the door when I saw what was wrong. I registered the things in the wrong order and this to dramatic effect. I realised that the trowel was no longer where I had dropped it. It was against the wall opposite the entrance. Had Pav or I kicked it? More grippingly, and I really only saw this when I was almost at the door, was that a hand stretched out into the corridor. The arm lay outstretched and I instinctively knew it belonged to my husband.

The camel was upon me again and I involuntarily clutched my chest as if it were possible to burrow my hand in and assist my labouring lungs. Shock overrode the depression that was to come. My earlier illness on the farm was nothing compared to what the next months would bring. Then I had been on the seabed, continually drowning, sometimes seeing light and gulping painful breaths of air. The depression to come would entomb me in a sarcophagus, itself buried below the seabed.

The person at the door was my husband. His lying position was a slouch, almost on his side, leaning back onto the floor units, the one arm stretching out as if testifying to an attempt to halt his buddy. And the man upon whom he had been leaning was gone. Khalid or Rashid, it didn't really matter, both were absent.

The thought of the Arab on the loose burdened the camel and I gasped for breath. I'd not heard another vehicle since Pav's departure and I had not noticed another missing which meant the man was on foot. Possibly in the lounge? Behind me? I turned away from the entrance, pressed my back against the corridor wall, and forced a deep painful breath in an effort to shift the weight of the camel.

There was something sticky on the floor and my sole peeled away from it with the sound of Velcro.

The metronome continued inexorably. Clack, clack, clack, clack. A hammer to an anvil. On and on. The world had been burnt to malleability and was being bashed into an unrecognisable form. Love, tenderness, touch, all had vaporised during the firing. There was no going back.

I was aware of the danger and saw the trowel. There would be knives in the kitchen. Yet, I didn't arm myself. Death wish, perhaps? Or its opposite. Strangely, I possessed a sense of invincibility. I was alive and everyone else was dead. I wished to join them and knew I would not.

Apart from my husband and the missing Arabs the bodies were positioned as before. At the behest of my parents my husband's body would be shipped back. I was in no state to make decisions. The British government picked up the tab. Ian was not transported. They were not willing to fork out the £10,000 or so for an orphan. He was buried in Bahrain's Christian cemetery. I believe Sparky was also buried there. Saudi prohibits the burial of Westerners and non-Muslims in its soil.

* * *

I left Saudi Arabia in early 1986 and the embryonic book was started in 1989. I completed and revised it and in 1991 a publisher accepted it. In that same year the Gulf War halted publication. By 1994 the climate had changed but not government hostility. Then in 1997, some 13 years after setting foot on the tarmac of Dhahran airport, I had a publishing date. A murder involving two nurses as suspects postponed publication on the grounds that it could jeopardise negotiations. As with all such incidents in the country, be it a nurse falling from a balcony or this new incident, they became muddied with the bureaucracy and took on the enigmatic dimensions of a presidential assassination. The nurses' sudden release in 1998 allowed the presses to roll again. This time I stopped publication. Actually I was under contract and was only able to delay it. The reason was that the furore over the nurses' case made my publication seem like a tasteless effort to jump on the bandwagon. Towards the end of 2000 more expats were interned. They were accused of bombings in the land, part of so-called bootlegging wars. The events of September 11th 2001 increased Western interest in the Arab world. But the nature of my book was considered damaging to the Saudis at a time when they were already in bad light. And the expats were still interned. So it was shelved again.

Now I'm happy to lead a pedestrian, even mediocre, life. For in those two years in Saudi Arabia I lived a lifetime. And in writing this book I have relived it. It is enough.

As to the question: is this a true story? I have to be careful how I reply. It is a truthful story. There is truth in it. It lies in the detail. My story contains equal measures of poetic and literal truth. After all I signed the truth away. That was the price of freedom.

* * *

I leave the building with uncanny calmness. I should run. Instead I stand at the top of the steps. Fear is the grip of sparrow's feet. Sharp but small. For just as my surroundings are reduced to a backdrop of tissue-paper consistency, so too the thought of one of them out here is dwarfed by the enormity of what has happened. I am numb. I cannot focus, yet I absorb all sensory signals. That duality of detachment and keen awareness continues to accompany me. The farm is as still as when the lads are out working. A buzzard that kept other birds quiet takes laborious flight.

I deny my thirst and teeter between sitting down and moving on. The wooden steps creak with my indecision. I stand there for what seems an age when a noise on the threshold of my imagination draws my attention. I do not move. My alertness is about to pan away when I hear it again. A groan. The sound of movement as a rasp of sand. I focus on Abdul's cruiser. It stands in front his demountable. There is no sound for a long time. Patience is my ally. When the groan comes I want it to be Mike but know it cannot be him. Curiosity tussles with dread and eventually I persuade myself to investigate.

For want of a better word my approach is weird. I walk over to the cruiser, but it is as if I am going there by chance. I do not move purposefully. I feel the young sun perforating the cool with tiny scalding needles: thinning the air with its prickling piercing. A streak of cats has dabbed the sky in a stampede of off-white paw prints: a pitter-patter heading to where parallel lines meet. The Chevrolet is gone and has left no tracks in the ground, just as the B-29 leaves no path in the Hiroshima sky. I am strolling over, looking nonchalantly this way and that for distraction or observation; almost abstractedly kicking the dirt. Weird.

I move around to the right, the front of the vehicle, allowing myself ample distance. Strangely I look at the door of the demountable before idly glancing down the side of the cruiser, between it and the building. I know that someone is there, but my distance is not merely physical.

At first I don't recognise the battered face in the shadow of the cruiser. Whoever it is presents no threat. I step closer and recoil when eyes snap open and stare at me.

I remain disconnected. Exhausted though I am, my emotional time is not over. I am still going through a myriad of emotions at lightning speed. Synapses are overheating, barely able to keep up with the conflicting signals, flapping and flickering, continually derailing any train of thought. Occasionally, I reach up into the gale of impulses and hold a thought before it is torn from my grasp. One is clear like a splash of ice-water in the face: I should kick him. Not for who he is, but what he represents. Hasn't there been enough violence?

His lips part and he speaks. I recognise the person to be our overseer. I take another step towards him. I'm standing over him, but our distance is immeasurably greater than the length of my body. The word he is repeating is water. His eyes plead with me. One side of his face is pebble-dashed with grit. After a while I realise that he's fallen silent. Still he looks into my eyes. Trying to find me. I give him nothing for I have nothing to give. I am not there. Caked lips mouth something, but I do not bend to listen. Has he resumed his litany? Is he gasping for water? Can't he see that he cannot get sense from me, let alone water? How can he ask me for water, when I deny it myself? I do not bend to listen.

Some distant urgency is building. I don't know why at first. A fresh awareness takes possession of me and I am both bound and jettisoned by a new storm of sensations. The wailing of hysterical ghouls is getting louder. Stillness carries sound. Madness is round. I'm lost if found.

No, he isn't asking for water. He is speaking English, using a word I recognise, but one to which I can attach no meaning. The wailing of the banshees is obvious, but I hesitate, as if the word is the most important thing in the world: the whispered secret I would listen for in the furious rush of the wind upon trees in leaf. This new word is not like his plea for water; this word is not for him, it is for me. When I flee I don't remember the word he repeated.

Now I run.

Stillness may carry sound, but when I run I can see the multiple blitzes of distant vehicles trying to strobe the daylight.

Banshees becoming sirens.

I run round the kitchen building, feeling the acid-burn of fingers at my shoulder. I race across the courtyard and into the old greenhouse. And I wait, hidden, cowering. Not thinking about Abdul's word. The word that was his attempt to reach me, his attempt to span the void he'd seen between us. The word he knew I knew. The one he thought could explain the inexplicable. I do not comprehend; I cannot comprehend. I cower. Only later, much, much later, does its meaning assume portent. The word being as simple as water and more significant than oil.

Pollution.

Learning to live. That was what I was doing. Long ago I'd boarded a pilot-less plane with limitless fuel and so relinquished responsibility. Doctors and therapists, to varying degrees of success had tackled and mastered the cockpit controls. They'd steadied and steered and finally landed the craft. Patiently they'd rebuilt my confidence and coaxed me from my seat, guiding me down the long aisle, and pushing me out on my own.

I'm waiting for the train with a horde of commuters. The truncated vehicle sweeps into the underground station and people edge nervously on the platform. The City can be such a selfish place. People converge on the doors and search for seats. The doors open and those alighting force the waiting commuters to jockey for new positions. But I am heedless of this rush. The sight of a butterfly distracts me. The train has come from over-ground where the insect must have inadvertently entered. I watch it flutter out as people board. Here there is no green. This is an alien place. A hostile world where no one can help. It flutters uselessly, high in a sooty corner. I feel its despair. Or more truly I despair for it. Once, certainly before remarrying, I would have fallen to my knees and sobbed. Now, although saddened, I jump into the train, as the doors are about to close.

www.ingramcontent.com/pod-product-compliance
Ingram Content Group UK Ltd.
Pitfield, Milton Keynes, MK11 3LW, UK
UKHW041258180426
11947UKWH00008B/550